ONE IN A MILLION

We slowly went upstairs holding hands, and walked to my bedroom door. I saw the longing in his eyes. Darryl kissed me softly, cupping my face in his hands.

"Angela, I'm all mixed up inside," he said huskily. "You know my background; my home training is really pricking my conscience right now." He kissed me again. "But I want you so much . . ." He kissed my neck, and murmured again, "so much . . ." against the hollow of my throat.

Abruptly, he pressed me against the wall, holding me so tight, I could hardly breathe. His lips crushed against mine roughly, as his hands started to caress my body. I pulled away slightly and looked into his eyes. I was no longer with Dare, the sweet, shy guy who couldn't drive one-handed. I was with Darryl, the whirlwind, the dynamo, and all that passion and power, instead of being diverted into a song was directed at *me*. He took possession of my lips yet again.

I was frightened by the strength and suddenness of his desire. He stopped, all at once, and pulled away from me. "I lost it for a minute. I want you so badly and . . ."

He started to kiss me again, more gently, but I stopped him. "Millions of women would think I'm crazy, and they'd be right. But I can't. It's too fast . . . my head is spinning. I need some time to adjust to this."

He smiled, took my hands and kissed each one. "I don't wants millions of women. I want you. I'll wait. You're worth waiting for, baby."

All For Love

Raynetta Mañees

PINNACLE BOOKS
KENSINGTON PUBLISHING CORP.

PINNACLE BOOKS are published by

Kensington Publishing Corp.
850 Third Avenue
New York, NY 10022

First Printing: September, 1996

Printed in the United States of America
10 9 8 7 6 5 4 3 2 1

This book is lovingly dedicated to the generations of women in my life; my mother, Lebertis; my daughter, Tiffani; and my granddaughter, Zayna.

And in loving memory of my dear friend, the late Beverly Ann Harper.

Acknowledgments

My grateful acknowledgment to Dr. Helen Byrd-Pinnock and Dr. Melinda Dixon (neé Love), my friends since high school. Their advice on sections involving medical questions was invaluable.

Also, my undying thanks to Marilyn and Fran, the friendly computer room assistants at Lansing Community College.

One

You've Got A Friend

"Welcome to Atlanta. Want help with your bags, miss?" the doorman asked.

I looked down at the suitcase and flight bag the taxi driver had placed on the curb, "Yes, maybe I do."

I usually didn't need a bellman. Having learned to travel light on business trips, one suitcase was all I normally took. But this trip, I had my biggest flight bag as well. Because of the formal company dinner the following evening, I'd had to bring evening wear and accessories.

He called for a bellman, then said, "We might be in for a wait. This joint has gone plumb loco over the past couple of days."

There *did* seem to be an unusually large number of people milling around. "Because of the Compu-Data conference? That's *my* company and most of our people are just arriving today."

"Yeah, it's gotten even worse today; but it's been nuts since Monday. Darryl Bridges is staying here, you know."

"Darryl Bridges? *The* Darryl Bridges?"

" 'The Wiz,' himself. He gave a couple of concerts here; one was last night, in fact. Ever since he arrived the place has been crawlin' with reporters, security people, and fans. And females go ga-ga over this guy."

What healthy woman under 85 wouldn't? I thought. Darryl Bridges could have been a major star if he was tone deaf. The man was *that* outrageously handsome. Warm deep sienna skin covered a face like a masculine angel, with those penetrating coal black eyes. He was tall and slender with broad shoulders and a narrow waist. He seemed even taller because of the clean, slim lines of his legs.

Even if the opposite were true—if he was butt ugly but talented—Darryl would have been a star. His talent was unparalleled. He had a four octave range and his voice could be mellow as a kiss or powerful as a volcano. He danced like a human hurricane, played six or seven musical instruments spectacularly, and most of the fabulous songs he recorded were his own compositions. No wonder he was called "The Wizard."

"Sure wish I'd known. I'd have come in a day earlier, and caught the concert."

"Not a chance, honey, unless you were willing to pay three or four hundred dollars for a scalped seat—*if* you could have found one. Those concerts sold out the day they went on sale. Don't tell me *you're* a Darryl Bridges fanatic, too?"

"Well, I don't know about 'fanatic,' but I *am* a big fan of his. I'm a musician—I admire him more for his talent than his looks."

"Yeah, sure," said he condescendingly. "And how does your *man* feel about this 'admiration'?"

"Well . . . I'm . . . uh . . . man-less at present."

"Now *that,* honey, is a seven day wonder . . ." he moved in closer, "and a crying damn shame."

Why, you old dog, I thought. He had to be old enough to be my grandfather. Well, as they say, "just because there's snow on the roof don't mean the fire's out in the furnace."

"Uh-huh," I said, ignoring this thinly veiled invitation. "Look, I don't think anybody's coming. I'll just try to get this in myself."

He was suddenly all business again, "I'd help you, but I can't leave the door. Want me to call the front desk? *They'll* get somebody 'round here."

I had already shouldered my burdens and was headed inside, "No, that's all right. I can make it to the desk and they can get someone while I'm checking in."

There was no help immediately available at the front desk either. "I'm so sorry, Mrs. Delaney. It'll be only a few minutes before a bellman's free, I'm sure," the desk clerk said. "Things have been a little helter-skelter around here of late." She leaned closer, "Darryl Bridges was staying here, you know," she whispered.

"*Was* staying here? You mean he's checked out?"

"Yes, just a few moments ago. He has a concert in Miami tomorrow, I understand."

Damn, just my luck! I had been hoping to catch a glimpse of him in the lobby or something. *Oh, well, back to matters at hand.*

"Could you help me out? I made the arrangements for my company's dinner tomorrow night and I need to check on the preparations. Can I leave my bags with you while I go to the catering office?"

I was our division's Human Resources Director. The Lansing Division had opened two years before when Michigan business got too brisk for the Detroit Divisional Office to handle it all. I was Assistant HR Director in Detroit. When my boss, Wes Zantinni, was picked as Division Manager for Lansing, he took me along and promoted me to his old job.

Wes's innovative management style made the Division an instant success. And he gave me free rein to try some employee and customer policies that sent satisfaction *and* quality ratings through the roof.

Now we were at a seminar hosted by the national office in Atlanta. As the "new-comer" of the company, Lansing was asked to "run" the Annual Awards dinner. When Wes asked me if I minded making arrangements for the dinner, I think he was afraid I'd feel he asked me because it was "woman's work."

I assured him I didn't mind. I knew Wes better than that, and anyway, it was more in line with my department's thing than most of the others.

"Certainly," the clerk replied. "But the catering office is in the basement. Wouldn't you rather check with our sales office? They're right down the corridor."

"No. I'd feel better discussing things directly with the people who'll be serving us, if I may."

"Of course. Go down that elevator and just follow the signs."

Easier said than done. When I got to the basement, it was obvious from the look and smell of the place that the walls had recently been painted. There wasn't a sign in sight.

Marvelous! Well, you're really batting a thousand today, girl. I eeny-meeny-miney-moed a decision to go left, and started out in search of the office. After wandering aimlessly for a minute or two, I heard an elevator bell from somewhere in front of me. I headed for the sound, hoping it was someone who could direct me.

I heard running footsteps and a voice cried, "Look out, man!" a second before something big came flying around the corner I'd just reached and smacked into me. I would have fallen, but a strong arm suddenly encircled my waist and held me erect. I looked up into the deepest, darkest eyes I'd ever seen.

"Hey . . . wow . . . I'm really sorry! Are you all right? Did I hurt you?"

"No . . . no, I'm fine," I gasped. I wasn't hurt, but sure had the wind knocked out of me.

"Man . . ." he said, looking down at the things that had flown out of my purse when I dropped it. "Look, let me help you pick this stuff up. That's the least I can do after almost maiming . . ." He turned, and looked at my face for the first time. "You . . ." his voice trailed off.

That's when I realized this man with his arm still around me was . . . Darryl Bridges!

He must have realized he was still holding me at the same

time. We abruptly stepped apart. I was still trying to catch my breath. "What's your hurry? Where's the fire?"

"I've got a press conference across town in twenty minutes—though that's no excuse for knocking a lady semiconscious. Miss?"

"Mrs. . . . Delaney, Angela Delaney."

"I'm Darryl Bridges."

"Yes. I know." This brilliant statement was all I could think of to say.

By this time a guy in Darryl's sizable entourage had picked up my things and handed me my purse.

"Er . . . could I drop you somewhere?" Darryl inquired.

"No, I'm staying here. In fact, I just checked in." I couldn't resist adding, "Besides, if you get in any bigger a rush, the reporters at that press conference will be interviewing a ball of flame."

Darryl started laughing just as an older guy next to him said, "Yeah, we'd *better* light a fire under it, man, you're due there in fifteen minutes. The limo's waiting." He gestured down the hallway. I surmised it connected with the parking structure next door.

"Yeah, Sam, okay." Darryl answered him, but didn't take his eyes off me. "Are you *sure* you're all right?"

I smiled, "Positive. But you'd better hurry. After all, it's not like they can start without you."

He laughed again before turning to go. "Guess you're right. Well . . . uh . . . goodbye."

"Bye."

They started off again. Darryl turned and waved just before they rounded the corner.

Mercy! What a man! I almost said aloud. *He's even more handsome in person! And why can't* I *find somebody that . . . nice?* I had to laugh aloud at my own foolishness. *Angie, you run into the most famous entertainer in the world and all you can think of was that he was "nice?"* But he was. Talking with him had been as easy and natural as if he was some guy I met in line at the grocery store. There wasn't any "kiss my ring—I'm a star" about *him.*

I went through the discussion with the caterers and my afternoon meeting in a daze. I was fortunate that *my* presentation wasn't until the next day. I wasn't thinking very clearly. I kept seeing Darryl's dark, probing eyes before me. I was grateful to finally get to my room after the seminar ended.

I took a shower and went over the notes and visual aids for my presentation the next day. Just as I was nearing the end the telephone rang. When I answered, a vaguely familiar voice said, "Hello? May I speak to Angela?"

I wasn't sure who it was but had the feeling it was someone I knew. "This is she," I acknowledged, half my attention still on my materials.

"Hi . . . uh . . . this is Darryl Bridges."

My first impulse was to say "Yeah, right—and I'm Aretha Franklin. Now who is this, really?" But something stopped me. Now I recognized the voice—it really *was* him. I didn't say anything—I couldn't think of anything to say. After a few beats he asked, "Are you still there?"

I focused a bit then, and feeling like a real jerk, answered, "Yes . . . uh . . . I'm still here. I'm . . . I'm just so surprised."

He cleared his throat, "I probably shouldn't have called out of the blue like this . . . if it's a bad time . . ."

That brought me back to life. "No . . . oh, no, Darryl. It's not a bad time at all. Excuse me, I was so startled *you* were calling I forgot my manners. How are you?"

"Just fine. Listen, I had to see if *you* were all right after having me line block you this afternoon." His warm mellow baritone sounded just as good spoken as it did in song.

"Right as rain. It's really thoughtful of you to call." Despite my best efforts, there was a small quiver in my voice.

"No problem. Sorry to just run off like that. Sometimes my schedule is tighter than a new shoe."

"I can imagine. I heard you have a concert tomorrow in Miami?"

"Right. We're on the way there now."

"You're driving down?"

"No, flying." He paused, "Can't see much, but I think we're close to Orlando right now."

"It must be exciting . . . traveling all over the world."

"It can be, but it can get old, especially when I'm near the end of a long tour, like now. Do you travel much?"

"I travel a fair amount for my job, although most of my business trips are a lot closer to home than Atlanta."

"Where's home?"

"Lansing, Michigan."

"Lansing . . . Lansing. That's the state capital, right?"

"Yes. You know your geography . . . but then I guess you *would.*"

He laughed, "Yeah, I do move around a bit." He paused then, "You live in Lansing with your . . . uh . . . family?"

"Most of my family lives in Detroit. I moved to Lansing two years ago for a promotion. My daughter Tiffani lives with me."

"Just your daughter? No *Mr.* Delaney? You're divorced?"

"No, widowed."

"Oh." he sounded ill at ease, "I'd noticed you weren't wearing a wedding ring. I'm sorry. Was . . . was it recent?"

"No, it's been sixteen years now. But enough about me," I said, quickly changing the subject. "Where are you going after Miami?"

We began discussing his tour. From there the conversation went on to travel in general and California, where he lived. I told him I'd never been there. I was surprised he wanted to talk to me for so long—someone he didn't even know. But talk he did. I got the feeling he not only wanted to, but *needed* to talk. It reminded me of years before when I'd done volunteer work at a community center. He reminded me of some of the people I talked to then, especially some of the older people, who maybe lived alone and had no one to talk to. Sometimes they'd go on and on while I was helping them, talking about everything under the sun. And I'd let them, knowing they were enjoying the opportunity to just *talk* to someone.

I got the same feeling with Darryl, but I enjoyed every minute of it. He was an awesome conversationalist. He expressed himself so well and had such astute insights. I was caught off guard by how bright he was and by his off-the-wall sense of humor. He'd traveled all over the world and I loved hearing about the places he'd visited. And he had one rare additional quality—he was a great listener. He really listened to me and his perceptive questions showed it.

We wound up talking almost an hour. Finally, he said, "We're about to land, guess I'd better get ready. It's been really great talking to you. Would you mind if I call you again sometime?"

I caught my breath. "No, of course not, Darryl." I gave him my telephone number. "I'll look forward to hearing from you."

"Fantastic! Well, gotta run. Talk to you soon."

I just sat for a while staring at the phone. Had I actually spent the past hour talking to Darryl Bridges? He'd proved to be as nice over the phone as my first impression led me to believe.

Three days later the conference was over. I hadn't told Tiffani about meeting Darryl Bridges. I wanted to do that in person, to see the look on her face.

"Honey! I'm home!" I called, entering with my luggage.

She came rushing out of her bedroom, purse over her shoulder. "Hi, Mama. How was the conference?" she asked, kissing me on the cheek.

"Oh, honey, it was terrific! My presentation dazzled 'em! And you'll never guess . . ."

"Mom . . . I'm sorry. I gotta go. Everybody's waiting for me at the mall. We're going to that new Benny Hawkins movie, and I don't want to make them miss the beginning. But I want to hear all about it when I get home, okay? I love you."

Before I could answer, she kissed me again and was gone. I watched her through the balcony doors as she drove away. *Well,* I thought, *she's eighteen years old now. This is what you've always wanted; prayed for. For her to be her own woman; have her own friends, her own goals. That's what you've worked so hard for—now the day is here.* Tiff had just graduated high school and was starting college in the fall. She had a part-time summer job she loved and even had her own car; my old one, since I'd finally bought a new one.

Not bad for a widow who finished college nights while raising a child alone. Tiff had even made a whole new group of friends since we'd moved to Lansing.

And you're not doing so bad yourself, old girl. The promotion had finally brought me the financial security I'd struggled for ever since Bobby's death. And since moving, I'd made friends, too. I'd joined a church, established myself locally as a singer and actress in community theater—I even had a date every now and again. *Then why do you feel so empty?*

Putting the luggage down, I went to my room to change. Against my will, Bobby entered my thoughts. I avoided thinking about him as much as possible. *That's all over and done with, girl—why torture yourself?* But it didn't work that night. I couldn't help remembering how bright life together seemed when we married. Even though we'd "*had*" to get married.

I went into the kitchen to get dinner started, cooking only for myself. Tiff would have a bite with her friends while she was out. Grabbing a Pepsi, I went into the living room, eagerly turning on the television.

"Ladies and gentlemen—stay tuned for the biggest television event of the year—Darryl Bridges—*live* from Carnegie Hall!"

Darryl had been one of my favorite entertainers ever since he burst on the scene . . . what . . . fifteen, sixteen years ago? Before then I'd always thought of him as a kid. He was younger than I, and anyway, he *had* been a kid when he first started. But I realized then that Darryl had to be in his thirties.

I wonder why he never married. There had been rumors Darryl was gay, but I hadn't believed them even *before* I met him. The press hadn't been able to link him romantically with anyone and they made a big to-do about the rare occasions he was seen with a date. A daring reporter once asked him point-blank, "Are you gay?" Darryl looked exasperated, and simply replied, "No." God knows Darryl could have any number of women on his arm if he so chose. Apparently, he *didn't* so choose.

The performance that night was a special charity concert for Homes, USA—the organization founded a few years before by several big stars to help the homeless nationwide. Darryl had been named that year's chairman and he was presiding with a vengeance. There was a short film after the concert which covered the many activities Darryl had sponsored and attended in support of the organization.

Moved by Darryl's compassion and his dedication to improving the plight of homeless people, I realized I had underevaluated this man. I'd always thought of him as just a bundle of talent wrapped up in a sexy package. But now I saw there was much more to him and became curious about him as a person.

The next day I checked out a biography on him at the library and read the most recent magazine articles about him. He was involved in a number of activities to help those less fortunate. And he was always gracious in the rare interviews he gave. The press, however, seemed to have a love-hate relationship with him. They were fascinated by him and most of his press was in praise of his talents and activities, but there were frequent digs, cheap shots, and unfounded rumors as well. Unfortunately, that kind of thing sold papers and magazines. From all I saw, Darryl was a hell of a person and deserved better.

I walked around in a daze for a week and jumped every time the telephone rang. After a while, I began to wonder if he'd *ever* call me back. Maybe he was just being what some people think of as polite?

The following Wednesday at around midnight I was settling into bed, just about to go to sleep, when the phone rang.

"Hello . . . Angela?"

It was him. "Hi . . . Darryl?"

"Yeah, it's me. How are you? Hey, did I wake you up? I'm

sorry. I ought to have better sense about making calls to other time zones by now."

"No, Dare, I wasn't asleep. Oh, I'm sorry. I've read some people call you 'Dare'—or do you prefer Darryl?"

He laughed that wonderful laugh of his. "Either one's okay. They both beat 'Dare-All,' or 'Burning Bridges'—although I kinda like 'The Wizard.' "

"I've seen those handles in print, but does anyone ever really call you that?"

"Yep—when I'm not around. The press treat me like Mr. Wonderful *during* an interview, but sometimes, afterward, even *I* don't recognize the 'quotes,' or the crazy names they call me."

"That couldn't be easy to take."

"No, but I've learned the best thing to do is just ignore it." I could tell he was uncomfortable discussing it. "But I won't bore you with my problems—what have *you* been up to lately?"

We talked until two o'clock in the morning. At last I said, "Dare, I love talking to you, but if I don't get a little shut-eye, I'll fall asleep at my desk."

"Sure, Angie. Listen, I'm sorry about calling so late. Next time it'll be earlier."

"It's great to hear from you anytime."

"You'd better watch what you say, lady. I'm known to be a dangerous man with a phone in my hand."

I had to laugh, "Well, Mr. Bridges, I'm no slouch with a phone myself. I think I can handle it."

That laugh again! "Well, I'd better let you get some rest. Talk to you soon. Write me!"

"I will. Goodnight."

Darryl began to call regularly. At first it was every week or so, but then the frequency of the calls increased. He'd call me from all over—Chicago, Toronto, Paris—wherever he happened to be. He'd given me an 800 number where I could leave a message he said would get to him wherever he was. I never used it. I didn't want to take the risk. If we talked when *he* called *me,* I could always be sure conversation was welcome.

Anyway, nothing ever came up that couldn't wait for his next call.

He'd also given me a special address, and I *did* write. It got to the point I'd write him once or twice a week. Sometimes it was just a short note; sometimes a long letter. And if I saw a funny card I thought he'd get a kick out of, I'd send it, too.

The calls and the letters went on for three months. Our relationship was like nothing I'd ever experienced. Sometimes I'd be driving along and one of his songs would come on the radio; or I'd be watching one of his videos on TV and it would hit me: "Hey! I *know* him!" That's the way I felt. We talked so often about so many things, it felt as though I knew him, although we'd only met once.

We talked about almost every subject: world politics, people, music extensively—and our families, our childhoods.

Darryl was, of course, the youngest of the Bridges family—the world famous gospel singers. Sylvia Bridges, Dare's mother, was a legend in the field, on par with Mahalia Jackson and Marian Anderson.

Darryl never recorded officially with the family; at first because he was too young—being seven years younger than the next oldest. Dare spent most of his childhood backstage, watching his family perform from the wings. They tried to incorporate him into the act when he was ten or so, but he was too shy to sing on stage. What they didn't know was much of the time he was alone, (which was a lot, the family being so often in rehearsal or recording sessions) he spent singing to himself and teaching himself to play many of the instruments that were always laying around. It was during this time that he began writing his first songs.

The family was dead set against it when at seventeen he told them he was starting a career in *popular* music. It caused a rift between them in the beginning, but now, he said, they'd come to accept his choice—in fact, they supported and were proud of him.

But there was one topic we didn't talk about—the romantic

sides of our lives. I didn't bring it up for two reasons. One, I didn't have anything on that score *to* talk about. I'd broken up with my last steady boyfriend when I moved to Lansing for my new job. He still lived in Detroit and felt I should have turned down the promotion in order to stay there, near him. Since then I had dated only sporadically. Secondly, I felt if Darryl wanted to talk about his love life—if he had one—or had questions about mine, he'd say so. He never did.

I'd told Darryl all about Tiffani, of course, and that I was widowed when she was less than two years old. I sensed he was curious about my marriage and how I wound up widowed so young, but I avoided the subject, and he didn't pry.

Bobby and I had been high school sweethearts and carried the romance with us into college. I had been a virgin until he convinced me it wouldn't be wrong for us to have sex. "We're getting married, anyway, aren't we, baby?" he'd said. It was the seventies, and like most young girls then, I wasn't very sophisticated about birth control. Neither was Bobby. I got pregnant.

We'd gotten married and I dropped out of college to work full time—supporting us, while Bobby continued with school. I, of course, had to stop working for a while right before and after Tiffani's birth. That's when things stared to fall apart. Bobby never had to struggle before. His parents sure weren't rich, but he was their only child, and up until that point Bobby had gotten everything he wanted—including me—without having to sacrifice for it.

What didn't help was his mother's attitude toward me. She resented me from the first, as she resented anyone she felt was a rival for the affection of "her boy," but the serious nastiness didn't start until she realized I wasn't just another of Bobby's revolving girlfriends. She'd begged him not to marry me, but for the first time in his life, he defied her.

I thought things would improve when Bobby got his degree and found a good job, but they only got worse. That's when his drinking started. That's also when his abuse started. Again, this was almost twenty years ago, and there wasn't a lot said then about battered women's rights. I suffered his abuse personally, but one day he pushed Tiffani, who was just learning to walk, because she was pulling on his pants leg, wanting "Daddy" to pick her up. She fell and cut her head on the edge of a table. I knew at that moment the man had killed my love for him forever, and my marriage was over.

I forced Bobby to leave; although he kept coming over, stalking me, begging me to take him back. The drinking worsened; he got fired. That day he came over to our apartment, begging me to let him in, but I wouldn't—I was afraid of him. That night I was awakened by the police; Bobby's car had run over an embankment—he was dead.

His mother blamed me. As far as *she* was concerned, I tricked Bobby into marrying me by getting pregnant and I killed him by "burdening" him with myself and Tiffani. And although Tiffani is the only grandchild she'll ever have, she resented Tiffani for being the cause of her son having to marry "that girl."

I'm not guessing Iris felt this way—she *told* me; screaming these things at me at Bobby's funeral. I was a twenty-year-old, penniless widow with a broken spirit, and a baby to raise alone. Her vicious words wounded me to my very heart. What hurt even more was her treatment of my child. At first Tiffani would try to contact "Grandmother" She would call her and invite her to school plays and such, to which she never came. Bobby Sr. didn't share her feelings—*he* wanted to see his granddaughter, but twenty-five years of marriage to Iris had broken any independent will he had.

As Tiffani grew older, it became obvious, even to a child, that her grandmother had no use for her. Tiffani was about seven when she asked me one day, "Mama, why does Grandma Iris hate us?" All I could do was hold her and cry.

I'd never told the whole story to anyone. Many knew Bobby and I had our problems, but no one knew the degree of his abuse. I was ashamed to tell anyone. Although, intellectually, I realized I was the victim, not the villain, I felt responsible. I felt I should have been able to do *something* that would have saved our marriage—and Bobby's life. Of course, I couldn't tell Darryl any of this.

Then came the Monday evening I was home alone watching an entertainment news show. The hosts were describing a charity concert Dare was doing in Los Angeles that coming Friday, arriving "home" for the final stop of his lengthy tour. Darryl had already told me about the concert, and I got that "I know him" feeling all over again. As if on cue, the phone rang: "Hi, Angie. It's Dare."

"Dare, where in the world are you? That sounds like the ocean in the background."

"No such luck—just a lousy connection. I'm in L.A., at the Coliseum."

"L.A.? I thought you weren't going there for the concert until later in the week."

"I wasn't, but there were some problems with the stage setup and I thought I'd better check them out personally. Listen, I just had a brilliant idea."

"Wiz, all your ideas are brilliant."

"Flattery, my dear, will get you anything—including a trip to L.A."

"Huh?"

"Didn't you tell me you'd never been to one of my concerts?"

"That's right. I haven't—to my lasting regret."

"Well . . . would . . . would you like to come out for this one?"

"Out? Where? To Los Angeles?"

"Yeah. Can you get away for a few days?"

"Well, sure, but . . ."

"Look, my staff will take care of everything—the travel and hotel arrangements—everything. And, of course, you'll be my guest."

I paused. "Darryl, are you serious?"

"I've never been more serious." His voice got softer. "We've become such good friends through letters and over the phone. It would mean a lot to me if you'd come. Will you?"

"I . . . don't know what to say," I stammered.

"Now, I can help you out there. Just say, 'Yes, Darryl, I'd love to come. Thank you for inviting me.' "

I couldn't believe it! I laughed, "All right, then. 'Yes, Darryl, I'd love to come. Thank you for inviting me.' "

"Great! Look, they're waiting for me, but I'll call you tomorrow with the details, okay?"

"Okay," I said, suddenly feeling numb.

His voice got soft again, "I'm really glad you're coming. Talk to you tomorrow."

"Okay," I repeated dully.

When I hung up, my first thought was, *What have I done?* Talk about a case of mixed feelings! I was overjoyed about seeing Dare again. But uneasy about it, too. Could he possibly be thinking that I'd . . . ? *Girl, please,* I told myself. *Now you're a fine looking woman—but Darryl is constantly surrounded by some of the most gorgeous women on earth; you're not in* that *league, honey. He's knows what a thrill it would be for you, that's all.* Still, although I wanted to go, I was afraid to. Our relationship was a friendship, not a courtship. I didn't deceive myself on that. But, even so, by the time he called the next day, I had worked myself into a near frenzy with anxiety.

"Hi!" he said in his usual breezy way.

"Hi." I wasn't feeling very breezy that day.

"It's me."

"Yes, I know."

"Why so glum? Is something wrong?" I guess we'd clocked in so many hours he was able to pick up my mood from just the few words I had spoken. "Are you and Tiffani all right?" he persisted.

"Yes, Dare, we're fine."

"You haven't changed your mind about coming out for the concert, have you?" He'd zeroed in on exactly what was bothering me.

"No . . . I haven't"

"Okay . . . so . . . what's up? I can tell something about this is bothering you. Talk to me."

"Well, it's just that . . ."

"Yes? It's just that . . . what?"

"It's nothing, Darryl. It's just that . . . well . . . I'm kinda . . . nervous about it."

"Why? *I'm* not nervous about it—well, maybe just a little bit. I guess under the circumstances, any two people would be a *little* nervous. But why are you *this* upset?"

"Because . . . because . . . well, Darryl . . . I'm a thirty-seven-year-old woman with a grown daughter, and I'm certainly no starlet."

"Why's that a problem? You think you're ugly or something?"

"Darryl, don't tease me, I'm serious."

"Okay, okay, I know you are, I'm sorry. But, Angie, believe me, you're getting yourself worked up over nothing."

"It's not 'nothing' to me, Dare."

"So I see." He hesitated a moment. "Angela," he said very slowly, "believe me, your looks are the kind many a starlet would kill for: long black hair, a truly beautiful face, a lovely figure and great legs. What's not to like? Besides, you've got a lot more going for you than just good looks. After all, how many people can be 'Innovator of the Year' with only two years on a new job?"

I was absolutely speechless.

"Angela? Are you okay?"

"Darryl," I said slowly, "I never told you about that award. How did you know?"

"Oh . . . right. Well, I . . . uh . . . now don't get mad. Let me explain . . ."

Then it hit me. "You've had me investigated!"

"Angela, I . . ."

"I don't believe it! You had me investigated! How could you! How *dare* you!"

"Now, Angela, give me a chance to explain!"

I was miserable. Here I was, like a fool, believing this man, this multi-millionaire megastar, could relate to me as one person to another, could really consider me a friend. And he had put someone up to *spying* on me! I was angry and humiliated and hurt. What hurt most was my disappointment in him. "Darryl, why didn't you just *ask* me anything you wanted to know? Did you think I'd have *lied* to you? After all the hours we've talked, all the thoughts we've shared, didn't you trust me at all?"

"It's not like that, Angela! Listen to me . . ."

I didn't want to listen. I couldn't bear to. I just wanted to hang up the phone and cry. But damned if I'd let him hear me cry, or think I was so upset I couldn't even continue talking about it.

He was still pleading, "Please, just listen to me. Be fair. Don't condemn me without knowing all the facts."

"Fine. Darryl superstar 'Mr. Wizard' Bridges . . ." I shot back "Go ahead. I'm listening."

He was silent for a moment, then said quietly, "Okay, Angela, we're even now. I insulted you. Now you've insulted me. Feel better?"

"What do you mean—I've insulted *you?*"

"Calling me Darryl Bridges superstar. You know we've never related to each other that way. We're friends, *good* friends, I thought. I have millions of fans, Angela, but I have very few friends. I've never come on to you like you were 'just a fan,' and you know it. I didn't deserve that." He sounded more than a little ticked off, but I didn't care. I was still more than a little ticked off myself.

"Friends? How can you say that when you had me investigated. You *did,* didn't you?"

"Yes, I did."

"Well, is that the way one friend treats another?"

"No, it isn't. And *I* never would have after I got to know you."

That slowed me down a little. "I don't understand."

"I know you don't. *Now* will you listen?"

I sighed, "All right, go ahead."

"After I called you in Atlanta, I wanted to talk to you again—but I had to make sure. You have no idea the kinds of hassles I've had dealing with people. I've been receiving death threats for years. I've had nine paternity suits filed against me, seven of them by women I never even *met,* and before you ask, no, the other two weren't valid either. Maybe I've gotten paranoid, but I've had so much turmoil come from the most innocent contact—especially with women—that I've had to be cautious about the simplest things, like picking up a phone and calling someone.

"So I had my staff check you out after I called that first time. That's how I found out about the award. I was just trying to find out if it was safe to call you, or if you'd go screaming to the press with some wild story about you and me.

"No, a friend wouldn't do that to a friend. That's why I'd never do that now, now that I know the kind of person you are. But then I didn't. *Now* do you understand?"

I felt like two cents—*after* inflation. "Yes, I understand . . . now. Darryl, I'm sorry I flew off the handle like that."

"Hey, it's all right. I can dig why you did. In your shoes I guess I'd feel the same. I'm glad it's finally out in the open. I've been feeling bad about not telling you before. I should have, but I didn't want you to be angry with me or, worse, to not trust me."

"I'm sorry about what I said, I didn't mean it. Forgive me."

"There's nothing to forgive. At least what you said was honest. What I did was dishonest . . . at least not telling you before now was. Do you forgive *me?"*

"Of course. I guess we'd both better 'Step Lively' and apologize, huh?" "Step Lively" was one of his biggest hits.

He laughed, "Yeah, now that we're friends, I want us to 'Stay That Way.' " It was another hit.

"Okay, Mr. B., enough with the record plugs. I already *have* all your albums."

He laughed again, but then his voice got very serious, "Angie, I value your friendship, and I'd never do anything to hurt you, please believe that."

"I do, Dare."

"Well, one purpose was served. Now you don't have to feel nervous about coming. I already know quite a lot about you Angela, and I like all I see. And as for the 'starlet' angle . . ." His voice lowered to a whisper, "I don't know why you'd ever be concerned. You're a very beautiful woman. Anyway," he finished briskly, "we're really friends now—we've had our first argument!"

I had to crack up at that. "Yeah, I guess you're right."

"Angela, you're an extremely sweet person, and it takes a lot to get you there, but, man! Do you have a temper when you get mad! Remind me not to ever make you mad again!"

We started to talk about my trip out. We decided I'd arrive on Friday morning and stay until Sunday. Dare said he'd keep Saturday open and show me around the city. Someone would call me after all the arrangements had been made.

"I won't be able to meet you at the airport personally," he said. "I'll probably already be at the Coliseum, and anyway, if somebody at the airport were to recognize me, it could get pretty hairy. But I'll make sure you're met by a car and driver."

"There's no need, Darryl. I could take a taxi and . . ."

"No, ma'am. I'm not about to let *you* loose on poor defenseless Los Angeles. I'll have somebody meet you."

"Darryl," I said, suddenly feeling shy, "I'm really looking forward to this."

"Me, too. And I'm looking forward to having one of our marathon discussions in person, being able to *see* you. I like to watch a person's eyes when we're talking."

"Is that why you wear dark glasses all the time, so you can watch and people can't see you watching?"

I think I caught *him* off guard *that* time. "Well, yeah, you got me there. I'll call before you leave to make sure everything's arranged."

The next day I got a call from an Anita Giles, Darryl's travel coordinator. She told me my plane ticket and boarding pass would be delivered by courier that evening at about seven. On Friday a limo would arrive at nine A.M. to drive me to Detroit Metro Airport. I was booked for the eleven A.M. flight non-stop to LAX—first class.

I'd be met at the airport by a driver; he'd have a sign bearing my name. A limo would take me to my hotel, the Los Angeles Regal. I was already pre-registered for Suite 1801. I'd be met at the hotel door with my key. She also said a packet of information for my return trip would be waiting in my room.

"Oh," she added, "I almost forgot. An American Express Gold Card will be included in the envelope with your tickets."

I silently gulped, but tried to stay calm, "And I'm to use the card to settle my hotel bill?"

"Oh, no. The hotel has already been taken care of and there's a $2,000.00 credit on your account with them, for any charges you wish to make to your suite. Any other questions?"

The courier came shortly after seven, and Darryl called later that evening to make sure I'd been contacted. When I tried to thank him he interrupted, "No . . . thank *you* . . . for coming."

I asked what types of clothing I should bring. He said "just casual stuff—jeans and whatnot. The weather's supposed to be in the low eighties and sunny."

He called again Friday morning at seven A.M. "Dare! It must be the middle of the night there."

"Yeah," he yawned. "I was going to call you when I got home after rehearsal yesterday, but it was two in the morning, your time, and I didn't want to wake you." I could have told him at two o'clock I was laying in the dark wide awake, too excited to sleep. "Then *I* fell asleep," he went on. "I just woke up. Glad I caught you before you left. Everything set?"

"Yep. I'm all packed. I was just about to hop into the shower."

"Well, go ahead and get dressed. Somebody will call you at the hotel about the concert arrangements. I will myself, if I can get away."

"All right . . . uh . . . will I see you tonight, after the concert?"

"What? Of course! I'll have someone bring you to my dressing room, okay?"

"Okay, Dare. Well . . . see you."

" 'Bye. Have a good flight."

I was dressed and ready when the limo driver rang my bell promptly at nine. He came up to my apartment and carried my suitcase and flight bag down to the limo. Everything went like clockwork. I got to the airport in plenty of time for my flight. After a short wait I was able to board. The plane left on schedule—I was on my way!

Two

If They Could See Me Now!

During the flight I gave myself a pep talk about Darryl. This was heady stuff. I didn't want to lose my composure and embarrass him . . . or myself. When we'd first started talking, my feelings for Dare were merely tremendous admiration and an ambiguous attraction. But he wasn't just a face on TV or a voice on the stereo anymore. Now he was my friend, someone I talked with, laughed with, and even argued with. I steeled myself to continue thinking of him as *just* a friend. Women all over the world adored Darryl—many of them younger, prettier, and more accomplished than me. I was four years older than Darryl to boot (though to my credit, I didn't look it).

He's an isolated, lonely man who needs a friend, Angela, I told myself. *As different as our circumstances are, we have a lot in common in the way we look at life. But that's all it is, girl, so don't fool yourself.* I sat back in my seat, contented. I could live with that. After all, I never imagined he'd ever even know I was alive. Now we were friends, and here I was on my way to spend a weekend as his guest. That was enough—that was more than I ever dreamed of. I was determined not to spoil it for either of us.

I dozed off and the steward woke me, touching me on the shoulder. "Pardon me, Mrs. Delaney; we'll be landing in about fifteen minutes." I didn't have time to get jittery. I was too busy tidying my hair and makeup. I didn't want whoever was meeting me to think Darryl was consorting with a slob.

In the gate lobby, I saw the young, muscular brother who'd picked up my things in Atlanta holding a sign bearing my name. I walked over to him; "Hi. I'm Angela Delaney."

He said "Hi," just as an older black man, who was standing next to him, turned around. "Mrs. Delaney?" the older one said. "Hello, I'm Sam Steele, the man's chief of security. This is Alex Winston, one of his assistants," he indicated the younger guy. "Pleased to meet you. Welcome to L.A." He was looking me over. "May I have your claim check? Alex can go for your bags while I take you to the car."

"Sure," I said, giving it to him.

He handed the claim check to Alex, who grinned at me, and took off. Then Sam said, "May I?" and took the flight bag I was carrying. He steered me toward a nearby door, taking me by the elbow with his free hand. "This way, please, Mrs. Delaney."

"Angela's fine, Mr. Steele."

He smiled at me then for the first time. "Nobody around Darryl calls me Mr. Steele, honey. I'm just plain Sam."

I smiled back at him. "Okay, Sam."

As we walked along, I caught him staring at me with sidelong glances. From what I'd heard, Darryl couldn't have women flying in to visit him very often. I knew how curious this man must be about me. Sam kept watching me out of the corner of his eye like he expected me to explode at any given moment. Then I realized I was giving him sidelong glances, too—watching him watching me. Suddenly, the whole thing struck me as funny, and I couldn't suppress a laugh.

Sam looked at me warily. "What's funny?"

"Nothing, Sam," I said. "I was just wondering why you're checking me out so closely. Is my slip showing?"

He looked sheepish. "I'm sorry. I didn't mean to be rude. It's just that you look so familiar. Have we met somewhere before?"

I grinned at him then. "Would it jog your memory if I dropped my purse and stuff flew out all over the floor?"

He looked puzzled at first, then grinned back, "Atlanta! I must be getting senile. You're not a woman a man could easily forget."

"Why, thank you, sir."

"And I see *Dare* didn't . . ." he muttered under his breath.

By this time we'd made it to the door. At the curb sat a sleek, black Mercedes limousine with dark tinted glass. Sam walked me to the rear door, and said, "Here we are," as he opened it. I ducked my head and got the shock of my life. There sat Darryl.

Sam said, "Get in, darlin', so I can close the door."

I slid in next to Darryl. He was wearing black jeans, a black shirt, and black loafers with no socks. That was it—no glitter and no smile, only black sunglasses. He looked as tense as I felt.

He turned to me, "Well . . . uh . . . hi."

"Hi, I didn't think *you'd* be here to meet me. What a surprise."

The side of his mouth quirked in a little lopsided smile; "A *pleasant* surprise, I hope."

I laughed, "Of course a pleasant surprise! Why didn't you tell me?"

"I decided to come after I talked to you this morning. There's so much commotion backstage after a show, I didn't want us to meet again that way."

"Well, I'm glad." I offered my hand, "It's great to see you again, Mr. Bridges." I smiled. "Although not quite as *striking* as our first encounter."

He looked startled for a second, then laughed, and shook my hand. "The pleasure's mine, Mrs. Delaney." He seemed to relax a little, "How was the flight?"

"Fantastic—I've never flown first class before."

Hearing the trunk of the limo open, I turned and saw Alex depositing my bags. Sam, who had been standing on the curb next to the door, got in the front. Alex got behind the wheel, and off we went. In a short while we were on the freeway.

Neither Darryl nor I said anything for the next five minutes or so. All at once, he leaned forward saying, "You guys don't mind if we have a little privacy, do you?" as he pushed a button. A glass partition started to rise between the front seat and the rear compartment.

Before it got all the way up, Sam retorted, without turning around, "Hell, no, Dare. Who wants to listen to you any more than they have to?"

Darryl settled back in the seat with a sigh. "There, that's better. I'm nervous enough without an audience."

"I thought you said you weren't nervous about this."

"No. If you recall, I said I *was*—a little bit."

"Why?" I gave him a wicked look. "You think you're ugly, or something?"

He started laughing, "Touché. Score one for Angela."

"That's better. I thought for a minute you were going to get shy on me."

"I *can't* get shy with you," he said. "You don't give me a chance to."

"That being the case," I replied, "how about taking off those shades? I feel like I'm talking to the Ghost of Christmas Yet to Come."

He laughed again, but took the shades off and put them in his shirt pocket. Once again I was riveted by the black velvet depth of his eyes, with their full brows and heavy black lashes. His deep bronze skin almost seemed to glow. His lips were full and, soft, his teeth a flash of white as he smiled at me. "Is this better?" he asked.

I looked him in the eye, "Much."

"Angela," he said, shaking his head, "you're a trip without a ticket."

I smiled at him. "Is that good?"

He looked me in the eye, "Very."

That broke the ice. He started telling me about the concert.

The limo would pick me up at the hotel at six, Alex would be my escort. After the concert, he'd take me backstage. "Poor Alex," I commiserated, "having to go to the concert with a blind date."

"Actually, he said he's never seen the show from 'up front,' and he's looking forward to it. To tell the truth, though, I think he *was* leery of accompanying a lady he'd never seen—or that he *thought* he's never seen. But from the way he's been watching you in the rearview mirror, I don't think that's a problem anymore." I looked up, and sure enough, my eyes met Alex's in the mirror. He quickly glanced away.

"One minor correction, though," Darryl added, "you're *my* date. He's just watching out for you while I'm working."

Darryl told me he and the guys were going directly to the Coliseum after they got me settled at the hotel. He liked to get to wherever he was performing early. He said that way he could avoid some of the crowd, make sure last minute changes were in place, and most importantly, get psyched to perform. He described for me the factors involved in pulling off a show of that magnitude (90,000 people—the place was sold out). It was spellbinding. He was totally absorbed, and I got a glimpse of the electricity and magic that are his trademarks.

We were still deep in discussion when we arrived at the hotel. Alex popped the trunk and got out. Sam lowered his window as a doorman approached. Sam said something to the man, who nodded, pulled a waffle key from his pocket, and handed it to Sam.

I turned back to Darryl. He had pulled a big black hat out from somewhere, and put it on. He'd put the sunglasses back on and was shrugging into a shapeless gray cardigan sweater. Surprised, I asked, "Dare, are *you* going in?"

"Sure. You don't think I'd let a lady go up to a strange hotel room in a strange city alone, do you?"

By this time Alex had my bags and Sam was opening my door. We entered the hotel and walked through the lobby. Darryl and I side by side; Sam in front and Alex behind. We didn't sprint, but we didn't stroll, either. We entered an elevator and Sam pressed the button for eighteen.

On the eighteenth floor, we quickly found Suite 1801. It wasn't hard; the only other "room" was suite 1802. Sam unlocked the door and stepped inside, holding the door open for me. The suite was fabulous: fully stocked bar, projection screen TV, a balcony garden, a full kitchen. Alex took my bags into the bedroom.

I noticed a large bouquet of red roses in a vase on the coffee table. The card read: "I'm glad you're here. See you soon. DDB."

"Oh, Darryl, the flowers are just beautiful! Roses are my favorite."

"Glad you like them. I wasn't sure what to send you, so I sent roses because they're *my* favorite."

I broke the stem off one of the roses, and put it into a buttonhole in his collar. "Well, let me share them with you."

He actually blushed! "Thank you," he said faintly.

He walked to the bedroom door where Sam and Alex had disappeared—we could hear them admiring the Jacuzzi in the bathroom. "Hey, you guys, come on," Darryl hollered through the doorway. "We gotta get moving. Let's get out of here and let the lady unpack."

Sam came out of the bedroom, and his eyes went straight to the flower in Darryl's collar. *This one doesn't miss a trick,* I thought. He walked up to Darryl, sniffed the flower, and quipped, "Nice corsage, boss."

Alex came over to me. "You know I'll be by for you at six?"

Darryl glared at him, "Take care of her," he said. "But don't get *too* attached, my brother. *I'm* taking over after the concert."

"Don't worry, man," Alex said. "She'll be safe as in her mother's arms."

"Yeah, well," Darryl replied warningly, "that's fine. Just remember that *you're* not her mother!"

Alex looked at me and shrugged, "There's just no pleasing some people." Then he grinned. "See *you* at six—sharp."

Sam was at the hall entry door, "Gentlemen, let's hit it." He waved at me, and he and Alex walked out. I walked with Darryl toward the door.

"Everything okay?" he asked.

"Okay? I'm so excited I feel like I'm going to jump out of my skin!"

"I hope not. My plan is to see you—with skin—later tonight."

Just before we got to the open doorway, out of sight of Sam and Alex, Dare stopped me with a hand on my arm. He leaned over and kissed me lightly on the cheek. "See you later," he said without looking at me, and quickly walked out.

I closed the door and just stood there a moment. *Steady, girlfriend,* I told myself. *Just friends, remember?*

Then I ran for the bathroom, suddenly reminded the last such visit was several hours and thousands of miles ago. I saw why Sam and Alex were so intrigued by the Jacuzzi; the thing was a work of art. Turquoise marble with gold faucets, it was big enough for several people to fit into comfortably.

The telephone rang. There was one on the wall, next to the Jacuzzi. I picked it up, thinking it must be Tiff, checking to see if I had arrived safely. A man inquired, "Hello, may I speak with Mrs. Delaney, please?"

"This is she."

"Good afternoon, Mrs. Delaney. I am Marshall Maitland, the hotel manager. Welcome to our hotel. I hope you enjoy your stay with us. Is there anything you require?"

"How thoughtful of you, Mr. Maitland. I'm fine. The suite is perfect."

"Would you like me to send a maid up to unpack?"

I was beginning to get into the spirit of this! "No, there's no need. I'm traveling very lightly this trip." I had to stop myself from adding "my good man."

"Very well, then. If I can in any way be of assistance, please don't hesitate to let me know."

I thanked him and hung up. *Well,* I thought, *now* that's *serv-*

ice with a smile! I wondered what triggered the call: Darryl Bridges's staff making the arrangements, or the $2,000.00 credit to the account.

I went into the bedroom, kicked off my shoes, and sat down on the bed. It felt so good that I swung my feet up on the bed, leaned back, and crossed my ankles, while putting my hands behind my head. *Hey,* I thought, *I could get to like this!* Then I picked up the phone and called home. Tiff was probably getting worried. We talked for an hour—I had to tell her every detail. As we said goodbye, Tiff warned, "Have a great time, Mom, but keep your eye on Darryl. Sounds like he's trying to put a move on you."

I had to laugh. "Girl, don't be silly. Do you think *that* man would have to send all the way to Lansing, Michigan—of all places—to find a woman to 'put a move on?' If he stood on the nearest street corner and crooked his finger, women would throw themselves at him like confetti. Anyway, if you had seen him when I first got into the car, you'd know he wasn't trying to put a move on anything . . . except maybe himself. I thought at first he was going to jump out of the window to get away from me."

"Why? Did he act stuck up, or something?" Tiffani demanded, and I could hear in her voice "He'd better not!"

"No, it was just that he seemed more edgy over us meeting again than I was. Although he tried his best to hide it. And he's anything but stuck up. Once we started talking, he relaxed, and he was just like he is over the phone—really nice, with a quirky sense of humor, and . . . just people. There's something sweet—and kind of sad—about him."

"Still, you watch him."

"Tiff, the man's been a perfect gentleman."

"Well, watch out anyway," she repeated. "He might be a wolf in sequined clothing." I laughed again. Then she asked, "What are you and he doing after the show?"

"*After* the show? Nothing. He hasn't said anything about us *doing* something after the show. He'll probably be worn out.

He said he'd see me backstage. We'll probably talk for a little while, and then he'll ask Alex to bring me back here."

"Watch that Alex, too. It sounds like he's got the hots for you."

"Tiffani, you think everybody's 'got the hots' for me. Alex is just a kid—he couldn't be over twenty-five."

"And he probably thinks you're under thirty, my young-looking mom, so don't think he won't hit on you."

I told her I'd call when I got in from the concert and not to worry about me. It was two-thirty. I had been too jumpy to eat before I left home. Not that I wasn't still jumpy, but I had to eat something to last through the day.

Back in the living room, I spied a humongous fruit basket on the bar. More goodies from Darryl? No, the card read: "Thank you for choosing the Los Angeles Regal—Marshall Maitland, Resident Manager." I picked out an apple, taking a bite as I went into the kitchen. I opened the refrigerator—and whistled. There was enough food to hold a political convention. Bottles of wine: red, white, and champagne; a large covered tray of cold cuts and cheeses; a giant bowl of paté; several jars of caviar; an enormous vegetable tray . . .

I found bread in the bread box on the counter and fixed myself a turkey sandwich (with Grey Poupon mustard, what else?). There was Pepsi in the fridge. Eating the sandwich I thought, *Well, better get unpacked,* and went back into the bedroom. I hadn't brought much with me: my outfit for the concert, jeans and some tops, a dress for Saturday evening, and a pants suit to wear home.

Unpacking, I caught a glimpse of myself in the mirror and was glad I had decided to wear a dress on the flight since Darryl thought I had "great legs." It was just a simple black dress with a V neckline and a gold and black belt, but I looked nice in it. I had almost worn jeans, but at the last moment decided not to.

It only took about fifteen minutes to unpack. I decided to take a long soak in the Jacuzzi; to just relax until time to get dressed. There were several thick terry cloth robes in the closet. I took one, undressed, and pinned up my hair. I found a large bottle of bubble bath in the bathroom, and took a shower while the Jacuzzi was filling. After the shower, I put on the robe, went into the kitchen and got another Pepsi. Taking it with me, I got my "Pivot Point" tape from my luggage and popped it into the stereo. Then I went back into the bathroom and slipped into the Jacuzzi—ahhhhh! Heaven!

Sipping the Pepsi, I leaned back, more relaxed than I had been in days. As the old song goes, "If my friends could see me now!" But they couldn't. Neither friends nor family knew I was here. Nobody knew anything about my friendship with Darryl except Tiffani; and only because I'd *had* to tell her. She'd picked up the phone a few times when he had called. They had even chatted a bit once or twice.

But I swore her to secrecy, explaining my relationship with Darryl was too juicy a secret for anyone to keep. I told her if word got out it could possibly *end* the relationship. Darryl never said anything about keeping things on the q.t., but I knew he'd absolutely hate it if the Lansing Journal's headline one day read, "Superstar Darryl Bridges Involved With Local Lansing Woman." Once I put it to Tiff *that* way, she understood, and kept mum.

Listening to the music, I closed my eyes and tried to picture Darryl the way he looked when I gave him the rose; trying to reconcile that image with the voice coming from the stereo.

I woke with a start. Good Lord! What time was it? There was a digital clock on the wall; it was 4:35. I'd been asleep in the Jacuzzi for over an hour! I jumped out of that seductive tub, put on the robe, and went into the bedroom to get dressed. The telephone message light was flashing. When I called the message center, the operator said, "One moment, ma'am. Yes . . . A Mr. Burns called at three fifty-five. He was sorry he missed you, and said he'd see you at seven o'clock."

Mr. "Burns"? I said aloud. *Mr. Burning . . . as in Bridges! Darryl! Of course he knew I'd realize it was him.*

By five-thirty I was dressed. I had agonized over what to wear. I wanted something simple and causal, but a little special, too. I finally decided on black jeans, an off-white, long sleeve silk shirt, and a black vest with off-white lace trim. No purse—I put my lipstick, a small comb, a roll of breath mints, a tiny tube of perfume, and my room key in my pockets. I didn't think I needed them, but I also tucked three twenty dollar bills into the fifth pocket of my jeans. A girl can't be too careful. Mama always said, "Have cab fare home."

At 5:45, I heard a chime. It must have rung three times before I realized it was a doorbell! I'd never stayed in a hotel room that had a doorbell before! Feeling like a rube, I went to the door. Showtime!

"Alex," I said, "Come in . . . you're early."

"Yes . . . and you're *ready?*"

"Yep."

"A woman that's not only ready on time, but early! Hallelujah!" He looked at me. "Hey, you look terrific!"

"Thank you. You're not so bad yourself." He had on a blue silk shirt and baggy jeans. I realized what a very attractive man he was.

"Thank *you.*" He motioned to the door, "Shall we?"

When we got to the limo, he started for the rear door. I protested, "I'd rather sit up front with you, Alex, if you don't mind the company."

He gave me a big smile, opened the front door, and replied, "I wouldn't mind one bit." He got in the driver's side and we pulled out. "I decided I'd better come for you a little earlier; the crowds around the stadium are worse than usual. It might take us a bit longer than I originally figured," he said, turning onto the freeway.

"Alex, this is probably a dumb question, but where are you going to find space to park this thing, once we get there?"

"Oh, we've got our own private area," he laughed. "Don't worry. I haven't mislaid the boss's ride once in all the time I've been working for him."

"How long is that?"

"Two years."

"How'd you get the job? It sure couldn't have been in the Want Ads."

He laughed again, "No. I was a Darryl Bridges scholarship recipient."

"You *were?*"

"Yeah. When I got out of high school I had good grades, but no money, you know?" I nodded. "So I went into the Marines—a two year hitch. I had *some* money for school, but not enough. I heard about the scholarship program, and applied. When I got it, I wrote Dare a thank you letter. He answered it, and we kept in touch. After I got my degree . . ." He looked over at me, "It's in mass communications. Anyway, after I got my degree, I couldn't find a job. Dare offered me one.

"I'm not just Darryl's driver. I work with him on a lot of projects, and I'm learning about the entertainment business—all aspects of it. Not only the music industry, but print media, TV, and film, too. Learning inside stuff—things you can't get in a classroom. And I'm picking up a lot about the commercial end of it, too. He's a hell of a businessman." After a short pause, he added, "Can I ask *you* something? Dare hasn't told us much about you. Apparently you guys kept in touch after Atlanta?"

"Uh-huh," I replied vaguely.

Alex smiled, "Not talking, huh? Okay, mystery lady, I'll back off." He looked at me again, "I always *did* admire the man's taste."

Just as traffic started to get heavy, he exited the freeway, "It's going to be one big parking lot from here on in. We'll make better time on the streets." In about ten minutes we were approaching the rear of the stadium. There was a police barricade all around it, and plenty of cops, too. Alex pulled up to a guard who must have recognized him (or the car). The guy immediately pulled aside a barrier, and Alex pulled the car into a lot designated "Stadium Staff Parking." Alex pulled the car right up next to a large door marked "STAGE." There were several uniformed guards nearby.

"Alex, you're parking *here?"*

"Yeah," he said, "Dare's got to get out of here fast after the show." He grinned, "He does have a *few* perks."

We went in the door. Several young Hulk Hogan look-alikes sat just inside. One said, "What's happening, man?"

"You got it," Alex said as we walked by.

We walked down a long, dim hallway, passing what I guessed were dressing rooms, walked up some stairs, and we were backstage. I could hear the audience talking, and yelling, and cheering. We were in the wings on the right-hand side of the stage. The stage was thick with haze from a smoke machine. Darryl was in the wings on the other side with some musicians. He was wearing a black and white satin shirt and white leather pants. He looked up, smiled, and waved. Then he frowned at Alex, looking at his wrist, as if to say, "What kept you?"

"Uh-oh," Alex said, "Guess we're late—the show's about to start. Let's get to our seats." 'I looked at my watch—it was 7:09.

I looked at Dare, pointed to my leg, made a gesture like breaking a twig, then pointed to him. He smiled and gave me a thumbs up. Alex was leading me by the hand now. It was so dark I could hardly see. We went down a short flight of stairs and along a narrow, shadowy corridor. Alex stopped and opened a door I hadn't even seen. We were out into the stadium. There were several burly guards just outside the door. Another guard was holding two front row seats, just slightly to the right of center, for us.

Just as we reached the seats, the sound of gently falling rain was heard. The smoke on stage started to get thicker and the sound of falling rain grew steadily louder and stronger, joined by the sound of thunder. All at once, there was the flash of a hundred strobe lights—like lightening—and Darryl jumped from a hidden recess to front center stage!

The audience went crazy. People were screaming and yelling,

whistling and crying. Darryl just stood there in a floor length black cloak, covered with sequined patterns of the moon and stars, motionless. The ovation never let down one bit—if anything, it got stronger and louder the longer he stood there. After whipping the crowd into a frenzy by just standing still, Darryl finally jerked off his cloak, tossed it aside, and launched into the first song, "Step Lively."

I was swept along with everybody else. I had never seen Darryl perform in person before. As dynamic as his performances on TV and in videos are, they hadn't prepared me for the impact of the real thing. He took command the second he set foot on stage, and never loosened his grip.

After two up-tempo numbers, he slowed the pace, sitting down at the piano, singing "Basic Needs," one of my favorites. It was just Darryl, the band, and the back up singers—no dancers. During the second verse, he left the piano, walked over, and stood right in front of where Alex and I were sitting. He smiled down at me, and blew me a kiss, pointing his finger as he did as if to make sure I'd know it was for me. All around me the crowd cheered, most of the women screaming. By reflex, I blew him a kiss back. He laughed, and moved off to the other side of the stage.

The show was two hours of non-stop phenomenon. Several women fainted and had to be carried out. Darryl was unbelievable. His voice and song delivery went from heart-breakingly pure and clear on the ballads, to raw, wild, and sexy on the fast numbers. His dancing was incomparable to anything I'd ever seen.

Alex was caught up as much as everybody else. Despite working for Darryl for two years, and seeing him almost daily, Alex was yelling and clapping like a maniac. At one point he turned to me and said, "Man! The Wiz is *really* on fire tonight!"

After the finale, the crowd didn't want it to end. They stomped and chanted, "Dar-ryl! Dar-ryl!" over and over again. Darryl did two encores. At the end of the second, Alex said,

"Let's go. He never does more than two encores. If he didn't set a limit, they'd keep him here all night." Dare's more knowledgeable fans apparently knew this; a lot of people were then starting to leave, although many were still whistling and cheering for Dare to come back one more time.

We made our way to the door backstage. A guard unlocked it for us. We retraced our steps, and were back at the dressing rooms. Only this time the hall was brightly lit, and full of people, many carrying instruments, costumes, or equipment. Alex led me to the side, out of the stream of traffic. "Wait here just a sec. Let me make sure he's dressed." He disappeared through a doorway across from where I was standing.

A tall, slender black guy I recognized as the bass player came by with his guitar in his hands. "Hey, pretty lady, what's your story? Why are you standing here all by yourself? Need some company?"

Before I could answer, Alex appeared behind him. "She's not by herself, Jesse. She's with me," he said, reaching around him for my hand.

The tall guy stepped back. "No offense, man. But you should know better than to leave a woman who looks *this* good back here all alone." He winked at me and walked off.

Alex led me over to the doorway he'd gone through. We were in a sort of reception room—there were sofas and chairs all around. A large table was set up against one wall, loaded with things to eat and drink. There were lots of people milling around. Some of them were Darryl's dancers, background singers, and musicians. I drew a lot of curious stares as Alex walked me to a door at the very back of the room. He knocked on the door and, without waiting for an answer, opened it and motioned me in.

Darryl was sitting with his back to the door at a lighted mirror, removing his stage makeup. He still had on his outfit from the last number. He looked into the mirror, saw me standing there, and smiled. Alex hadn't come in with me, and had closed the door as he left. Darryl stood and turned to face me,

"How'd you like it?" He was still flushed, as well he might be, after the spectacular display he'd just put on.

I didn't know how to answer. I couldn't think of any words that came even close to how I felt. Then Darryl looked sheepishly at the chair next to his, "I guess the first thing you'd 'like' is a seat, huh? Sorry, I get carried away." He held the other chair out for me, "Please."

As I sat down he asked, "Do you mind if I take this stuff off my face while we talk?" His teeshirt was stuck to his chest. He followed my gaze and looked down at himself. "I get kinda sweaty out there," he added apologetically as he sat down again.

"Well . . ." he said, looking into the mirror and taking a tissue to the makeup again. "So, what's the verdict? How'd you like it?" When I didn't answer straightaway, he stopped removing the makeup and turned to face me. "You did *like* it, didn't you?" He said this with a laugh, but there was a sliver of uncertainty in his eyes.

"Darryl, I'd never seen you perform in person, before tonight. I wasn't prepared for . . . for *this*. It was electrifying," I finished simply.

He smiled again—with his eyes as well, this time—"Thank you, ma'am. High praise indeed for a man without manners enough to offer you a seat."

"I was thrilled when you blew me a kiss."

"The least I could do for a lady who came three thousand miles to see me perform."

There was a knock at the door. When Darryl answered, a rather short, fiftyish woman entered. She looked at me and said, "Oh . . . hello." Unlike the other people around Darryl I'd encountered, she didn't seem at all surprised to see me.

Darryl turned to me, "Angela, I'd like you to meet the woman who keeps me sane. This is Mary McCoy, my personal assistant. Mary, Angela Delaney."

"Hi, Mary."

"Nice to meet you. How was your trip out?"

Darryl looked at me, "Mary authorized your travel arrangements."

"Good to meet you, too, Mary," I said. "Everything went as smooth as silk, and my hotel suite is divine."

"Glad to hear it."

As she and Darryl went on to discuss some messages he had received, I looked around the room. It was a mess. Not dirty, but it was very untidy. There were costumes thrown everywhere. I saw at least three pair of Darryl's shoes scattered across the floor. At 5′11″, he was only a few inches taller than average for a man, but he had some mighty big feet. I resolved to check out the shoe size, if I got the chance.

The dressing table, where we were sitting, was covered with makeup containers, fan letters, and several bouquets of flowers. Then I smiled. There on the counter, in a glass of water, was the rose I'd given him at the hotel.

"Oh . . . and Dare," Mary was continuing, "one of Paulo Pagnelli's people called, wanting to know when you'd make it to the party at Smarty's. I told him *my* calendar shows the party's not for another two weeks, but he said Paulo had talked to you about changing the date." I wondered why Paulo Pagnelli, an opera star, would be calling Dare.

"Damn, he did! I forgot! Mary, I forgot to tell you, and then I conveniently forgot all about the change myself. Call him back, and tell him I'll be there about eleven." Mary nodded and left.

Darryl looked at me, "Paulo Pagnelli arranged a club gala to foster celebrity support for Homes, USA. He called me about moving it up to tonight because of the concert, to generate more publicity. I've got to go. You don't mind *too* much, do you?"

I *was* disappointed. I'd hoped to spend a little more time with him that evening, but those are the breaks. If the party was for Homes, USA, I knew he *did* have to go.

I stood up, "No, Dare, of course I don't mind. I'd better get out of the way, so you can get ready. Can someone take me back to the hotel?"

He looked surprised, took my hand, and gently pulled me back down to the chair. "Whoa. I didn't mean 'Do you mind excusing me,' I meant 'Do you mind going with me'?"

"Going *with* you?"

"Sure. You agreed to be my date for the evening. I'm not about to let you renege on me. So far this evening has been me, you—and about 90,000 other people. That's not much of a date. You're going to have to do better than that."

Although the thought of being in the midst of a bunch of celebrities was intimidating, my heart soared at the thought of going with Darryl. Then it sank again. "Darryl, I'd love to go . . . but I can't. I don't have anything with me to wear." I looked down at my outfit, "I can't go in *this.*"

"Well, I guess that's my fault. I did tell you strictly casual, didn't I?" He looked over my outfit. "You're right. Cute as that is, it's not going to cut it for this soiree." He gave me a devilish look, "But you're not getting out of it *that* easily." He picked up a phone on the dressing table, and punched a couple of numbers. "Get Marcel in here, pronto," he said and hung up. "Surely I have enough clout in this town to get a lady a party dress at only . . ." He looked at a clock on the counter, "9:45 on a Friday evening."

There was a knock at the door, and at Darryl's response, in walked a tall, slender man with wavy blond hair, wearing an ultra sharp double-breasted suit. "What's up, ducks?" he said to Dare, but looking inquisitively at me.

"Angela, this is Marcel. He's the best costumer in the country," Darryl began.

"In the *world,* sweetie," Marcel corrected him.

"Marcel, this is my friend Angela. She's from out of town, and needs an outfit for a party tonight because someone who should have known better—me—told her to bring only casual clothes. Can you help us out?"

Marcel walked over to me. He looked about thirty-five, and

reminded me for all the world of a young Liberace. "Stand up, doll," he told me. I did. "Turn around, honey." I did that, too.

"Are there any dress shops that are still open or that you can *get* opened?" Dare asked.

Marcel shrugged, "Why bother with that? I can take the lady over to Monumental Studios, and she'd have acres of outfits to choose from. Suits?"

Darryl bowed to him, "Marcel, you're a genius!"

Marcel spread his hands, "But, of course."

Darryl looked questioningly at me, "Hey, we haven't asked how *you* feel about all this. Maybe you wouldn't like going to a party in an outfit that was somebody's costume for a movie."

"Are you kidding? I'd *love* it! What a kick!"

Dare shook his head, "My kind of woman!" he laughed. Then he said to Marcel, "Why don't you two go on over to the studio and I'll meet you there." He turned to me, "It'll take me about an hour, okay?"

"Sure, Darryl, that's fine."

Marcel opened the door for me. "Madame," he said, and escorted me out of the dressing room. If people gave me wondering looks when I went into the dressing room, they outright *stared* when I left with Marcel. Most of the stares were just nosy, but one small, pretty Eurasian girl, gave me a positively poisonous look.

We went into the corridor and ran smack into Alex. "Hey, where're *you* going?"

I explained the situation. "Oh," he said, "Okay, see you in a bit." He stared at Marcel, "This is a real special lady, man. So take it slow."

Marcel just sniffed at him and turned to me saying, "Come, darling," and walked away. He added, "Such a crass young man," as we walked down the hallway.

Outside, Marcel led me to a white Ferrari. "Buckle up, hon," he said, as we took off—and I do mean took off—that man did forty in the parking lot. When we got on the freeway, he really opened it up. "Boy," I gulped, "we must be doing eighty."

"Eighty-five," he corrected. "But don't worry, dear. I'm the world's best driver. What's the use of having a sports car if you don't sport in it?"

I made no comment.

He glanced over at me, "So, where are you from?"

"Michigan."

"Michigan? I'm originally from Detroit myself."

"You're kidding."

"Nope. Graduated from Cass Tech High School. If you're from Michigan, I'm sure you've heard of it."

"Heard of it? I'm a Technician, too. Class of '76."

" '76?," he peered at me, "How old were you when you graduated—five?"

"I only wish, but thanks for the compliment," I laughed anxiously, hoping Marcel would get his eyes off me and back on the road.

We talked about Detroit and how it got such an undeservedly bad rap in the media, "Detroit can be dangerous, but name me any city that size that isn't. L.A., New York, Chicago, Dallas; they all got crime, crime, and more crime. Drugs and corruption through and through. But Detroit gets singled out."

"I've felt that way a long time. I'm glad to hear somebody else has come to the same conclusion."

"No 'bout a-doubt it," he said. Yep, he was a transplanted Detroiter, all right; he had the lingo. Then he added, "But if you're from Michigan, how'd you run into Darryl?"

"It's a long story."

He smiled at me, "Okay—I know Dare doesn't like putting his business in the street. Well, at least you're having better luck with him than *I* did."

I must have had a strange look on my face, because then he said, "Hey, look, doll, the man is gorgeous, famous, talented, sexy, AND rich. I had to try—but no dice. Don't you worry about *that.* Whatever rumors you may have heard, he's—alas—straight as a ruler. Every guy of the persuasion in show business has hit on him at one time or another and he's just not interested. I know. We've got our own grapevine on who is and is not."

He'd exited the freeway and was approaching the guard station at the studio entrance. "Please have someone with a key meet me at the costume shed," he told the guard. We drove on until we came to a cavernous warehouse of a building—this was the costume "shed?" There was a guard standing by the door. "Here we are, sweetie," Marcel said. We got out of the car, and the guard let us into the building.

Marcel led me to a large dressing room near the entrance, "Just wait here. I'll go see what I can find."

"All right . . . uh . . . I wear a size . . ."

"I know the dress size, dear. That's my business." He tapped my hip, "A tad too much here, but otherwise—not bad. I can't stand bony, shapeless broads. But I do need your shoe size."

I told him. He whistled, "My! We're a bounteous girl all over, aren't we? Not to worry, some of the world's most famous women have generous feet. Back in a flash. Why don't you peel down and put on one of the robes over there?" and he left, closing the door.

I went to the row of robes on hooks he had indicated and found one my size. I took everything off but my bra and panties, and put on the robe. There was a knock at the door. When I answered, Marcel came in with several dresses over his arm and hung them on a hook near the door. "Here you are, honey. You can have your pick, but for *my* money . . ." he reached into the dresses, and pulled one out, "this is the winner."

The dress had a strapless red satin bodice and a wide waistband of the same fabric. There was a loose cap-sleeved sheer black chiffon overblouse that disappeared into the top of the waistband. The skirt was three layers of softly gathered black chiffon over a black taffeta underskirt. It hung straight down from the waist, but was very slightly ruffled at the hem on each layer with a narrow strip of red satin binding. The fabric was sprinkled with diminutive sparkles, twinkling like tiny diamonds.

I gasped, "Marcel! It's heavenly!"

"Of course it is—it's one of mine. And it'll show off your best assets: that tiny waist, those legs, and those marvelous boobs. Try it on while I get some goodies to go with it." He left again.

I took off the robe and my bra, and stepped into the dress, praying, "Please let it fit!" I pulled it up, fitted my bosom to the bra built into the dress (bless you, Marcel!), and reached back. It zipped up without a hitch. I closed my eyes and turned around to face the large mirror over the counter. The dress looked like it had been made for me. The bodice reached to just below the cleft of my full breasts so that a tiny amount of cleavage showed. The waistline fit perfectly on my slender midriff, and the hem fell to just below my knees. My hips are a size larger than my "marvelous boobs," so the skirt, instead of hanging straight down, flared out slightly at the hips, making my waist appear to be even smaller. The effect was elegant and polished, but sexy.

I ran my hand over my hair, glad now that I *hadn't* decided to cut it last summer. Now it reached to my shoulder blades, turning just under. It looked like black satin under the bright light of the room.

Marcel knocked again. I let him in. "Well?" I asked, twirling.

He looked me over, "Perfection," he pronounced, "But then . . . what did you expect?" He was holding a pair of red satin pumps with two inch heels and a small matching envelope bag. "Slip on the shoes, love—and pray." I did both. The shoes fit; they were snug, but not tight.

Marcel pulled pantyhose and what looked like two small red roses out of his pocket. "This completes Madame's ensemble." The roses turned out to be red satin earrings—clips; he'd noticed that my ears weren't pierced. The guy really *did* know his business. "There's all kinds of combs and makeup in those drawers along the counter," he added. "Are you set? Need anything else?"

"Nope. You've thought of everything."

"I know. Okay, then I'll leave you to do your thing."

I took the dress off carefully, hung it back up, and pulled on the pantyhose. Sheer as they looked, they had support. The panty had tummy control, and my legs felt rejuvenated.

I took my things out of the pockets of my jeans, and put them on the counter. Then I put my clothes in a small plastic bag I found in a drawer. Finding blush and mascara, I made my face a little more dramatic than I had for the concert. Then I put my things into the handbag. I had just slipped the dress back on, when there was a knock at the door. "Marcel?"

"Yes, it's me," he said. " 'Dare's here. He's waiting just outside. Are you ready?"

"Almost," I replied. "Give me five minutes. Oh . . . Marcel . . ." I went to the door and opened it a crack, "Please ask Alex to put this in the trunk for me," I said, handing him the bag containing my clothes. I leaned a little further out the door, and kissed him on the cheek, "Thanks for everything, fellow Technician."

"You're more than welcome, love. Just name the first one after me." He reached out, turned me around, and zipped up the dress. "Don't dawdle, now." He looked me up and down, "Another Marcel triumph!"

After closing the door, I slipped into the shoes. I sucked a breath mint while I dabbed a little perfume on my wrists and neck. I was ready—scared, but ready.

What are you scared of? Everybody at the party will be people just like you. They put their pants on one leg at a time, too. The guy you're with is the man of the hour, and he's *confident you won't disgrace him, or he wouldn't have asked you in the first place. You look sensational, if I do say so myself—so let's go!*

Putting the remains of the mint into a wastebasket, I picked up the purse, and walked out of the room and through the exterior door.

The limo was parked near the door. Dare, Marcel, and Alex were standing next to the car, talking. Dare was wearing a black tuxedo and a red dress shirt with rows of tucks down the front. Instead of a bow tie, he wore a large black broach at his throat, and in his lapel was a red rose. Even wearing the inevitable black shades, he looked like a prince. Hearing the click of my heels, they all turned. Darryl just stood there a moment, watching as I approached. He reached up, slowly took off the shades, and put them in an inside jacket pocket. Then he began to walk toward me.

About two feet apart, we both stopped. After a few seconds, I felt self-conscious under his gaze and glanced down. When I looked up again, he was still staring at me. He moved a step closer. "You're breathtaking," he said, so quietly I barely heard him.

He turned and offered his arm. We walked to the limo where Alex was holding open the door, and, waving to Marcel, rode off into the night.

Three

After the Dance

"Dare, stop staring. You're making me nervous."

"I'm sorry. It's just that you look so beautiful in that dress. Not that you wouldn't look beautiful without a dress . . . I mean . . ."

I stopped him with a hand on his arm, "It's okay, Darryl, I know what you mean." I smiled, "Thank you."

The glass partition was still up. Alex was sneaking peeks, but couldn't hear us. Darryl slid a little closer, "Not nervous about the party, are you?"

"Well . . . a little."

"Don't be." He took my hand, "We'll only stay for an hour or so. We'll just put in an appearance and split, okay?" I nodded.

"You're really something," he continued. "At the airport you looked like a socialite. At the concert you looked like a PYT, and tonight you look like a goddess. Just how many sides *are* there to you, anyway?" He smiled, but there was some contemplation under his words.

"I'm a versatile woman, Mr. Bridges," I replied. "Anyway, *you* should talk. This morning you were a shy young man, at the concert you were a human tornado, and tonight you're Prince Charming. I *have* to be a quick change artist just to keep pace with you." After a beat, I asked, "Is that the rose I gave you?" He beamed and nodded, looking about ten years old.

We were in the heart of L.A. now. Darryl started pointing out various points of interest as we passed. In a short while, we arrived at the club. Again, police barricades lined both sides of the path from curb to entrance, with police on both sides as well. There were about three hundred people behind the barricades. Alex came around and opened the curb door. Darryl was next to the door, so he got out first, and the crowd gave a massive shout; some of the women screaming. He stood waving at the crowd with both hands for a moment, then turned back to the limo, extending his hand to me.

As I slid across the seat, the thin fabric of the skirt began to rise. I swung my legs to get out and as I put my feet on the curb, the dress rose to mid-thigh. The crowd let out another roar. This time it was the men who were yelling. I heard a loud wolf whistle, and another guy said, "Oooo-weee!"

When I took Darryl's hand and quickly stood my skirt fell back into place. Darryl had a peculiar look on his face—I hoped I hadn't embarrassed him. He put my hand through the crook of his arm and escorted me to the door, smiling at the crowd and waving with his free hand as we went. I didn't wave (nobody was there to see *me)*, but I did smile.

We entered a spacious vestibule. A roly-poly tuxedoed man met us, "Mr. Bridges! As always, a pleasure." He nodded to me, "Good Evening, miss." Turning back to Darryl, he said, "They're waiting for you, sir. This way, please."

Darryl nodded and said, "Lead on, Tony."

Tony led us not to the closed double door straight ahead, but across to and through a door at the side of the foyer. We were in the kitchen. The cooks and kitchen helpers gaped and grinned as we walked by. When one guy stuck out his hand, Darryl stopped to shake it and say hello. Tony led us to a double swinging door. He turned to Darryl, "One moment, Mr. Bridges, I'll let them know you're here," and he went out the door.

Through the doors' small glass insets, I could see Tony making his way through the dim room beyond and going to a man seated at one of the front tables. When Tony said something to him, the man got up, and approached the stage, where a small band was playing. At the same time, Tony headed back toward us. The man in the room went up on stage. As the man signaled the band, I saw he was Paulo Pagnelli. The band stopped just as Tony, along with two waiters, re-entered the double doors and stood in front of Darryl and me.

Darryl smiled, putting his free hand over mine, which was still resting in the crook of his arm. "Ready?" I swallowed, trying to smile back, and nodded.

The band gave a flourish. Pagnelli took the mike. "Ladies and gentlemen, may I introduce our guest of honor this evening, this year's chairman of Homes, USA . . . Mr. Darryl Bridges!" Pagnelli gestured in the direction of the kitchen doors. Just then, Tony went through the doors. The two waiters each took one door, swung them inward, holding each door open.

"Here we go," Darryl said.

We stepped forward into the room. A spotlight hit us and the band began to play "Step Lively." After about three steps, Darryl stopped and waved around the room. He kept my hand on his other arm, pressing his arm, and my hand, close to his side. I hoped he couldn't feel my trembling.

We then followed Tony across the room. Everybody was standing. Some people were standing on their *chairs,* whistling and cheering. Tony led us to an elevated booth at the side of the room. As we approached, I saw a woman sitting in the booth—the dancer who had given me the malicious look back at the stadium.

Darryl looked at her in surprise, "Jasmine, what are you doing here?" Dare and I were still standing, with the ever faithful Tony hovering nearby. The crowd was still applauding and cheering.

Tony inquired, "Mr. Bridges, is there a problem?"

Darryl quickly answered, "No. No problem at all," and gestured for me to sit on the side of the booth opposite the girl. I did, and scooted over so he could sit next to me. The spotlight went out and the ovation died down, as the band began to play Darryl's song "Love From the Shadows."

Tony asked if Darryl would like his "usual." Darryl responded, "Tony, tonight I'd like something a little special. How about a bottle of Dom Pérignon?"

Tony said, "At once, Mr. Bridges," and hurried off.

"Jasmine," Darryl repeated, turning to her again, "what are you doing here?"

"I hooked a ride with Ronnie Tripper," she said smugly. Ronnie Tripper was an up-and-coming stand-up comedian.

"That explains why you're at the party, Jazz, but it doesn't explain what you're doing *here.* If you're Mr. Tripper's date, shouldn't you be at *his* table?"

"Oh, he wandered off somewhere. Anyway, I thought you'd want me here when you arrived, so I told the head waiter I was with *your* party." She gave me an insolent stare, "Aren't you going to introduce me to your . . . companion?" The way she said "companion" made me sound like a toothless ninety-year-old woman on a walker.

Darryl started to say something, changed his mind, and curtly replied, "Certainly. Angela, this is one of my dancers, Jasmine Bryant. Jasmine, my good friend, Angela Delaney."

"Hello, Jasmine," I offered.

"Don't recall seeing *you* around before," she slurred. The lady apparently had a tad too much to drink.

"Mrs. Delaney is visiting from out of town," Darryl said frostily.

"Oh . . . so it's *Mrs.* Delaney, huh?" she said to me. "Well, let's hope *Mr.* Delaney doesn't find out you're here," she added, sounding like she'd just *love* to be the one to tell him.

I was getting a little perturbed with this broad. I fixed her with a look, "*Mr.* Delaney is deceased."

At least she had enough sense to be embarrassed, "Oh . . ."

Another guy would have hinted around for her to leave, or motioned for somebody to come and get her, or left *with* her, hoping to ditch her, and double back. Darryl didn't do any of those things. He just leaned over, looked her in the eye, and said, "Jasmine, Mrs. Delaney and I would like to talk privately. Would you excuse us?"

"Okay, Darryl . . . sure," she said, quickly rising. "See you later, okay?" Darryl didn't answer as she left the table.

"Angela, I'm sorry. I had no idea *she'd* be here, let alone here trying to start something. I took her with me to another charity function a few months ago. I thought she'd get a kick out of it, and the publicity could help her career. She's been acting bizarre ever since, but I never thought she'd pull a stunt like this."

"Darryl, you don't owe me an explanation."

"I just want you to understand."

"She's a stunning woman." I couldn't resist adding, "Too bad her behavior doesn't match her looks. She has such unusual coloring."

"Her father's black and her mother is Vietnamese. I gather she's had a pretty hard way to go. I guess that's why I've tried to overlook how she's been acting lately."

Tony came back then with two fluted glasses, followed by a waiter carrying a champagne bucket. Tony made a big production of opening the bottle and pouring some champagne for Darryl to taste. After Darryl's approval, Tony filled the glasses, and left. Darryl lifted his glass, "To roses."

"To roses," I echoed, touching my glass to his.

People started coming by. I met Denzel Washington, Robin Williams, Whoopi Goldberg, and on and on. The constant visitors were harder on Darryl than me. Whenever the visitor was a woman, Darryl, gentleman that he is, would stand. He kept popping up and down, and could hardly get to his champagne.

I looked at my watch and thought I would call Tiffani. I asked Darryl to excuse me, and he stood so I could leave the booth. "I'll be right back," I told him, and made my way to the door I thought must lead to the entrance hallway. A lot of people were checking me out as I went; not staring, but surveying me when they thought I wasn't looking. Some even smiled and nodded, or said hello. Out in the lobby, I saw a sign for the women's room, and went inside. There were a couple of telephone booths in the sitting room. I entered one and called home.

"Mom! Where have you *been?* I've called the hotel twice! It's three o'clock in the morning!" Tiffani scolded.

"Slow down, honey. It's only a little after midnight here, remember?"

"Gong! That's right—*I* feel like a blockhead. How was the concert? Are you back at the hotel now?"

"The concert was phenomenal. No, I'm not at the hotel. I'm at a party with Darryl."

"All right!" she cheered. "I told you he'd have something up after the concert." Suddenly she probed, "It's not one of those Hollywood orgy parties, is it?"

"Kid, have you lost your mind? It's a perfectly respectable party in a perfectly respectable club in downtown L.A. Look, honey, I don't want to be gone long. I just wanted to make sure you were all right, and let you know I was still out."

"Yeah, Mom, I'm fine. Call me when you get back to the hotel, okay?"

"Sure, but it might be late. Don't worry about me, I'm in good hands."

"Just make sure he keeps his 'good hands' to himself! Love you, Mom!"

I went into the next room, and entered a stall to straighten my pantyhose. Just as I was preparing to leave, someone came into the room. "I *told* you not to drink so much!" a voice said angrily. "If you don't cut it out they're going to throw you out on your ass!"

"I don't give a damn!" another voice shot back. "That fat bitch! Who does she think she is, coming in here making toasts, acting like the Queen of Sheba?"

"Jasmine, calm down," the other voice said. "She hasn't done a damn thing, and you know it. You're just jealous. You tried, but it just wasn't in the cards. Forget about him."

"He can't see being with me, but he shows up with *that* frump!"

"The woman's hardly a frump. Even Ronnie said, 'Hey, who's that fine babe with Darryl?' And she's not fat either. She's sure not skinny, but I'd call it voluptuous." The friend sounded like she'd had a few too many herself—she could hardly pronounce that last word. She added wistfully, "I wish I had just *part* of her chest. Who the hell *is* she, anyway?"

"Who knows?" Jasmine snapped. "Some hick stray Darryl pulled out of a haystack somewhere."

Okay, girlfriend, how do you deal with this? *Well, damned if I'm going to be trapped in a bathroom stall by two lushes. I'm* ready *to leave, and I'm* going *to leave.* I smoothed my dress, stuck my nose in the air, and sauntered out of the stall.

The two of them looked at me thunder-struck, not moving a muscle. Walking up to a mirror, I took out my lipstick, gave them my mellowest smile, and said, "Good evening." Then I took my sweet time applying lipstick and patting my hair before I waltzed past them to the door, and pulled it open. I started to walk out, then stopped and turned. "Oh . . . and Jasmine . . ." I said with a smile, "we moved all our haystacks out of the city limits *years* ago, dear." I batted my eyelashes twice, and left.

I made my way back to the table. The band had taken a break, and recorded music was playing when Benny Hawkins came by. "Hey, Darryl, what's happenin'?" They shook hands, then Benny turned to me. "Well . . . good evening . . ." he extended his hand, "I'm Benny Hawkins. It's a real pleasure to meet *you.*" Darryl introduced me, and without asking or being asked, Benny sat down. "Yes, indeed, a pleasure. Are you new to L.A.?"

The sound system started playing Darryl's "Mellow Movin'." Darryl grabbed my hand and started to rise, "Come on, Angie, let's dance."

I looked up in surprise, "What?"

But he pulled me up, said, "Excuse us, man," to Benny, and

started for the dance floor, leading me by the hand. When we got there, he turned to face me, and held out his arms, "Don't worry; I'll take it easy on you."

Oh, you will, will you, I thought, *well, we'll see about that.* I can't dance like Darryl Bridges (who can?), but I've been known to hold my own on a dance floor. I twirled twice and spun into his arms just as "he" began to sing the lyric. His eyes widened in surprise. Then, as we started dancing, he threw back his head and laughed. We moved into the music in perfect sync—his doing, not mine. He was so easy to follow.

At the end of the first verse he said, "Let's give them something to talk about. Hold this position," and we did, swaying in place to the music. As the chorus started he asked, "Do you remember the bop?"

"Try me," I challenged, and we swung into that.

We went through the rock steady, the bump, the hustle, and the tango hustle, with Darryl whispering the transitions to me as we went. Everybody else on the dance floor backed up and watched, cheering us on. We did the last chorus "free form," with Darryl doing some of the steps he's most famous for, and me doing my disco best. As the record was fading out, Darryl took my hand and turned his back to me placing my hand on his shoulder. He led me off the floor *a la* John Travolta in *Saturday Night Fever.*

The place went up in commotion. People were jumping up and down, waving and throwing napkins. It was a madhouse. Darryl led me back to our booth, Benny Hawkins had left, and we sat down. They wouldn't stop clamoring. The spotlight came on our table. Darryl stood up, bowed, and offered his hand. I thought, *what the hell,* stood, and took a bow myself. Then we took our seats again. They finally turned off the spotlight, and the uproar began to fade as the band, having come back, began to play—what else?—"Mellow Movin'."

Dare looked me over, "You're just terrific. I didn't know you were a dancer."

"I'm not. I love to dance, but I'm not *that* good at it. Out there was just me following you."

"No, it wasn't," he disputed. "You have to be a dancer in your soul to move like you just did."

Visitors really started to come by then. Dare and I hardly had a minute to ourselves. Tina Turner was chatting with us, when Benny Hawkins came back. "Mind if *I* ask your gorgeous friend to dance, Darryl?"

Dare didn't look too crazy about the idea, but he said, "Not if *she* doesn't mind."

Benny turned to me, "May I?"

I didn't want to. I'd rather have stayed with Darryl and I didn't like the look in Benny's eyes. "I'm still a little winded from the last dance. Maybe later."

But he wouldn't take no for an answer, and took my hand. "Oh, that was half an hour ago, and this is a nice slow one."

I knew if I objected further, Darryl would be forced to intervene. I didn't want to cause a scene—everybody was looking at us. So I smiled, said, "All right," and followed him to the dance floor.

The band was playing "Me And Mrs. Jones." Benny put his arm around me and held me close. Too close. I pushed back from him.

"You're a sight for sore eyes around here," he said.

"I am? Why?

"An honest-to-goodness sister. You're a rarity in La-La Land. Most of the *pretty* women of color in the circles *I* run in are phony and full of it . . ." his hand slid down to my butt, "and so skinny."

"Now, wait a minute, buddy." I moved his hand back up to my waist. "I don't care *who* you are. I don't play that, okay? Movie star or no, keep your hands where they belong, or I'm outta here."

He laughed that crazy laugh of his. "I knew it! A sister through and through! All right, I'll behave."

We danced in silence for a while, before he said, "Baby,

you're all woman. You look good, you feel good, you even smell good. What in the world are you doing here with *Darryl Bridges,* of all people?"

"What's that supposed to mean?" I retorted. Benny apparently let his macho man screen image go to his head. "I'm here with *Mr.* Bridges because he *asked* me. Why do you think?"

"Oh . . . and do you always do the things men ask you to do?" he sneered.

"That," I said pointedly, "depends on who's doing the asking, and what he's asking for."

"Suppose *I* was doing the asking? How about a telephone number where I can reach you? or better yet . . ." he pulled me close again, "why don't you and I just slip out of here?"

"What about Darryl?" I asked, pushing back again.

"What *about* Darryl? What's *he* gonna do—beat me up? Anyway, you're a real woman, baby, and what you need is a *real* man."

Mercifully, the song was coming to an end. "I *came* with a real man, Mr. Hawkins, and since I'm a real *lady,* I intend to leave with him. Thank you for the dance. No, I can find my way back to my seat." I left him standing there.

When I got back, Darryl was talking to Paulo Pagnelli, and introduced us. Seems there had been a short program and a film about Homes, USA before we arrived. Now Darryl was going to say a few words. He told me, "After I do this we can go, if you're ready."

"That's fine, Darryl."

"Are you okay? You look flushed."

"Yes, I'm fine; just a little breathless from dancing, I guess."

"Well," he said doubtfully, "If you're sure you're all right." He motioned for Tony, who had been lingering in the general area of our table almost all evening, and asked to have the car brought around. As Tony left, Dare said, "This will only take a minute. Be right back."

Paul and Darryl went on stage, and after a flourish from the band, Paul introduced Darryl. (Why do people say someone "needs no introduction"—then proceed to do just that?) Dare spoke for a few minutes about Homes, USA—its mission, and progress to date. Then he thanked everyone for their contributions and support, and announced that the evening had produced over a quarter million dollars for the charity. The assembled guests gave Darryl—and themselves—a big hand. Darryl said good night, and came back by the table for me. As we left, people reached out to shake his hand, or pat him on the back.

Alex and the limo were at the curb outside. The pack was now thinner, but many die-hards were still there. Darryl stopped once or twice to give autographs. A young black guy called out, "That's one fine looking lady you got there, man!"

Dare looked at me, then hollered back, "Yeah, man . . . I know!" That started them all whistling and laughing. Darryl took my hand and we walked the rest of the way to the car, where Alex was holding the door.

We both leaned back. "Angela, this has been the most marvelous evening I've had in a long time, but I'm bushed. Call it a night?"

"Yes, I'm about done in, myself. But you're astonishing. It's a wonder you're still on your feet, after the show, and all."

"I'm always pumped after a show. It takes me hours to gear down where I can sleep, but I'm about there now. You're the one that's amazing. Not many women could have handled that party the way you did. You carried yourself like a queen. The place was buzzing about you."

"About *me?* Darryl, even if that's true, it's only because I was with you."

"Maybe that was partially it at first. I mean . . ." he smiled ruefully, "I have a date so seldom, I guess it *is* news. But people kept watching you, especially after we danced. Everybody was wondering who you were. When you were dancing with Benny Hawkins, Gregory Peck came by, wanting to meet my 'charming dancing partner.' "

"Gregory Peck? I missed meeting *Gregory Peck?"*

Darryl chuckled, "I'll introduce you to him, I promise." He paused, "Speaking of Benny Hawkins, what did he say that upset you?"

This man's radar was sharp. Too sharp. Nothing escaped his notice. "It was nothing, really, Dare. He was just flirting a little." Darryl didn't say anything, but I could tell he didn't like it one bit.

Alex turned a corner and we were approaching the hotel. There was a crush of people outside the door. Dare leaned forward, lowered the glass panel, and asked, "What's going on?"

Alex replied, "Don't know, Dare. There's a whole mess of people out there, though."

"Don't stop, man. Drive past and we'll call from down the street."

Alex drove past the hotel. Some people turned to squint at the car, but I knew they couldn't see inside. I heard one woman say, "Is it him?" as we went by.

Alex drove down about six blocks and turned into a parking lot. He picked up the car phone, punched up the hotel, and asked for the night manager. "Hi, this is Alex Winston. I'm calling for Mrs. Delaney, your guest in Suite 1801. She's attempting to return to the hotel, but there seems to be some commotion outside. What's going on?" Alex listened for quite a while, then said, "I see . . . could you hold, please?" and he pushed the hold button.

"What's up?" Darryl asked anxiously.

"You're not gonna like it, man. Seems word's gotten out *you're* registered to Suite 1801, and apparently some girls spotted you leaving the lobby today. The hotel management's told the crowd you're not staying there, but nobody's buying it."

"Great!" Darryl said disgustedly. He turned to me, "I'm sorry about this, Angie."

"It's not your fault, Dare."

"Well, you sure can't stay there now. It wouldn't be safe.

Even if we could sneak in a back way or something, I wouldn't let you stay in that suite alone now."

"Yeah," Alex interjected. "The manager said they already caught some fool trying to break in." Alex looked at me, "He didn't get in, though, so your stuff's safe." He turned back to Darryl, "They offered to post a guard at the door, compliments of the hotel."

"No way, man," Darryl replied. "She'd be like a prisoner in there. And it's still too risky."

"The manager's also offered to call around to other hotels in the area, to locate a vacant suite. He said they'll deliver Angela's bags wherever we say."

"I've got a better idea." Darryl turned to me, "Now, Angela, don't take this the wrong way—but why don't you stay . . . with me?"

"With *you?*"

"Sure. I rattle around at home all by myself most of the time. You'd have your own suite there, too. Tomorrow I could show you around the place. It'll be fun." He looked me in the eye, "No funny business, I promise. And this way, I'll know you're safe." He looked at me compellingly, "And I would really welcome your company."

It took me all of about three seconds to make up my mind, "Well . . . If you're sure I wouldn't be a bother . . ."

"A bother? Woman, please! Alex, tell the hotel to have Angela's stuff packed and delivered to the house as soon as possible. Give him the directions, and . . ."

"Darryl," I interrupted, "could you ask them to bring my roses, too?"

He gave me a gentle little smile, "Sure . . . Alex, tell the man to bring the lady's roses, okay? Then call ahead and ask Monroe to prepare a guest room."

While Alex was still on the phone, he pulled out of the parking lot, and we were soon on another freeway.

"Darryl, if Tiffani calls and they tell her I've checked out, she'll be worried to death. Can I call her from here, or should I wait until we get to your house?"

"Oh, you can call her right now." He pulled a telephone out of a recess near his seat (a car with *two* telephone lines?). "Let me dial it for you." He punched out the numbers and handed the phone to me. "Here you are."

"Hello?"

"Tiff? It's me, honey. Listen, there was a problem at the hotel, and . . ."

"What problem? Are you okay, Mama?"

"I'm fine, honey. It was nothing like that. But I'm not going to be staying at the hotel. I'm . . . I'm going to be at Darryl's," I said quickly.

"What! Mom, have you gone crazy?"

"Tiffani, I'll be all right, and . . ."

"But what if he . . ."

"Tiff, I know what I'm doing . . ."

Darryl touched my arm, "May I speak to her?"

I nodded. "Tiff, Darryl wants to talk to you." I handed him the phone.

"Tiffani," he said, "I know you're concerned about your mother. I promise you she'll be fine. I've got a big house. She'll have her own suite and all the privacy she needs," which I thought was a very circumspect way for him to say what we all knew he was saying.

"Dare," I whispered, "can you give her a number where she can reach me?" He gave her the number, then said, "Don't worry, I'll take good care of her. Good night. Here's your mom back."

"Mama? I guess it's okay. He sounds really nice."

"He *is* really nice, baby," I said looking at Darryl with a smile. He gave me a bashful smile back, and looked away. "I'll call you tomorrow. I love you."

Darryl had let the glass divider up while I was talking. After replacing the phone he said, "It'll take about forty minutes to get there, so just relax. Care for something to drink?" He pointed to a small refrigerator under the seat opposite us.

"No, Darryl, thank you."

"How about some music?" He flipped open a case full of CDs. "Anything special you'd like to hear? Long as it's not one of mine."

"Anything you like is fine. In fact, I'm curious what you listen to."

He put on Earth, Wind, and Fire's classic "That's the Way of the World" album. "Is this okay?"

"Perfect," I said, "It's one of my favorites."

"Sorry about your things being delayed. We'll find you something to sleep in, and your stuff should be out by morning."

"That's about the tenth time tonight you've apologized to me, do you realize that?"

"Really? Uh, no . . . I hadn't realized that. . . I'm sor . . ."

I put a finger to his lips, "Hold it. I refuse to hear that word from you one more time within the next twenty-four hours. Especially when what you're doing all this apologizing about has been one of the most glorious nights of my life."

He kissed my finger and said softly, "Was it really?"

I replied, even more softly, "Yes, it was . . . really."

He took my hand and kissed it, looking into my eyes. Then he leaned forward and kissed my lips, gently, gingerly. He drew back searching my face, clearly trying to assess how I felt about the kiss. I put my head on his shoulder. He put his arm around me and leaned over. His lips brushed my hair, "Sleepy?" he asked quietly. I could feel the velvety touch of his breath on my ear.

"Yes, a little."

"That's jet lag. It's almost six o'clock in the morning in Michigan. Your body thinks you've been up all night."

"Well, if it does . . ." I looked up at him, "I hope it knows I've enjoyed every second of it."

He kissed me on the forehead. "Just sit back and relax, honey. I'll let you know when we're there."

Then, in Darryl's car, on my way to Darryl's house, with Darryl's arm around me, and my head on Darryl's shoulder, I fell asleep.

Four

Getting To Know You

I opened my eyes to a sunlit blue ceiling, and remembered where I was—a guest room at Darryl's. We had sleepily made our way from the car the night before and gone straight upstairs. Since we'd decided we were too tired to eat, Darryl had shown me to my "room." It really *was* a suite—a large sitting room, a larger bedroom, and bath.

I smiled, remembering him saying good night. He kept hesitating—his bravado in the dark of the limo apparently gone. Being a woman of the '90s, I resolved the dilemma by kissing *him*—just a peck on the cheek. But he didn't seem to mind. He had a big smile on his face as he left.

Sitting up, I gazed around, soaking up the beauty of the room. Everything in it was blue. Everything. But each a slightly different shade of blue. It was heavenly. Suddenly a splash of red caught the corner of my eye. I turned—there were my roses, in a royal blue vase on a dressing table. Then I noticed my bags were right inside the door. What benevolent genie had put them there?

The telephone rang. "Hello?"

"Good morning." It was Darryl. "Did I wake you? Did you sleep well?"

"Good morning. No, you didn't wake me. And yes, I slept like a baby, thank you, sir. But where are *you?*"

"Down the hall, in my room. I'm on the intercom." I looked down at my phone; it had four lines, and the intercom line was lit. My room was intercom nine.

"My room is seven and the kitchen is zero, if you want a snack or something," he continued. "There should be a house directory somewhere near the phone. I sneaked in about half an hour ago to put your stuff inside. I hope you don't mind." A smile crept into his voice, "I kept my eyes closed the whole time."

So it was him! I laughed, "No, of course I don't mind, but how long have you been up? What time is it, anyway?"

"It's about 8:15. I've only been up forty-five minutes or so. It's a beautiful day. Would you like to have breakfast on the terrace?"

"Sounds great. I wasn't hungry last night, but now I'm famished."

"Me, too. Nine o'clock?"

"Fine. How do I get to the terrace?"

"Downstairs, at the end of the left hallway."

"Okay, see you in . . ." I spied a clock on the bedside table, "thirty-nine minutes."

I quickly called home to make sure Tiff was all right, let her know I'd spent a restful and CHASTE night, and tell her I'd call later with all the juicy details. Then, jumping up, I went to my bags. All my stuff was there, including the bag containing my concert clothes. There were also two Los Angeles Regal bathrobes, compliments of the ever solicitous Marshall Maitland.

I rapidly put my stuff away. The few things I hung up looked lost in the cavernous walk-in closet. I picked out things to wear: white jeans, a black top, and black lace-up shoes. Looking in the mirror over the dressing table I thought, *Thank God!* My hair still looked decent.

I went into the bathroom. Everything there was blue, too, including a baby blue toilet and a navy blue Jacuzzi. I took advantage of one and looked longingly at the other. Then I took a fast shower, put on a tiny amount of daytime makeup, and dressed. I looked at my watch—8:58—good, I didn't want to keep a hungry man waiting. I opened the outer door of the sitting room, and there was Darryl, leaning against the hallway wall opposite. He straightened and smiled. "Mornin'." He was wearing white jeans, a black and white striped pullover at least two sizes too big, and black Nikes.

"Dare! I didn't know you were waiting for me."

"It's only been a few minutes. I didn't want you to have a hard time finding your way. I'm starving—shall we?"

I hadn't seen much of the house the night before. It had been dim and I had been groggy. I looked around now as we headed downstairs. We were in a long hallway with tables and chairs against the walls at irregular intervals. Some of the tables held bouquets of live flowers. I recognized one from Darryl's dressing room the night before. He pointed to the last door before the stairs as we passed it, "This is my room." The door was closed. I was dying for a peek inside.

We went down the stairs I dimly remembered climbing the night before and came upon a large circular entryway. The floor was tiled in a varied mosaic pattern. There was a huge crystal chandelier overhead. "This way," he said, gesturing to the left. "I really live on this side of the house. The other side has the formal living room, the dining room, a library, and, believe it or not, a ballroom. I don't entertain very much, and when I do it's mostly informal. I keep a lot of my books upstairs, and read there." I had heard he was a voracious reader.

He pointed out rooms as we passed: a comfortable looking living area with a grand piano he called the music room; his practice room, lined with mirrors; and a projection room. As we approached the end of the long hallway, I could see what I had taken for a large bay window was actually a glass wall. It was a solarium. Darryl opened the door and we entered.

All around were lush plants of every description. There was a rubber plant—no, a rubber *tree* that reached almost to the ceiling. There were orchids, ferns, climbing vines, and many more plants I couldn't even name. "Darryl, this is just magnificent." I took a deep breath, "Smell the flowers—it's almost overpowering. I love it!"

"It's one of my favorite spots in the whole house." He smiled, "It smells great now, but it's not so hot on days the gardener fertilizes!" He pointed to the door on the other side of the greenhouse. "This way to breakfast." He opened the door for me, and we were out on a long broad terrace, overlooking a kaleidoscopic garden and an immense swimming pool.

Darryl led me to a white wrought iron table, with two matching padded chairs. He held one of the chairs for me, and as I sat down asked, "What would you like?"

There was a rolling sideboard with a small breakfast buffet: scrambled eggs, mixed fruit, croissants, sausage, bacon, and . . . grits! "Grits! Darryl, do you like grits?"

"Love 'em. Been hooked on them since I was a kid. My mother let the cook prepare the other meals, but always cooked breakfast herself whenever we were at home, and she always fixed grits." He took the plate that was in front of me, "May I serve you, madame?"

I started to rise, "Darryl, you don't need to . . ."

He silenced me with, "What'll it be, toots?" in a Humphrey Bogart accent.

"Okay, you win, Mr. Belvedere," I laughed. "I'd like scrambled eggs, sausage, fruit salad, and a croissant."

"What . . . no grits?"

"I like them, too, but not this morning."

He prepared my plate, placed it in front of me, quickly fixed his own—*with* grits—and took the seat opposite. He asked, "Shall I say grace?" I closed my eyes and bowed my head. He said a brief prayer. Then he asked, "Coffee?"

"Are you having some, too?" He nodded. "Then allow me," I poured first for him, and then myself. We dug in. Neither of us had eaten since early the previous day, so we were busy for the next several moments. After a while I remarked, "Dare, your home is absolutely beautiful."

"Thanks. Later on, I'll give you the five dollar tour."

Just then, an older man in jeans and a blue chambray shirt, with a phone in his hands, came out of another entrance to the terrace, and approached the table. "Monroe," Darryl told him, "I'm not taking any calls this morning."

"I'm sorry to disturb you, sir," Monroe said in an impeccable British accent, "but it's Mr. Stewart. He says it's imperative he speak with you right away."

Darryl sighed, "Okay, I'll take it." Monroe sat the phone down on the table near him, nodded good morning to me, and left. Dare looked at me, and started to say the "S" word.

I gave him a warning look, "Oh, no, you don't. It hasn't been twenty-four hours yet."

He chuckled, "All right. Excuse me, I'll only be a moment." He picked up the phone: "Okay, Stew, you got me. Now what's so urgent? What? What are they doing here *today?* Yeah, I know, but no can do . . . It's none of your business, but if you *must* know, I'm entertaining an out-of-town guest—a lady." He looked at me and smiled, "Yes, she is—*very* pretty. Well, maybe she would. Hold on, I'll ask her."

Dare put the call on hold and saw the question in my eyes. "It's Dalton Stewart," he told me. Dalton Stewart produced all of Darryl's—and many other performer's—recordings. "There's this gospel group from Philly he's really hyped on to sing back-up on a song I just finished," he continued. "They were originally scheduled to audition yesterday, but due to the concert, it got moved back to this coming Friday. The problem is, some clown forgot to tell *them* that. They're here now. He wants me to come down to the studio to hear them. Would you go with me, if I do? It won't take long, maybe an hour or so."

"I've never been inside a real recording studio before. I'd love to go. I wouldn't be in the way?"

He gave me a look, "As if I would go without you."

He pushed the hold button again, "Okay, man, you got me, thanks to my understanding house-guest. We'll be there in about an hour. You owe me, man." He hung up, "Take your time finishing breakfast. They can wait *that* long."

He picked up the phone again, "Monroe, see if Alex is around. If he is, ask him if he's free to drive us into the city. If he's not, let Dave know, I need him to drive, and I need the limo brought around right away."

After hanging up he explained, "I told Alex he could have the weekend off. He has an apartment here, but he also has a condo—and a girlfriend—in L.A. I thought I'd drive us around today, but since we're going to the studio, that probably isn't such a good idea."

"Should I change? Is this okay to wear?"

"Sure, that's fine. I'm going just as I am, too."

"Dare, who's the dude who brought you the telephone?"

"Monroe? Oh, he's my butler." He saw my eyebrows raise in surprise. "The jeans? I don't ask the household staff to wear uniforms and stuff. It makes me uncomfortable to see somebody else uncomfortable. They can wear what they like, long as it's within reason."

The phone rang again; the intercom line this time. "Okay, thanks, Monroe," Dare said and hung up again. "The car's out front. Seems Alex didn't fly the coop. He probably stuck around just to eyeball *you* another day. Are you done? Would you like a second helping?"

"Nope. As my grandfather used to say, I have dined sufficient."

He laughed, and came around to pull out my chair, "He sounds like *my* grandfather! Well, let's go face the world." We retraced our steps to the reception room, "Need anything from upstairs?"

"Yes."

"Me, too." He walked with me to my door. "I'm just going to duck into my room for a second. See you in a few."

I made a quick bathroom stop, put the stuff from the evening bag into my pockets, and took a minute to check my hair and make-up. There was a knock at the door. "Ready?"

Dare had covered his hair with an L.A. Dodgers baseball cap. "I've never seen you in a baseball cap before. It makes you look different."

He winked, "That's the whole idea."

Alex and the limo were waiting outside. The three of us talked about the concert on the way to the studio. "You were sizzling last night, man, just smoking!" Alex told Dare. "What got into you?"

"Well, the sight of a certain pretty face may have inspired my performance," Dare said.

"Now, you do have a point," Alex concurred. "I know a pretty face can do a lot for my motivational level. That could have been it."

The studio was a squat two-story building in Hollywood. As unimposing as it looked outside, it was totally high-tech inside. We went through a door marked "Studio A," and were in the control room of the studio. It reminded me of the bridge of the "Enterprise"—all around were banks of electronic equipment with dials, levers, and lights. The two technicians there greeted Dare.

Through the glass panel of the control room, which bordered the actual studio on one side, we could see Dalton Stewart talking to six young people; three guys and three girls. None of them looked much over twenty, and one appeared to be still in his teens. Stewart turned and waved to Dare, who was heading for the door leading to the studio proper. "Should I wait for you here?" I asked.

"Hell, no," Dare replied, "I want Stew to meet you, and those kids look like they would welcome another friendly face." Indeed they did. When they saw Darryl entering, they all jumped, and looked scared to death. You could hardly blame them; the course of their lives could be drastically changed by the next hour.

Stew came over to meet us. "Hello," he smiled. "You must be the lovely visitor." He stepped back and looked me over in appraisal, "A very apt description. I'm Dalton Stewart."

"Angela Delaney," I said, offering my hand. "I'm a great admirer of your work, Mr. Stewart."

"Thank you, my dear, but my father was Mr. Stewart. I'm 'Stew' . . . Angela?" I nodded. "It's a pleasure to meet you. Sorry to interrupt your Saturday, but I really needed our friend here," he said, gesturing to Darryl with his head. Stew turned, "Let me introduce everybody."

The group was called Harmony. Two of them were brother and sister. Stew introduced Darryl and me to each of them. I could see how awed they were by Darryl, and I could certainly understand why.

Preliminaries out of the way, Dalton prompted, "Okay, folks, let's get to work. Why don't you guys do the a cappella number for Darryl?" Harmony lined up, while Dare, Dalton, and I sat on some nearby stools. One tall kid, Marvin, who seemed to be the leader, gave them the pitch on the studio piano. They started singing, and sounded like anything but their name. It was gruesome.

After about fifteen seconds, Darryl stopped them. "Okay, you guys, this *ain't* what I heard on your demo. What gives?"

"I'm sorry, Mr. Bridges, I . . . I guess we're kinda nervous," Marvin stammered.

Darryl walked over to them, "Oh . . . I think I see the problem. You're under the impression you're singing for some dude named Mr. Bridges and his hard-hearted friend. The real deal is that you're singing for Angela and Darryl; two major push-overs for a good gospel sound." That got a laugh from them, and they seemed to loosen up a little. "Now, let's try it again," Darryl said, walking back to his stool.

They were tentative at first, but hit their stride by the middle of the first verse. They were fabulous. The harmony was sweet, tight, and original. At times one voice supported another, yielding three, four, or five part harmony. At other points each voice held it's own line, for full six part harmony. The occasional brief solo line or section of unison singing had that extra punch, in comparison.

Near the end of the song, Dalton leaned over to me. "What do you think?" he whispered, still watching the group.

"Me?" I asked incredulously.

"Yeah," Dalton said, looking at me expectantly.

"Well, Stew, I think they're great. The tenor goes a little flat on the forte sections, but other than that, they're dynamite."

While I was speaking, Stew kept staring at the group, nodding his head. When I finished, he looked at me, "You've got a good ear. Do *you* sing?"

"A little."

"Tell your buddy to bring you over some evening. I'd like to hear you."

Before I could respond, Harmony finished the number. The three of us gave them a very honest standing ovation. They *were* marvelous. They were laughing and hugging each other as we went up to them. Dalton said he'd gone over Darryl's new song with them earlier and asked for a playback of the accompaniment tape as he and I took our seats again. Darryl remained standing with Harmony.

The music started with a single piano. It was joined by a string section. A strong drum beat was added. Then Darryl started the verse. It was "His Footsteps Were There in the Sand." It was captivating. Darryl's silvery voice floated across the room. Harmony supported him with a layer of vocals that were not only beautiful within themselves, but also made Darryl's solo line that much more poignant. I was transported. At the concert I was thrilled. overwhelmed. But today I was moved, touched, and awed. Not only by Darryl's singing, but by the fact that he'd composed this hauntingly beautiful piece of music. What manner of man was I dealing with here, anyway?

When they reached the end, there wasn't a sound. Darryl wasn't looking at Dalton, he was looking at me—with the same expression he'd had in the mirror the night before. "How'd you like it?" was written across his face. I smiled at him, and simply nodded my approval. No words would have sufficed. He smiled diffidently back and looked down at his hands. The two technicians in the control room were applauding like mad—we could see them, even if we couldn't hear them. Darryl looked up over at Stew this time, "Well, there's no doubt, is there?"

Stew shook his head, "Nope. No doubt at all."

Harmony really started whooping and hollering and hugging, then, Marvin even hugged *me!* Then Stew said, "Shall we discuss the details?" Marvin and his sister spoke for the group. The two of them, Dalton, and Darryl started to discuss contracts, recording schedules and other minutiae. The other four kids were just wandering around the studio in a daze.

I walked up to one of the girls; Ruby. "You all are just fantastic . . . unbelievable," I told her.

"Thanks," she giggled. "I was so *nervous.* At first my voice wouldn't even come out of my throat! Singing for Darryl Bridges. And now I'm going to be *recording* with Darryl Bridges! I can't believe it! He's just the best there is." She looked over to where Darryl was standing and talking. "And he's so nice!" Turning back to me, she lowered her voice, "Are you his girlfriend?"

Startled, I quickly replied, "No . . . no, I'm not. We're just friends."

Ruby gave me a disbelieving look, but "Uh-huh" was all she said.

Darryl was coming over to where Ruby and I were standing. "Well, I guess that's it for today, baby," he said, rubbing his hands together. "Ready to go?"

Ruby gave me a look that said, "just friends, huh?" I don't think Darryl even realized he'd called me "baby." He was so excited about finding Harmony and how they sounded on the song. He was like a kid on Christmas morning.

Darryl turned to the others, "We're going to take off now, but I'll be seeing you guys again real soon. Stew, I owe *you* one, man." He led me out through the control room.

Back in the limo he turned to me, "Well, would you like to drive around a bit? See the city?"

"That would be great," I replied. Alex drove us around, and Darryl pointed out the sights: The Hollywood Bowl, Mann's Chinese Theatre, Little Tokyo, UCLA.

After a while he said, "I guess it kind of limits sightseeing if you can't get out of the car, but that probably wouldn't be a good idea. I'm . . ." he stopped himself before he said the "word." "I wish we could, so you could get a closer look."

"Darryl, I'm having the time of my life," I said happily.

"Well," he said, uncertainly, as he scrutinized my face, "As long as you're enjoying yourself."

After driving around a couple of hours, Darryl declared it was time for lunch, and we went to the Estralita Restaurant. The place was packed with celebrities. I had to force myself not to stare. Darryl was greeted by several people as we walked in. After the waiter took our orders, Darryl excused himself. It was like watching a wave cross a lake as he left the room; heads and bodies turned to follow his progress.

Alex smiled at me, "I haven't had much chance to talk to you today. How're you doing?"

"Fantastic. I've never *had* so much fun."

"How'd you sleep last night?"

I knew what he was speculating and I decided to tell him, "Alone."

"I wasn't asking *that*."

"No, you weren't—exactly—but I know you were wondering."

"Well, Angela, after what I saw go on in the back of the car last night, can you blame me?"

"No, I don't blame you, Alex. I'm not angry. I just want you to understand the nature of my relationship with Darryl."

"And that is?"

"That we're friends. Pure and simple. Just friends."

"Then why did he kiss you last night?"

That was a question I had been trying not to ask *myself*. I didn't know the answer. So far that day, other than calling me "baby" back at the studio, Darryl's attitude toward me had just been that of a chivalrous friend. I'd followed his lead, and played it strictly platonic. *But why* did *he kiss me last night?* I said the first thing that popped into my head: "Well, last night was a magical kind of evening and I guess we both got a little carried away." That sounded lame even to *me.*

"Angela, who are you trying to fool; me or yourself? He might be just a friend to you—I doubt it, but I'll grant the possibility. But I *know* you're not just a friend to him. I've never seen him act this way before. He's not the same person around you. And I heard through the grapevine you two really got down on the dance floor last night."

"So we danced. Rather, *he* danced, and I tried my best not to get in his way . . . so what?"

Darryl was across the room, returning to the table. Alex leaned toward me, and whispered, "So the rumor mill's buzzing because he's never been known to get up and dance at a party like that—*never.* I gather since he was a teenager, nobody's seen him dance other than professionally—either performance or rehearsal." I was glad Darryl was too close for me to reply to that. I didn't *have* a reply to that.

Shortly after Darryl's return, the waiter brought our orders. I was in the company of two handsome and attentive men, the food was delicious, and the service flawless, but my enjoyment of the meal was hampered by being constantly watched.

We were sitting at a table toward the back of the room, next to a wall. I wondered if Darryl planned it that way, or if this was "his" table. It was great being next to the wall; it left one direction I could look and not be looked back at. Nobody stared. They were too sophisticated for that. But every time I looked into the room, several pairs of eyes were quickly averted. I knew one reason why. Several people in the room had been at the party the night before. Seeing me with Darryl again today—at lunch no less—fueled their interest considerably. The implications being: did they have breakfast together? Did they spend the night together? Most of them were probably wondering, as Jasmine's tipsy friend had put it, "Who the hell *is* she, anyway?"

There was, however, apparently an unwritten law at that joint: you could greet anybody you liked (and hope they'd greet you back), but you didn't stop at anyone's table unless asked. Seated where we were, there wasn't much excuse for anyone to stroll by, so they contented themselves with waving and lifting glasses to Darryl when they caught his eye. The shocker was, some people even waved at *me*. We ate in relative, if surveilled, peace. Darryl made good on his promise of the night before. When Gregory Peck arrived, and greeted Darryl on his way in, Dare waved him over and introduced us.

Toward the end of the meal, Darryl turned to me and said, "How'd you like to go on a boat ride?"

"Sounds like fun," I answered. "Where?"

"You'll see," he replied mysteriously.

After Darryl settled the check, we waited at the door for the valet to fetch the car. Darryl turned to Alex, "You can have the rest of the weekend, if you want, man. I'll drive, or get Dave."

"Okay, man. That's cool."

"We could drop you off, since we're already in town."

Alex drove us to a sharp looking condo complex and we all got out. Darryl told him, "I'll be fine until Tuesday, if you want the time."

"Great. See you Tuesday morning." He turned to me and said, "Guess I won't see you again before you leave, Angela. It's been a real pleasure. Have a safe trip home."

He offered his hand, which I promptly ignored, and stood on my toes to kiss his cheek. "It's been wonderful to meet you, too, Alex. Thanks for going with me to the concert."

"Anytime."

Dare said, "Come on, Angie, let's ride." We were all on the passenger side of the car. Alex opened the front door for me while Darryl went around to the driver's side. "I know I'll see you again . . . soon," he whispered as I got in. He stood on the curb waving as we left.

I didn't expect Darryl to be a very good driver, after all, how much driving could he do? I was apprehensive. I'd already seen that the L.A. freeway system was a force to be reckoned with. But he was fine. He drove slower than Alex or the "sporty" Marcel, but he was doing all right. "These L.A. freeways are really something," I commented, looking out the side window.

"Huh?"

"I said," I repeated a little louder, "this freeway system is really something else."

"I can't hear you," he replied, even louder. "Maybe because you're all the way over by the door." He glanced down at the seat beside him, then smiled at me.

I slid closer until we were almost, but not quite, touching. "How's this?" I whispered.

"Perfect," he declared. "You're coming in loud and clear."

He told me where the CDs were (there were some in the front of the car, too), and how to put one on. "Pick anything you want," he said, "as long as it's . . ."

"I know . . . 'not one of mine,' " I finished for him. We didn't talk much. We were both into the music. At one point, he reached over and took my hand, but then started having trouble controlling the car. He put his hand back on the wheel. "I don't drive too well one-handed," he said, apologetically.

"That's okay. If you can't hold my hand, I'll hold yours," and I put one hand over his as it gripped the steering wheel. And, silly as it sounds, we rode all the way to his house that way.

We were there before I knew it. I didn't remember any of this from the night before. I had been asleep. Darryl pulled up to a large iron gate and blew the horn. The gate opened. We were going along a slowly curving drive through a lightly wooded area. The foliage started to thin as the drive curved sharply to the left, and there was the house. The lawn surrounding it was lush and green, the landscaping impeccable.

The house wasn't what I think of as a "mansion"—no marble columns and stuff. It was a house. But it was a BIG house.

The center section rose in a large "A" shape, with two long extensions on each side. I could see the edge of the terrace, where we'd had breakfast, off to the side. Darryl didn't turn into the circular off-shoot from the main drive, which led to the house, but drove past to a smaller structure to the rear.

"Let's get some different wheels," he said, as he approached the smaller building.

A short red-headed man came out of the building. "Afternoon, Mr. B," the man greeted Darryl as he got out of the car. "She giving you trouble?" It took me a second to realize he meant the limo.

"No, Dave, it's running great, as always. But I'm driving myself today, so I'd better get something smaller, before I wrap this around a tree." Dare was on his way over to the passenger side, but I got out first. "Angela, this is Dave. Dave, my friend, Mrs. Delaney. Dave does a little of everything around here, Angela, but his main trade is keeping the cars running fine."

"Was in somebody's pit at Indy twenty years running. Afternoon, miss." I smiled and nodded a greeting. He turned back to Darryl, "What's it to be, Mr. B?"

"The baby 'Benz, Dave."

"Just washed and polished her yesterday, sir. Be right out." He walked back into the building, which I had correctly deduced was a garage. Less than a minute later one of the large overhead doors began to rise, and Dave drove out in a bright red Mercedes two-seater.

Off we went, and after about twenty minutes arrived at a marina. Darryl parked the car in a lot right next to the dock. He started to get out, then saw me reaching for my door handle. "Oh, no, you don't. You don't open doors for yourself when you're with me. That's *my* prerogative."

We walked along the dock. There were only large craft in the water. Some more substantial than others. Suddenly, Darryl stopped, "Here we are." I looked up. We were standing by a huge yacht.

"This is *yours?*" I asked. He nodded proudly. The name of

the vessel was "M & M." I laughed, "Oh, no—'Mellow & Movin'?"

"Guilty as charged," he chuckled. He took me to a gangplank, "Watch your step, now. I don't swim too good, and if you fall in, my rescue attempt would probably kill us both."

A youngish guy in whites greeted us. "Good afternoon, commodore," he said to Darryl, and touched his cap to me, "Ma'am."

Commodore?

"Angela, this is Captain Ahab. Captain, Mrs. Delaney."

"Captain *Ahab?*"

"It's really Habe, ma'am. Aaron Habe. The 'Ahab' stuck from the Navy." He touched his hat again to Dare this time, "Ready to cast off whenever you say, sir."

"Let 'er rip, captain."

"Aye-aye, sir," Ahab replied, and gave Darryl a snappy salute.

Darryl snapped one back. As the captain was walking away, Dare leaned over and whispered, "I *love* doing that!"

Five

Taking A Chance On Love

We stayed out about two hours, relaxing in deck chairs, drinking iced tea and just talking. It was the first time we'd had a chance to have one of our "marathon discussions." I'd wondered if we'd have difficulty talking like this—like we were used to doing over the phone—in person. It was even better in person, because we could draw so much from the other's facial expressions and gestures. And yes, he *did* watch my eyes.

On the way back to the house, Darryl asked, "Well, what would you like to do this evening? We could go out to dinner, and go dancing (dancing! I remembered what Alex had said), or I could invite some people over, and have a little get-together. Whatever you like."

"What do *you* want to do, Dare?"

"Well . . ." he said slowly, "we've done so much yesterday and today, and I've relished every minute of it. But what I'd rather do tonight is just spend a quiet evening with you."

"You would?" I whispered.

"Yes, if you wouldn't be bored to death. I'm not much of a nightlife person. I spend most of my evenings, when I'm not working, home alone. It would be a treat to spend an evening at home with you to share it."

I looked out the side window, "That's what I really wanted, too," I said hesitantly.

Neither of us said anything for a long while. "You know," he said finally, "there was a draw-back to taking this car I hadn't considered."

"What's that?"

He looked at me mischievously, "It's got bucket seats."

Back at the house, I asked, "Will you excuse me for an hour or so? I'd like to freshen up and call home."

"Sure, I could probably do with a little freshening myself. I'll meet you in the music room. Can you find it all right?" he asked as we were climbing the stairs.

"Yes, I think so."

He walked me to my door. "Are we dressing for dinner?" I asked.

"Are you kidding? I'm the guy with a butler that runs around in jeans, remember? Whatever you're comfortable in is fine." He was still standing there, shifting from foot to foot.

"What's the matter, Darryl? Is something wrong?"

"No, no . . . ah . . . well . . . see you in a bit." He turned, and walked down the hallway toward his room.

I closed my door and sat on a nearby sofa. Time for a little self-analysis. When I got off the plane, Darryl was just tremendously exciting and I honestly believed that's how things would stay. But they hadn't. Despite all my "he's just a friend" denials to Tiffani, and Alex, and Ruby, I couldn't make myself believe that anymore. I was falling in love. I wasn't there yet, but I was well on my way.

I wouldn't have been concerned if I were falling in love with DARRYL BRIDGES, the superstar, the world renowned entertainer, the multi-millionaire. I'd had crushes on celebrities before. What woman hadn't? When I was ten years old, I'd had a crush on Soupy Sales, of all people. I suddenly remembered when I was in my twenties, not long after Bobby's death, and Darryl still a teenager, that I'd even had a slight crush on *him,* before I told myself how silly it was.

But I wasn't falling in love with Darryl Bridges. I was falling in love with a guy with a shy smile. Who had old-fashioned manners, treated a woman like a lady, and made her feel like a queen. Who, despite being at the pinnacle of his profession, was equally as gracious to unknown beginners like Harmony, as to his peers. Who would reach back to help a broke, talented brother like Alex. Who cared about his employees' comfort. Who liked grits. *This* was the man I was falling in love with, and I knew that man would be impossible to forget.

I started to cry. I was angry at myself for allowing this to happen. I felt I'd betrayed his friendship. The man trusted me, believed he could be himself with me, and not have to worry about giddy complications. I knew Darryl liked me. In fact, from his behavior the last couple of days, I thought it even possible that Alex was right, and that Dare was romantically attracted to me as well. But I also knew, as I was sure *Darryl* had to know, that the gulf between us was insurmountable. The distance alone made the situation impossible. Throw in who he was and the life he led, and he might as well have been on another planet.

I dried my eyes and stood up. This was the last evening I would spend with him. I was going to make sure it was a pleasant memory for both of us. I wanted him to remember me and say, "I really enjoyed being with her," not, "Boy, she sure was a drag that last evening," or, worse, "Poor Angela, I didn't mean to hurt her."

I called home and talked to Tiff for a while. She was in a hurry, on her way out for the evening with her "posse." I told her I'd be home the next day about nine P.M., our time, allowing for the hour drive from the airport.

Going to the closet, I looked over the few things I'd brought with me. I didn't have much left to wear. I pulled out a pair of blue jeans, but wanted something a little special to wear with them. I decided on a white lace blouse and the white tank top I always wore under it.

The dress I'd worn to the party was still hanging there. I'd have to remind Darryl to have it returned. I held the dress against me. I'd never forget how I felt that evening—like a princess in the tender care of a devoted prince. The tears began again, but I stopped myself. *No, I won't allow this. I've had the dream of a million women come true. I wouldn't have this weekend not happen for worlds. And I won't allow that sweet man to find out my heart will be breaking when I walk out of his life tomorrow.*

I quickly showered and dressed. Leaving the suite, I opened the outer door tentatively, half-expecting Darryl to be there. Nope, he wasn't. I started down the hall. Just as I got to the stairway, a tremendous crash came from Darryl's room, followed by, "Damn!" and then, "Ouch!"

I went to the door and knocked, "Dare! Are you all right?"

After a few seconds he opened the door. "I'm okay, but my hand's not." He held out his right hand. There was a cut running from the bottom joint of his middle finger to the middle of his palm, and it was bleeding heavily. As I watched, some drops of blood dripped onto the green carpet.

Instinctively, I took his hand, and came into the room. "We've got to stop the bleeding," I instructed. "Let's go into the bathroom." There, I held his hand under cold running water, to staunch the bleeding. "Keep that there," I told him, as I looked in the medicine cabinet and found a first aid kit. I got out disinfectant, cotton, and bandages.

By then the bleeding had almost stopped and I could see the cut wasn't as long or as deep as I had feared, although it was bad enough. "Well, Mr. Bridges, looks like you'll live, but you've tried your best to become the first nine-fingered Grammy winner in history. Sit down, and let me bandage it."

He put down the toilet lid, and sat on it, while I pulled up a nearby padded stool and sat with the first aid kit balanced on my knees. Against his vigorous protests, I cleaned the wound, painted it with disinfectant, and covered the cut with bandages. "Dare, you should see a doctor about this," I counseled.

"Naw, it's fine. It hardly even hurts now."

"But you could get an infection."

"Not with the prettiest nurse in the world taking care of me." He grinned, "You know, you're a good person to have around in an emergency."

I really looked at him then. Whatever happened, it must have been while he was dressing. He had on blue jeans, but no shoes and no shirt. When Darryl was younger he had been skinny; *really* skinny. But over the years his frame had filled. Though he was still slender, he was skinny no more. He had very broad shoulders and his arms and chest rippled with muscle. Not the body-builder kind, but muscle all the same.

It suddenly hit me that I had rushed, unbidden, into his room—into his *bathroom,* for God's sake—while he was only half dressed. I became tremendously uneasy. "Uh . . . well . . . I'd . . . uh . . . better get out of here, and . . . and let you finish dressing," I stammered, and started out of the room.

He reached out with his left hand and grasped my arm. "Girl, what's the matter with you? Haven't you ever seen a man with no shirt on before? Come back here." He stood up, "Hey, there's blood on that pretty blouse."

I looked down. There were two small spots of blood on one side near the collar. Probably from when I held his hand up to look at. He grabbed a wash cloth and awkwardly, with his "good" hand, moistened it with cold water. Then he came over to me, and started dabbing at the spots.

"Dare," I protested, "It's no big deal, really."

"No," he insisted, "we've got to get this out before it dries and sets in." The spots *were* coming out. "There," he said, "that's got it." He looked up, "I was almost finished dressing. Stay with me while I put on a shirt and we'll go downstairs together."

I followed him back into the bedroom. I had been too intent on his injury to notice the room when I first came in. I looked about me now. The room was part of a suite, like mine, only bigger. We'd rushed through the sitting room and were now in the back, where his sleeping quarters were. It was huge, airy, and done in shades of green and blue. It was beautiful, at least

I thought it *would* have been beautiful—if I could have seen it. But I couldn't really tell *what* the room looked like because there was stuff everywhere: books, clothes, record albums, audio and video tapes, shoes, maps, letters, flowers, suitcases, hats, stacks of music. I could see the condition of his dressing room the night before had been no fluke.

He read the look on my face, "Well," he said with chagrin, "My secret is out at last—I'm a closet slob. The maid won't do anything in here but dust, vacuum, and change the linens, because every time she moves any of my stuff, I complain I can't find anything."

In the middle of the floor was an overturned audio cabinet, lying on it's side, and spilling out of it was a stereo unit that would never play again in *this* life. Wires were sticking out of cracks in a couple of spots. The cabinet had a glass door, which had shattered into several jagged pieces.

"I was trying to roust this dump up a bit and *that* thing," he said, pointing to the dead stereo and cabinet, "took a header when I was moving it. I went to pick up the glass and the rest, as they say," he held up his lacerated hand, "is history."

"And you're still running around with no shoes on, with all that glass on the floor," I scolded. His Nikes were in a chair nearby. I picked them up and went over to him. "Put these on. Just because I bandaged your hand doesn't mean I'm willing to bandage your feet, too, amigo."

He sat on the bed and tried to put on the Nikes, but his hand was giving him trouble, more from the limitation in motion imposed by the bandages than the injury, it seemed. He reached under the bed, pulled out a pair of black loafers, and slipped into them instead. Glancing ruefully at his feet, he lamented, "Gunboats, huh?"

"Yeah," I concurred, "but don't feel like the Lone Ranger." I stuck out one of my feet, "I was amply blessed in that department myself."

"Yeah . . ." he said with a sly smile, "I noticed."

He grabbed a white shirt lying on the bed, put it on, but

couldn't button it. I went over and did it for him. "Now, why are men's shirt buttons always on the wrong side?" I teased. I finished buttoning the shirt and looked up, expecting a smile. But he wasn't smiling.

He put his arms around my waist. His eyes were like lasers. He abruptly pulled me closer and kissed me. Not like the night before. This time he really *kissed* me . . . like he meant it. His lips were soft, but probing, demanding. I felt hypnotized. Spontaneously, I put my arms around his neck. When we finally broke the kiss, he whispered, "I've been wanting to do that since that first day . . . when I held you in my arms."

"Darryl, I . . ." but he smothered my words with another kiss.

The phone started to ring . . . and ring, and ring, and ring. Darryl finally said, "Damn!" and sat down on the bed to answer it. "Hello!" he bellowed quite rudely, actually. "Oh, hello, Mom," he continued. I stifled a giggle and started walking around the room.

As he talked, I explored the room and saw a computer and laser printer on a desk in an alcove. I went over and turned them on. The PC was state of the art, loaded with several software programs I was familiar with. I was still fiddling with it when he hung up the phone a minute or so later. "Okay, you can run, but you can't hide. Where are you?"

"Over here," I said, waving my hand above the monitor.

He came over and put his head on top of the monitor, facing me. "Well," he said with a blank look, but crossing his eyes, "that was my mom." We both burst out laughing. "And wouldn't you know the first thing she'd say would be 'What are you doing?' Hey, can you actually drive this thing?"

"Sure. It's got some of the same software I use at work."

"Well, maybe you can show me. Every time I try to use it, it just beeps."

"It's not as bad as it looks," I replied, and hit a button to print up the document I'd just created. He pulled the page from the printer and cracked up. It said in big, bold letters, **"DARRYL BRIDGES SURE CAN KISS!"**

That smokey look came back into his eyes, "Thank you. But you know what they say, 'practice makes perfect.' " He started behind the desk.

I jumped up and walked past him, back into the room, "Uh . . . what's in there?" I said, changing the subject and pointing to a double door I'd just noticed in the wall across from his bed. There wasn't a similar door in my room.

"Another bedroom," he said, opening the door. I went inside. It was a suite identical to his in size and shape but it was empty; no furniture, and an ugly, worn, maroon carpet on the floor. The walls needed painting.

"Why no furniture?" I asked. He had followed me into the room.

"Well, this whole section is the master compartment. This suite would be for the lady of the house, if there *was* a lady of the house. Since there isn't, I just left it alone. I don't need it as a guest room." He came up behind me, put his arms around me, and buried his face in my hair. "In fact, you're the first person to set foot in here since I bought the joint. Ummm . . . your hair smells good." I walked out of his embrace. "Come on, Angie," he said. "Don't walk away like that. You know we need to talk this over. There's something going on between us we've got to deal with."

"I . . . I know, Darryl, but I don't think you had talking on your agenda just then, and I don't think we should talk about it here. Let's go downstairs."

"Are you mad at me for kissing you like I did? I didn't plan it that way, honest. But you were standing so close to me, and . . ."

"How could I be angry at you for . . ." I looked down at the floor, "for something I wanted . . . just as much as you did?"

He came toward me and started to speak, but I took his hand

and started for the door. “Didn’t you say something about a grand tour?” I asked, leading him into the hallway.

We went downstairs and Darryl showed me the entire house. It was beautiful, but most of it seemed unlived in, almost cold, except for rooms he spent most of his time in, like the music room. I loved the kitchen. It was huge, with large windows in a niche looking out on the terrace and the garden beyond.

“Unless I have a lot of people over, I always give the staff Saturday night off, so I’ll cook for us. I used to be a pretty fair cook, though I admit I haven’t done much cooking lately.”

“Darryl, I’ve got an idea. Let’s have a picnic!”

“A *picnic?* Angie, it’ll be dark out in a few minutes.”

“Yeah, I know. I’ve always wanted to have a moonlight picnic, but I never have. Have you?”

“Me? I’ve never had a *daylight* one.”

“You *haven’t?*”

“No. By the time I was ‘picnicking’ age, my family was touring all over the world. My folks thought I was better off with them than left at home with relatives and sitters. So most of the time I traveled with them, even though I wasn’t performing.” He looked away, “I guess there wasn’t much ‘normal’ about my childhood.”

I’d touched a nerve. But I wasn’t about to let him get moody on me. “Well, then, it’s high time you were initiated. Have you got a ‘pic-a-nic’ basket, as Yogi would say?”

He laughed then, “No, I don’t think so. Hey, wait a minute . . . I’ll be right back!” He dashed out of the room.

I started looking for picnic goodies. I found a half a ham and Swiss cheese in the refrigerator, as well as lettuce, tomatoes, and cucumbers. I got eggs out and started them boiling.

Darryl came back with a deep, wide wicker basket with handles on both sides. “How’s this?”

“That’s great! Where’d you find it?”

“Promise you won’t laugh.”

“I promise to *try* not to laugh.”

“I got it from the greenhouse. There was a potted plant in

it, but there's no dirt in here. See?" he demonstrated, tipping the basket to show the inside. He was as excited as a kid on the last day of school.

"Well, it's perfect," I pronounced. "You *are* a wizard." I was rewarded by his five-hundred-watt smile.

"What can I do?" he asked eagerly.

I had him line the basket with towels, and fetch a tablecloth and blankets. While he did, I cut meat and cheese for sandwiches. When he got back, I had him make the sandwiches, while I fixed a green salad. He got out plates, glasses, and napkins while I made deviled eggs. I found strawberries for dessert and made a large thermos of lemonade.

When the basket was packed, Darryl tried to lift it, but put it back down in a hurry. "The handle goes right across the cut in my hand," he explained.

"No problem. I'll take one side and you take the other." Dare put the tablecloth and blankets over his right arm, and we headed out on the terrace with the basket between us, then down the steps to the garden. The night was perfect; warm with a slight breeze and only a few wispy clouds in a star-filled sky, keeping the full moon company. Finding a likely spot near a flower bed, we put the basket down, and I started to spread out the tablecloth with blankets on each side.

"I'll be right back," Darryl said suddenly, and ran back into the house. I spread out the feast while he was gone. In a few minutes he was back with a "boom box" and several tapes. "Got to have some music," he said. Would this man never cease to amaze me? What he put on the box was the original cast recording of "Cabin in the Sky." He saw the disbelief on my face. "I can change it if you'd rather hear something more . . . contemporary."

"Lena Horne and Ethel Waters?" I said, sitting down on a blanket. "That stuff is timeless. I'm just floored because when we've talked about music, you never mentioned being into show tunes."

"Well, when we talked about music, you never told me that

you sing, either." I was embarrassed, as he sat down on the blanket on the other side of the tablecloth, across from me. "I heard you tell Stew you sing. You can't sing for him unless you sing for *me* first."

"I . . . I will, Dare. But don't change the subject. How long have you been into show tunes?"

"When I was coming up, my folks wouldn't allow any music in the house except religious music, classical music, and show tunes. They said other types of music were too 'worldly.' I was weaned on this stuff. I can remember my mother singing me to sleep with 'Oh, What a Beautiful Morning' from 'Oklahoma!' " He bowed his head, said a short prayer, and we started eating.

When "Taking a Chance on Love" began, I said, "I *love* this song! Darryl, sing it for me? Please?" He started to sing along with the recording. I reached over and turned down the volume, so the music was more in the background. His voice was (and is) truly an instrument. As many times as I had heard him sing, it never sounded so lyrical.

When he finished, he gave me an embarrassed smile, "Guess I should leave Broadway to Robert Gulliuame."

I smiled, "That was magic. I only wish I'd been recording it. Thank you."

As we were finishing, he said, "I think this may have been the finest meal I've ever had." I reached over and popped a strawberry into his mouth. He caught my hand and kissed it. "But I know I've never had a more enchanting dinner partner." He came over and sat next to me. "Angela, I heard what that girl said to you today."

"What girl, Darryl?" I knew *exactly* what girl, but he'd caught me off guard. I was stalling for time.

"The girl in Harmony. Ruby was her name."

"About being nervous?"

"No. When she asked you if you were my girlfriend."

I didn't trust myself to look at him, so I looked down at my hands. "I don't know what could have given her that impression."

"I do—us. The way we relate to each other." He put one finger under my chin and tipped my face up to look into his eyes. "The way we look at each other." His eyes were searching mine. "We're not 'just friends' anymore . . . are we, sweetheart?"

He kissed me softly. Then, as he gently pushed me back onto the blanket, his kiss became seeking, yearning. I put my arms around him and we lay that way, kissing in the moonlight, a long time. Finally, he pulled back slightly. "I'm crazy about you, Angela," he said hoarsely, "and I think Ruby had a very good idea."

"Darryl . . . we . . . we just met."

"We didn't just meet. We met months ago. And I've been intrigued with you since the beginning. I have a confession to make. I *was* concerned that you weren't hurt, but I really called you that first time to satisfy my curiosity about you—so I could *stop* thinking about you.

"Instead, once I started talking to you, I really couldn't get you out of my mind. I'd be in Hong Kong, or someplace, and when I saw something interesting, my first thought would be, 'Wait 'til Angie hears about this.' Finally I told myself I had to see you, to figure out why I was so fascinated by you." He buried his face in my hair and whispered, "Now I know."

"Darryl," I said, looking up at the moon, "I . . . I feel that way, too," I laughed sadly. "A couple of hours ago I was crying because I thought I might never see you again."

He looked into my eyes and touched my cheek, "You were?" I nodded. "Well, baby, you don't have to worry about that. You're going to be seeing a lot of me for a long time to come."

I rolled away from him, stood, and walked away a few steps, "But that's a big part of the problem, honey. Come Monday, I'll be back in Lansing and you'll be here."

He came over to me, "A minor inconvenience." His eyes were shining. "Especially since you just called me 'honey.' Now I *know* you care."

"How could you have had any doubt?" I put my arms around

him and kissed him; the way I'd been longing to kiss him. I twined my fingers into his hair. As his tongue sought mine, I felt my breasts crush against his chest. When we finally broke apart, I was shaken. He was, too.

"Darryl, this is happening so fast . . . too fast. I . . ."

"Under normal circumstances," he began reflectively, "a man wouldn't ask a woman to be his lady on their first date." He looked at me quizzically, "Or is this our second date?"

I smiled at his precision, "I think this could properly be called our second date."

"Okay, their second date," he continued. "But these are not normal circumstances. Unfortunately, given the crazy life I live, the circumstances will *never* be normal. But *we're* normal, and what could be more normal than a man and woman who care about each other making a commitment to each other?" He took both my hands, "Angela, I know it's not going to be easy, but I have faith in you and me. What we feel is not something that comes along every day. It's up to us. We can make it work if we want it bad enough. I'm willing to try. Are you?"

"Dare, I feel that way, too, but . . ."

"But what? Is there something else? Is there some*one* else? Do you already have a man?"

"No," I laughed, "I don't."

"Well, lady, don't look now," he took me in his arms, "but there's a skinny man from Kansas City applying for the job." He kissed me again.

I held him close, but paused just long enough to whisper, "You're hired."

We sat there in the dark, holding hands and talking far into the evening, working out how to best handle things . . . now. We agreed our relationship had to be kept confidential, not that either of us wanted to (I *wanted* to tell the *world!*), but because Tiffani and I would be hounded to death, perhaps even be in danger, if it were known.

It turned chilly and, in the thin lace blouse, I began to shiver. Darryl declared, "Better get you inside. You're not going to catch pneumonia on me." We packed all the stuff and went inside, leaving everything in the kitchen. We slowly went upstairs holding hands, and walked to my bedroom door. I saw the longing in his eyes. He kissed me softly, cupping my face in his hands.

"Angela, I'm all mixed up inside," he said huskily. You know my background; my 'home training' is really pricking my conscience right now." He kissed me again, "But I want you so much . . ." He kissed my neck and murmured again, "so much . . ." against the hollow of my throat.

Abruptly, he pressed me against the wall, holding me so tightly I could hardly breathe. His lips crushed mine roughly, almost cruelly, as his hands started to caress my body. I pulled away slightly and looked into his eyes. I was no longer with Dare, the sweet, shy guy who couldn't drive one-handed. I was with DARRYL, the whirlwind, the dynamo, and all that passion and power, instead of being diverted into a song, or a dance step, was instead directed at *me.* He took possession of my lips yet again.

I was frightened by the strength and suddenness of his desire and he was hurting me, bruising my lips with his. I struggled feebly in his embrace. He stopped then, all at once, and pulled away from me. "Honey? Oh, baby, I didn't mean to come on to you like a madman. Did I hurt you?" I shook my head. "I lost it for a minute," he continued. "I want you so badly, and . . ." he smiled sadly, "Well, it's been a hell of a long time for me."

I looked up at him, "Me, too," I whispered.

He started to kiss me again, more gently, but urgently. After a few moments, I stopped him, putting my palms against his chest. He reluctantly drew back a bit. I took a deep breath, "Millions of women would think I'm crazy, and they'd probably be right . . . but . . . I can't. I just can't. It doesn't feel right. It's too soon. Darryl, I believe everything you've told me, and God knows I feel the same. But so much has happened so fast, my head is spinning. I need some time to adjust to this—to you and me."

He smiled, took my hands, and kissed each one. "I don't want 'millions of women'—I want you. Okay, sweetheart, I understand. So, bad as I want you, and . . ." he smiled at me again, "horny as I am . . ." he was standing close to me and I could *feel* how horny he was, "I'll wait." He brushed my lips lightly with his. "You're worth waiting for, baby." His voice had taken on that gravelly quality again. "And when it does happen—" he pulled me closer, "and it *will* happen, Angela—it'll be the way we both want it to be."

Surprisingly, he began to chuckle, "Maybe I should be like a medieval knight, and sleep across the door of my lady's chamber for her protection. But that would be senseless—the only one you need protecting from around here . . ." the glint came back into his eyes, "is *me*."

A lock of hair fell across his eyes. I brushed it back. "You're the most spellbinding man I've ever known, do you know that?" I moved closer to him, "Darryl, maybe . . ."

"No . . ." he decided, holding me at arm's length, "no 'maybes.' I want you to be sure. I have to *know* that you're sure. Goodnight, sweetheart." He embraced me tenderly and gave me a long, lingering kiss. Then he opened the door to my room, and pushed me gently inside as he blew me a kiss and left, closing the door behind him.

I almost ran after him, but stopped myself. Instead, I busily got ready for bed and packed most of my things in preparation for leaving the next day. I lay down and turned off the light, thinking about going home. Home. I looked around the room in the moonlight. In just a few hours this had begun to feel like home, too. I couldn't sort out all that had happened that night. I was too numb, too incredulous. I fell asleep seeing Darryl's smile.

I drifted back to consciousness. It was still dark. *This,* I thought, *is proof how shook up you are, girl. You never wake up in the middle of the night like this.* I turned to look at the bedside clock—and stopped. Darryl was there beside me, asleep. He was still fully dressed, shoes and all, lying on top of the covers. It was a king-sized bed and I was pretty much to one side, but he was all the way over on the other side, on the very edge of the mattress. If he had rolled over, he would have fallen on the floor.

That was it. In that split second I went from falling in love with Darryl to *being* in love with him—totally, hopelessly in love. "My sweet, gallant knight," I whispered.

I stood, smoothed back the covers I had been lying under, and lay back down on top of them, scooting over until I was next to Darryl. I kissed him softly. He stirred, but didn't quite wake up. So, snuggling even closer, I kissed him again. This time he opened one eye, looking directly into my face, and said "Uh-oh."

He rose on one elbow, "Now, don't be mad, honey. I couldn't sleep. I couldn't stop thinking about you going away tomorrow . . . today, and I just wanted to be near you. I won't touch you. I promise."

I rose on one elbow, too, and looking him in the eye, crooked my index finger and summoned, "Come here, Sir Galahad."

A flame flickered and ignited in his eyes, "Are you sure, baby? Are you really sure?"

I kissed him. In a wild flurry of movement my nightgown and his clothing flew all about the room. He held me so tightly I could hardly breathe, but it wasn't his embrace that had me breathless; it was my own passion.

He spanned over me like a bridge, covering my neck and breasts with kisses. "I'm so hungry for you, baby." He whispered gruffly in my ear. Suddenly he stopped, and looked down into my eyes. "This ain't no one night stand, Angel. There's a lot of excitement in the life I live, but a lot of headache—and heartache—too. You'll have to deal with both, if you're my woman. Are you down with that, baby? Can you accept that—and me?"

I put my arms around him and pulled him close again. As

he embraced me in return, I lay back, and let the whirlwind sweep me away.

I opened my eyes and saw an expanse of male chest. With a smile, I closed my eyes again, remembering who that chest belonged to, and why it was there. Stretching reminded me even more—every bone in my body ached. It had been two years. Two years of sleeping alone. I thought I was used to it. I began to accept it. But I realized now my body had been crying out for release. I wondered if I'd ever again feel close enough to a man for this type of intimacy. I looked over at the gentle giant sleeping beside me, and smiled. It wasn't at all difficult to feel close to *this* man.

And *whew!* If the women of the world only *knew*—armed guards and barbed wire couldn't keep them away from him. He made love like he sang; full of fury and fire. And tenderness. We'd made love until sunrise, drifting off only then out of sheer exhaustion.

Oh, my God! I thought . . . *what time is it* now*?* I quickly looked at the clock. It was only 8:05. My plane left at noon.

I heard a soft knocking somewhere nearby. There it was again; no, it had stopped. I kissed Darryl on the forehead and started toward the bathroom when there was a knock at my outer door. Quickly grabbing one of Marshall Maitland's robes, I pulled it on as I went through the parlor to the hall door and opened it a crack.

It was Monroe. Today he was wearing Bermuda shorts and a Mickey Mouse tee shirt. "Sorry to intrude, miss, but there must be something wrong with your telephone." There certainly was: Darryl had taken it off the hook the night before. "I can't locate Mr. Bridges," Monroe continued. "He wanted an eight o'clock call, but he's not answering his telephone, nor his door. Do you know if he perhaps went out?"

Just then, Darryl stirred, and called out in a blurry voice, "Woman! Where are you?"

Monroe turned three shades of red. "Beg pardon, miss," he said, backing away from the door. "Please forgive me for interrupt . . . uh, disturbing you," He started to walk away, but stopped and turned back. He gave me a thumbs up, and with a straight face said, "Good show, miss," and left.

I went back into the bedroom. Darryl was still in bed, stretching and yawning, but smiled when he saw me. "Hey, what's the deal here? You ravish a man all night, then get up at the crack of dawn, and leave him alone in a cold bed. What a heartless wench."

I leaned over and kissed him. "This bed is hardly cold. After last night, it's a wonder it didn't burst into flame. Anyway, who ravished whom? I was the ravishee here, mister. I'm sore all over."

"Yeah," he said, rubbing his chest, "so am I." He reached for me. "You know what the best cure is for *that*—a hair of the dog that bit us."

I pulled back a little, "Darryl, come on, now, honey. My plane leaves in less than four hours."

"Four hours? That's an eternity. And I only want about twenty minutes." He pulled the belt of the robe, causing it to fall open.

It was more like forty minutes.

As we lay back exhausted, I cautioned, "Darryl, if we don't get out of this bed right now, I'll never make it to the airport."

"I wouldn't have a problem with *that,*" he retorted. He took my hand, "Really, can't you stay another day or two?"

"I could, honey," I conceded, "but that would just make it harder when I *did* leave. Anyway . . ." I said deliberately, "I think we *should* be apart for a while right now. We said some pretty heavy things to each other last night. I think we need some distance between us, to see how well they hold up."

"What do you mean?" he asked abruptly. He pulled me over so I was looking down into his eyes, "Do you think I said those things just to get you in the sack?"

"No, Darryl . . . of course not. I know you better than that . . . but . . ."

"Angela, I meant every word I said to you last night—every word. No amount of distance will change that. Do you still mean what *you* said?"

"You know I do," I answered softly.

"Then that means you're my girl now, right?"

I laughed nervously, "Darryl, we're a little old for 'going steady.' "

"Whatever you call it, I'm talking exclusive here, Angel. I need to know you're my lady, my woman. Are you?"

"Darryl . . ." I hesitated, "Are you *sure* that's what you want?"

He sat up and stared at me, "Yes, of course I'm sure that's what I want. And I thought it was what *you* wanted, too."

"It is, sweetheart. I'm sure of how *I* feel, Dare. But are *you*—really? I mean, look at how you live. Look at who you *are*. Dare, we're from two different worlds, and . . ."

"Bull. There's only *one* world, Angela, and we *both* live in it. What's going on here? Do I strike you as the type of man who'd make a blasé decision about this?"

"No, Darryl, but . . . well, there literally *are* 'millions of women' who would gladly come your way, and . . ."

"Oh, so then it's my *occupation* that's bothering you. Don't go 'star-struck' on me *now*, Angela." He grasped my shoulders and forced me to look into his eyes. "You wouldn't feel this way if I was some man at your office, or the mechanic who fixes your car. What ever else I may be, I'm also a thirty-three-year-old man who's been lonely a long time."

He took my hand. "I'm not lonely anymore," he whispered. "Why you? I couldn't explain it in words. All I know is that there's a spark, a chemistry between us that I've never encountered with any other woman. I think I've known it was there all along." He lay down and took me with him, holding me tightly in his arms, "And you know it, too. Don't you, baby?" he whispered.

I looked into his eyes and my doubts evaporated, "Yes . . . I do."

"Now, if we've got *that* all squared away, let me ask you, again." He looked into my eyes, "Are you my lady, Angela Delores Seymour Delaney?"

I gave him a shaky smile, "Yes, Darryl Douglass Bridges."

He held me close and kissed me very gently, running his fingers through my hair. Then he reached behind me and smacked me on the rump. "Good. Well, now that that's settled—get the hell out of my bed."

"Your bed? This is *my* room, buster."

"Oh, so it is . . . so it is." He got up and put on the robe one of us had thrown on the floor. "Well, since I don't have a change of clothes in here, I guess I will have to step out for a minute or two. I'd have Monroe serve breakfast up here, to save time, but I don't want to embarrass you by giving away that we . . ."

"Don't have to worry about *that.* He already knows, Dare."

"He *does?* How?"

I told him and he started to crack up. "I bet *that* unstiffened his upper lip," I added.

"Don't let that 'veddy' British veneer fool you. Monroe is a cool dude and he's probably overjoyed." He looked down at the floor. "He's seen me during some pretty desolate times." He brightened, leaned down, and kissed me. "See you in half an hour. Don't mess around. I'm hungry." He went to the sitting room door. "I'd better close this. I wouldn't want Monroe to have heart failure if he brings breakfast in while you're dressing," he teased as he left.

I ran around like a crazy woman, but managed to get showered, dressed in the red dress I'd brought for Saturday night, and almost finish packing before there was a knock at the door. "Are you decent?"

"Yes, honey."

He opened the door, "Aw, shucks." He was wearing a red

shirt and black slacks, "Well, anyway," he gestured to the sitting room, "breakfast awaits."

While I was dressing, Monroe had served breakfast in my parlor. "Would you say grace this morning?" Darryl asked.

I bowed my head, "Dear Lord, thank Thee for the many blessings Thou hast given us. Please bless this meal and this house. And please keep Darryl and I safe until we're together again. Amen."

"Amen," he echoed softly.

We ate and talked—by our standards, talking, very little, dreading the separation that was now imminent. As we were finishing, Darryl said, "I have something for you; hope you like it." He reached into his pocket and pulled out a ruby tennis bracelet.

I gasped, "It's beautiful . . . but Darryl . . ."

"There's an inscription on the charm," he interrupted, handing the bracelet to me.

The inscription read: "AD/DB June 16-18," and a rose was embossed on each side. "How in the world did you manage to . . ."

"I ordered it yesterday. They just delivered it this morning. Here, let me put it on," he said, coming over to me. He knelt next to my chair, put the bracelet on my wrist—clumsily, because of his cut—and kissed me. "Unless the brothers in Michigan are deaf and blind, there's got to be a slew of them who'd be only too glad to park their shoes under your table. Now, when those Lansing dudes start grinning in your face, look at this, and tell them you're spoken for. Hear me?"

"Yes, sir. And when those starlets and models give YOU the eye, look, but don't touch."

He laughed, "Yes, ma'am. That won't be hard. That's what I've been doing for a long time, anyhow. But now . . ." he kissed my hand, "I have a real reason not to." He looked at his watch and stood, "Much as I hate to acknowledge it, I guess it's time to head for the airport. Are you all packed?"

"Almost. Come in with me while I finish."

We went into the bedroom, and while I packed the last few items, he sat on the dresser, swinging his legs. "Dare, my bracelet is so lovely. I just wish I had a gift for you."

"You've already given me what I wanted most in the world," he said, "and I'm not talking about the lovin'. Although . . ." he jumped down and started toward me, "I sure wouldn't turn down a return bout."

I ran to the other side of the bed, "Oh, no, you don't!" I had a hotel robe in my hand. "Hey, why don't you keep this? It's not much, but at least it's something to remember me by."

"Darlin', I've got all I need to remember you by right here," he said, tapping his forehead. He sat down on the bed. "But I already have the other robe like that. I wore it to my room, remember? I'd rather keep that one. You wore it . . . it smells of your perfume."

"Then I'll keep this one, and we'll have a matching set."

He came over and hugged me, "We've got a matching set, all right," he intimated, rubbing his pelvis against mine.

"Cut it out, lover boy," I murmured, not really meaning it, and rubbing back.

He backed quickly away from me, "Hold it! I can't take much more of this. If you expect me to let you out of here anytime today, we'd better leave—NOW. Are you ready?"

I looked around the room, "Yes, I think that's everything . . . Oh, wait!" I went to the vase of roses and broke one off.

"Baby, you don't have to take that with you. I'll get you a *million* roses."

"But they wouldn't be *these.* These will always be the first flowers you ever gave me." I took a couple of tissues from the dressing table, carefully wrapped the rose, and put it into my makeup case. "Now I'm ready."

Dare carried my suitcase downstairs. The limo, Dave, a huge man named Cortez, and surprisingly, Sam, were waiting outside. Once we got underway, Darryl put his arm around me. I looked down at his bandaged hand, "Dare, I want you to see a doctor about this cut."

"Baby, it's not that bad, really."

"Still, I want you to have a doctor look at it, for my peace of mind, okay?"

He laughed, but said he would. Then said, "There's one more thing . . ." He cleared his throat, "I don't know how to say this . . . diplomatically."

"You don't have to be 'diplomatic' with me, hon. Whatever it is, just say it." He was getting all tongue-tied again. What in the world could it be?

"Well—as you probably know—I have a few bucks," he began, which had to be the understatement of the century. "Well, Angel, I don't want you or Tiffani to want for *anything*."

I should have known this was coming. "We don't, Darryl. I mean, I'm certainly not wealthy, but we've got everything we need."

"You're not going to make this easy for me, are you? Okay. What I'm saying, Angela, is that I want to give you some money."

"What on earth for?"

"What *for?* Clothes, jewelry, cars—anything you want. Now, don't misunderstand me, baby. I respect you too much to try to buy you. I just want to share what I have with you. Isn't there anything you need? Anything you want?"

"Yep. You've already given it to me . . . and *I'm* not talking about the lovin', either." I took his hand, gently, since it was the injured one. "Dare, I know what you're saying, but honestly, we're all right. And if something happens, and I get in a jam, I'm not too proud to ask for help."

"Just my luck to get myself a self-reliant, independent . . . and completely lovable woman. Well, will you at least keep the credit card, in case a problem comes up, and you need something in a hurry?"

"Yes, honey. Of course." I had forgotten all about the credit card. I hadn't taken it out of my purse since the day I got it. And I had no intention of using it. But if keeping it made him feel better, I'd keep it.

That settled, we were quiet, holding hands until we arrived at the airport. Sam got out and took my bags into the terminal.

"He'll get your bags checked, honey, and come for you when your plane starts to board." He sighed, "It's going to be lonelier than ever around here now. I have to go to London this week for some contract negotiations. I'm not sure how long it'll take, but I promise you, we'll be together soon . . . real soon."

"Didn't you tell me last night I was worth waiting for?" He nodded. "Well," I said quietly, touching his cheek, "You are, too."

Sam came out of the terminal then, walked to the car door nearest me, turned his back to us, and waited. "He's giving us a chance to say goodbye," Darryl said in a subdued tone. We embraced, and shared one last, lingering kiss.

I buried my face in his shoulder, "Don't forget what I said about those models," I tried to joke, determined not to cry.

He chuckled softly. "Well, don't let me catch some man answering the phone, either."

I looked up at him and smiled, a real smile this time. I suddenly knew what he said that morning was true: no amount of distance could change the bond that had developed between us. "If you do . . ." I teased, "it means my grandfather's visiting."

He really laughed this time. Then his eyes became very serious, as he looked deeply into mine. "I'm so glad you came into my life; and my plan is to keep you there."

I smiled and touched his cheek "I'm not going anywhere." Then I turned and opened the car door. Sam helped me out and walked with me toward the terminal. I didn't look back until just before I got to the door. Of course, I couldn't see Darryl; the car windows were too darkly tinted. But I knew he was watching. I blew him a kiss, turned, and walked into the terminal; out of his sight. But I knew now, not out of his heart.

Six

Anticipation

"So what happened? Tell me everything!" Tiffani was almost bouncing up and down on the sofa.

"Honey, *please.* I just got in! Give me a chance to catch my breath!" I laughed.

The trip home was uneventful—no delays or foul-ups, which was fortunate. I wasn't in the best shape to handle any sort of conundrum at that point, anyway.

I called Tiff when the limo was about twenty minutes away and she had been watching for me from the balcony. Now, she was bursting at the seams, impatient to hear about my adventure with the rich and famous.

"All right, where shall I start? What do you want to know first?"

"I want to know everything! Start at the beginning, and don't leave *anything* out!"

"But, Tiff, I've already told you about . . ."

"I don't care. Tell me again. You might have missed something!"

So I started with being met by Sam and Alex. I'd gotten to the mini-confrontation in the women's room when the phone rang. "Oh, shoot," Tiffani said, "Just as you were getting to the *good* part."

She answered it and her eyes became round as Frisbees.

"Mama," she whispered, her hand over the mouthpiece; "It's *him!*" "Yes, she's home" she continued into the phone. "She just got in. . . . Sure, I always miss her when she's away, but I'm glad she got to see the concert. I know she had a great time . . ." Her eyes got wider still, "Well, yes, I'd *love* to. Really? When? I'm looking forward to meeting you, too. Yes, she's right here. One moment . . ." She put her hand over the mouthpiece again. "Mama! He said 'next time' he wants *me* to come with you! What does he mean 'next time'? What's going on?"

"Tiff, don't keep the man holding. Does he want to talk to me?"

"Yes, but what . . ."

"Let me talk to him, baby. Then I'll fill you in." She handed me the phone, "Hello, Darryl," I said happily.

"Hello, my American Beauty Rose. Did everything go all right on the way home?"

"Yes, honey." At the word "honey," Tiff's eyebrows shot up under her bangs. "Everything was fine. The plane arrived on schedule and the limo was waiting."

"Hope I didn't let any cats out of bags with Tiffani just now. I gather you haven't had time to tell her about us."

"No, I haven't yet, but I'm going to in the next few minutes," I answered, looking at Tiff with a grin. She was silently mouthing the word "what?" I said into the phone, "So what have you been up to since you kicked me out?"

"Taking a nap . . . in your bed. *Our* bed, the one we slept in last night. I miss you, sweetheart."

"I miss you, too." Tiffani was on the verge of apoplexy.

"Listen, now that I know you're home safely, I'll let you talk to Tiffani and get settled. I'll call you back in a couple of hours to tell you goodnight." His voice lowered to a husky whisper, "I just wish I could tell you goodnight the way I did *last* night."

"So do I," I whispered back.

By the time I hung up the phone, Tiffani was ready to explode, "Will somebody *please* tell me what the hell is going on?"

"Watch your language, young woman," I warned.

"Okay, Mama, okay. I'm sorry. I'm sorry! But . . ."

"Tiff," I started slowly, "Darryl and I have found that . . . that our friendship is deeper than we realized."

"And?"

"And we've discovered we care for each other very much . . ."

"And?"

"And . . . he asked me to be his girlfriend."

"And you told him 'yes'? Please, Mama, say you told him 'yes'!"

"Yes, Tiffani, I told him . . ."

"Aaaaahhhh!" She screamed, jumping up from the sofa. "My mother is going with *Darryl Bridges!* I don't believe it! I don't . . ."

"Tiff! *Tiff!* Stop that screeching and sit down! Do you want the whole building to know?"

"Yes! I want the whole *city* to know!"

"Tiffani," I had to laugh at her hysteria, "I know how you feel. I feel the same." I stopped laughing and walked over to her, looking at her intently, "But what I told you before about keeping this under your hat is even more critical now." I smiled and stroked her hair. "Now will you please stop running around like a maniac and sit down? Don't you want to hear the whole story?"

That got her to settle down—a little. I told her all about the weekend. Well, not *all* about the weekend. I left out one part. When I finished, she said, "Mama, are you pulling my leg? You're kidding, right?"

"Oh, so you think it's not possible for a man like Darryl to want a broken-down, old hag like your mama for a girlfriend, huh?"

"Oh, Mama, you know that's not what I meant, but . . ." Her face got very concerned. "Mama, are you sure about this? I know he's famous, and fine, and rich, and all that, but there should be more to it than *just* that."

"There *is* more to it, dear. He's thoughtful, and smart, and funny, and sweet, and . . . I do really care for him, baby. Care for *him* the person, not him, the 'superstar.' " I gave her a roguish smile. "Of course, I don't hold it against him *too* much that he's 'famous, and fine, and rich, and all that.' "

"So what happens now?" she asked worriedly.

"What do you mean, 'what happens now?' "

"Are we moving to California or something?"

"No, dear. Why would we move to California?"

"Well, if you and Darryl are . . ."

"Tiffani, listen. Darryl and I care about each other very much. But we're not *engaged,* and you know I'm not the 'kept companion' type. We're each going on with our own lives. It's just that now we'll also be a part of each other's lives, as well."

"Well, *that* doesn't sound like much fun. Don't you want to be with him?"

"Of course I want to be with him, sweetheart. But his home is in California and my home is here. I have a career here, and," I smiled, "he's a self-employed businessman who travels a lot. But he promised we'd see each other often."

"How, Mama?"

"I don't know, hon," I replied, "but I know he'll find a way."

Dare called back just as I was climbing into bed and we talked for an hour or so. I understood then why the man is such a successful songwriter—he was more romantic over the telephone than any ten other men could have been in person.

After we hung up, I lay there, turning my bracelet around and around on my wrist. If not for it, I could have believed I'd dreamed the whole thing. I loved Darryl and I knew I meant a lot to him, too, but I'd had, or tried to have, long distance relationships in the past. They seldom lasted, and this was not your routine relationship to begin with. I fell asleep saying a silent prayer for him, for myself . . . and for us.

The next day at work was a typical Monday—crazy. I was

on the phone with Chicago trying to work out a training schedule for some people we'd promoted, when I heard a man ask for me out in the lobby. As I hung up the telephone, my secretary, Clara, walked into my office, lugging an enormous florist's box. "Damn, Angela, what's *in* this thing—a body?"

I opened it. Inside were three dozen long-stemmed red roses. The card read: "Thank you for the most unforgettable weekend of my life. Here's the first installment on that million. I miss you. Love, Doug." Doug? I laughed aloud. That was his middle name.

"Who's Doug?" Clara asked, reading the card over my shoulder.

"Nosy," I evaded, smelling one of the roses.

"A new fella, huh? Must have more money than sense; three dozen roses! And it's about time. You haven't had a date since Truman was president."

"For your information, Mrs. Dembrowski, I wasn't even *born* when Truman was president."

"See what I mean?" she came back with one of her uncontestable rebuttals. "Come on, now, Angie, what gives? Who are they from?"

"Well, Clara," I said, feeling impish, "if you *must* know, they're from Darryl Bridges."

"Right . . ." she gave a disgusted snort, "and I'm married to Ringo Starr." She flounced to the door. "If you didn't want to tell me, all you had to do was *say* so," she huffed as she left.

I sat down at my desk and laughed until I cried.

When I despaired over the poor odds of a long distance relationship, I hadn't taken into account Darryl's ingenuity, devotion, and virtually unlimited resources. He called at least daily; frequently more. A few days after my return from California, a UPS manager called me to arrange a "substantial delivery." It turned out to be a PC and printer, just like the one in Darryl's room.

The following Monday, Darryl arrived back from London.

We were talking, and saying for the umpteenth time how much we missed each other, when he proclaimed, "The hell with this! How would you like a weekend guest?"

Startled by what I thought was an abrupt change in topic, I elegantly replied, "What?"

"I said, dear, how would you like a weekend guest?"

Still not catching on, I, again suavely, asked, "Who?"

"Who? How quickly they forget! Me! Remember me, your devoted suitor? The guy you physically assaulted not two weeks ago? *Me!"*

"You?"

"Honey, have you sworn off words of more than one syllable? Yes, me—Dare, Darryl, your man, your lover. It doesn't make sense for us not to see each other when we're less than five hours apart." He hesitated, "It's okay if I come out to see you, isn't it? I have a lot of nerve inviting myself like this, but . . ."

"Sweetheart, there hasn't been one moment since I've been home I haven't longed to be with you. But it never occurred to me *you'd* be able to come *here."*

"If we're careful, I think we can pull it off. I'm so impatient to see you, baby, I'd face a whole platoon of reporters and fans to do it. But hopefully that won't be necessary; not if we play our cards right."

"Darryl, I can't believe you're serious!"

"Well, I am." His voice softened. "I want to see you, Angel. And I won't ask you to do all the traveling. Anyway, I want to meet Tiffani and see where you live." He paused, "The only thing that worries me is if this gets out, you and Tiff would be in for a rocky ride. Maybe I shouldn't try it. I guess it's selfish of me to put you at risk that way."

"You're not selfish. It's proof how *un*selfish you are that the notion even occurred to you." I paused a moment this time. "Dare, when we made a commitment to each other, we knew this was something we'd have to deal with. I want you to come.

I want to be with you . . . I *need* to be with you. About the rest, I'll take my chances."

We worked out the details. Darryl said he'd staged incognito missions before. He, Sam, and Alex would arrive early Thursday evening. He asked if there was a hotel nearby. I told him about the Holiday Inn just five minutes drive from my apartment complex. "Great! We can get rooms there, and be right at your door."

"What do you mean 'we?' If you think you're coming to Lansing, and you're staying anywhere but with *me*, you're sadly mistaken, bucko. I don't have enough room for all three of you—I wish I did—but *you're* staying here with me."

"You wouldn't mind? It would be so much easier for us to be together that way, if it wouldn't be a problem."

"A problem? Mr. Bridges, that's the way it's going to be. I'll brook no nonsense about it." I hesitated. "But, Dare, there is one thing. With Tiffani here, we . . ."

"Say no more, sweetheart. I know. But I'm a desperate and resourceful man. I assure you, ma'am. We'll find a way!"

I knew I'd have no problem taking Friday and Monday off, so we planned for him to stay until Monday evening. I told him Tiff and I would pick them up at the airport. "No need there, honey," he said. "Alex and Sam will need a car while we're there anyway, so we'll rent one at the airport and drive ourselves into town."

When I told Tiffani, she got—predictably—hysterical, "He's coming *here?* To Lansing?"

"Yes, hon. He's bringing Alex and Sam with him, and *they're* staying at the Holiday Inn, but Darryl's staying here, with us."

"Here? In our apartment? Awesome," she said reverently.

"I figured he could sleep in my room and I'd bunk in with you." I wanted to let her know the lay of the land upfront.

"Well, Mom, this might work out well, because I was thinking of going down to Detroit this weekend. Marlowe's friend Kimberly is getting married and Marlowe wants me to go to the wedding with her. Kim's father rented a club for the reception and it's gonna to be the throw-down of the decade."

Marlowe was my niece, my sister's daughter. Marlowe was only a year and a half older than Tiffani, and also an only child. They were more like sisters than cousins. Since we'd moved to Lansing, Tiffani often went to Detroit on weekends to visit her cousin, see her grandmother, and to "hang out" with her old crowd.

I felt bad about not telling my family, at least my mother and sister, about Darryl. But I knew Mama would worry, though she'd pretend not to. And Celeste—much as I love her, and she loves me—couldn't keep a secret *this* big if her life depended on it.

But I still had concerns about Tiffani's trip. "Tiff, you don't have to make yourself scarce because Darryl is coming. He wants to meet you, and I want you to meet him."

"Even if he *weren't* your new fella, do you think I'd miss meeting *Darryl Bridges?* No way!" She looked at me narrowly. "Anyhow, haven't I checked out every boyfriend you've ever had? I have to scope this dude to make sure he's worthy."

"Tiffani," I laughed, "he's worthy. Believe me."

"I'll judge *that* for myself," she retorted. "Just because he's Mr. Grammy doesn't automatically make him good enough for my Mama. But, this way, I'll be here with you all part of the time and you can have some time alone, too. And I really did plan to go visit Marlowe this weekend, anyway."

So, that's how we resolved it. She'd be home until Friday afternoon and take the train down to Detroit. She'd come back Sunday afternoon, in time for work on Monday.

We cleaned house like two demons Tuesday evening, and Wednesday I washed my hair and did my nails. Dare's plane was scheduled to arrive at six-fifteen Thursday evening, so we were expecting him about seven-thirty or eight.

After leaving work Thursday, I stopped by the market for a few last minute things and got home about five-thirty. As I was walking from my parking stall, a tall man in a very off-the-rack gray business suit, a big hat, and horn-rimmed glasses got out of a dark green Cadillac parked near my front door. Just as I passed him, he said, "Pardon me, miss, but can you direct me to the nearest florist shop? I want to get my girl some roses." I dropped the grocery bag as I ran back and into his arms.

A few moments later I heard Sam say, "You two better break it up before the neighbors call the cops." He was standing near us with a big grin on his face.

Alex had retrieved my bag, but was holding it out, away from his body. "Yeah," he agreed, "let's get inside. This thing has sprung a leak."

Darryl got out a large suitcase and they followed me to my apartment. As Dare and Sam took a seat in the living room, I went into the kitchen with Alex. He deposited the soggy sack in the sink and proceeded to wash his hands. I called to Dare and Sam, asking if they'd like something to drink. Sam wanted a beer and Dare wanted a diet Pepsi.

"Told you I'd be seeing you again soon," Alex whispered, as we walked back into the living room with the drinks.

Alex gave Sam the beer he'd carried in for him and sat down next to him on the sofa. I sat next to Dare on the loveseat and handed him his Pepsi, saying, "Darryl! You startled me half to death! Why didn't you tell me you'd be here earlier?"

"Wanted to surprise you, baby. When I got up this morning, I just didn't feel like waiting. We decided not to take my plane—too much attention. So we went out to the airport and got on the first thing smoking."

"Did you have any trouble finding your way?"

"Your directions were perfect, Angela," Sam volunteered, "but 'Wrong-Way Corrigan' here insisted on driving . . ." he nodded to Dare, "and we almost wound up in Canada."

"What's the problem?" Darryl challenged. "We're here, aren't we?"

"Yeah," Sam came back, "after you finally let Alex take the wheel."

The guys stayed long enough to finish their beers, then set

out for the hotel. As I closed the door behind them, Darryl called out, "Now come back over here and let's get properly reacquainted."

As I approached, he pulled me down on his lap. "I'm too heavy to sit on your lap, honey," I objected.

"No, you're not," he said, hugging me. "You're like Baby Bear's porridge . . . 'just right.' "

"I thought in the Bridges household Baby Bear ate grits, not porridge."

"Whatever," he replied, and kissed me. "God, I missed you! Darlin,' you said we needed to see if we'd still feel the same after we'd been apart." He held me a little tighter. "*I* still feel the same. How about you?" He got a kiss for his answer.

After we "reacquainted" a while, I said, "Look, friend, my daughter will be home any minute. We'd better cut it out, or we'll be caught in disreputable circumstances."

"I'll just tell her the truth—you shamelessly attacked me the minute I stepped through the door."

I stood up, "You would, too, wouldn't you? Well, before you enlighten my only child on her mother's bohemian ways, let's get you settled. Let me show you to your room."

He picked up his bag and followed me to the bedroom. "Is this your room?" he asked.

"Need you ask?" I pointed to a picture he'd sent me before my trip to California, now framed, and on my bedside table. "When I got this, I never dreamed the real McCoy would be standing in this room one day." I looked up at him and our eyes locked. We started to walk toward each other.

Just then, I heard the front door opening, followed by, "Mama, I'm home. Where are you?"

"In my room. Out in a minute, hon." I grinned at Darryl. "Boy, is *she* in for a surprise!"

He was rubbing his hands together anxiously. "Man . . . I hope she likes me."

"She will," I predicted in a whisper, taking his hand. "She

has her mother's good taste. Well," I added, leading him out of the room, "let's go meet the Pepsi generation."

Tiffani had gone into the kitchen for a glass of water. She was standing with her back to us as we approached. "I was late leaving work . . ." she was saying. "Why is this grocery bag in the sink? Of all days to be held up! They'll be here in an hour or so." She took a sip of water and said, as she turned toward me, "Oh God, I hope he likes . . ." Her voice trailed off as she saw Darryl and I standing in the doorway.

People considerably older and more experienced than Tiffani have lost it upon coming face-to-face with Darryl. This poor kid had to contend with meeting him unexpectedly, and as her mother's new boyfriend, to boot. My firecracker child had many wonderful qualities, but keeping a cool head was not yet among them. I braced myself for the explosion. But she just stood blinking at us for a moment, then simply said, "Oh . . . Hello."

"Tiffani," I said warily, "this is Darryl. Darryl, my daughter, Tiffani."

Darryl, bless his heart, made the first move, "Hi, Tiffani. I feel as though I already know you. It's wonderful to finally meet you."

Tiffani put down the glass and wiped her hand on her jeans, "It's great to meet you, too," she said calmly, shaking his hand. I was flabbergasted. "I love all your stuff," she continued.

"Thanks," Dare said with a smile.

"But I didn't know you wore glasses."

"I don't," Darryl said with a chuckle, taking the specs off. "These are plain glass—camouflage," he added in a conspiratorial whisper.

"Hey, you two, what are we standing around in here for?" I asked. "Let's go into the living room." We did, and Darryl began asking Tiff about school and her job. Since he started her talking about everybody's favorite subject—themselves—she was off to the races.

The telephone rang. It was my friend Bev, wanting to know my plans for the weekend. I went into the bedroom to talk, since Darryl and Tiff were already deep in conversation. "A friend from out of town is visiting this weekend," I cautiously told her.

"A 'friend,' huh? Male or female?" she probed.

"Decisively male."

"Oh, *that* kind of friend. You've never said anything about this mystery man. Who is he? How long have you known him? Where's he from? And, most importantly, does he have a friend for *me?*"

"Hold on, girl," I laughed. "I can only answer one question at a time!"

"Well, you haven't answered *any* yet, so start talking—and start with that last question first!"

I laughed again, "Bev, I haven't met many of his friends yet, so I don't know."

"Well, when you do, keep me in mind. Now tell me the rest."

Thinking fast, I remembered the flowers Darryl had sent me, "His name is Doug," I fibbed, "and he's from California."

"He lives there now? How long have you known him? And how in hell did you meet him in the first place?"

"We met months ago—but it's a long story. I'll tell you all about him later, Bev, I promise, but now I need to get back. He only arrived forty-five minutes ago."

"All right, Angie, I won't hold you. I know how it is. Are you going to bring him to the club this weekend?"

"I don't know," I said hesitantly. "I mean, we live so far apart we can't see each other often and . . ."

"Don't say another word. I know how *that* is, too. But you two have to come up for air *sometime.* Why don't you bring him out Saturday night?"

"I don't know," I repeated, "I'll ask him and see."

"Okay, girlfriend. Well, call me next week if I don't see you before then, and . . . good luck!"

As I hung up the telephone, Tiffani's laughter floated in to me, along with the not nearly as dulcet tones of her new favorite rap tune. Back in the living room, Tiffani and Darryl were in the middle of the floor dancing.

"Mom! Darryl's teaching me this new dance called the 'Turbo Booster.' I've got it, too—watch!"

She had it, all right. Those two nuts proceeded to 'Turbo Boost' all over my living room. "I'm going to be the first one in town to know it!"

"Come on, Angie, get a piece of this," Darryl said. "And don't pretend you can't dance, either. I know better."

"Okay. You want a 'Turbo Booster?' I'll *show* you a 'Turbo Booster.' " And I busted a move, too. I wasn't as good at it as either of them, but I held up my end. That damn tape was one of those "house music" mixes that go on forever. We were only too ready to retire from the field of battle when it finally ended.

"Mama," Tiffani panted from where she'd settled next to me on the sofa, "Darryl knows MC Smoke!" MC Smoke was the brain behind the opus we'd been dancing to. "Darryl says maybe one day he'll throw me a party and ask MC Smoke to come!"

I gave Darryl, who was sitting on the loveseat across from us, a look that clearly said, "Thanks a whole heap, pal." His return gaze innocently answered, "So? What's wrong with that?" I forgave him. Obviously the man hadn't attended a teenage party since he was a teenager himself, if then even. He didn't know what he had gotten us into.

"Hey, Mom," Tiff asked suddenly, "What's up with that grocery bag in the sink?"

"Oh, my God!" I wailed, running to the kitchen. I had forgotten all about it. Mr. Murphy and his law were in full effect—the contents of the bag were ruined, and along with them, my plans for dinner. "Oh, no," I groaned.

"What's wrong, Mama?" Tiffani called to me.

"Nothing major, dear. But we'll have to go to plan B for dinner."

Darryl came to lean against the kitchen doorway, "Actually, I was hoping to take you ladies out to dinner this evening."

"But Dare, I wanted to cook for you. Anyway, do you think it would be . . . uh . . . wise . . . for us to go out?"

"I think so. Being recognized depends a lot on people expecting to see me, like in a city I'm scheduled to appear. Nobody expects to see me here, so most people who look closely will just think, 'Wow, that guy sure looks like what's-his-name.' "

" 'What's-his-name,' indeed!" I laughed. "Your name is slightly better known than *that,* Dare."

"Be that as it may," he replied, "I think we'd be okay."

"Afraid to eat my cooking, eh? I'll have you know I'm a very good cook, sir."

"I don't doubt that for a minute, hon, and you'll have ample opportunity before the weekend's out. I like to eat. But it's not often I have a chance to take *two* beautiful women out to dinner."

Sam and Alex wound up going with us. When Darryl called to let them know we were going out, they wanted me to recommend some places to eat and some local night spots. I told Darryl they might as well come with us. Dare and I changed clothes. I put on a blouse and slacks, but Dare stepped out in a jogging suit that was much too big, dark glasses, and the baseball cap again.

When the guys came by for us, I offered to take the wheel, since they didn't know the city. I drove with Darryl sandwiched in the front between me and Tiff, despite Alex's protests from the back that he was "hogging the women."

"Eat your heart out, man," Dare threw over his shoulder, then leaned back and stretched his arms along the back of the seat behind Tiff and I, hugging our shoulders. "Ah! Now *this* is living!" he sighed.

I drove around the city for a bit, showing them the sights. Lansing's smaller than most places Darryl has visited, but it's a nice city. Since it's the state capital, I took them by the Capitol Building. It's a beautiful sight, especially at night. They loved Moore's River Drive. The roadway curved within mere yards of the river, and people parked there with their vans and RVs to fish.

We went to "Just Like Mama's," one of the few soul food restaurants in town. Its casual, down home atmosphere was almost as big a draw as its fantastic food. Those men ate like food had just been invented. The place featured an all-you-can-eat buffet, and they substantially lowered the owner's profit margin for the night. They all went back for seconds, and I think Sam went three times. "It's been a long time since I've had food like this," Sam explained. "We don't run across good soul food too often."

After leaving the restaurant, we were passing one of the malls, when Tiffani mentioned she and her friends often hung out at the video arcade there.

"Arcade?" Darryl repeated.

"Oh, man . . . *now* you've done it," Alex told Tiff.

We were at the arcade until it closed at eleven. Darryl was a Skee-Ball zealot, like Tiffani, and I thought I would have to drag them both out by their respective belts. It looked like the jig was up at one point, when Darryl went to get change for yet another twenty. Dare had taken off his dark glasses in order to better see the video screens, and the young guy behind the counter said, "Hey, man, do you know you look just like . . ."

"Yeah, man," Darryl replied in a bored voice, "People are always telling me that. I wish that dude would grow a beard or something." The guy nodded and walked away. I couldn't believe he bought it!

Alex and Sam dropped us off at home and took off for an evening at my favorite club, after I gave them directions. When we got inside, Tiff said, "I'm really beat. Think I'll call it a night. Night, Mama," she said, kissing me on the cheek. "Night, Dare. Thanks for dinner and everything."

"You're welcome. And thanks for beating me at Skee-Ball. I demand a rematch!"

"You've got it, anytime," she laughed. "Well, good night, you guys."

"Tiff is a special person, Angela," Dare said, as we settled on the sofa. "She does you proud."

"I am proud, Dare, and extremely thankful," I said. "Now if I could only get her to stop being so hyper."

"I wouldn't worry about that. That'll come in time. It's great she's so full of life. Too many girls her age are so jaded, they're old before their time."

I turned on the tube. The "Blues Brothers" was on. It turns out we both love that movie, and sat on the sofa cackling like two lunatics. I examined his injured hand. He had gone to his doctor, as I had asked. Fortunately, no stitches were needed and it was healing fine.

When the movie ended, Darryl, who had his arm around my shoulders, pulled me closer, and started to sing softly in my ear, "Anticipation . . . anticipa-a-tion is making me wait . . . It's keeping me wai-ai-ai-ai-ai-ai-ting . . ."

"Dare," I said slowly, "I guess I'm being old-fashioned. Tiff's not a child anymore. Although I haven't been celibate since Bobby died, I've never . . . uh, entertained a lover at home before while Tiff was here, and . . ."

"No problem, honey. I've never been in a situation like this before, and I'm willing to defer to your judgment. I have to say, though, I don't think I'd feel comfortable handling it any other way myself. I can wait. We'll have tomorrow and Saturday." I'd told him about Tiff's trip to Detroit. "In fact, we'd better turn in, too," he said as he he stood up. "I want both of us to get plenty of rest tonight . . ." the glint I remembered came into his eyes as he pulled me up from the sofa, "we're both going to need it."

We walked back to my bedroom, took turns with the bathroom getting ready for bed, and wound up in our hotel robes, kissing good night in the hallway. "This is déjà vu for sure," he said. "I've got to find a way to stop telling you good night *outside* the bedroom door."

"Anticipation . . ." I started to sing.

"Hey, you *do* have a lovely voice. You still haven't sung for me yet and don't think I've forgotten. But I think this song is more appropriate, 'Tomorrow . . . tomorrow . . . I'll love you tomorrow . . .' "

"I think that goes . . . '*I* love you, comma, tomorrow,' honey."

"Whatever," he said, pulling me close and kissing me. "Good night, my Angel. Until tomorrow."

I quietly went into Tiffani's bedroom, trying not to wake her, and slipped into the empty twin bed.

"Mama?" Tiff whispered.

"Yes, baby. Sorry I woke you. Go back to sleep."

"I like him, Mama."

"I'm glad, dear. He likes you, too."

"He's really crazy about you, Mama. It shows in his eyes when he looks at you."

"I'm glad about that, too . . ." my whisper grew even softer, "because *I'm* really crazy about *him*."

"I know. It shows in *your* eyes."

"That obvious, huh?"

"Transparent as glass—both of you. What are you all doing tomorrow?"

"No plans yet," I yawned. "I guess we'll just wing it."

"If I didn't like Dare anyway, for himself, I'd like him for making you so happy. Good night, Mom. I love you."

Seven

Raindrops On Roses

I opened my eyes and one of Tiffani's stuffed bears was staring back at me. She slept in one twin bed, but the one I was in was the usual home of her menagerie of stuffed animals. This had apparently been missed when Tiff turned back the covers for me the night before.

I heard Darryl and Tiffani laughing. Looking at her clock, I saw it was a few minutes after nine. I rarely slept that late, even on weekends. Grabbing Tiffani's comb and brush, I smoothed my hair, put on my robe, and went out to see what was so funny.

Tiff was in her robe in the kitchen, cooking breakfast. Dare was sitting at the kitchen table with a cup of coffee. Tiffani had taken her portable TV into the kitchen; one of the morning cartoon shows was on, and they were laughing at the antics of Daffy Duck.

"Morning, sleepy head," Darryl said. "We were just about to wake you. Breakfast is almost ready."

"Yep. About five minutes. Morning, Mama."

"Morning, sweetheart," I walked over and kissed her on the cheek. Then I went to Darryl and said, "Morning, sweetheart," again, as I kissed him, *not* on the cheek. "Five minutes will give me just enough time to feel human. Excuse me."

When I came back from the bathroom, Darryl pulled out a

chair and handed me a cup of coffee. Then he resumed what he had apparently been doing—setting the table.

"Darryl, let me do that," I objected.

"Do what?" he said, putting out the last pieces of silverware, and sitting down himself.

Tiffani served breakfast and Darryl said grace. The meal was, like everything Tiffani cooks, delicious. My cooking is good, but hers is fabulous. This morning she prepared what I called her "everything but the kitchen sink" omelet, which featured ham, cheese, potatoes, tomatoes, onions, and green peppers. That and blueberry muffins made for a meal fit for a . . . superstar.

"Best omelet I ever had in my life," Darryl pronounced, patting his stomach. He was wearing his hotel robe, too. Tiffani must have noticed it was just like the one I had been wearing since my return from California, but she didn't comment on it.

"Do you all mind if I have first crack at the bathroom?" Tiff asked. "I want to pick up my paycheck and do a little shopping before I leave. I have to get a wedding present, for one thing."

"Glad you said that. Excuse me. Be right back," Darryl said, rising from the table and going into his room. Tiff looked at me and mouthed silently, "What's he doing?" I shrugged and made a "beats me" face back.

In a few moments, Darryl came back with two black velvet boxes. "Just a couple of small gifts for my charming hostesses," he smiled, taking his seat again, and handed a box to each of us.

Tiffani opened hers first. Inside were a pair of diamond stud earrings; each one a full carat, or *I'm* a vegetable homonym. She drew in her breath, "Darryl! Oh, I don't believe it! Thank you! I'm going to go put them on right now!" she dashed into her bedroom.

I looked at Darryl, "A couple of 'small' presents, huh?"

"You haven't opened *yours* yet," he said, looking at me pointedly. I opened my box. Inside on a slender golden chain was a pendant. The center piece was an oval shaped diamond surrounded by ten or twelve small rubies. The detail of the setting was like tiny golden leaves, making the rubies look like miniature roses. I just sat staring at it, watching the stones twinkle in the morning sunlight.

Darryl was watching me closely. "You don't like it," he said disappointedly.

I looked up, but his image was wavering. "Oh, Darryl . . ." I breathed. I could barely squeeze out the words. I blinked, and one fat tear slowly slid down my cheek.

He leaned over and kissed away the tear. "Guess that means you do like it, after all," he said softly, taking my hand.

Tiff came rushing back in, hair swept back from her ears and wearing the earrings, "Just *look* at them! They're . . . Mama! What's wrong?" I tilted the box so she could see inside. "Great day in the morning!" she exclaimed, "Talk about a piece of the rock!"

Darryl and I burst out laughing. He took the pendant from the box and fastened it around my neck. I looked from Darryl to Tiffani, and back to Darryl again. "Well, how does it look?"

Tiff gave me the Okay sign. "It's phat, Mom." "Phat," in the latest hip-hop parlance, so I'm told, means what *we* used to call "out-of-sight."

"How do you like it on me, Dare?" I asked, shyly turning to him.

"It's lovely . . . but can't compare with the beauty of the woman wearing it," he said, kissing my hand and looking into my eyes.

"Ahem . . ." Tiff cleared her throat, "well, maybe I'd better take that shower now," she said, beating a hasty retreat.

Dare and I moved to the sofa, having a second cup of coffee. We held hands and watched cartoons. About a half hour later, Tiff came flying out of her room, diamond studs in attendance. "Be back in a couple of hours, Mama," she said, kissing me. "See you, Dare," and out the door she went.

Darryl and I looked at each other.

"Be gone a couple of hours, she said," Darryl began, taking my hand.

"Probably more. That kid takes 'shop 'til you drop' as a directive."

"Still," he said, standing, drawing me with him, "we should wait until later."

"Yes, we really should," I agreed, following as he led me to the bedroom.

"After all," he continued, taking off my robe once we got there, "we've waited this long; we could wait a few more hours."

"Easily," I conceded, kissing his throat as I slipped off *his* robe. He was wearing a bottom, but no pajama top.

He slid the straps of my loose nightgown down over my shoulders. It fell in a puddle at my feet. He took me in his arms and held me tightly. "But I don't want to wait another second . . ." he said gruffly. "Do you?"

My "no" was smothered as his lips descended on mine.

The interlude was explosive and sweet, but brief. Darryl was concerned Tiffani would come back and find us in a "compromising position."

"We've been in a number of positions the last hour or so, sir. Which was the compromising one?"

"None of your lip, woman. Just get up, and let's get dressed. But I want you to know," he said, stopping me as I started to rise, "this was just the appetizer. We're going to have the feast later this evening."

"Ooooo, I'm scared of you," I said with a shiver.

"With good cause, my dear, with good cause. Now get up."

I could have told him Tiffani was savvy enough to not come back without warning us first. Sure enough, she called about an hour later to say she'd be home in about twenty minutes. By the time she called, Darryl and I were both showered and dressed. Today he was wearing jeans, a baggy blue tee shirt, and his Nikes. We were out on the balcony, relaxing in the rocking lawn chairs, when the telephone rang. A woman's voice asked, "Hi, is this Mrs. Delaney?"

"Yes, it is. Who's calling?"

"This is Mary McCoy, Darryl's assistant. Remember me? We met a couple of weeks ago at his concert."

"Yes, of course I remember you, Mary. But I'm Angela, not 'Mrs. Delaney.' How are you?"

"I'm fine, thanks. Darryl said it would be all right if I called with his messages. I hope you don't mind."

"No, I don't mind a bit, as long as you don't tell him anything that'll cause him to leave."

"Eager as he was to get there, Angela, I couldn't pry him out with a crowbar, let alone a phone message," she laughed, "and anyway, it's just routine stuff."

I laughed, too. "Okay, Mary. Hold on a minute, I'll get him." Since the telephone was cordless, I took it out to Darryl on the balcony.

Tiffani came back while he was still on the phone, "What's going on?"

"Nothing, honey. Darryl's just talking with his office."

"Well, I gotta finish packing. My train leaves in a little over an hour."

I trailed her to her bedroom. "Are you sure you're not doing this just because you think Dare and I want to be alone?" I asked worriedly.

"No way, Mama, I really want to go to this gig. I wouldn't go if I didn't. I like hanging out with Dare. He's cool. Anyhow," she added with a smile, "you're not telling me you *don't* want to be alone with him, are you?"

I made a face at her, "No, Miss Smarty-Pants, I'm not telling you that."

"Well, then, what's the problem? We both get to do something we really want to do, and I'll be back Sunday to ride herd on you two love birds."

By the time Tiffani was packed, Darryl was off the phone.

He added the baseball cap and dark glasses to his ensemble, and we climbed into my car and headed for the train station.

We sat in the parking lot, right next to the tracks, waiting for the train to arrive when a thought occurred to me. "Tiffani," I queried, "you don't have your earrings with you, do you?" She wasn't wearing them.

"Uh . . . what earrings, Mom?"

That told me all I needed to know. "You know 'what earrings,' young lady. The diamond earrings Darryl just gave you. I don't think you should take them."

"Oh, Mama, what's wrong with taking them with me? I want to wear them to the wedding."

"No way, girlfriend. Give them to me."

"But, Mama . . ."

"Tiffani, this is not open to discussion."

"Well, I'm not a child. I'm eighteen years old, you know."

"I'm very aware of how old you are . . . to the second—Miss Thang. I was there, remember?"

"I don't see why . . ."

Darryl interrupted. "Angela, are you worried about her losing them? They're insured. Your necklace is, too."

"No, Dare, that's not it. I'm concerned about someone hurting her to take them. Most people will figure they're cubic zirconium, and she got them at K-Mart for $19.99. But there may be some genius who'll recognize them as the real thing. I lived in Detroit a lot of years. I know it's not as bad as the media tries to portray it. I also know, just like any other big city, it's a place to watch your step. She's going to be at that reception with a lot of strangers, and I know the younger set is going to split off into some sort of after party on their own. Taking those earrings is just asking for trouble."

"Oh, Mama, you're just being . . ."

"Tiffani," Darryl interrupted again, "I think your mother's right. Fork 'em over."

"But . . ."

Darryl didn't say anything. He just turned to the back seat, and looked at her. Then a miracle occurred. She reached into that sack of a purse she always carries, took out the black velvet box, and handed it to me. "Oh, all right."

"Tell you what," Darryl said then, "how about taking this, instead?" He took off the thin gold chain he was wearing. It had a small "D" initial charm. "See, the initial even matches your last name. How about it?"

"Hey! Great!" Tiffani exclaimed, taking it and putting it on. "I'll take good care of it, Dare, and give it back when I get home Sunday."

"Give what back?" he asked.

Tiffani looked puzzled, "Your chain."

"That? Oh, that's *your* chain."

"Really? Oh, Darryl! Thank you!" She hugged him around the neck, across the back of the seat.

"Hey, hold it! You can't have the neck! I want to keep *it!*"

The train arrived then, saving Darryl from being strangled to death by Tiffani's gratitude. Dare got Tiff's bag from the trunk and we walked to the boarding platform.

"Mama?" Tiff said quietly, "I'm sorry about the earrings. I understand why you don't want me to take them. *I* think it would be safe, but I don't want you to worry about me. And I didn't mean to be so bitc . . . snippy about it."

"It's okay, babe. Just another mother-daughter negotiation peacefully concluded. Maybe I *am* being over-cautious, but that's a mother's prerogative. Be careful, and take care of yourself. You know the rules."

"I will, Mom. See you Sunday." She kissed me on the cheek. "Dare, see you Sunday, too. Have a great weekend, and take care of my Mom."

"Will do," Dare smiled. "Enjoy the wedding, honey."

"Love you, baby," I said, as she stepped up onto the train. "Call me as soon as you get there!"

"I will, Mama! Love you, too! 'Bye, Darryl . . . and thanks again!"

I looked around quickly, but no one seemed to have paid any attention to just who this particular "Darryl" was.

Tiff went to a window seat and waved as the train left the station. We stood with our arms around each other, waving back, watching until the train was out of sight. Then, holding hands, we walked back to the car.

Leaving the parking lot, Darryl said, "Angie, maybe I shouldn't have given Tiffani those earrings. The kind of problem you're concerned about honestly never occurred to me—and it *should* have. Even isolated as I am from the 'real world' by the glass prison I live in, I *do* read the papers and watch the news, and I know those things happen. If anything ever happened to you or Tiffani because of something I gave you . . ."

"Darryl, the gifts are like everything else about you . . . thoughtful and generous. The problem's not with the gifts. The problem's with greed and crime, and *they* existed long before you or I arrived on the scene. Don't worry, we'll be careful. I know what is and is not a good time for us to wear our 'rocks,' as Tiff would say. But while we're on the subject . . . Darryl, that jewelry had to cost a fortune. I love my necklace, I truly do," I touched it fondly, "but I love it because *you* gave it to me, not because of its value." I gave him a gently reproving smile, "A less expensive gift would have been just as much loved, hon."

"I know, Angel, *that's* one of the reasons I want to *shower* you with gifts. You're right, the jewelry *did* cost a fortune but I *have* a fortune—several fortunes, in fact." He gave me his roguish smile, "And I can damn well spend one of them on my woman, if I so choose."

I gave him a resigned smile, and shook my head. "What am I gonna do with you?" I asked him dejectedly.

He put a hand on my knee, "I've got a couple of suggestions."

"Oh, really? But I thought you might like to sight-see a while."

"Nope." His hand began to travel up my thigh.

"Or maybe stop somewhere for lunch?"

"Wrong again." The hand was still migrating.

"How about a movie?"

"How about putting the pedal to the metal and getting this car back to your place before I ravish you in the back seat?"

"You can't ravish me in the *back* seat while I'm driving, honey."

"Okay, then . . . in the *front* seat."

Soon we were at my apartment complex. Darryl kept grabbing at me as I opened the door. After we entered, I turned to face him, one hand on my hip, "I believe you made some rash statement earlier about this morning being just an appetizer, did you not?"

He slowly walked toward me, "Lady, my mouth don't write no checks my body can't cash." He put one arm around my waist and pulled me to him, so tightly and quickly it took my breath away. He entwined the fingers of his other hand in my hair and swiftly, but gently, arched my head and body backward, as he took possession.

We didn't "come up for air," as Bev had put it, until hours later. In the interim, Tiff had called to say she'd reached her aunt's house safely. After her call, Darryl called the guys to let them know we'd be in the rest of the evening (in case they wanted to go out) then he'd taken the phone off the hook. After that, for the next several hours, no one existed in the universe for us except each other.

A long time later, as my heartbeat slowly returned to a normal pace, I breathed a long, contented sigh from the cradle of Dare's arms. "Are you all right, my darling?" he asked.

"Yes, sweetheart, the most 'all right' I've ever been in my life. I was just thinking. Six months ago, who could have foreseen this?"

"I marvel at that, too. If we hadn't just happened to be in the same place at the same time, we never would have met."

He stroked my hair. "Do you know what just knocks me out about you?"

"My itty-bitty feet?" I asked, looking down to where my feet were rubbing his—four battleships passing in the night.

He laughed, "No!" He kissed my forehead. "You're so genuine; so for real. It's a quality that can't be learned or faked—you either have it, or you don't. And you're confident enough of your own identity to treat everybody around you like a . . . a *person;* Stew, the people at the party in L.A., and especially me."

"Well, hon, you *are* a person . . . Uh, you *are,* aren't you?" I feigned uncertainty.

"Yes," he laughed. "Contrary to some folks' popular belief, I am." His face clouded then. "There *have* been times I've felt more like some kind of a freak than a person."

"You're not a freak. You're a perfectly normal, perfectly healthy . . . *very* healthy . . ." I amended, "human male." I paused, "Dare, you *are* different; there's no denying *that.* I think one reason there are so many phony stories about you is that people can't . . . can't *categorize* you. *And* because you can do so many things so well most people can't do at all."

"But that's what I do. And I admit it's a big part of me, a critical part of me. But it's still only a part. It's still only what I *do*—not what I *am.*"

"I . . . I understand, honey."

He kissed me. "You really do, don't you, Angel? You see me as *me* . . . the person that guy on stage is only a part of."

That started us off again. The next time we surfaced it was almost eight o'clock. "Darryl, we haven't eaten since breakfast. I'd better see to dinner." I started to rise, but he put out a hand to stop me. "Where're you going?"

"I told you, honey, to start dinner."

"Do you have to?"

"Aren't you hungry?" I asked, surprised.

"Yes," he said, reaching for me again. "Now that you mention it, I sure am."

I slipped out of his grasp, "Look, you—dinner first, dessert later."

I put on my robe and made a quick stop by the bathroom. Then I went into the kitchen and began taking out the ingredients for dinner. A few minutes later Darryl followed me, tying the belt on his robe. "Can I help?"

"Yes. You can wash and chop those mushrooms."

We worked together getting dinner started. He *did* know his way around a paring knife and saucepan. I'd put on some soft music (not his), and we both hummed along to it as we prepared the meal.

While it was cooking, we relaxed on the sofa with a bottle of white wine. I turned off all the lights and opened the balcony blinds so we could look out on the starlit night and the lovely landscaping surrounding the complex.

"Okay, Angela," Dare said after a few minutes of silence. He reached over and turned off the stereo. "Even though you're the hostess, tonight you're going to have to sing for your supper."

"Excuse me?"

"I want to hear you sing. What little I've heard so far sounds pretty good."

"Oh, Dare . . . not *now*."

"Why not? You've stalled long enough. After all, I've sung for *you*. Turn-a-about's only fair. Let's have it."

"I don't have any music."

"A real singer doesn't need music, and I've got a feeling you're a real singer. I'm waiting . . ."

I pondered what I could sing for him. Then I remembered his love of show tunes—and roses—and sang "My Favorite Things."

After I finished, he just sat there with his hands clasped, looking down.

"That bad, huh?" I asked faint-heartedly.

"You're not going to try and tell me you've never done any singing, are you?" he asked, still not looking up.

"Well . . . no, Darryl. I've been singing since I was a little girl. I've been in several singing groups, and I've done a lot of local musicals and plays. I've done a fair amount of solo work, too. Just amateur stuff, but I love it."

"And when were you planning on telling me this?" he asked, still looking at the floor.

"Well, Dare . . . I . . . I felt . . . self-conscious telling you about my small claim to fame when you . . ."

"Angela," he finally looked up, right at me, "you've got one of the most beautiful voices I've ever heard in my *life.* I don't believe it. This is unreal." He gave me a piercing stare. "Is there anything you *can't* do?"

"Yes," I replied, "wear a size eight shoe."

We both lost it then, winding up on the floor laughing. When we finally stopped, Darryl said, "Let's sing something."

"Okay. What?"

"Let's try 'Stay That Way.' " He started singing and I joined him. On the second verse, he left me with the melody and made up a harmony part for himself as he went. After we finished, he said, "How about doing a duet with me?"

"I just did, silly."

"No, I mean *record* a duet with me."

"What?"

The oven timer went off, saving me from once again being caught speechless. I rushed into the kitchen to rescue our meal from flames, but my beloved was not to be diverted so easily. He followed me.

"What do you say, Angel?" Oh, God. He had that charged-up look on his face again.

"Oh, Darryl. Be serious," I said, taking the casserole out of the oven.

"I *am* serious! Honey, I never kid around about my music. We sound *spectacular* together! Our blend is perfect. You've got a good ear, as Stew so accurately pointed out. Couldn't you hear how good we sound together?"

I went into the dining room to set the table, but he was right behind me. "A lyric soprano! Who would have guessed it from that sexy, alto speaking voice! I don't have anything ready now that's right for us, but I'm going to start writing something the minute I get home!"

I decided this had gone far enough. "Honey, I'm touched and flattered but . . ."

"I'm not saying this because of how I feel about you, Angela. You're *good* and you've got the potential to be great! And don't tell me that you don't love to sing—it's all too obvious you do."

"Yes, I *do* love to sing. Under other circumstances I'd be thrilled to death, and if I had to, I'd *crawl* to California to get to that studio. But I don't see how we could do this *now.* Wouldn't it raise a lot of questions if this unknown, untried, unheard of female popped up from nowhere to record with one of the world's biggest stars? It would blow our cover for sure."

"Oh . . ." he said, stopping short. "I hadn't looked at it *that* way."

"Praise from a musician of your caliber is praise worth having. I'm honored you'd even consider me a serious vocalist. But I don't see how we could get away with it now, Dare."

"Well, I admit you have a point. But I don't give up easily. I'll figure out something."

"That's what I'm afraid of," I said under my breath.

I got him off the subject by wafting the casserole under his nose. The poor thing was hungry; it had been hours since we'd eaten, and we'd both burned a lot of calories.

I lit two tall candles, and after turning off all the lights again, we had our meal under their flickering romantic glow, with soft music in the background (classical this time).

As we were finishing, Darryl proclaimed, "Darlin', if Tiffani's a better cook than you, I'd better leave now, before I wind up weighing three hundred pounds. Now let's see: you sing, you dance, you're a great businesswoman, a fantastic mother, a fabulous cook, and . . ." he looked contemplative. "I'm forgetting one of your many talents." The gleam came back to his eyes again as he leaned toward me, "Oh, yeah . . . *now* I remember."

The dinner dishes remained on the dining room table overnight.

Eight

Alone With You

I opened my eyes, savoring the magic of waking in Darryl's arms. I lay still, looking at him, trying to freeze the moment in my memory, thinking how wonderful it would be to wake beside him *every* morning.

"Hold it!" my common-sense override cut in. *"Danger! You're about to go into imagination overload!"* I tried to stifle the next thought, but it was too late. How do you tell yourself *not* to think about something? The thought refused to be derailed. *Angela Bridges . . .* Mrs. *Darryl Bridges . . .*

I sighed and stroked Darryl's hair. His eyes opened, looking directly into mine. Without a word or sound, he kissed me, then pulled me deeper into his embrace. He kissed me again and we said good morning to each other in the sweetest possible way.

An impassioned hour or so later, we wandered into the kitchen and I cooked breakfast while Dare loaded the dishwasher with the previous night's neglected plates and utensils. He laughed when I pulled a huge, unopened box of grits out of the cabinet.

"For me?"

"For you," I confirmed with a nod.

Over breakfast, he inquired, "Well, Angel, what's on the agenda? Anything in particular you want to do?"

"Just to be with you," I told him with a grits-y kiss. "But you're the 'company,' what would you like to do? Uh, *that's* a given," I added, as he grinned, scooted his chair closer, and put his hand on my knee.

"What do you usually do Saturdays, sweet stuff?"

"Usually? I clean house, do laundry, go shopping, and sometimes I go to the club on Saturday night."

"Well," he said, glancing around, "if this place were any cleaner it would squeak, and I don't see any monster bags of laundry hanging around. So let's go shopping."

"Do you really want to? Do you think it would be okay?"

"Sure, we won't run into any problems. We've been doing all right the last two days, haven't we? As for wanting to, hon, do you have any idea how long it's been since I've gone shopping like a normal person?" He paused and looked thoughtful. "Come to think about it, I've *never* gone shopping like a normal person."

"I don't know if you'd like my kind of shopping, Dare. Almost every Saturday I make the rounds of the local re-sale shops. I just love it. I've found some treasures in those places." I pointed into the living room at the pride of my acquisitions. "See the coffee and end tables?"

"You got *them* at a re-sale shop?" he asked, incredulously. "They're gorgeous." And they were: a matching three piece set in dark mahogany, the tops with beveled glass centers. "Well," he said, "what are we waiting for? Let's go shopping!"

After we dressed, I asked, "Aren't you going to call the guys?"

"I did, while you were in the shower." He chuckled, "They've both got hangovers. Seems the Lansing nightlife is too much for those two smooth operators."

"Oh, no! Well, maybe they don't feel up to shopping."

"Oh, we're not taking *them*. Today is our day, baby. Just you and me."

Darryl was like a kid in a candy store at the re-sale shops. He kept nosing into everything: opening furniture drawers, thumbing through books, examining glassware, chatting with the store owners.

One place sold vintage clothing, and I found a wonderful man's evening scarf. It was of heavy brocaded satin in cream, black, and maroon paisley. There was long, thick, black silk fringe on the ends. I took it over to where Darryl was fiddling with an old camera. He flipped over the scarf.

"I've never seen one like it," he said, running his hands over the magnificent fabric.

I put it around his neck, "Then it's yours."

"Honey! I *love* it, but you don't . . ."

I gave him a fierce look, "Listen, buster, this is an equal opportunity romance. I can damn well spend part of *my* fortune on you if *I* so choose." The crazy man insisted on wearing the scarf during the rest of our rounds, strange as it looked with jeans and a casual shirt.

On several occasions I saw people do a double take when they looked at Darryl, and twice folks came up to him, remarking on his resemblance to you-know-who. Each time his somewhat weary, "Yeah, so I've been told," response worked like a charm.

By three o'clock, we decided to stop for a late lunch at my favorite Chinese restaurant and discovered this was yet another passion we shared. After a long, leisurely meal, we headed back to my apartment. As we were driving along, Darryl suddenly called out, "Hey, baby, hook a right!"

I turned right at the next corner, pulled to the curb, and asked, "What's wrong, Dare?"

" 'Nuttin,' honey.' Be right back!" he said. He jumped out of the car and sprinted back around the corner. Less than five minutes later he was back with a bouquet of red roses. "You didn't think I'd forgotten, did you?" he said, presenting them with a kiss.

Back at the apartment, he suggested we go out to the club that evening. "Sam and Alex said they had a great time there the other night. I don't want you to think I'm the kind of guy who never takes his lady out on the town. Anyway, it sounds like fun."

"I don't know. Most of the people that hang out there are big fans of yours. Going undetected *there* might not be so easy."

"Sometimes you gotta gamble a little," Dare urged. "I'm game. Come on, baby, let's live dangerously!" I apprehensively relented.

"What time does the 'in-crowd' show up?" he asked.

"It usually starts to get crowded about ten."

"All right. We'll get there a little before ten and get seated in an out of the way spot." He saw the concern on my face. "Don't worry, Angel. The guys said they were going again tonight. So if anything jumps off, they'll get us out of it in a hurry."

I looked at my watch. "It's only a little after six now," I said, walking toward the bedroom. "Hmmm . . . Whatever can we do to keep occupied for a couple of hours?" Still walking away, I turned and crooked my finger, "Oh . . . *I* know . . ."

"What?" he asked eagerly.

I turned to him, and slowly unbuttoned his shirt. Wrapping my arms around him, I began to rub his back as he embraced me. He pulled my tee shirt over my head, and in one deft move, unhooked my bra.

"Angela, your beauty staggers me," he murmured, his face buried between my breasts. My need for him surged through me like a bolt of lightning. Soon all our clothing was on the floor, and we joined it, too eager for the last few steps to the bedroom.

"I can't get enough of you," he whispered into my hair, as his strong, yet gentle hands caressed my thighs.

The DARRYL part of him that exploded on stage made its spellbinding, turbulent presence felt most off stage when we made love. He was a symphony of contradiction: tender, yet fierce; sweet, yet riotous; impassioned, yet leisurely; giving, yet unquenchable. We lay there on the carpet a long time afterward, both too depleted—and too content—to move.

About nine we started getting ready to go out. Dare showered while I anguished over what to wear. I took my shower and was still in the bathroom putting on makeup, when his reflection appeared in the mirror. I turned to face him. He was wearing a black suit with baggy, cuffed trousers, a black shirt, and a black silk tie. He had his "new" scarf hanging loose around his neck, outside the jacket, but tucked under the lapels. In the jacket breast pocket was a kerchief the same shade of maroon as in the scarf. He had pulled his hair back into a knot at the nape of his neck. Suddenly he whirled, executed a complicated step, and pulled one pant leg up a bit to let me see his maroon socks. "Well," he said, holding out his arms, and turning around, "you likes?"

I applauded and whistled. "I likes. I likes big time. I'm going to have to take a whip and chair to keep women away from you. But, sweetheart, in that outfit you're hardly inconspicuous."

"Got that covered," he said, ducking back into the bedroom. He came back seconds later wearing a black fedora with a wide soft brim, and the shades. "These will get us in and seated. Once the place fills up, I can take them off."

"I don't know," I replied skeptically. "The shades perhaps; indoors, at night, wearing them might call more attention to you than going in without them—but maybe you'd better keep the hat on."

His outfit settled what I would wear. I had a black jersey dress I loved, but hadn't worn in years. I found it, and tried it on. Hot damn! It still fit! It was a simple cut dress with a halter neckline, a slightly flared skirt, a matching wide belt with a rhinestone buckle, and practically no back. The back of the bodice was merely two criss-crossed straps holding the sides together.

I added black pantyhose, a small black velvet purse, and three inch black pumps that made me only a scant inch shorter than Darryl. The only jewelry I wore were the necklace and bracelet Darryl had given me.

When I walked into the living room where Darryl was waiting for me, he gave a soft wolf-whistle. "Mercy! Baby, you could start a riot!" I turned around and gave him an over the shoulder smile. "Holy mother of pearl!" he exclaimed, seeing the back of the dress. "Uh . . . are you *sure* you want to go out? I mean, we could . . ."

"Oh, no. Going out was *your* idea, and a damn fine one at that. Let's boogie!"

When we arrived at the club, it was only about half-full. Everybody in the joint turned to look when we walked in the door. I guess a couple, both attractive (I'm modest, but precise), both dressed almost entirely in black, and both almost six feet tall *was* somewhat of a sight.

Several people I knew greeted us as we walked to a table, and I stopped once or twice to introduce "Doug." We made our way to a table toward the rear, on the side closest the dance floor. A waitress I knew, an older woman, came to take our order. "Hi, Angie. You haven't been in for a while. How you been?"

"Just fine, Reesie. You?"

"Can't complain, honey, and it wouldn't do no good if I did," she said with a throaty laugh, looking over at Darryl. "I can see why you haven't been coming out lately. If I had somebody like *him* at home, I'd *never* leave!"

I laughed. "Reesie, this is my boyfriend, Doug."

Darryl nodded, "Pleased to meet you, Reesie."

"Honey, I'm *very* pleased to meet you. Next time you come in, leave your old lady at home," she said with a wink.

After she left to get our drinks, I turned to Dare. "I didn't mean to introduce you as my boyfriend. It just slipped out."

"What's wrong with that? I *am* your boyfriend."

"Yes, but we agreed . . ."

"We agreed to not broadcast our relationship, true enough. The people here can't know my identity, but—whoever I am—

I'm your man. I'm proud to be your man and I don't care if every damn person in here knows it."

All at once I heard, "Well, girl, I see you *did* manage to make it after all. Good to see you. Now, introduce us to your handsome companion." I turned to see my friends Bev and Charlie who'd apparently just come in.

Dare stood while I did the introductions. "Would you ladies care to join us?" he asked.

"Well," Bev said, quickly taking a seat, "if you're sure it's not an intrusion." She swept her long braids away from her face and smiled at me with a suggestive twinkle in her light brown eyes.

"We'd be delighted," Darryl replied, holding out a chair for Charlie. "In fact, we're expecting a couple of my buddies to join us shortly. I know they'd love to meet you." Sure enough, about fifteen minutes later, Sam and Alex arrived. I did the introductions all around, Charlie correcting me when I introduced her.

"Charlene," she rectified, offering one long-nailed hand to Alex, while patting her auburn beehive with the other.

I emphasized to my friends how Sam, Alex, and DOUG were here on a brief vacation. I knew the guys had caught on when a few minutes later Sam asked "Doug" how long we'd been there.

We had a great time. The music was marvelous; the best of the new stuff, liberally mixed with oldies. I was proud that a lot of the recordings of *both* groups were Darryl's. If the crowd only knew the creator of so much of the music they were grooving to was right there in their midst!

All three men asked each of us to dance at one point or another. Darryl was careful to keep his dancing in check. He might have been able to mask his appearance, but if he started dancing the way only he could, it would have been a dead giveaway. Then he might have just as well set up a neon sign pointing to his head saying "DARRYL BRIDGES!". I saw a slightly cramped look on his face while he was dancing to a fast number with "Charlene."

"It's killing you, isn't it?" I asked him later, when we were alone at the table; the others all out on the dance floor.

"What?"

"Dancing like an accountant."

"You noticed, huh? But it's worth it to be here—dancing with you."

A while later, Bev and I excused ourselves and went to the ladies' room. As soon as the door closed, she said, "Okay, Angela; what in the world are you doing here with Darryl Bridges?"

I was dumbfounded. "Huh?"

She started laughing. "Angela, Doug looks just like Darryl Bridges! Well, not *just* like him. Doug's more muscular, and I think he's even better-looking. But surely you've noticed the resemblance!"

"Sure," I quickly recovered. "People are always coming up to him saying that. I guess I've gotten so used to it I don't really notice anymore."

"How did you meet these guys? They're handsome, sophisticated . . . and loaded. They were fighting over who'd pay for the next round of drinks! I've died and gone to man-heaven!" She paused while applying lipstick to her full, pouty lips. "Angie, Doug's fine as he can be, but Sam's more my type—the older man-of-the-world. Is he married?"

"Do you think I'd let him get away with outrageously flirting with you—the way he's been doing all evening—if he was?"

"Well, what are we waiting for?" she smoothed her dress over her petite, slender frame in anticipation. "Let's get back out there before some heifer tries to move in on our territory!"

When we got back to the table, Charlie invited us all to a party one of her co-workers was throwing. Alex and Sam jumped at the invitation, but Dare and I begged off, saying we were going to make it an early night.

"I bet," I heard Bev say under her breath.

After they left, Darryl and I had one last slow dance. On the way back to the table he said, "I'll never make it back to your place without a pit stop. I won't be long." He saw me back to my seat and continued on to the men's room.

I was pawing in my purse for the car keys, when someone sat down across from me. I looked up and inwardly groaned. It was Richard, a guy I'd gone out with twice and never wanted to date again. He was a guy who wouldn't take no for an answer. And a guy who'd apparently been drinking—a lot. "Hello, beautiful. Man, you look hot tonight! Haven't seen you around for a while. Where you been hiding?"

"I haven't been hiding." I didn't want to hurt his feelings. Richard was a nice guy. I just couldn't see us as a "love connection," as Chuck Woolery would say. "Listen, Richard," I said gently, "I'm not here alone. I'm with someone."

"Yeah, I know. I saw the scrawny bastard leave."

That got me ticked. "My *escort* didn't leave, but *you* should. He'll be back any minute."

"Who is that punk, anyway? I've never seen *him* in here before. What is he . . . some big dope man from Detroit?"

Now I was insulted on my own behalf, as well as Darryl's. Richard knew damn well I would never knowingly go out with *any* kind of "dope man," big or otherwise. Plus, Detroit was my home town, and I didn't cotton to anybody insulting *it*, either.

"Why would you say a thing like that?" I asked angrily.

"What other kind of dude would step in *here* in a two or three thousand dollar suit?"

I didn't know beans about men's clothes. I didn't know Darryl's suit was so exclusive. But that was none of Richard's business, anyway. "He's my boyfriend," I snapped.

"Boyfriend? You told me you didn't *have* no boyfriend."

"Then I didn't. Now I do."

"So how does *he* rate? That chump doesn't even know enough to take off his hat when he's out with a lady. And he dances like he's got a stick up his ass." He reached for my hand. "He might have the money, but he can't do anything *else* for you I can't do better, baby."

"Look, Richard," I said as I snatched back my hand, "you've known for some time now what the score is between us. And I've got a commitment with someone now. He wouldn't appreciate finding you in his seat."

"I don't give a damn *what* he wouldn't appreciate."

"That's your *second* mistake," Darryl's voice said quietly from behind me.

Richard looked up. He hadn't seen Darryl approaching, he'd been too busy giving me a hard time. Now he was going to get bad with Darryl.

"Oh, yeah? And what was my *first* mistake, big man?" I guess the "big man" was Richard's lame attempt at sarcasm, since he was about two inches taller than Dare, and had him by a good forty pounds.

"Your first mistake," Darryl shot back, moving up next to my chair, "was messin' with *my* woman to begin with."

"And just what do *you* plan to do about it, Rocky?" Richard countered.

I could see what was coming. "Dare . . ." I began, so rattled I called him by his "real" name.

Never taking his eyes off Richard, Darryl cut me off with an abruptly raised hand, a gesture that said more plainly than words, "Butt out—I'll handle this."

"The lady asked you to leave," Dare continued in a softly menacing tone. "Now *I'm* asking you to leave. You can try me if you want, but you've already got two strikes. I wouldn't go for three."

Richard stood up, his eyes locked on Darryl's. My eyes were level with Darryl's right hand, and I watched while it clenched into a fist. "Oh, no," I whispered.

Richard suddenly dropped his gaze, muttered, "Screw it," and walked away.

Darryl sat in the chair he'd just vacated. "Are you all right, Angel?"

"Yes, I'm fine, but let's get out of here."

Darryl's exchange with Richard had been so brief and quiet that in the now crowded club it hadn't drawn attention. We just got the standard waves and good nights from my acquaintances as we left.

Except for Richard. His eyes followed us from his perch, sulking at the bar, as we neared the door. Out in the parking lot, I tensed for the door to open behind us, but it didn't. When we got into the car, my hands were shaking so badly I couldn't get the key in the ignition.

"Hold on!" Darryl told me. "You're trembling like a leaf. It's over, darlin'. There's nothing to be frightened of. Look, you'd better let *me* drive."

"Darryl, we should get out of here! He might come out to start something any minute!" Just as I said that, the door from the club opened, and I jumped, but it was just another couple leaving.

"Angela, calm down, honey. He's not coming out *here* until he thinks we're gone."

"How can you be so sure?"

"Because I know *he* knows I'd mop up the asphalt with his butt, that's how. That's what that stare-down in there was about. I was letting him know I could do it, and he—wisely—believed me."

"Darryl, I know you're fit, but Richard's *bigger* than you, and . . ."

"Angel," Darryl interrupted. He paused to make sure I was listening and finished quietly. "I'm a black belt."

"You're a what?"

"I'm a black belt in karate, dear. Sam decided years ago my best security option included being able to defend *myself*. I started studying karate." He shrugged. "And I liked it. Now—let's switch. I'll drive us home."

We switched places and Dare pulled out of the parking lot, turning left, following my directions. "Who *was* that jerk, anyway?" He said suddenly. *"Richard?* You *know* him?"

"He's not a jerk, honey. At least, up to now I didn't *think* he was. I went out with him twice about a year ago. Even after the second time, nothing clicked. I never went out with him again—but he's never stopped trying. I've never seen him act this way before." I paused. "And I've never seen him sloshed before, either."

"He watched us from the minute he walked in."

"He did? I didn't even see him."

"I did. I never should have left you alone. I knew *something* was up with him. Not that he was the only man looking at you." He grinned at me, "You're very 'lookable,' baby. But Richard was the only one who *kept* staring. Well, in a way, I feel sorry for the guy."

"You *do?* Why?"

"I know how *I'd* feel if I saw you out with another man."

"There's no danger of *that,* Mr. Bridges."

"Better not be. Angel, there's never *any* excuse for a man forcing his attentions on a woman. He was way out of line there, and I would have cheerfully cleaned his clock for that. But as for how he *felt,* look at it from his standpoint. He'd struck out with you, gotten nowhere after a whole year of trying, only to see you pop up on the arm of some Johnny-come-lately. No wonder the poor slob got tanked." He stopped talking abruptly. His face twisted into a frown.

"What's wrong, Dare? You don't think Richard and I . . ."

"No, I believe you, honey. It's just that this situation has forced me to see a problem I've been having in a new light."

"What problem?"

"Jasmine. I didn't realize until the night of the party how intensely she had a . . . a . . .thing for me. I was disgusted with her that night, and to tell the truth, she hasn't been acting much better since." He looked at me sheepishly, "She cornered me after rehearsal a few days ago and made an offer that left no room for . . . misinterpretation."

I turned around in the seat to fully face him, and looking him up and down asked, "And your reply was?"

"Oh, come on, baby," he said with an uncertain smile, "you know what my reply was. Give me *some* credit." He paused, "You *are* kidding, aren't you?"

I laughed, "Of course I'm kidding, honey. You trust me—I trust you."

"Thank God! It would be kinda difficult if you were the jealous type—given my current . . ." he looked extremely embarrassed "popularity with the ladies."

"No problem there. No other woman can 'take' a man from me unless he's more than willing to go. In which case, I didn't have much of a relationship to begin with. God knows I've got my faults, but jealousy isn't among them."

"What faults? I haven't seen any. And *your* man's not going anywhere."

"He better not. So Dare, what are you going to do about Jasmine?"

"I don't know. I had just about made up my mind to fire her, but now, I think I'll give it a little more time to see if she snaps out of it on her own. She needs the job, and it would hurt her career if I let her go, especially if it got out *why* I let her go. And she really is a great dancer . . ." he gave me that devilish grin, "almost as good as you."

"So you like my moves, huh?" I said, turning on the radio.

"You know it . . . *all* of them," he replied wickedly.

Darryl's song "Just When I'd Stopped Believing" was on. He tensed and reached to change the station, but I stopped him, placing my hand over his. "Honey, why don't you like listening to your music?"

"I love listening to my music, Angel—most of the time. I do when I'm alone, or performing, or in a crowd. But it makes me uncomfortable when I'm in a small group or with just one other person."

"Why?"

"It makes me feel so self-conscious, so *different.* How many people do *you* know who turn on the radio and hear their own voice coming back at them?"

"*I* don't know any others, but *you* do. It's got to happen to you recording artists types all the time. And why does it only bother you if you're not in a crowd?"

"Performing is one of the things I enjoy most in this world, and when I'm performing . . . well, I'm *supposed* to be the center of attention, you know? I mean, that's the whole point—my career would be in a whole mess of trouble if I wasn't. And being in a crowd is essentially the same thing. But when I'm one-on-one with somebody, I just feel like I'm on display . . . like I'm an exhibit, or something."

I touched his shoulder, "Do you feel that way with me?" I asked softly.

He looked at me in surprise, "No, sugar. You know I don't feel like that with you."

"Then let's just enjoy the music." I put my hand over his as he gripped the steering wheel, as I had in California. I could feel him relax. By the song's end, we'd reached my apartment complex.

He pulled the car into my parking stall and turned to me with a smile. "You're a new lease on life for me, you know that?"

"The feeling's mutual . . . 'big man.' "

He laughed and opened his door. "You're gonna pay for that."

"I hope so," I replied with a leer. This time, I knew him well enough to know *he* knew enough to open my door, unlike many other "gentlemen" I'd dated.

We went up to my apartment, and as I closed the door, I remembered we hadn't had dinner. "Darryl, aren't you hungry? We haven't had anything to eat since lunch."

"Yeah, I could do with a bite. Any of that good goop left from yesterday?"

"Sure, there's plenty," I said going into the kitchen, after kicking off those killer heels. "And, fortunately, I put it into the fridge before we got . . . uh, otherwise occupied. But I'm not about to feed you leftovers, hon."

"Why not? That stuff was great. And anyway, Angel . . ." he took my hand and kissed it, "your leftovers are better than anyone else's main course."

He took off his jacket and hung it on one of the dining room chairs, while I put the casserole in the microwave to reheat. Wandering around the living room, he said, "Angela, your place is just fabulous. It looks like where you'd live—it reflects your personality." He pointed to a small gold plaque on the wall. "Another Saturday shopping treasure?" he asked. I nodded. He walked over to it and read it silently. Then he bowed his head slightly, looked up again, and read it out loud:

WOMAN

Made by God from the rib of Man
Not created from his head to be superior
Nor from his feet to be stepped upon

She was made from his side
To be equal to him

From beneath his arm
To be protected by him

Near his heart
To be loved by him

I walked over while he was reading and stood next to him, reading along silently.

"And that's just how you feel about it, isn't it?" he asked, still facing the plaque. "Well, you're by my side . . ." he looked at me with a grin, "and I think we both know you're my equal—and *then* some."

He put an arm around my shoulders, "You're beneath my arm, and I *did* have to protect you tonight. He turned me to face him and put his arms around my waist. "This way, you're even nearer to my heart." His lips lightly brushed mine and his arms tightened around me as he pulled me closer, looking solemnly into my eyes.

"Angela, you're everything I've ever wanted. More than I ever even dreamed of . . ." He glanced away for a second, licking his lips, then looked up into my eyes again, even more intensely. "Angela . . . I . . ."

I stopped him. "Darryl . . . don't."

"Why not?" He looked at me anxiously, "I'm not in this thing by myself, am I?"

I walked out of his embrace and over to the balcony doors. "Darryl, you've got to know how I feel about you," I whispered, looking out into the night. "But we've only been together twice. We only first spent time with each other two weeks ago."

He came up behind me and put both his hands on my shoulders. "That doesn't matter. The only thing that does matter is how we feel. Everything else is just a detail." He hesitated a second. "I don't think that's what's really troubling you, anyway. He turned me to face him, "I'm not *him,* Angela."

I flinched and looked away. "Who, Darryl? I . . . I don't know what you're talking about."

"Yes, you do. Robert . . . Bobby . . . your husband—you know who I'm talking about. We've talked about everything under the sun, but you've never talked in any detail about *him.*

"I bet Richard *isn't* a bad guy, when he's not plastered and caught up in a jealous rage. He couldn't be, or you'd have never gone out with him once, let alone twice. And what really happened with the man you were seeing in Detroit? Did he break it off, or did *you?* What are you afraid of, Angela?"

I tried to walk away, but he grabbed my arms and held me there. "It must have hurt you a lot, baby," he added softly. Taking my hand, he led me over to the sofa. "Tell me now, Angel."

Slowly, haltingly, I told him about my marriage to Bobby . . . and how it ended. The entire time I was talking he didn't speak, he just nodded from time to time, listening intently and holding my hand, squeezing my fingers during the most agonizing parts. As I finished, the tears I had been fighting to hold back overcame me. I sobbed helplessly as I remembered all that hurt, and pain, and fear, and loss, and turmoil. Darryl didn't say anything, and he didn't try to stop my tears. He just held me like a baby and rocked me, softly crooning a soothing melody.

When I finally stopped crying, I looked up. My tears and makeup had smeared his shirt. "Oh, Darryl, I smudged your shirt!" I sniffed.

He wiped the last of the tears away and tipped my face to look into his eyes. He gave me a fragile smile. "That's what my shoulder is for, baby. For you to cry on—and lean on—whenever you need to." We sat silently for a moment, then he said, "That explains a lot. Now I understand." He paused. "I *really* understand, Angela." He looked down at his hands. "I lost someone I once loved, too," he whispered.

"You *did?* Oh, Darryl, I . . . I never knew."

"Nobody does. Not really. A few people knew *something* was going on, but even they didn't know the degree of our involvement." He looked into the distance. "It was Tonya Carol."

Tonya Carol was the beautiful, talented, wild spirit that captured the imagination of movie audiences all around the world five or six years before. Until she was found dead in her dressing room minutes before she was due on the set; dead of a cocaine overdose. I didn't know what to say. He had already been holding one of my hands. I joined our other hands, as well.

"Tonya was wonderful; so sweet, smart, loving—but she was so insecure about her talent, so afraid of failure. I found out afterward that at first she turned to drugs only once in a while, for the false courage it gave her. But it quickly reached the point where she couldn't even step in front of the camera unless she was high.

"Her agent supplied her with the stuff." His face turned dark. "I almost *killed* him when I found out. But by then it was too late. She'd hid it from me until she was past rescue. Even then, I never gave up hope until it was, eternally . . . too late."

I moved closer and squeezed his hand tightly. "I walked around in a daze for months," he continued, "not knowing day from night—or caring. I'd stay in my house for weeks on end." I remembered that period. Some of the press had said Darryl was afraid he couldn't compete with newer artists.

"Then, when I finally snapped out of *that,* I threw myself into my music, working 'round the clock, until I almost collapsed." I remembered that, too. Other segments of the media had said Darryl was an egomaniac, who couldn't stand to share the limelight with anyone else.

We sat there in silence a long time, just holding each other. Finally, the timer went off, bringing us back to the present. I went to the microwave while Darryl got out plates and silverware, and we sat down to eat. He bowed his head. "Dear Lord, Thou knowst how much we can bear. We thank Thee for standing by us, for sustaining us in our hours of darkness, and for bringing us back into the light. Amen."

"Amen," I said softly.

"Honey?"

"Yes, Dare?"

"I never told anyone before." He took my hand, "I'm glad I told you."

I leaned forward, kissed his hand, and rested my cheek on it. "So am I."

That night, there was a new closeness between us. Glorious as our lovemaking had been, right from the start, now there was a new tenderness; a deeper intimacy. Afterward, I lay with my head on Darryl's shoulder, one arm across his chest. We hadn't spoken for a long, long time, and I thought he had fallen asleep. He must have thought *I* had, because just as I *did* start to doze off, he leaned forward and gently kissed my forehead. "Sleep peacefully, my love," he whispered. "The past can't hurt us anymore. Yesterday is behind us, today was sweet, and we'll spend ten thousand tomorrows together."

He started to hum softly. I could feel the vibration deep inside him. It was the same melody he'd crooned to me earlier. I didn't know what it was. I'd never heard it before. But it was entrancing, enveloping. Lulled by this impromptu concert for one, I drifted off to sleep.

Nine

Keep The Faith

I opened my eyes to see Darryl's, looking at me intently. "Morning," I whispered. "Have you been awake long?"

"Just long enough to see an Angel greet the morning," he smiled. "It's a glorious sight . . . one that bears frequent viewing," he added, taking me into his arms. "Honey, you know what I'd like to do today? I'd like us to go to church."

"To church?" I asked in surprise.

"Yes, I haven't been to church in more years than I can remember. I was raised with a religious background and many parts of it I miss. Do you mind if we do that this morning?"

"No," I said softly. "I'd like that very much."

"When do services start?"

"Well, they have two morning worship services. One at eight o'clock and one at 10:45, with Sunday School in between."

He looked over at the clock, "It's seven-thirty now—too late for the early one. Let's go out to breakfast and make the 10:45 service, okay?"

"Okay, darling."

He pulled me closer, "I love it when you call me 'darling,' darling."

After a short interlude, we dressed; Darryl in his nerdy accountant's outfit, complete with the glasses and the addition of a phony—but very realistic—mustache. We had breakfast at

Big Boy's and deliberately delayed getting to the church, to arrive shortly *after* service had started; slipping into one of the back pews.

Several people nodded and waved to me, especially my fellow choir members. My choir sang on first and third Sundays. Since this was a second Sunday, many of them were in pews nearby. Darryl drew many a curious glance. Nobody had ever seen me attend church with anyone but Tiff before, and they all knew I wasn't married. They had to be wondering who the handsome man in the ill-fitting suit was.

The children's choir was singing today, and their young voices were celestial. Darryl and I clapped along with everybody else as they sang "Swing Down Chariot-Stop and Let Me Ride." Darryl whispered, "They're wonderful—I'd love to work them into a project I'm thinking about." Later in the service, DeJuan Morris, who's about ten, sang the solo on "Lead Me, Guide Me." As his innocent soprano rang out, Darryl looked very pensive. *"That* brings back memories," he said under his breath, more to himself than me.

Alter call was next, when the assistant Pastor prayed aloud, and all who wished could approach the altar and pray silently. As always, many people did. I would have liked to, but I knew Darryl shouldn't, and I didn't want to leave his side. So we just stood where we were and bowed our heads, along with everyone else who hadn't gone up. As I stood there with my eyes closed, Darryl's hand gently took mine. He was at the very top of my prayer list, and I had the feeling I was prominently placed on his, as well.

Pastor Matthews was in fine form, delivering a sermon on faith: "When I was a seminary student, about a hundred years ago . . ." This brought a titter of laughter from the congregation. "A young man there was struggling with the concept of faith. This fellow was torn between becoming a minister or a mechanic; you see, he loved to tinker with things—to take them apart to see what made them tick. It tormented him that faith required belief in so many things he couldn't touch, feel, see, or measure in some tangible way. He began to doubt his calling, and to seriously consider leaving the seminary." He stopped for a sip of water.

"He talked it over with one of his instructors, who advised him to let God guide him to the right path. The student even cut out the letters 'LET GOD' from construction paper, and pinned them up on a bulletin board in his room.

"Finally, after hours of trying to reconcile his feelings, he left his room one night to go for a walk, slamming the door in frustration. While out, he decided the ministry was not for him, and determined to leave the seminary the next day.

"When he returned to his room, the first thing he saw when he opened his door was his bulletin board. He'd slammed the door so hard when he left that he'd jarred one of the letters of his reminder loose, and it had fallen. The bulletin board now read, 'LET GO.' "

Cries of "Amen!" and "Hallelujah!" echoed through the church.

"He realized then," the Pastor continued, "that he had been holding back, not giving his all, reserving a part of himself that should have been dedicated to the future the Lord intended for him. He started to let his heart, not his head, take control—and stayed with the ministry." He took another sip of water. "You know," he added, "I never *did* find that 'D.' "

After benediction, I tried to sneak us by the Pastor. He was, as was his custom, at the main entrance, greeting the congregation as they left. But as I attempted to maneuver through the crowd to a side exit, he called out to me, "Sister Delaney. So good to see you out this morning."

Caught, Dare and I turned to face him, "Good morning, Pastor Matthews," I said.

"I looked for you last Sunday, when your choir sang; I wanted to hear my song." I did a solo on "His Eye is on the Sparrow"; the Pastor's favorite song. "But you'll sing it for me next week, won't you?" he was continuing. He looked over at Darryl expectantly.

"Pastor Matthews, may I present my friend, Darryl . . . uh, Douglass?" I silently added the "Bridges"—so I didn't like lying to my Pastor . . . sue me.

Pastor Matthews extended his hand, "A pleasure, Mr. Douglass. Welcome."

"Thank you, Reverend," Darryl replied, shaking his hand. "I truly enjoyed your sermon."

"Thank *you,* son. You know, one of the privileges of being old *and* a pastor is getting away with nosing into other people's business." He looked at me. "Sister Delaney here is a fine young woman, and I promised her former pastor I'd look out for her, especially since she and her daughter have no family here in the city." He looked back to Darryl. "Are you two *just* friends—or are you serious about her?"

Embarrassed, I started to intervene when, without missing a beat, Darryl looked the pastor in the eye and answered, "I'm *very* serious about her, sir."

"I see," the Pastor replied. "Well, in that case, I'm sure I'll see you again. I don't know what miracle brought you two together, but God bless you both." He leaned closer to Darryl, "I've always loved your family's music—and yours, too, son."

Darryl looked like I felt—stunned.

"Don't worry," Pastor Matthews winked at us. "I won't tell a soul," and he turned to greet another parishioner, while Darryl and I stumbled for the door.

Back in the car, we just sat and looked at each other. "How in the world did he know?" Dare finally said, in wonderment. I just shook my head.

By the time we returned to my apartment and (after a short pause for our favorite cause) changed clothes, it was time to pick Tiffani up at the train station. She babbled on about the wedding festivities all the way home. I gave Dare a look, and he nodded silently, acknowledging he *now* understood why one of my nicknames for Tiff is "Motor-Mouth."

Dare called the guys. I asked him to invite them for dinner.

After all, *they* were my guests, too, and I felt I had been neglecting them.

Darryl, Tiffani, and I worked together, bumping into each other in my small kitchen, fixing a huge spaghetti dinner. Dare made the spaghetti, after sending Tiff to the store in the process to get some spices I didn't have. I sampled the sauce as it was cooking. It was a work of art. "Fabulous," I whispered. "And what other hidden talents do *you* have that *I* don't know about?" I quizzed him, harkening back to his grilling me about my singing.

"That's for me to know . . . and you to find out," he whispered back, giving me a squeeze in a rather indiscreet spot while Tiff wasn't looking.

By the time Sam and Alex arrived, all was ready, and we sat down to eat. My dining room table was small and normally seated only four comfortably, but Dare and I didn't mind being squeezed close together on one side of the table.

After dinner, Alex spotted the small trophy in the living room. "What's *this?*" he said, picking it up and reading it; " 'Bid whist second place champion, 1993?' "

"You're looking at her."

"Well, I ain't got no *trophy,*" he said slowly, putting it down, "but in *some* circles I'm known as a pretty mean whist player myself."

I couldn't let *that* challenge go unanswered, so we got out the cards and started play. Everybody wanted to play. I had taught Tiff, and as it turned out, Sam had taught Darryl. Cards weren't allowed in Dare's house when he was a kid. Since there were five of us, we worked out a system. Whenever a game was lost, each of the losing team would draw a card. The low-card holder would then get up and let the person waiting take his/her seat for the next game.

This rotational play went on for about an hour, until chance paired Sam and I. Try though they might, Darryl, Tiff, and Alex, in all three possible combinations, couldn't unseat us. After this became excruciatingly obvious, Darryl declared,

"Okay, now what's going on? Are you two passing signals, or what?"

"I didn't win that trophy for nothin'," I answered Dare, but looking pointedly at Alex.

"Damn straight," Sam joined in. "She's the best whist partner I've had . . ." he leaned back in his chair and grinned at Alex, "since I won the St. Louis *first-place* spot in '81."

That ended the game. Shortly afterward Sam and a much subdued Alex left to take Bev and Charlie to a movie. Tiff spent most of the evening in her room, on the phone, telling her Lansing friends about the wedding. Darryl and I sat out on the balcony, sipping ice tea and talking until it was time to go to bed.

Once again, we found ourselves kissing good-night outside Tiff's bedroom door. "I don't want the day to end," he said looking deep into my eyes. "Angela . . . I . . ."

I stopped him with a kiss. God knows I *wanted* to hear it, but I didn't want him to speak prematurely. I was sure of how I felt, but I wanted *him* to be sure. I couldn't bear it if he found out later he was mistaken.

He pulled back and smiled. "Lady, you change the subject with the most pleasurable diversions I've ever known. Okay, you win, I'll wait . . ." tenderness shined in his eyes, "but not for long."

The next day went quickly. The three of us had breakfast before Tiff went off to work, and Darryl and I spent the rest of the day lounging around the house; listening to old records, looking at soap operas (which he followed, often being home when they were on), all in each other's arms.

Five o'clock rolled around too soon, and Sam and Alex came by for Darryl. They came up to tell me and Tiff, who was by then home from work good-bye, and went down to the car to wait for him. Then Tiffani told Dare good-bye and—thoughtfully—went into her bedroom.

Darryl turned to face me, "Honey, let's say good-bye here. I don't want you to come down to the car. Until I see you again,

I want to remember you standing here in this room where we shared so much."

"Okay, Dare," I said softly.

"God, I wish we could make plans right now for when we'll see each other again, but with the way things are going—who knows?" he sighed in disgust.

He was leaving in two days for a video shoot in Spain. The shooting schedule was fouled up by a strike and the resultant red-tape. Now he wasn't sure *how* long it would take to get the video "in the can." I couldn't come with him, or even visit him there, because I didn't have a passport. Dare said he could possibly pull a few strings and expedite getting me one, but neither of us thought it was a good idea to draw that much attention to our connection.

"Honey, we've already found out distance can't diminish the way we feel. I don't think time can make much of a dent in it, either," I said, touching his cheek. "What do you think?"

He took me in his arms. "I think I'm the luckiest man on earth," he said softly, and kissed me. Without another word, he picked up his bag, turned, and walked out the door.

I stood there in the middle of the room, willing myself not to cry, when suddenly the door burst open and Darryl rushed back in. His bag dropped to the floor with a bang, and with quick, purposeful strides he came to where I was still standing. Before I could utter the "Wha . . ." forming on my tongue, he swept me into his arms and held me close.

"I love you, Angela, and there's no way I'm leaving here without telling you." He pulled me even closer and kissed me. I felt caught up in the eye of a hurricane. When we finally broke apart, he said, "I couldn't leave, especially not knowing how long it'll be before I see you again, without telling you how much I love you. I'd bust if I didn't tell you now . . ." He looked at me with his soul in his eyes. "And find out if . . ."

"I . . . Yes, I do . . . I love you, too, Darryl," I replied unsteadily.

"Are you sure?"

I realized he was holding his breath, waiting for my reply as though his life depended upon it, and it suddenly hit me we had the same fear; being in love, and not being loved in return. That *I* could hurt *him* never occurred to me before. Once it did, I couldn't get the words out fast enough. "Yes, Darryl, I'm sure. I love you with all my heart."

He released his breath with a sigh. "Good," he said tenderly, cupping my face in his hands, "because there was also no way I was leaving until I heard you say so." He kissed me one last time, again grabbed has bag, and left, blowing me a kiss just before the door closed behind him.

The days stretched into weeks. Snafus dragged the video shoot on and on. As always, Darryl called me every day, but we yearned to be together, especially now. At one point he even decided to scrap the entire project, and just come home, but I wouldn't let him. He already had over a million dollars invested in the video. To walk away he'd have to write the whole thing off as a loss.

"Being with you means a whole hell of a lot more to me than a million dollars, baby," he rebutted.

"I know, hon. So the million-dollar lady will wait patiently until her million-dollar man comes home."

Even then, I think he still would have dumped the project if it hadn't been for Alex. Alex was directing this video. The concept had been his idea, and he had such a clear image of how it should be filmed, Darryl had suggested, "Well, why don't you *direct* it, man?" At first Alex didn't realize Dare meant it. Alex had never directed a film before, although he'd assisted in the production of many. But Dare really thought he was the man for the job. Once Alex realized that, he was ecstatic. And Darryl knew how important the video was for *Alex's* career.

I made light of the situation for Dare's sake, but it wasn't easy. I missed him—so deeply at times it was almost a physical ache. And I knew the words we'd spoken when we'd last seen each other were just the first act of a play still being written.

About two weeks after Dare left for Europe, I was crossing the parking lot to my car on my way to work, when a man in a late model car got out as I approached. "Mrs. Delaney? Mrs. Angela Delaney?"

I looked at him quizzically, "Yes? I'm Angela Delaney. Do I know you?" He looked like a younger, slimmer Ned Beatty.

He chuckled, "No . . . no, ma'am, you don't. My name is Chet Mitchell." He flashed a leather folder, holding some sort of I.D. at me. "I'm with American Scene newspaper—Los Angeles bureau."

At the words "Los Angeles" I froze. Gathering my composure, I replied, "You're a long way from home. What can I do for you, Mr. Mitchell?"

"I'd like to talk to you about your relationship with Darryl Bridges."

The shock on my face had to be more genuine than my feeble attempt to laugh, "Darryl Bridges? The only Darryl Bridges *I've* ever heard of is *the* Darryl Bridges, the entertainer."

"That's the guy I mean," he said, leaning against his car.

"My relationship with *him?* What is this . . . some sort of fan survey? Did you get my name from his fan club roster? Look, I'm a major Darryl Bridges fan, but I'm almost late for work. I'm not going to risk making my boss mad, not even to talk about Dare." I turned, and started for my car again, hoping I'd gotten away clean.

"His fans almost always call him 'Darryl,' " Mitchell said softly. I stopped short. "The press and his fans almost invariably refer to him as 'Darryl,' " he continued, slowly walking up behind me. "Usually, only people who know him . . . who *talk* to him . . ." he was standing directly behind me now, "call him 'Dare,' " he finished, even softer.

I turned around slowly and this time really looked at him, "What did you say your name was?"

"Chet Mitchell."

"May I see your credentials again, please?" He handed the leather folder to me. I looked his press I.D. over carefully before handing it back. "Why are you telling me all this, Mr. Mitchell?"

"Because I believe you have a close, even intimate, relationship with Darryl Bridges."

My eyes narrowed, "What are you implying?"

"Nothing improper, Mrs. Delaney, I assure you. I'm simply saying I think you're Darryl Bridges's . . . significant other."

"I don't know why I should waste my time a second longer listening to you make these crazy . . ."

He'd taken something from his pocket while I was talking, and wordlessly handed it to me. My voice trailed away. It was a grainy snapshot of Darryl and me leaving the party in L.A. Darryl had me by the hand, leading me to the limo.

I looked up at Mitchell. Before I could speak, he added, "I've also got records—unofficial of course—of telephone calls made from Darryl Bridges's limousine. In the past few months there have been over fifty calls to your telephone number."

I looked him in the eye. "What do you want from me?" I asked bluntly.

"Just to talk to you, Mrs. Delaney."

I paused, then said, "Would you like to come in?"

"Yes, I would. Thank you."

He followed me into my apartment, I offered him a seat and coffee. While the coffee was brewing, I called my office to tell them I'd be late. After serving the coffee, I sat down, and said, "Okay, Mr. Mitchell, I'm listening."

"Please call me Chet. May I call you Angela?"

"Sure, why not?" At that moment, what he called me was the last thing on my mind. "Okay, Chet, shoot."

"For years there's been speculation about Darryl Bridges's love life—or lack of one. That he has an ongoing relationship with *any* woman would be news. But a relationship with a woman like *you*—a career woman with a grown daughter . . ." This was worse than I thought. He'd obviously done a fair amount of checking up on me already. "Why, that would be a bombshell!"

"So why not ask Darryl? He's the one who's experienced in dealing with the media . . . I'm not. Or is that the very reason *I* got picked?"

"To be honest with you, that *is* part of the reason. The other part is that Darryl Bridges has the most air-tight security of any celebrity I know. It's virtually impossible to get to him without going through channels. I didn't want to approach him that way and tip my hand."

He put his coffee cup down and leaned forward. "Angela, I have more than enough information already to run a story about you and Darryl. I'd like to do it with your input. Not that I'd let you dictate what I write, but I want it to be accurate and fair, and I'm certainly willing to take anything you say into consideration."

I still hesitated. When I didn't speak, he added, "Angela, I'm going to run this story, whether you talk to me or not."

"Chet," I said finally, "let me ask *you* something. What's your opinion of Darryl Bridges?"

"I'm a reporter—a good one. I don't report my opinions. I report facts."

"I understand that, but surely you've formed a personal appraisal of him."

"Well, personally, I'm a big admirer of Darryl's. Have been since the beginning. I guess that's why covering him has become sort of a specialty of mine. I've covered his career from the start. I think he's a unique talent, and one hell of a human being."

"He is—both."

He leaned forward again, "So you admit you know him?"

I smiled weakly. "In light of all that dynamite you have, a denial would be pretty pointless, wouldn't it? Yes, I know him. He's sat on that very sofa, right where you're sitting now."

Chet looked very excited, "He has? He's been *here?*"

"Yes, he has. Look, you've been frank with me, let me put my cards on the table. Can we go—what do you media types call it—off the record?"

"I can't make any promises."

"Fair enough. Chet, Darryl and I care for each other very much. Our relationship is precious to us, and we've tried our best to keep it as it should be—private. If you've followed his life as you say, you know despite his phenomenal professional success, or maybe even *because* of it, privately Darryl's spent most of his adult life as a lonely, and often unhappy person."

For the first time, Chet looked uncomfortable. "Yes, I know that."

"He's not lonely or unhappy anymore because of his relationship with me. I don't know how much you know of my background . . ." He started to fidget again, "but I've had many lonely years, too. *I'm* not lonely anymore because of *him.*

"Our relationship is deep and strong, but it's still new. It's still developing. All we want is a chance to let it develop on its own, without the whole world picking it—and us—apart at every turn.

"You see where and how I live, Chet. I live here alone with a teenage daughter. You know, probably better than I, how vulnerable we would be to the media, and to all sorts of curiosity seekers and weirdos, if you print that story."

"Let me get this straight: are you asking me not to print the story, *at all?*"

"Yes. That's precisely what I'm asking. In return I promise you this: if the day comes when Darryl and I decide to go public with our relationship, you'll be the first to know, and we'll give you full details ahead of anyone else."

I could see the indecision on his face. "You're asking a hell of a lot."

"I know I am. But three lives hang in the balance here. I've pled the case for my daughter and myself. Now I'll plead Darryl's. Chet, after all that he's given with his music, and donations of his time and money, and of . . . of himself to help other people in so many ways, I think Darryl deserves at least this much of a break."

"Look, it's not that I don't appreciate your predicament, or that I'm unsympathetic to it. Hell, I *like* the guy. But Darryl is one of the most famous people in the world." Chet leaned forward again with his hands open. "People are interested in everything about him, even down to the clothes he wears, what he eats."

"No one has as crucial an interest, or investment, in our relationship as *we* do, Chet."

"Surely you didn't think a development in his life of this magnitude would go undetected, unreported."

"We'd hoped it would—at least for a while."

"That's not realistic. Darryl's a public figure, Angela."

"Darryl's a public *person,* Chet—emphasis on 'person.' He's a celebrity, but he still has needs and feelings—and so do I. I guess being allowed the same degree of privacy most other people take for granted *was* too much for *us* to hope for." I lifted my chin and looked him dead in the eye. "So go ahead and run your story, if you must. I love Darryl and he loves me. We'll weather this."

I started to rise. "I don't have anything more to say. If you'll excuse me, I have to call Darryl. He's in Spain, as you probably know. He's going to want to get back here fast—now."

He reached out and gasped my arm. "Hold on a minute," he said quickly. I sat back down and we just studied each other for a moment.

"I won't print the story, at least not now," he said finally. He looked at me and grinned. "Because I can see right now I'll just be *postponing* it. But I have three conditions. One, you *do* give me the scoop if and when you go public. Two, you agree if this leaks out through some other source, I'll *then* run the story—*including* this conversation—as an exclusive. Three, you don't tell Darryl about my visit. That guy has too much clout. I don't need a man that powerful angry with me, especially when I don't even have publishing the story he's angry about in compensation. Agreed?"

"You've got a deal." We shook on it, and as I walked him

to the door, I asked, "Chet, how did you get on to me, anyway?"

He chuckled, "Well, a good reporter never reveals his sources, but that's no problem in this instance. I don't *know* my source. A package arrived in the mail with the picture and the limo phone records. It also had your name, address, and telephone number. I have no idea where it came from, other than the envelope being postmarked in L.A."

I opened the door for him and offered my hand, "Good-bye, Chet. Have a safe trip home . . . and thank you."

"You're welcome," he said, as we shook hands. He held on a second. "You know, despite his problems, I've always thought Darryl Bridges was a lucky guy," he smiled, "now I *know* he is. Good-bye."

I didn't tell Darryl . . . at least, not then. The decision didn't come easily. I didn't want any secrets between us. And it wasn't lost on me this complication carried a very serious implication—somebody in Darryl's camp was leaking information. The picture could have been taken by anyone, perhaps even a fan. But the telephone records and my address . . . those almost certainly *had* to have come from someone on the inside.

But in the end, I decided I should wait to tell Darryl. He had more than enough on his mind with the video shoot fiasco. I was a pretty good judge of character (look at the man I picked to fall in love with!), and I believed Chet would keep our bargain. I watched the papers and listened to the news very anxiously for the next few days. Nothing. Not a peep about Darryl and me. I silently blessed Chet Mitchell.

Three weeks after Darryl left for Spain, the video was *finally* finished and Darryl was coming home that Friday. He was flying directly to New York City for an award ceremony. When he called to tell me, he asked if Tiff and I would like to come.

"My plan is to see you the first day I set foot back into the good old US of A," he said. "If you don't want to come to New York, I'm coming to Lansing. Don't matter to me, baby, as long as I'm with you. They can *keep* that award before I'd let it keep me away from you another day. But I thought you ladies might like a weekend in the Big Apple."

"Like? Wiz, got any wild horses? That's what it would take—and more—to keep us away!"

Ten

Whenever We're Apart

"Mama! This is too much!" Tiffani was running around the hotel suite, looking into rooms, touching the furniture. She finally stopped in the middle of the living room and started spinning, arms held out wide. The precedent setting restraint Tiff had shown when meeting Darryl had flown, and her usual pyrotechnics once again held sway.

"Honey, my goodness! If you don't quiet down we're gonna get thrown outta here!" I teased.

"Fat chance," she retorted, "considering who our host is." She looked closely at me. "How much is Darryl shelling out for this joint, anyway?"

"I have no idea, hon. His staff made all the arrangements." I stopped and looked around myself. "A pretty penny, though, I would imagine."

This trip had begun much like my trip to L.A. The competent Anita Giles had called with travel details and a limo had arrived, as before, to take us to the airport. When we arrived at Kennedy, a limo had been waiting to take us to the hotel; a hired car and driver this time, since Alex and Sam were still en route from Spain, with Dare. Darryl's flight wasn't scheduled to arrive until six o'clock that evening. This was cutting it awfully close; the award ceremony started at eight, but Dare said it was the best that could be arranged.

"Ma! Come here!" Tiff called from her bedroom.

When I went into the room, Tiff was pointing to a large bouquet of red roses. She handed me a small envelope. "This was with them. I didn't read it . . . yet," she added with a grin. The envelope was addressed "Mrs. Delaney." The card inside read simply, "I can't wait! DDB." This man of mine was incredible. Although he was still in Spain (or en route from), the card was in his handwriting.

I took the flowers into the room where my luggage had been deposited and ran into another surprise. "Oh, Miss Delaney," I called to Tiff, "Could *you* step in *here* a moment, please?"

"What's up, Mama?" she said, appearing in the doorway. I pointed to a large bouquet of *white* roses, and wordlessly handed *her* an envelope. Her eyes lit up, "Oh, Mama!" She opened the envelope, laughed as she read the card, and then handed it to me. "For the world's prettiest Skee-Ball player. I'm ready for that rematch! See you soon. Love, DDB."

Tiff picked up the vase. "Mama, no wonder you feel the way you do about Darryl. He's awesome." She looked wistfully at the roses. "He makes me realize how much we've missed . . ." She brightened again, and started singing, "It's so nice to have a man around the house . . ."

"Well, I'm going to take these into *my* room, where they belong!" and she sashayed off with the flowers.

The doorbell rang. *This* time I recognized what it was right away, and went to the door. "Who is it?" I asked, not looking through the peephole.

"Room service," a muffled voice replied.

But it would have taken far more than a hand over the mouth to disguise the voice I'd been hearing in my dreams. I broke a nail turning the dead bolt and flung the door open wide. There was a blur of motion, and I was in his arms. We kissed each other like . . . well, like two people in love who haven't seen each other in weeks. After the first surge of reunion, we stood quietly, still clinging to each other, my head on his shoulder.

"I missed you," he whispered in my ear.

"Oh, Darryl . . ." was all I could say.

"'I missed you, too' would be the standard and preferable response, my love," he needled.

I put my arms around his neck, "Okay, then. Well, how about this . . ." I looked deeply into his eyes. "I love you, and I've dreamed of being with you every second we've been apart." I kissed him, and his enthusiastic reciprocation showed me *that* reply was fully to his liking.

"Mama, what was that . . . Whoops!" Tiff had come out of her bedroom, but seeing Darryl and I in a clinch, had begun to turn her to head back into it—quickly.

"Wait a minute! I thought we were friends! What kind of way is that to greet a friend who's been imprisoned in a foreign land lo these many weeks?" Dare walked over to Tiff, put an arm around her shoulders, and kissed her cheek. "Did you forget what I looked like, or what?" he demanded indignantly.

"Oh, Darryl, stop teasing me," Tiff said shyly, but she stood on tip-toe to kiss his cheek in return. "Welcome back, and thanks for my flowers. They're gorgeous."

"You're welcome. Now . . . you two fine broads come on over here." He took each of us by the hand, leading us to the sofas, "and tell me what you've been up to while I've been out of your collective hair."

"Honey, when did you get here?" I asked. "It's only . . ." I looked at my watch, "three-thirty. I thought your flight didn't arrive until six."

"I decided I couldn't wait that long to see you."

"But I thought there wasn't an earlier plane."

"There wasn't. So I bought one."

"An *airplane?*"

"Well, I'd been thinking about getting another one, anyway. And I wasn't going to let a little thing like charter scheduling keep me away a minute longer. I'd timed it so I could meet you and Tiff at the airport, but we ran into a head wind, and you guys had left for the hotel by the time we landed."

We were all starving, so we went into the kitchen, and talked while preparing and devouring a leisurely late lunch. At about five Dare said, "Well, I'd better get outta here, so you all can get ready for the evening's festivities. We're in the suite next door." Tiff's head was turned, and Dare winked at me as he said this. I knew why—I'd noticed the door in my bedroom.

"I trust you ladies found evening gowns to your liking?" he continued. The affair was formal, and I'd finally used the credit card for dresses for the occasion. I had to. Darryl had threatened to send Marcel to Lansing with a truckload of formals if I didn't, and I wasn't entirely sure Dare had been kidding.

"Yes, Mr. Blackwell," I answered him. "We've both got new ensembles . . . from head to foot."

He turned to Tiffani, "What color is yours, hon?"

"It's emerald green, Dare—that's my favorite color—trimmed in white. Why?"

"So I can make sure your corsage matches it, is why," he decreed.

"And aren't you going to ask about *my* dress? Don't I get a corsage, too?" I asked, with one hand on my hip.

"You sure do, Angel. But I don't need to ask about *your* dress. There's only one flower in only one color for my American Beauty."

I walked with him to the door. He took me in his arms. "Have I told you today that I love you, lady?" he asked.

"No . . . no, I don't believe you have," I said, hugging him and looking up with a smile.

He stopped smiling and tenderly cupped my face, looking at me with his heart in his eyes. "I love you."

"I love you, too. Welcome back . . . 'big man,' " I whispered softly.

He kissed me. "We'll be by for you guys at seven sharp," he said as he left.

The next couple of hours were a flurry of activity as Tiff and I got all dolled up for the evening. We were running around doing each other's nails and hair like two girls getting ready for a prom. Just as we were completing the final touches, we heard voices outside, and went to a window. There was a sizable crowd in front of the hotel, many of them carrying signs. Even from the fifteenth floor, we could see some of the signs just said "Darryl!" in huge letters.

"Wow! Mom, Dare's so down-to-earth it's easy to forget who he *is*. I hadn't thought about him being mobbed by fans, but it sure looks like that's a possibility. What are we going to do?"

"Don't worry, baby. Darryl's used to this. He *lives* with it. He and his bodyguards will have things under control."

"Bodyguards? I never thought of Darryl as having bodyguards!"

"Honey, what do you think Sam is? I mean, I know after all the years they've been together, their relationship is much more than employer/employee. Sam treats Darryl like a younger brother. But Sam is Darryl's chief of security. In other words, his chief bodyguard."

"Man!" Tiff had to sit down on the bed to absorb all of this. "I just never thought about it before. Has anybody ever tried to hurt Dare?"

"Yes, dear." I sat down next to her. "He receives death threats on a regular basis. He told me last year his people caught a man with a gun trying to sneak backstage at one of his concerts. The guy said God told him Darryl was evil and had to be destroyed. The man was later committed to a mental institution." I shivered, as I had when Darryl told me this. Every time I thought about it, one name kept repeating in my mind—John Lennon.

"It never got reported," I continued. "Dare's PR man tries to keep stuff like that out of the press, for fear of 'copycats' making the situation worse. Dare's also gotten bruised up several times being rushed by fans; people who didn't mean to hurt him—but did—in their enthusiasm to get near him."

"Poor Darryl! It's got to be rough living with that stuff all the time."

"It is, sugar, but it's like I've always told you, everything in life has it's price, and often the heaviest prices we pay are not in terms of money. What Darryl lives with is unfortunately one of the prices of fame. And Darryl's about as famous as they come."

"You know, with all he's got, I feel sort of sorry for him. What does he do when he just wants to be himself? To just go out to the mall, or the movies, or something?"

"He can't do those kinds of things, honey. At least not without a whole lot of special preparation—guards and disguises and such."

"Mama, aren't you worried about something happening to him? And for that matter . . ." she looked at me with something very akin to fear on her face, "aren't you worried about something happening to *you* when you're with him?"

"I worry about *him* all the time. But I don't worry about myself." I looked at her intently. "You can't live your life in fear, love. You have to be smart, and not take stupid chances. And you have to do everything in your power to better the odds in your favor. But in the long run, there are no guarantees.

"Now I don't want *you* to go worrying about this. Darryl's staff are professionals. The best. And I don't want you worrying about me, either. Darryl would die before he'd let anything happen to me. Anyway," I said, looking away from her, "I'll face anything I have to—to be with him."

"You love him—don't you, Mama?" she asked softly.

"Yes, baby. I do."

"And he loves you." This was a statement, not a question.

"Yes, he does."

"Has he told you so?"

"Yes, sweetheart."

"Wow . . ." she whispered. "What are you and Darryl going to do?"

"Well, Tiff, we're just playing it by ear, for now."

The doorbell rang. I was glad. The conversation had taken a turn I wasn't prepared to deal with . . . not just yet. "Well, speak of the distinguished devil. I think Prince Charming is here to take us to the ball. Are you all set, Cinderella?"

"Oh, God! I need to check my eyeliner! Tell him I'll be right out!" and she ran into her bathroom.

I went to the door, and there stood Darryl, resplendent in a black *leather* tuxedo and a white silk evening shirt. When Dare said "we'd" pick us up, I'd assumed he meant Alex, or Sam, or both. But with him, in a more conventional tuxedo, was a young man—a very young man—I didn't recognize.

"Good evening, Mrs. Delaney," Darryl said with a sweeping bow. "May I say you look incredibly radiant this evening?"

"Thank you, Mr. Bridges," I said with a curtsy. "And may I say you look indescribably handsome tonight? Won't you come in?"

He laughed, and they came inside. "Honey, I'd like you to meet a friend of mine, Michael Smith."

"Hi, Michael."

"Michael, this is my lady, Angela Delaney," Darryl said proudly, putting an arm around my waist.

"My pleasure, Mrs. Delaney," Michael said in a surprisingly resonant voice."

"It's just Angela, Michael."

Darryl turned to me, "I didn't think Tiffani would want to go to this gig with just us old fogies for company, so I asked Michael to come with us."

Tiffani came out of her bedroom, took one look at the three of us, and exclaimed, "Oh, my God . . . MC Smoke!"

"Mr. 'Smoke' is your escort for the evening, Tiffani—if that's okay." Dare proceeded to introduce them. Tiffani most definitely had no objection to "MC"—who preferred to be called Mickey—as her date. Michael Smith, a.k.a. Mickey Smith, a.k.a. MC smoke, turned out to be a soft-spoken, well-mannered young man. He presented Tiffani with a wrist corsage of white orchids.

"And these are for you," Darryl said to me, taking a spray of red roses out of the box he was carrying and slipping it on my wrist. "Shall we?" he asked, offering his arm.

Dare had an abundance of security people this trip. There

were some six or seven of them in the corridor. They escorted us to a freight elevator. We went to the sub-basement, and when the elevator doors opened, *two* limos, Alex, Cortez, and Sam were waiting. Alex gave first Tiffari, then me, a kiss on the cheek in greeting, as he helped us into the second car.

"Because it's so remote, the hotel doesn't use this exit any-more," Darryl told us, "except to help out guests in situations like this." Alex, Sam, and Cortez, got into the front seat of our limo. The others got into the lead car. We followed the other limo through a short corridor and up a ramp, and soon we were in the hotel parking structure. We exited into an alley, which in turn led between two buildings to the street behind the hotel. No crowds there. A few people glanced at the cars, but they couldn't see through the heavily tinted glass. And no one did more than that—just glance. As I quickly discovered, stretch limos in Manhattan on a Friday night are no rarity.

We were going to the Golden Note—the songwriter's—awards. This award program was not televised; one factor Darryl and I considered in deciding I would accompany him.

Another one of the many ways Darryl is extraordinary is that he writes almost all of his own material. Most hit songs are not written by the artists who perform them.

Songwriters, in the main, are a group pretty much unknown to the general public. Still, this was a very prestigious, and very closely watched award, especially for those in the music industry. They know, better than anyone, that a great musical performance starts with a great song. There was, therefore, press coverage. That was guaranteed at any event Darryl attended, anyway, whatever it was, by his sheer presence.

We didn't go in the main entrance, where most of the nominees were making the best of publicity opportunities, but instead slipped in a side door. We were quickly seated, third row back on the center aisle. We arrived just before the house lights dimmed, but in those few minutes, I saw heads turn as people realized Darryl was there. Several people waved at him, and a few others unabashedly stared at me. People I recognized from my visit to the west coast. They seemed particularly interested to see me with Darryl again, this time on the opposite side of the continent.

But I focused my attention on the stage. I was as guilty as the next average person, in that the names of most of the songwriters being honored were not familiar to me; although their songs were.

One feature of the program was some writers performing their own songs. This produced pretty dismal results in some instances, but others were sensational. The show stopper occurred when Darryl slipped from his seat, to appear on stage a few minutes later, performing his most recent number one hit, "Look Again." He didn't dance to this number; a slow, dreamy ballad. It was just him, on a bare stage, seated on a stool with his guitar and the orchestra in the pit unobtrusively accompanying him. It brought down the house, getting the longest standing ovation of the evening. As he was taking his bows, he looked down at me and smiled. I thought my heart would burst with pride and admiration for this genius I loved.

Darryl won awards in two categories that evening and Mickey won one, too; a rap music category having recently been added. As it turned out, Mickey had written the number Darryl, Tiff, and I had danced the "Turbo Booster" to back in Lansing. Tiffani clapped so hard when he went up to accept his award, it was a miracle her corsage didn't fall off.

During the finale, we slipped from our seats and back to the limo. Tiff and Mickey wanted to go to the after-party being thrown by the sponsors of the event. Dare and I didn't. We hadn't had any time alone the entire day. Alex took us back to the hotel, and several of Dare's security team came down to the "secret" entrance to meet us. As we walked to the elevator, I asked, "Do you think Tiff will be all right?" as any mother would, whose only daughter was going off to a New York party with a rap star she'd just met.

"I haven't known Mickey a long time, but I think a lot of him, he's got his head on straight. Alex and Sam will stay with them every minute—and not many people would deliberately get on the wrong side of Cortez." I heartily agreed. Cortez looked like Steven Segal's huskier brother.

The security team saw us back to my suite. Darryl unlocked the door, standing back as I entered. I went in, and as I turned around, he grabbed me, holding me tight, covering my face and neck with kisses.

"Angela, do you have any idea how desperately I've missed you? It's been all I could do all evening to keep my hands off you." He picked me up and carried me into the bedroom, kicking the door closed behind him. We tumbled onto the bed, his hands caressing my body. "Do you know how much I've longed for you? How much I've *ached* for you?" His hands were underneath me now, unzipping my dress.

"I haven't been able to sleep at night, thinking about you," I murmured in his ear. "I missed you so." I took off his jacket, threw it on the floor, and began to unbutton his shirt. Moments later, our clothes scattered all over the bed and the floor, we were locked in love's oldest embrace. As powerful and passionate as our intimacy had been up to that point, I wasn't prepared for the tidal flood of desire that overcame us.

Much later, as we lay still entwined, spent and panting, Darryl kissed me feverishly. "I love you, Angela. I never imagined it was possible to love this much. I'll never let us be apart this long again."

"These past few weeks have been the longest of my life." I cradled his head on my breasts. "Sometimes I'm . . . I'm almost afraid of how much I love you, Darryl."

"I know," he whispered into my hair. "It's been a long, long time since I opened my heart. I feel that way, too, at times." He looked at me with a shaky smile. "But it's not gonna scare me away from you." He stopped smiling. "Nothing will *ever* take me away from you . . ." he held me tighter, "except death."

After a long moment, he said, "Honey, seeing each other a

couple of days a month just isn't enough. Can you get away for a couple of weeks?"

"I think so, love. Why?"

He propped himself up on one elbow. "I want you to come out to the coast. We'll take a vacation together—God knows we both deserve one. Can you?"

"I'm pretty sure I can, but I need to give my boss a little notice, and it'll take me at least a week to arrange my department to handle my absence for that long."

"Okay, then. Let's say you'll come out next Friday night. Tiff can come too, and I'll show my two favorite ladies the town—or maybe we'll go down to the Bahamas. Would you like that, sweetheart?"

"I'd *love* it! I've never been to the Bahamas!"

"They say it's 'better in the Bahamas,' " he started to kiss my breasts again. "But, baby, you and I are going to make it *best* right here, right now!"

"Darryl," I said anxiously, "Tiff will probably be back soon. I know she'll come in to tell me goodnight."

"Don't worry, sugar. Alex will call when they're on the way. Now don't distract me. I'm busy."

Alex called a couple of hours later. We tidied the room, and Dare went to the door connecting the two suites. "After you tell Tiff goodnight, why don't you come on over to *my* place?" he said with a lascivious grin.

"I just might take you up on that." I looked at the door. "I've seen plain old hotel *rooms* that had connecting doors, but I never thought you'd find a connecting door between two *suites,* especially ones as luxurious as these."

"Yes, it's very uncommon. This hotel doesn't have 'em."

"But . . ." He gave me that devilish grin again. "Darryl! . . . You *didn't!*"

"Sure did. Why not? They'll put the wall back like it was after we leave." He kissed me. "See *you* for Part II in an hour or so, hot stuff," he said, as he slipped through the door.

The rest of the weekend was terrific. We went sight-seeing,

shopping (Tiff was in heaven!), out to dinner, and even caught a play, sneaking into the balcony after the house lights had gone down. We had a ball, even though Dare's security team had to go with us. Everywhere we went, one of the biggest sights seen by everybody *else* . . . was Dare.

But I was due for a major disappointment when I got to work that Monday. There was a training session in Chicago the following week I was scheduled to attend. Darryl was dismayed when I told him that evening.

"You've *got* to go?"

"I could probably wheedle my way out of it, Dare, but I really should go. The training involves a major change in procedure for *my* department, and I need to get the new information first hand. But it'll only delay things another two weeks; the week in Chicago, and a week to get things squared away after that. Would that be okay for *your* schedule?"

"I'll *make* it okay. I don't have a performance for the next six weeks, and I'll move any meetings and stuff either up or back."

That was one of the reasons I loved this man. He had millions, and could have said, "The hell with Chicago. In fact, why even bother with a job? You don't need to work anymore. I'll take care of you." But he didn't. He knew me well enough to realize two things. One, as I said to Tiffani, I wasn't the kept companion type. And two, my job meant more to me than just money. He understood how I felt on both scores without me needing to spell it out.

"Are you upset with me, honey?" I asked faintly.

"What? Of *course* not. I'm *proud* of you—and you waited for me when I was in Spain doing *my* job. I'll wait for you while you're in Chicago doing yours. Go ahead, and take care of business, my executive lady, so when you get out here . . ." I could *hear* that spark come into his eyes, "your mind will be clear to take care of *me*."

So the following Monday found me, not in California, but in Chicago. The training sessions were going well, but I missed

Tiffani, as I always did on a business trip—and now I had to contend with missing Darryl, as well. As always, he faithfully called me every day.

That Tuesday night, the telephone's ringing woke me. I looked at the clock. It was after midnight. Who could be calling so late? I'd already spoken to both Darryl and Tiffani earlier. I picked up the telephone hoping it wasn't bad news about either of them.

"Angie, honey, it's me," said the voice of the man I love, sounding strangely hollow.

"Dare, where are you? You sound like you're calling from the bottom of a well. Are you all right?"

"I would be if my woman wasn't such a sound sleeper. I was knocking at your door five minutes ago. Will you please get up and let me in?"

I sat straight up, "Honey . . . where are you?"

"Downstairs in the lobby, calling from this damn house phone."

"What! But how . . ."

"Look, baby, I gotta book—too many people wandering around down here. I'm on my way back up. Don't go back to sleep!"

Go back to sleep! Was he crazy? I jumped out of bed, ran to the bathroom, brushed my hair and my teeth, and went to the door. The minute I heard the elevator bell, I opened the door, and my nerdy accountant rushed in. Even with a million questions buzzing in my head, first things came first. I held him tightly as he kissed me.

But when we finally broke the embrace, I said, "Darryl! What on earth are you doing here? Is something wrong?" I removed the phony glasses.

"Yes, something was very wrong. My woman and I were on different sides of the country!"

"What!"

"I missed you, honey. I wanted to see you. And I decided to be like any other man for once, and go see my girl when I felt like it. It's been a week already. I wasn't about to wait another two." He kissed me tenderly, "I told you we'd never be apart that long again. I meant it. So . . . here I am."

Something wasn't right here. "Dare . . . where's Sam and Alex?"

"Uh . . . Who?"

"Who? Darryl, did you come out here *alone?"*

"Well . . . uh . . . yeah . . . I sorta did. What's the big deal?"

"The big deal? Oh, honey, *anything* could have happened to you. You could have been mobbed. You could have been kidnapped . . . *anything."*

"You want me to leave?" he asked, turning toward the door.

"No!" I grabbed his arm. "No, Mr. Smart-Alec, I don't want you to leave. Oh . . . come here." I wrapped my arms around him, "Honey, how could you have taken such a chance? If anything had happened to you . . ."

"Well, nothing did. But . . ." he added, looking down the neckline of my rather low-cut nightgown, "I sure wouldn't mind something happening to me *now.* Got any ideas?"

We both had several ideas. We had just finished investigating one when the phone rang. "Who could it be, now?" I wondered aloud. On cue, the comedian next to me started singing the song of the same title, as I picked up the phone. "Hello?"

"Hello . . . Angela? This is Sam—Sam Steele."

"Well, hello, *Sam,"* I said glaring at Darryl, who groaned, and pulled the covers over his head. "How are you?" I continued into the phone.

"Oh, I'm fine. I got your number there from Tiffani. I hope you don't mind. Uh, how are *you?"* he asked, as though it was the most natural thing in the world for him to call me at two o'clock in the morning—when I was on a business trip, no less.

"Just great, Sam," I answered . . . and waited. Obviously, my beloved had jumped ship without telling anyone. I could only imagine the panic at the other end of the line. Poor Sam was trying to find out if I could shed any light on Darryl's disappearance, without frightening me with the news he was missing.

"When was the last time you spoke to Dare?"

Now we were getting to the real purpose of the call. I decided to put him out of his misery. "About thirty seconds ago . . . Yes, Sam, he's here. Do you want to speak to him?"

In the conversation that ensued Darryl told Sam that he, (Darryl) could go anywhere he damn well pleased. Sam told Darryl that he (again, Darryl) could in that case also damn well find himself another chief of security, because he (Sam this time) couldn't be bothered with dumb stunts. After they got through telling each other off, it was agreed Sam, Alex, and Cortez would come out to Chicago the following evening to escort Dare home.

I slipped away from the next day's session early, and rushed back to the hotel. Dare had spent the whole day there, watching cartoons and soap operas. He hadn't even shaved, saying he was enjoying "just being a slob." But he managed to tear himself away from the tube when I came in. The fellas got in about six-thirty and stopped by, but left Dare and I to enjoy a candle-light room service dinner alone.

Their plane left the next morning at eight. Dare had a recording session scheduled for that afternoon. I wanted to go to the airport with them, but the still unshaven Darryl insisted I didn't. He didn't want me coming back into the city alone. "See you a week from tomorrow," he said as he walked through the door.

That day at work was endless. I couldn't concentrate. When I returned to the hotel, the room seemed so empty with Darryl gone. There on the table was a bouquet of red roses. Next to it was a small, flat package. I opened it. It was an audio cassette—just the cassette, no note. I always took my radio/cassette player with me when I traveled (which Darryl knew), so I sat down on the bed, put the earphones on, and put the cassette into the machine.

"My love," Darryl's voice said, "since among all the wonderful things you are, you're also a wonderful singer, I wanted you to be the first to hear a song I just finished—especially since it's dedicated to you." A piano started to play. Darryl began to sing:

You can be alive without living;
You can offer gifts without giving;
You can sing with your voice,
but cry within your heart.

You can look and still not see.
When the world comes between you and me,
That's the way I feel whenever we're apart.

You can listen, and not hear a word that's said
  around you,
'Cause you're listening for the voice that isn't there.
People all about, but loneliness surrounds you
And without you here, it's more than I can bear.

The only thing that keeps me going,
and that comforts me, is knowing
That you've felt the same for me right from the start.

Someday soon we'll end the yearning,
and we'll feel the joy returning;
When we find a way to never be apart.

Tears filled my eyes. I recognized the melody as the one he had hummed to me back in Lansing. I realized he must have composed it that night, while we were together. The strongest feeling of tenderness came over me. *This incredible man loves you,* I told myself, *and he* needs *you.* As articulate as Darryl was with the spoken word, he expressed his deepest feelings most powerfully through his music. This song told me everything I knew he wouldn't—or couldn't—say to me verbally. He needed me; he needed me *there*, with him. We both knew the only way I could be there with him would mean giving up my career—and virtually all of my present way of life. And I knew he was hesitant to ask that of me, at least not outright, not in words. I wasn't sure if he was even aware of the message he was sending me now through this song—but *I* was . . . and I knew what I had to do.

I called the hotel manager. He put me on hold a few minutes to get the information I required. But, once he got back on the line, a short conversation—and the credit card Darryl had given me—took care of everything I needed there. Then I called home, and spoke to Tiffani. Then, for the first time, I called the 800 number Darryl had given me all those months ago. A woman answered, saying simply, "Answering service."

Foolishly, I was startled. *Well, what did you expect for her to say "This is Darryl Bridges' secret, top-priority message center. May I help you?"*

"Hello," I said out loud. "This is Angela Delaney. I know Mr. Bridges is at a recording session, but it's important I get a message to him as soon as possible."

"Your name again, please?" she asked politely.

I told her. She asked me to hold, but was back on the line again in seconds. "Yes, ma'am," she said, even more attentively. "I'll make sure Mr. Bridges gets *your* message immediately. May I have it now?"

I took a deep breath, "Please tell Mr. Bridges I'll be arriving at LAX on United Airlines flight 126 at nine p.m. this evening, L.A. time. I'd like him to have someone meet me."

"Yes, ma'am . . . I'll get word to him right away. Any further message?"

I hesitated only a second, "Yes . . . tell him I said 'I love you.' "

Eleven

You Are My Lady

Once the plane was in flight, the doubts rolled in. The only thing I was unshakably sure of was my love for Darryl. I'd had no doubts there since my first visit to L.A. But I began to wonder how he'd feel about me coming like this, so unexpectedly. What if he had plans or obligations for the weekend? Darryl's obligations left little room for last minute absences. Maybe he'd even moved some things up to clear the deck for next weekend, when I was *supposed* to show up. Maybe he wouldn't be all that pleased to have me pop up now. He'd probably still be at the recording session—his sessions tended to run pretty late. I assumed I'd be taken to his house to wait for him there. Would he be annoyed when he arrived?

I tortured myself with these thoughts all the way to L.A. When the plane landed, I looked anxiously around the lobby. Did my message even *get* to Dare? Was anyone here to meet me? How would I get to his house if there wasn't? I didn't know the way to his house, and would his staff let me in even if I did?

Out of the corner of my eye, I saw someone wave. I turned, and there stood Alex, Sam, and Cortez. Next to them was a scruffy looking dude in jeans and a sleeveless plaid shirt. The disheveled one walked rapidly toward me, and I just as rapidly went to meet him. Before I could say a word, he wrapped me up in his arms, and kissed me so fervently his dark glasses almost fell off.

"I'm all for touching reunions," Sam said, looking around uneasily, "but I suggest you two finish *your* touching in the car, before somebody spots us."

We started swiftly for the exit, but just before we got there, a kid of about nine or ten materialized out of nowhere. "Excuse me," she said adoringly, "are you Darryl Bridges?"

Dare looked down. He didn't have the heart—or lack of one—to try to fool this child. He smiled at her, "Yes, I am." The kid's mother was standing behind her, looking as though she'd seen a ghost.

"Can I have your autograph?" the little girl asked, handing Darryl a small paper bag she was holding.

"Sure." Alex handed Dare a pen. "What's your name, honey?" Dare inquired.

"Angela."

"Angela?" Dare smiled over at me. "That's my favorite name in the whole world."

After he'd finished writing the autograph on the bag and was handing it back, Angela's mother offered another piece of paper. "My name is Emma," she croaked in an awed whisper.

Dare smiled, and signed an autograph for her, too. Handing *it* back, he said, "Look, we'd really appreciate it if you ladies didn't tell anyone you saw us until we've gone. Okay?"

"Sure, Darryl," Angela said. Her mom just gave a dazed nod.

"Thanks. Nice to meet you, Angela . . . Emma."

The guys really hustled us out then. The brief encounter had drawn some attention. Someone approached Emma just as we reached the door; no doubt to ask her, "Who *was* that?"

We quickly got to the limo, and departed with Cortez arriving with my luggage at almost the same time. I turned to Darryl with an uncertain smile and held out my hands. "Surprise."

He took off the shades. "Best one I ever had in my life."

"And *I'm* surprised *you're* here. I thought you'd still be at the studio."

"With *you* arriving? Not likely. I'm just glad you called early enough for me to cut the session short and get out here."

"You cut the session short? Oh, Darryl. You didn't have to do that . . . I could have waited."

He pulled me into his arms. "Honey, we've both waited long enough already."

When we arrived at the house and went upstairs, I was half-way down the hall before I realized he was no longer beside me. I turned and he was still standing near the top of the stairs at his bedroom door. "And just where do you think *you're* going?" he asked with a bemused smile. I'd been heading for the blue room, where I'd slept before. But, last time, I'd entered this house as the proprietor's newest friend. Now I was his *best* friend . . . and his lover. Dare laughed as I went sheepishly back and we entered his suite.

All the piles of stuff were gone, and this time I could clearly see just how beautiful the place was. There were bouquets of flowers but no roses.

As we walked through the parlor to his bedroom, I said weakly, "Darryl, I hope I'm not interfering with any plans you had for this weekend."

He didn't answer, but went over to the dresser to deposit my flight bag. "I mean," I went on, "I know we'd planned for me to come out next Friday, not today."

He studied me in the dresser mirror, but still didn't speak. "I mean . . ." I was really floundering now, "I understand if there are things you have to do. I don't mind waiting."

"I already told you. No more waiting, Angela," he announced, still contemplating me in the mirror. He turned to face me. "Come here, sweetheart."

I went to him, and he embraced me, holding me tight. He kissed me tenderly, then lifted his head slightly. "Angela," I looked into his eyes—*my* eyes widening in comprehension of the question I saw there before it left his lips, "will you marry me?"

My eyes told him all my questions, and doubts, and fears. And his eyes answered and conquered them—all in the span of a heartbeat. So all I *said* was, "Yes, Darryl."

A long time afterward, we lay still, breathing in sync. I kissed him, and murmured, "Darryl?"

"Yes, darling girl."

"I love you."

"And I love you. Welcome home."

The balance of the night was spent in joyful, passionate, grateful celebration—no details were discussed then. The things we said to each other then were said without words.

But the next day, after Monroe served brunch in Darryl's sitting room, and we were finished eating, I said, "Darryl, there are two things we need to talk about before we go any further."

He looked solemn, correctly divining these two things were important to me. "Okay, honey, what are they?" he inquired, moving his chair next to mine.

"Well, the first is my age. You know I'm four years older than you?"

"Yes?"

"Well?"

"Well . . . what?"

"What do you mean 'what?' You know 'what,' Dare. How do you feel about that?"

"That *is* how I feel about it, baby—'*So* what?' Maybe *some* people would have a problem with a man marrying a woman four years older . . . obviously I'm not one of them. I love you for the beautiful soul inside, not for the beautiful body that houses it; although I sure appreciate the packaging. But since *you're* so concerned about me marrying an old broad, let me elaborate: you're drop-dead gorgeous; you dance like a teen-ager; you could easily pass for four years *younger* than me; you're healthy, fit, and you've got the finest big legs on this or any other planet. Next question."

I laughed, but quickly grew serious again. "Dare, I guess I already knew how you felt on that score, but I needed a way to lead into my *real* concern." I looked down at my hands. "Darryl, I know how much you love children. I've read you wanted a houseful one day." I looked up at him. "Honey, I'm thirty-seven years old. I don't know if I can have even *one* child, and it's pretty certain I can't have anything even close to a 'houseful.' Darryl, I want you to be happy, and . . ."

"Hold it! Hold it right there!" Darryl commanded. "I'm only going to say this once, Angela. Listen up, you'll need to remember it for the next thirty years or so. I asked you to marry me because I love you; because I want to spend the rest of my life with you. Period. The only way I'm *going* to be happy is if I'm with you." He put his arm around me. "Now, as far as children are concerned . . . are you willing to try?"

"Yes! Oh, yes, sweetheart, but . . ."

"Angela, a baby is a gift from God. There would be no guarantees, even if we were both twenty. So, my only love—if the doctors give us the go-ahead—we'll try . . . and we'll pray. Okay?"

I leaned my head on his shoulder. "Yes, Darryl."

He kissed my forehead. "Anyhow, the day I marry you, you'll be giving me *one* child right off the bat. I thought Tiff would be one of the 'things' you wanted to talk to me about."

"No. I don't need to. I already know how you feel about her, and how she feels about you. *I* feel truly blessed."

After that, we talked for hours, making decisions, making plans. Darryl declared, "I won't stand for any long engagement," so we set the date for September seventh; four weeks away. We wanted to have our families and friends around us as we took our vows, so we had to allow some time for arrangements to be made. "And even *that's* too long a wait," Darryl quipped, "for a man who's ready to get hitched fifteen minutes from now."

"I don't think we could accomplish that, honey—unless Monroe is ordained."

Dare laughed, "He'd probably give it a go, if we asked him. But then it wouldn't be legit, and I have one inflexible demand of whatever ceremony we choose. That when it's over . . ." he kissed me lightly, "you're my wife."

We decided on who'd officiate (my pastor, Reverend Matthews—and what better choice?), and where the ceremony would be (at Pivot Pointe). We also decided Dare and I would fly back to Michigan to talk to my family the next day, and bring Tiff back to California with us. We would live with Darryl. Dare and I knew once the engagement was announced Tiff and I would need security. Darryl offered to stay somewhere else himself, and leave the two of us the house, if I felt it was improper for us to live there with him before the wedding.

"No, my chivalrous one, I don't see any sin in us staying with you now—and if anybody else does, too damn bad."

Darryl abruptly jumped up, taking my hand, drawing me with him. "That reminds me. Follow me!" As if I had any choice; he still had hold of my hand and was pulling me behind him. By then I'd seen Darryl many times when a fit of excitement was on him. The best thing to do was just go with the flow.

He walked rapidly into the bedroom, over to the double doors leading to the adjacent suite, and flung them open wide. I entered, looking about me in astonishment. The room that had been abandoned and forgotten the last time I was here was now completely furnished and redecorated. It was bursting with color, done all in shades of pink and blue—except for a huge bouquet of red roses.

"I told you this suite was for the lady of the house. As of the moment you said 'yes' last night . . . that's you." He came up behind me and put his arms around me, just as he had the first time we'd stood here together. "I had it done in the colors of your bedroom in Lansing, but you can change anything you don't like. You can redo the whole thing from scratch if you want."

"I wouldn't change a thing," I whispered.

"There's one major drawback, though. You have to also take the weirdo next door." He tightened his embrace. "Of course, he won't *be* next door very often," he whispered, nuzzling my ear, "if you're in *here*." Unlike before, *this* time I didn't walk out of his embrace—my new bedroom got christened right then.

"You were fairly confident I *would* say yes, weren't you, friend?" I teased him later.

"Yeah, pretty much," he said matter-of-factly. "But I was one hundred percent positive I *wanted* you to say yes, and I was going to keep asking until you did."

"But I wouldn't even be here now, if I hadn't made that unscheduled mad dash cross county."

"On the way back from Chicago, I made up my mind to ask you to marry me the next time I had you alone. That just turned out to be now rather than next weekend. As for the suite . . ." he looked around, "I started having the work done on *it* right after I left Lansing."

"You *did?*"

"Yes. I knew then I wanted to marry you. I've just been waiting for a signal you wanted to marry *me*. Something like your 'mad dash' is what I've been hoping for."

We put on our robes and went over to a loveseat facing the balcony doors so we could look out at the garden while continuing the discussion we'd started in his room. "Honey . . ." he took my hand, "how . . . how would you feel about joining me in a press conference? I think that would be the smartest way to go. There's going to be a whole lot of curiosity about you. I think we can derail some of it if you and I just meet the media together."

"Okay, Darryl, I'm game, if you think that's best."

"Man! What a cool customer! You mean it? You're not uncomfortable about it?"

I wasn't uncomfortable about it—I was petrified. But I'd had a talk with myself while Darryl was sleeping. I was going to be the wife of the man many people believed to be the most celebrated entertainer in the world, maybe even in *history.* Indirectly, *I* was going to be famous, too, for being married to *him.* I sure didn't crave the fame, but it was inevitable. I wasn't going to make the situation worse by having the man I loved worry about me handling it.

"No, honey," I lied. "We have to make some sort of formal announcement, and naturally, we should do it together."

Dare flopped back against the loveseat and stared at me. "Well, raise my rent! Woman, you never cease to amaze me! And here I stayed awake half the night composing a speech to brace you for all the media attention you're going to get from now on."

"I'm well aware, sir, that my future husband has achieved some small degree of prominence in the music industry."

" 'Some small degree?' Okay, lady," he said, as he tackled me, "you asked for it!"

A couple of hours later, we started getting ready to go back to Lansing. I decided I'd better tell Tiff beforehand, and called while Dare was showering. After our hellos, I said guardedly, "Honey, Darryl and I are flying back to Lansing this evening."

"What? Why? What's wrong? Did you two have a fight? No, you couldn't have, or he wouldn't be coming back with you."

"No, we didn't have a fight. In fact, just the opposite." I took a deep breath. "I wish I could tell you this in person, but I want you to have time to think about it before we get there." I moistened my lips, "Tiff . . . Darryl and I are getting married."

"Hot *damn!* I knew it! I knew he wouldn't wait much longer to ask you! And Alex said a year!"

I was so shocked I didn't even pause to discourse on her language. "Tiffani, what *are* you talking about?"

"Sam and Alex and I made a bet in New York on how long it would take you two to jump the broom. Alex said a year. I said six months. But Sam won—he said three more months, tops."

"Do you mean to tell me you all were making *bets* on when

Darryl and I were getting married? And what made you miscreants think we *were* going to get married? *We* never even discussed it before yesterday!"

"Mama, the way you two act has wedding bells written all over it! It was just a matter of time. Oh, Mama, I'm so happy for you!"

"Honey," I said softly, "it's going to make some major changes in *both* our lives—and not all of them for the better."

"I know," she quietly replied.

"Dare and I will talk all this over with you when we get there, dear, okay?"

"Okay, Mama." She brightened again. "I can hardly wait to see you . . . *and* Dare."

I told Darryl about the nuptial pool on the plane. He cracked up. "Stop laughing, Darryl Douglass Bridges! That's not funny!" I scolded him with an almost concealed smile.

"You know it *is,* honey, and you don't know the half of it! Samuel Steele is *not* a betting man! He won't even buy a lottery ticket!" He looked back to where Sam was sprawled out asleep, a couple of rows behind us.

"Well," he continued, taking my hand. "I guess Sam was waiting to put his money on a sure thing, so I'd better make sure of you, before you back out on me."

"No chance of that, 'O great engage-ed one. You're snared now, pal."

"I'm a cautious man and I believe in confirming all my transactions." He reached into his pocket and pulled out a small red velvet box. The ring was the most beautiful piece of jewelry I'd ever seen. It was the same pattern as my pendant; a diamond surrounded by rubies, with the same leaf pattern to the setting. But, my God, the diamond was stupendous! Yet the ring wasn't ostentatious, it was too delicately crafted for that. Darryl put it on my finger and leaned over to kiss me. "There. You're really mine now," he whispered.

"I have been since the first time you kissed me, my love."

Tiff was watching for us. She ran down to the parking lot

and hugged me first, then Darryl. If the guys thought they had enjoyed a soul food feast the last time, it was nothing next to the spread Tiffani had prepared. She had outdone herself: fried chicken, hamhocks, collard greens, yams, corn muffins, corn on the cob, and for dessert, banana pudding. Cortez ate more than anybody else (of course, he was *bigger* than anybody else), and during dinner, I found out why he'd been on the scene so much lately. Darryl was grooming him to take Alex's place. Alex was ready to move on to bigger and better projects on Darryl's behalf.

But Alex's mind wasn't on business just then. After we started eating, he turned to me. "Angela, Dare's got *you* sewed up, but if Tiffani can cook like this, I might just take *her* off your hands."

"You'll have to talk to her *parents* about that, old son," Darryl said sternly.

After dinner, the guys didn't stick around long, correctly concluding the three of us needed to be alone. After I saw them to the door, Darryl, Tiffani, and I moved into the living room and sat on the sofa—Darryl in the middle. We looked awkwardly at each other for a few moments, then Darryl said, "Well, ladies, shall I go first?" We both nodded. He looked at Tiff. "I want to say first that I love your mother with all my heart and soul, and my plan is to spend the rest of my days making her happy."

I took his hand. "You already have," I said gently.

He squeezed my hand and turned back to Tiff. "Which brings me to my second point. You and I start off with two very important things in common. We both love this woman and she loves both of us." He reached over with his other hand to take one of Tiff's. "I think you're terrific. You've got some of your mother's best qualities, and you've got a lot of your own, as well. If we let it happen, I think maybe you and I can grow to love each other, too, and complete the circle. Can we give it a shot?"

For her answer, she hugged him. I leaned my head against

Dare's back, my heart full of joy. I knew something Tiffani didn't—yet. Darryl wanted to adopt her. We'd discussed it on the plane. I'd wondered if he *could,* since Tiff was already eighteen. But, thorough as always, Dare had already checked with his legal team, and found it was no problem, especially once he was her mother's husband. After all, she was still under twenty-one. We'd agreed not to discuss it with her then, but to wait until some of the dust died down, before he asked how she'd feel about it.

We turned in then, wanting to get an early start for the next day's drive to Detroit to talk to my family. Tiff was already in her room by the time Dare and I left the living room. As we walked down the hallway, I stopped by Tiff's room, "Dare . . . ," I began, looking at him beseechingly with my hand on Tiff's doorknob.

"Oh, no! As a famous man once said, 'déjà vu all over again!' All right, my discreet darling—since this is the last time."

"Thank you for understanding, sweetheart." We kissed goodnight, but when I tried to open the door, I found it was locked. The only way it *could* be locked was from the inside.

Darryl started laughing. "Well, looks like Tiffani's giving you her blessing to spend the night in the same room with your soon-to-be husband."

"That's right," Tiffani's voice came through the door. "Now will you two stop all that talking? I'm trying to go to sleep in here!" So we went into my room and closed the door; doing very little *talking* indeed for the rest of the night.

Preparing to leave the next day was weird. After leaving my mother's house, we were going directly to Detroit Metro Airport to fly back to L.A. I was leaving this home forever. But although I was moving farther than I had ever moved before, I was taking less. Our baggage was strange because we were only taking things of sentimental or legal value. For instance, I had packed all our photographs; a folder containing documents, like our birth certificates; and another containing Tiffani memorabilia; her old report cards, and the like.

After a lot of thought, I also took a bundle of love letters Bobby had sent me before our marriage. I hadn't looked at them for years—it had been too painful. But this was yet another gift Darryl had given me. Now that I had finally faced what happened with Bobby, I was able to remember the good times with him, when I still loved him. I decided to keep the letters. God rest his soul, Bobby would always be a part of my past, and because of our relationship, I had one of the people I loved most in the world—my daughter.

Although we did take some, there wasn't even a need to take clothes. Darryl's staff had gotten hold of the shop where I'd, purchased our New York outfits and obtained our dress and shoe sizes. Dare had seen to it our new closets in our new home were far from empty. "But I didn't get a lot, baby," he told me. "I haven't met a woman yet who didn't want to pick her own clothes, so you and Tiff will have to go shopping when we get back."

Tiff stepped out of her room with two of her stuffed animals sticking out of her flight bag. She insisted on keeping all of them, saying they were her "children." Darryl promised each and every one of the critters would be packed and shipped to California.

A security team would be moving into the apartment before we held the press conference. Dare said that was necessary to keep people from vandalizing it for souvenirs. I thought he was being overly cautious there, but went along. He said a moving team would come in the following week, to make sure my things were disposed of as I wished. Most of the stuff would be given away to family, friends, or charity. The team would ship to the coast anything left behind that Tiff or I still wanted.

Walking out for the last time was a curious feeling. Darryl sensed my reflective mood and put his arm around me. We walked out the door together.

We had a regular convoy going down to Detroit. I took the

lead in my car, with Darryl riding shotgun and Tiff in the back seat. Cortez was following in Tiffani's car, and Alex and Sam were following him in the car we'd rented the day before at the airport. We were taking the cars down to Detroit because—although they didn't yet know it—I was giving mine to my mother, and Tiffani was giving hers to my niece, Marlowe.

I knew Darryl wouldn't have any problem with me playing his music, since it was just "us," so I popped "Pivot Point" into the tape-deck. We sang along to it all the way to Detroit. When the album ended, Darryl proclaimed, "Angela, that voice of yours deserves to be heard. I'm still thinking about that duet. *Now,* we can go for it!" Before I could protest, he turned to Tiff, "But I won't make it a trio. You inherited your mother's good looks, honey," he smiled as he shook his head, "but not her voice."

"Yeah, I know," Tiff sighed.

"But it's not all bad news," Darryl added, looking over the top of the seat down at her dainty shoes. "You also didn't inherit her feet."

I gave him a poke in the ribs. "You've got *your* nerve. Have you looked down past *your* ankles lately? Well, she can't sing, but she does have musical talent. She's been playing violin since she was eight years old."

"Yeah?" Dare said, really interested. He turned to Tiff and asked, "Are you any good?"

"Damn good," she said smugly.

"Hmmmm," Darryl said. "Now that's intriguing." Oh, no. We'd started that creative brain of his bubbling again. Blessedly, before my intended could go off on a tangent, we were pulling into my mother's driveway. Cortez parked Tiff's car behind mine and got in with Alex and Sam. They told Dare, "Good luck!" and drove off. They were to come back for us in a couple of hours.

"Boy!" Darryl exclaimed, as we walked up the steps, "I'm more nervous about meeting your family than I was meeting the queen!"

"And rightly so—my family is even nuttier than *hers!*" I joked, trying to put him at ease. I took his hand. I knew he really was jittery about this. Who wouldn't be, meeting new in-laws? I didn't even want to *think* about my meeting with *his* family, which we'd planned for the next day.

Mama was listening for us, and opened the door as we reached the porch. I'd only told her I was bringing a friend I wanted her, my brother, and my sister to meet. I only had one parent for Dare to meet; Daddy died when I was twenty-five.

Tiff walked in first, followed by me, and then Darryl. Tiff and I hadn't seen Mama for a couple of weeks, so she had to give us both a big hug. Then she looked over at Darryl and started. My mother is one of those wise people who believe what their eyes tell them, no matter how unlikely it seems. Darryl was sophisticatedly dressed in slacks and a sport jacket, looking his handsome best. No disguise—he flatly refused to meet his new mother-in-law "looking like a bum." So he looked exactly like who he was—Darryl Bridges.

Mama looked at him a long moment, then began, "Oh . . . please excuse me. It's just that you look so much like . . ."

"He *is,* Mama."

She looked at me in wonder. "What! But . . ." Other than Darryl and Tiffani, my mother knows me better than anyone in the world. She looked me in the eye and *knew* I wasn't kidding. Her eyes replied, "You've got a lot of explaining to do later, young lady!"

But my Mama is a lady of down home hospitality. At that point, she wasn't as concerned with *who* Darryl was, but rather, *what* he was—a guest in her home, and her daughter's friend. Mama turned back to Darryl, extended her hand, and said, "Mr. Bridges, I can't tell you what a surprise . . . and a pleasure it is to meet you. I've loved your singing since you were a teen-ager. Don't just stand there in the doorway, come in, come in!"

Darryl stepped farther into the entryway and shook her hand. "It's a pleasure to meet you, too, Mrs. Seymour. But please, call me Darryl."

I could hear my sister and sister-in-law talking. "Where is everybody, Mama?" I asked.

"They're all in the kitchen. Why don't you all have a seat in the living room and I'll let them know we have company."

To Mama you're either "family" (related or not) or "company," there's no middle ground. I touched Mama's arm and looked into her eyes. "Darryl isn't 'company,' Mama," I said softly.

She looked down at my hand and saw my engagement ring. Taking my hand to look at the ring more closely, she gasped, "Angela Delores! You couldn't mean . . ."

"Mrs. . . . Mrs. Seymour," Darryl interjected anxiously, "I love Angela. And she's made me the happiest man alive by saying she'll be my wife."

Mama looked back to me again. "We're going to be married next month," I whispered. "Please be happy for us, Mama."

Although her brain had to be ready to explode with questions, she believes in first things first, too—that's where *I* got it from. She threw her arms around me. "Oh, baby, I *am!*" Then she grabbed Darryl and hugged him. "I can't believe it! I don't know how this all happened, but welcome to the family!"

The four of us went to the kitchen, which is the general meeting place in Mama's house. Just before we pushed through the swinging door, my brother-in-law, Tony, called out, "What the hell is all that laughing about out there?"

We walked into the room. They all looked at Darryl—and jumped. Nobody said anything for a moment. Deciding I'd better not give them both barrels at once, I said, "Well, family, I'd like you to meet my . . . *friend,* Darryl Bridges." To my amazement, they burst out laughing.

"Angie," Tony said, "would you get real? Although I have to admit, my brother . . ." he continued, turning to Dare, "*you* look more like Darryl Bridges than *he* does. Well, nice to meet you, whoever you are."

They *really* started laughing then. And it was infectious; Darryl, Tiffani, and I were laughing, too—though not for the same reasons. But Mama didn't see anything funny in the situation. "Tony, you stop acting a fool! What's wrong with you all? Can't you see? *Look* at him. He *is* Darryl Bridges!" They stopped laughing then. They all knew Mama's sense of humor—what there was of it—didn't extend to this kind of joke. That meant Mama really believed this man to be Darryl Bridges. Which in turn meant either he *was* Darryl Bridges or Mama was in serious trouble. Either alternative fostered sobering thoughts. The room grew silent.

Finally, my sister, Celeste, said, "Angela, *what* is going on here?"

"Introductions, to begin with." I introduced Dare to all of them, including my brother, Roy, and his wife, Ida, both of whom, so far, hadn't said a word. From the looks on their faces, it was possible they never would again.

"I'm really happy to meet all of you," Dare said nervously, taking a chair once my mother, Tiffani, and I were seated.

"You know," Tony suddenly put in, "there was a blip on the news last night; a wild rumor that Darryl Bridges had been spotted at Metro Airport . . ." He stared over at Dare, "but the newscaster make a big joke out of it, said nobody knew of any reason he would be in town . . ." his voice trailed away.

"Well, now *you* know, Tony—he came to meet *you,"* I replied somewhat peevishly. I liked my brother-in-law, but sometimes he could be a little hard to take.

"You couldn't really be Darryl Bridges," Celeste said, still not believing.

"Well, I was when I woke up this morning," Darryl countered, with a smile.

"Then what in the world are you doing *here?"* Celeste persisted, not being rude, but trying to make some sense of the whole thing.

Dare looked to me for help. "Look, you guys," I said, "is Mate around?" Mate was nine, and my brother's youngest. Her real name was LaWanda, but she earned the nickname Mate at an early age. "MATE" stood for "Mouth Almighty; Tongue Everlasting." That was Mate; anything she knew, she told. If Mate was somewhere listening, Dare and I wouldn't have to hold a press conference. The whole world—or at least this corner of it—would know about us in a matter of hours.

"No, she went down the street to play," Roy finally found his tongue. "What's *that* got to do with this?"

"Well, Roy, what Darryl and I are here to tell you all has to stay confidential . . . at least for the next couple of days."

He suddenly looked excited. "Are you finally going to do something professional with your singing, Angie? Is *that* what this is all about?"

"No, Roy." I gave them a much condensed version of how Darryl and I met, gotten to know each other, and fallen in love, ending with, "and I said 'yes.' "

There was a silence again, until Tony, looking back and forth between me and Darryl, said skeptically, "Get outta here!"

Darryl laughed, and stood up. "No, my brother, it's all true. Are you sure your name isn't Thomas?" he added with a grin. He pulled out his wallet, removed his driver's license, and handed it to Tony. They passed it around, examining it closely.

"I know this must seem kinda sudden to you, and I realize you know me only by reputation. But believe me when I tell you I love Angela more than anything in this world, and I'll take good care of her and Tiffani."

"You really *are* Darryl Bridges? And you all are really *engaged?"* Ida exclaimed, speaking at last. I held out my hand, and showed her my ring. Then all hell broke loose. Suddenly, everybody was laughing and crying and hugging and kissing. Roy slapped Darryl on the back so hard I feared for Dare's vertebrae.

We heard the side door open, and Marlowe, carrying a grocery bag, came up the steps into the kitchen. "What on earth is going on?" she asked, probably thinking her family had, after years of threatening to, finally lost their minds.

"Marlowe! Marlowe!" Tiffani cried out, and I could tell how

hard it had been to hold in as major a secret as Darryl all these months. "My mother is getting married! . . . And she's marrying Darryl Bridges!" Marlowe looked at Tiffani as if to echo her father's "get real" to me a few minutes before—then saw Darryl standing there.

"Hi, Marlowe. Tiffani's told me a lot about you. I'm glad to meet you," Darryl said.

"Hey!" Tiff interjected, "it just dawned on me! Marlowe! Darryl's going to be your *uncle!*"

Marlowe opened her mouth to speak and fainted dead away. Fortunately, her father caught her and Tiffani caught the bag, before either hit the floor. After *that* excitement died down, Mama, Darryl, and I went into the living room, while the others continued the celebration in the kitchen with the booze Tony had sent Marlowe to the store to get.

Darryl and I explained our plans to Mama. "But, honey," she said when I got to that part, "you can't give me your *car!* It's brand new—you haven't had it a year!"

"Darryl's got several cars, Mama. I won't need it now," I explained gently. She regarded us silently for a prolonged moment. My mother is not a person driven by material wealth. Up to now, she'd just been happy her daughter, who'd been lonely so many years, had found the love of a good man. This was the first time it really hit her that her daughter had found the love of a good—and *wealthy*—man.

When I told her Tiffani and I were leaving within a few hours to move to California, she cried. That was the only point since I began my relationship with Darryl when I regretted any aspect of it. My mom called me the "meat," the middle child. My younger sister and older brother were the "bread." Although I know she was overjoyed for me, it hurt her to think of Tiffani and I living so far away. She'd been upset when we'd moved to *Lansing,* for goodness sake, which is only an hour drive from Detroit.

Darryl moved to the sofa next to Mama and put his arm around her. "Don't cry, Lillian," she'd told him he couldn't call her "Mrs. Seymour." "Angela and Tiffani will be back to see you often—anytime they want. And you're going to have to come out and spend some time with us. And don't forget you promised to come for the wedding a week early. We really need you to help us get things ready—don't think we're gonna let you get out of *that!*"

She smiled at Darryl through her tears. If I hadn't been unequivocally in love with the man already, that would have done the trick.

The guys came back for us a short while later. We hugged and kissed and cried all around one last time, and then the three us got into the back seat of the car to go . . . home.

Twelve

Family Reunion

When we arrived at Pivot Pointe that evening, I thought we were going to have to call a doctor to give Tiffani a sedative. The kid went absolutely ballistic; running around looking into rooms, checking out the cars in the garage, talking about taking a dip in the pool. Then when I finally got her up to *her* room (I'd decided to give her the green suite, next door to the blue one), she just sat in it over an hour, drinking everything in. She didn't want to leave it, even for dinner, so we had Monroe serve dinner for the three of us in her parlor. "At this rate, we're *never* going to get to eat in the dining room, Darryl," I told him.

We spent the evening talking, and retired early. This was the first time Darryl and I had slept together and not made love. We were just too exhausted. But it was wonderfully serene to just curl up in his arms and fall asleep. In spite of that, the next morning I was soon jittery as a cat. I knew I'd be meeting his family in a few hours.

Darryl had invited all of his family who lived within a reasonable drive for a barbecue lunch and family meeting. That was unusual enough in itself. The members of the busy Bridges clan had family gatherings infrequently, he told me. His parents were basically retired, but still performed from time to time for special occasions. His brothers and sisters were all still active in the business. Cassandra, of course, had followed in their mother's footsteps, and was one of the most popular gospel soloists around. Dare's brother Rick had made a career as an actor. The others were involved in behind the scenes activities like record production and filmmaking.

"But even if we got together more regularly, they'd know something was up today, because *I* called this meeting," he said. He explained the only other meeting *he'd* convened had been sixteen years before, when he'd called them together to announce he was branching off into popular—not religious—music. "*That* meeting was a lollapaloosa; let me tell you," he said, rolling his eyes. I'd silently just *bet* it was—and prayed *that* this day didn't wind up rivaling it.

We planned to tell the household staff that evening, after the family left, but Darryl decided we'd better tell Monroe beforehand. Monroe knew about the family gathering, of course, but he didn't know why. We called him into Dare's office.

When Dare told him, Monroe didn't bat an eyelash. He looked at me and began, "Mrs. Delaney . . ." Up to then I had been "Miss"—not disrespectfully—just informally. But now, since I was going to be "Madame," Monroe apparently thought more formality was requisite.

"I wish to offer my most sincere felicitations," he continued. "You may rely on me to ensure your wishes concerning household affairs are carried out to the letter. I am available to discuss them at your convenience, ma'am."

He turned to Darryl, "And, Mr. Bridges, may I extend to you my most heartfelt congratulations. I wish you and Mrs. Delaney every happiness. Now, if you'll excuse me, I'd better see to the luncheon." I was sitting near the door and it didn't close completely after him. As he was going down the hall, I heard a whispered and spirited, "Yes!"

Cassandra was the first to arrive. Dare and I were still in his office when Monroe came to tell us she'd entered the gate. As luck would have it, Darryl was on the phone in an involved conversation with his PR man, Jeff Mason. Jeff had called to discuss our press conference scheduled for the following day. I knew Dare's conversation was important, so I nervously left with Monroe to greet her on my own, without interrupting Dare to tell him she was there. "You don't have to stay, Monroe," I said, as we walked down the hallway together. "I'll get the door."

Monroe replied, "Very good, Mrs. Delaney," adding, "Good luck!" in a whisper, as he walked toward the kitchen.

I watched through a window, carefully planning what I'd say, as Cassandra left her car in the drive and came up the walkway. When she reached the door, I opened it, but all I got out was, "Hello, I . . ."

"Hi," she said briskly. "Boy, it's warm out today! Would you put these up somewhere until the rest of my family arrives?" She thrust two shopping bags into my hands. "They're gifts for my nieces and nephews," she added with a smile.

"Sure, I'd be glad to," I managed to squeeze in, "but . . ."

"And would you bring me a glass of something cold? Ice tea, pop, anything. I'm parched!" She started walking down the left corridor. "Tell Mr. Bridges I'm waiting for him in the music room, okay?" And she was gone.

I was still standing there befuddled when Dare came looking for me a few moments later. "*There* you are. Why are you standing out here, honey?" he said, coming up behind me. When I turned, he continued, "What's with the bags? You been shopping?" he joked. "That's the fastest, shortest shopping spree *I've* ever seen." Then he looked up at my face. "Hey, babe. What's the matter? You look like you've lost your best friend."

"No, thank God, I haven't . . . *you're* my best friend. But I *am* off to an inauspicious start with my new in-laws." I told him about my brief encounter with Cassandra.

"Oh, honey. I'm sorry." He took my hand. "But don't be mad at her. It was just an innocent mistake. It's not her fault, it's mine. I should have been out here to introduce you two and not back there running my mouth on the phone."

"No, Darryl. I should have told her who I was. I just didn't know how to do it without sounding . . . sounding . . ."

"Don't worry about it, sweetheart. You two will hit it off great. You'll see."

He took the shopping bags, put them in a closet, and we walked down to the music room. Cassandra was sitting on a sofa, leafing though a magazine. "Hi, baby brother," she said to Darryl, standing to hug him. "Now, what's this big mystery meeting all about?" She laughed, "You're not going to give Mama conniptions, like last time, are you?" She looked over at me, clearly wondering why I was standing there (and probably wondering where her drink was).

"No, I'm not going to give Mama a fit," he put his arm around me, "but your new sister-in-law might give *you* one—for mistaking her for a maid."

"My new . . . my new *what?*"

"Sister-in-law. Well, sister-in-law to be, technically. The wedding's not until next month. Cassie, this is my . . . fiancée, Angela Delaney."

"The *wedding?* . . . Oh, Darryl!" She hugged him, tackling him so hard, he had to spin her and himself around to keep both of them from falling. Then she turned to me. "Oh, I'm so sorry—and so embarrassed. You must think I'm an absolute idiot. Can you ever forgive me?"

"Hmmm . . . well, I'll decide *that* after I see how much you're going to help me with the wedding, but in the meantime . . ." I held out my arms. "I'm getting married, too. Don't *I* get a hug?"

I most certainly did. We sat down, and Darryl started telling her about how we met, but didn't get very far before his brother Larry arrived with his wife and two teenagers. After more hugging and kissing, Dare started the story again. But then family started arriving in earnest. Dare moved them out to the yard, where the staff was barbecuing, and I went upstairs to see what was keeping Tiffani.

When I returned outside with Tiff, Dare's parents and his

grandfather, Clarence Jones, who lived with them, had arrived. "And here they are now, Mama!" Darryl said. He met us, put an arm around my waist, took Tiff's hand, and led us over to where his parents were sitting. "Bet you never thought your troublesome son could get a lady this fine to marry him, did you?" He kissed me, and then said, "And this is Tiffani, your new granddaughter."

At sixty-nine, Sylvia Bridges was still imposing and still beautiful. I'd seen her on television many times, of course; she was one of the greatest gospel singers of all time. I knew Darryl looked like his mother, and his father, too, for that matter. But now that I'd come face-to-face with Sylvia, I knew where he'd gotten those eyes; those penetrating, probing eyes that seemed to see into your soul.

She hesitated a beat too long before saying, "I don't know what to say! Darryl's overwhelmed me in the past, but he's outdone himself this time! Welcome to the family, dear." She embraced me with her arms, but I could tell, not with her heart. Then she turned to Tiffani and started to hug her, as Darryl's father and grandfather moved in on me.

Quinton, Dare's dad, hugged me and kissed me on the cheek. But before he could say anything, Granddad took over. He stepped back to appraise me for a second. "Mmm-*Mmm!* Pretty as a plate of red beans and rice! Boy . . ." he said, nudging Darryl, "it took you long enough to find yourself a woman, but you sure didn't do no half-steppin' when you finally did!" He turned back to me. "Come here, and give Grand-daddy a big kiss, honey! And you, too, baby," he added, grabbing Tiffani.

Shortly afterward the food was ready, and we sat down at picnic tables all around the deck to eat. Q.T. (that's what Quinton told me to call him) said a prayer, thanking God for the two new additions to his family, and asking the Lord's blessings on the marriage of "my youngest son, and his lovely lady."

At one point during the meal Tiffani called Clarence "grandfather," and he corrected her. "No; it's Grand*dad,* baby. They all call me Granddad. I'm *old,* you know," he started cackling. "Speaking of which, boy," he added, turning to Darryl, "you got any of the *beverage* of that name around here? Or anything else with some kick to it?"

Sylvia frowned at him. "Now, Daddy . . ." she warned.

"Girl, don't look at me with those moon eyes like your mother used to do whenever I had a little nip. I'm ninety-one years old, and a drink can't do nothing worse to me than time's already done!" Darryl did have a fine wine cellar, mostly for guests, so they let him have a little wine, and that mollified him.

After the meal, we broke up, as family gatherings tend to, into male and female circles. Of course, the main topic of discussion in our group was the wedding. Everybody wanted to give me their ideas on dresses, flowers, reception menu—everything. And I appreciated it. It had begun to dawn on me that I had a lot to do, and not a lot of time to do it in. They all offered to help however I needed them.

Sylvia had stepped away, and I saw her, Q.T., and Darryl in lively conversation over by the pool, where Tiff and the other "young people," her new cousins, were having a ball.

I felt someone tugging at my sleeve. It was Dougie, Dare's sister Barbara's three-year-old; the baby of the family. All Dare's other nieces and nephews were at least teenagers. Barbara told me when she and her husband found out about this latecomer, they decided to name him after Darryl, since it looked like Darryl might never have any kids of his own. Dougie was slavishly devoted to "Uncle Dare," and Dougie had become fascinated with *me,* since I was going to be Uncle Dare's wife. I don't think Dougie really understood what a "wife" was, but he knew I was special to Dare.

"Auntie Angel?" He had started off calling me just "Angel," as he had heard Darryl do. His mother told him to add the "auntie."

"Yes, Dougie. What is it, honey?"

He was standing next to my chair. His face screwed up in a

puzzled frown. He pushed me forward slightly and looked at my back. "What did you do with your wings?" he finally asked. I thought his other aunts and cousins were going to die laughing. Poor Dougie was offended by their frivolous reaction to what was—to him—a very serious question. Since his mother had gone into the house for a moment, he took refuge in my lap, where he promptly fell asleep.

After Barbara returned and took Dougie, I went into the house to go to the bathroom. As I approached the first floor powder room, Sylvia came out. "Uh . . . hi," I said stupidly, not knowing what else to say.

She smiled at me. "It's really getting warm out there, isn't it?" she asked, friendly enough. But she didn't stop walking, and didn't seem inclined to stop and chat any further.

I decided to go for it. "Sylvia?" I petitioned.

"Yes, dear?" She stopped, and turned around.

"I . . . I thought perhaps we could talk alone a while."

She looked at me speculatively. "All right, Angela. I guess maybe we should." We went down the hallway to the music room and closed the door. We sat on sofas across from each other, and neither of us spoke for a moment.

Finally I said, "Sylvia, I know you know nothing about me; never even heard of me until a couple of hours ago." I paused. She was listening and looking at me closely; not unkindly, but as though she was making up her mind. She still didn't seem inclined to speak. *Jump in any time,* I thought as I struggled on.

"I know Darryl's happiness is important to you. It's important to me, too. I love Darryl, Sylvia. I love him with all my heart, and I know I can make him happy."

"That's what he tells me," she said, looking at me with Darryl's eyes. "He says he loves you, too, and you've already made him happier than he's ever been in his life." She didn't say this with much conviction.

I forged ahead, "Maybe I'm just a hysterical bride, and seeing things that really aren't there, but I'm getting the impression you're not entirely pleased about our engagement. Am I right?" She didn't answer right away. "Don't be afraid of offending me," I added. "How you feel about this is important to me."

She didn't mince any words then, "Angela, you're right. I *don't* know you. It takes me a while to get to know people. I have nothing against you personally, dear. From the little I've seen so far, you and your daughter seem like fine people. And it speaks well of you to have raised such a lovely child, especially alone. But three things concern me very much about you and Darryl marrying."

"What are they, Sylvia?"

She looked at me a long moment. "Okay, you asked me to speak my mind, so I will. Angela, Darryl tells me you and he only first began seeing each other in June."

"Well. . . yes, that's true, but . . ."

"Yes. He told me about all the time the two of you talked on the phone, and wrote letters to each other before then. But, in my book, that's not the same as 'seeing' someone. And, even if I conceded it was, you've still known each other less than six months. That's not very long to build a lifetime on.

"My second concern is Darryl's—well, I'll be frank—Darryl's . . . uh, resources. He told his father and I the two of you are not going to have a pre-nuptial agreement . . . although in all fairness, I have to tell you he said that was *his* idea."

"Right on both counts. He told me we weren't going to have a 'Hollywood' marriage; we were going to have a real marriage. He feels if we were insecure enough to need a pre-nuptial, we wouldn't have any business getting married in the first place."

"How do *you* feel about that?"

"I agree if there was any doubt—on either side—we shouldn't marry at all . . . but I'd have no problem signing an agreement. I don't want his money. And when we discussed it, my point was—what harm would it do to have one, since we were never going to need it?"

"*That's* exactly what *I* said to him, but he absolutely refused to discuss it further."

"And *that's* what he said to me. 'Angela, this is not negotiable.' Sylvia, since he feels so strongly about it, I'm not going to push him to change his mind. But in the event Darryl and I ever separate or divorce . . ." It was difficult for me to even voice these alternatives, "I wouldn't take any more out of our marriage than I had when I came into it." I paused again. "And I can tell you right now the only way we'll ever part is if Darryl decides he doesn't want me anymore—and in that case . . ." I looked away from her, "worrying about money would be the least of my misery."

She looked very concerned. "Now I *have* offended you. I'm sorry, I didn't mean to, truly. I'm not trying to accuse you of . . ."

"I know you're not, Sylvia. I'm not offended. This is what I wanted—a genuinely open discussion between us. Let me paraphrase something Darryl told Tiffani." I reached over and took her hand, "You and I both love Darryl, and he loves both of us. I'll do almost anything for you and I to get along—for his sake, if no other reason. But I've admired you all my life; I hope we can become friends . . ." I squeezed her hand, "just because we *want* to."

She scrutinized my face. Finally she said, "I see why my son feels the way he does about you. Angela, I'm an old woman . . ." I started to protest, but she went on. "Dear, I'm *glad* to be an old woman: seeing as when I was born, today I'd have to be an old woman . . . or dead." She smiled at me for the first time, "Of the two, I prefer old."

Then she became serious again. "I'm old, and when *I* was a girl, it wasn't considered quite . . . fitting for a woman to be older than her husband." I started to object again, but again she pressed on. "Yes, yes. Now even *I* know that's asinine. So I guess my third concern isn't much of one. I was thirty-six when Darryl was born. Barbara was thirty-nine when she had Dougie. Having a baby late isn't much of a hurdle these days, if a woman is healthy—and you look *very* healthy." I wasn't sure if that was a compliment—or not.

"Well . . ." she patted my hand and stood, "we'd better get back out there before Darryl sends a search party after us."

We went back out, and sure enough, met Darryl coming in just as we reached the terrace. He threw a hand up in front of his face, as though he saw a blinding light. "Whoa! You two excellent babes can't walk around *together* like that! Don't you know the human male can withstand only so much beauty at a time?"

Sylvia gave him a fond shove. "Dare, stop acting a fool, and go get your mother some iced tea."

"Okay, gorgeous." He kissed her cheek. "Would you like some, too, Angel?" he asked.

"Yes, honey, thank you," I replied, and he kissed me—*not* on the cheek.

"Back in a minute," he said.

Sylvia looked pensively after him. "To the world he's some kind of idol, but to me . . . he's the last baby I carried. Well, one thing's for sure—*something's* made him happy. I haven't seen him this carefree in years." She turned to me. "He's an exceptional man, Angela, and he's been hurt enough already. I couldn't bear to see him hurt more." Before I could answer, Darryl came back with our drinks.

Shortly afterward, Larry announced his group had better head home; they had a long drive. I learned it was a tradition for the family to sing together before parting. A lot of people would have paid a pretty penny to hear the Bridges family sing together one more time. Darryl suggested they sing, "Leaning on the Everlasting Arm" (what a fellowship).

"But Linda usually leads that, Dare," Rick pointed out. Linda was the one sister who wasn't there. She lived in Texas.

"Why don't *you* lead it, Dare?" Barbara urged.

"No," Darryl said, "I think one of the newest members of our family should." He pulled me from where I was sitting with the "non-singing" family members, and looked at me with so much love, there was no way I could decline, hesitant as I was to sing before *them*. I sang the verses, and Darryl took my hand as they joined in on the chorus. Tears rolled down Cassandra's cheeks as she took Darryl's other hand.

After everyone left, Darryl called all the household staff to the terrace. He told them our news, although they already knew; the ones who'd overheard the family discussions quickly spreading the word. They all seemed overjoyed. One of the older maids grabbed Darryl in a bear hug.

Darryl, Tiffani, and I sat out on the terrace for a while talking. Tiffani was all excited. Her new cousins were throwing a party that coming Saturday to introduce her to their friends. I was elated. Although this major upheaval in our lives bode fair to improve the quality of Tiffani's in a million ways, I knew she would miss all the friends and family we'd left behind. I did, too, but I had the man I loved to sustain me. Of course, Tiffani had the two of us, and I was beginning to see signs of more than "like" developing between her and Darryl. But still, it was only natural she would want the company of people her own age.

Since we were holding the press conference the next day, Darryl and I figured a few people knowing ahead of time would make little difference now. So we told Tiffani it would be all right for her to call any friends she wanted to tell. She became a human blur as she hastily kissed us both good night, and made a headlong dash for her room—and her phone. I again considered calling a doctor, sure we'd need someone to amputate the telephone receiver that would certainly be permanently attached to her ear by morning.

We went up to our (*our!*) suite then, for me to do the same with my friends. Darryl lounged around on my bed, while I sat at my desk making calls. I frequently called to him to pick up the extension, as some of my friends didn't believe me until *he* talked to them. In fact, a few didn't believe us even after *that.* One friend, who's a doctor, thought I had slipped a gear. She kept saying things like, "Have you been putting in long hours at work again?" and, "Angela, you really need to think about finding yourself a man."

Bev was at first a little peeved. "Do you mean to say that really *was* Darryl Bridges we hung out with that night? And you didn't *tell* me? Angela, how *could* you?" But my invitation to be a bridesmaid went a long way toward assuaging her displeasure.

I called my boss, Wes, with my resignation. Wes was the greatest boss in the world, and I apologized profusely for leaving with no notice.

"Well, Angela," he said with a chuckle, "I hate like hell to lose you, but under the circumstances, I don't think any offer I could make would beat out the competition's."

We talked about him replacing me with my assistant department head, Edwardo Chaidez. Eddie was ready. I always made sure he was up to speed on what was happening in the department. He was a go-getter, and great with the staff. He'd accompanied me on the trip to Chicago, even filling in for me on that last day, the one I'd missed when I left for the coast. I was pleased my happiness would make him happy, too, giving him a promotion he so definitely deserved.

The last call was to my pastor, Reverend Matthews. By then it was quite late in Michigan, and I apologized for waking him. I started off by saying, "Reverend Matthews, I'm not in Lansing. I'm in California, and . . ."

"Well, congratulations, Sister Delaney," he interrupted. "When's the wedding?"

"How . . . how did you know?" I stammered.

"Oh . . . I've got connections, honey," he said.

We asked if he'd come out to perform the ceremony, and he accepted. Then he asked, "Does Darryl know Lena Horne?"

Darryl was on the line, "Yes, sir, I know her well. I plan to invite her to the wedding."

"Well, son, that's the fee for my ecclesiastical services: an introduction to Miss Horne. I've wanted to meet her all my life."

Hanging up, I decided now was the time to broach the subject I'd been postponing: Chet Mitchell's visit. I finally told

Dare. He sat for a few moments rubbing his chin, as he tended to do when deep in thought.

"Are you mad at me, honey?" I asked timidly.

"What?" he said, coming out of his rumination, "No . . . no, I'm not mad at you, babe . . . although you *should* have told me this before. No more secrets between us from here on out—even well intentioned ones—understand me?"

"Yes, sir," I said submissively.

" 'Yes, sir,' my foot. Woman, you've never been meek in your life, and you know it. And you'd better not change on me now. I like you the sassy way you are. But . . ." he said, returning to matters at hand, "I don't have a problem with what you *did*. You kept your head and got us out of a jam. What does bother me is Mitchell being *sent* that information. It smells like an inside job. I don't like *that* at all."

"I thought so, too, and one name *does* come immediately to mind."

"Jasmine? Yeah, I thought of her right away, too. She appears to have both the motive and the inclination—but she wouldn't have had the opportunity. Jasmine wouldn't have had access to my limo phone records, let alone your address and telephone number. No, I don't think it could have been her. But we're gonna have to watch our step until we get to the bottom of this, honey.

"In the meantime, we owe Chet Mitchell. Nine out of ten reporters would have printed that story no matter what. The man's got integrity. I've met him, Angie. He's interviewed me a few times. I've always thought he was a straight up dude, and it looks like that was justified. Well, we'll call him tomorrow first thing, that'll give him a four or five hour lead on the competition."

We turned in then. Darryl and I weren't "too exhausted" *that* night.

The next morning early, we called Chet Mitchell at home, catching him as he was preparing to leave for his office. We thanked him for keeping our secret, and told him of the engagement. We also gave him our blessing to use the interview he had with me in Lansing, saying we'd fax him the information sheet that was going to be handed out at the press conference.

"I'm glad you got back to me before I had to get back to *you,*" he said. "Ever since the awards program, there's been a movement afoot to unearth the identify of Darryl Bridges's 'mystery lady.' I was just on the verge of calling you to warn you—I couldn't hold out much longer. I knew you were a lady who'd keep her word, Angela. Thanks for the scoop. My boss will *have* to give me that raise now!"

"My pleasure, Chet. As for keeping words, we're awful glad you're a man who sticks by his."

"Thanks. And I wish you guys all the best, you both deserve it. But, look, gotta go . . . I've got a story to write!"

Dare and I then left to meet briefly with his performance group before the press conference, which was at noon. The "crew" (as Dare always called them) were told to be there at eleven. No one knew why except Sam and Alex. Once Darryl made the announcement, the reaction was electric. Some of them really went bananas and started dancing across the rehearsal hall where we were meeting—practicing for the "show" they said they'd put on for our wedding reception. They were ecstatic—all except one. Jasmine didn't say anything. She didn't even look up.

The "crew" had almost all left, when I excused myself to go to the woman's room. As I was returning, I heard loud voices coming from the practice hall. "And how could you *possibly* want to marry *her?* Hell, you're only fifteen years older than her daughter!" It was Jasmine. I stopped. Entering the room would only make the situation worse, and I knew Dare was *more* than capable of handling it himself.

"And what's *that* supposed to prove?"

"Darryl . . . please . . . listen to me, baby . . ."

"No! *You* listen to *me!* And don't call me 'baby!' And take your hands off me, girl! Have you lost your mind?" Apparently

Jasmine had tried to attach herself to some part of Darryl's anatomy.

"Jazz, you're a great dancer, you really are. And professionally, you're an asset to the crew. But if you want to *stay* with the crew, you're going to have to make a major attitude adjustment—fast. I'm your *employer.* I tried to also be your friend, but you won't let me. You insist on trying to make our relationship into something it never was and never will be.

"Angela is the woman I love. The *only* woman I love—got that? And barring an act of God, in a few weeks she'll be my wife. And you know what? In a few weeks she'll own half of everything I have. That means she'll own half my corporation-and *that* means *she'll* be your employer, too. *In fact,* we've discussed you, and if she'd merely indicated she didn't want you around, you would have been gone *already.* She didn't object to me giving you another chance; so you've got *her* to thank you're here even now. Don't make either of us regret that! I mean it, Jazz! If you're snotty to Angela, or get in my face like this *one more time,* you're history!"

Jasmine bolted past me as she ran out of the room sobbing. She didn't say a word, but the glare she shot my way was corrosive enough for battery acid.

Jeff, the PR guy, was coming up the stairs at the end of the hallway just as Jasmine reached them. She started past him, but he grabbed her upper arm—surprisingly roughly—and said something to her. I was too far away to hear what it was. Jasmine snatched back her arm and slapped Jeff—hard—before she continued down the stairs.

Now, what do you suppose that *was all about?* I wondered. But I didn't have time to worry about it. Alex and Sam were hustling Darryl and I downstairs where the press was assembling in a small auditorium. In what seemed like no time, Darryl and I were waiting in the wings, while Jeff settled the crowd.

"Ready, Angel?" Darryl asked, putting his arm around me.

"Ready as I'm going to be, I guess." I was trembling, and he felt it.

"Baby, you don't have to do this. I can make a brief announcement on behalf of us both and cut questions to a minimum, or just not entertain questions at all."

"No, honey. We agreed this is the best way to do it. I'll be okay, just hold my hand when I get out there."

He winked at me. "You got it."

The reporters had finally quieted down. Jeff said, "And now, ladies and gentlemen of the press . . . Darryl Bridges."

Darryl kissed me on the cheek and walked out on the stage to reverberating applause. He went to the podium and adjusted the mike. "Good afternoon and thank you for coming. I've stood before you many times in the past to announce a new recording, video, or tour. Today I'm here to make the most joyful announcement of my life." He paused and the room went dead silent. He looked over into the wings at me. "I've met the most wonderful woman in the world." He turned back to the assemblage. "We've fallen in love and we're going to be married."

There was a huge rumble of surprise. Several reporters rushed from the room. Photo-flashes were going off like crazy. All over there were cries of, "Who is she? Who's the lucky lady? Is she here? Can we meet her?"

Dare laughed a bit, "Yes, she's here. I'll ask her to join me in a moment, but first, my staff is handing out informational sheets about my fianceé." I melted—as I did every time he referred to me as "my fiancée." The reporters were avidly reading the bio sheets. "We've planned the wedding for September seventh, at our home in Eventide."

He smiled over at me. I nodded. "And now . . . my beautiful bride-to-be, Angela Delaney." He held out his hand and started walking toward the wings. I took a deep breath and walked out on the stage to meet him. The glare of the camera lights was blinding. We met about mid-stage. Darryl put his arm around me and we stood for a minute or two, away from the podium, for pictures. Then he took my hand and led me back to the mike. "We'll answer questions now," he said, still holding my hand, out of sight beneath the podium.

A man shouted out, "How long have you two known each other?"

Dare answered, "About six months."

A woman asked, "Are you planning a big wedding?" Darryl looked at me, then nodded his head toward the mike.

"It'll be fairly large," I answered. "We want all our family and friends to be there. We haven't drawn up a guest list yet."

Another man probed, "Why the rush? Weddings take a lot of planning, and September seventh is less than four weeks away."

Dare took that one. "We're in love." He leaned forward to stare at the guy. "Have you ever been in love, man?" This brought a laugh.

One of the questioner's colleagues called out, *"Him? . . .* Hell, no!" which got an even bigger laugh.

"If we could arrange the kind of wedding we want more quickly," Dare was continuing, "we'd get married next week, tomorrow, today." He fixed the reporter with a stare. "There's no other reason." (In other words, "No, buddy, she's not pregnant"—everybody knew what Dare meant.)

A woman said, "Angela, your bio shows your birth date. Is it *correct?"* I nodded. "But," she continued in an incredulous tone, "that would make you four years older than Darryl."

"Yes, that's right. I am," I replied, then added in a stage whisper, "But it's okay, he already knows." That got a big laugh from them all.

"Have you signed a pre-nuptial agreement?"

"Sorry," Darryl said firmly, "but that's a personal detail we don't care to discuss publicly. Next question."

Somebody else called out, "Is the ring you're wearing from Darryl? Can we get a better look at it?"

"Yes, this is my engagement ring," I said, and held my hand out over the edge of the podium. Flashbulbs dutifully recorded every sparkle. Somebody said, "What a rock!"

"Angela, how does it feel knowing women all over the world fancy themselves in love with the man you're going to marry?"

"Well, it's going to take some getting used to, I guess, but frankly . . ." I looked over at Darryl, "I can't blame them." This got another laugh. Poor Dare. He actually blushed a little.

"Darryl," one reporter asked, "you said the wedding would be at *'our'* home in Eventide. Is your fiancée living there now?"

Darryl looked her in the eye. "As of yesterday, yes, she is. Her daughter Tiffani is there with us as well. As you see, Angela and Tiffani are from Lansing, Michigan. They lived there alone, just the two of them. I felt they'd be better protected here with me, once our engagement was announced."

A man asked, "How did you two meet, anyway?"

"We just bumped into each other," I said simply.

"It must have been one hell of a bump," the guy rejoined with a smile. That got a laugh, too.

"It was," Darryl chuckled. "I almost knocked her down—it's a wonder she didn't slug me. I called later that day to make sure she was all right."

He paused and turned serious. "As far as I'm concerned, the chain of events from then to now was inevitable. You folks don't need me to tell you how beautiful this woman is, you can see that for yourselves." He looked at me and put an arm around my waist. "But what you can't see is the loveliness of the person inside."

He looked at the reporters again. "Look, we're gonna get outta here now. Angela's not used to this kind of thing—yet. I don't want her to get spooked and change her mind before I can get her in front of a preacher! Thanks again for coming."

As we turned to walk away, several of them called out, "Kiss her! Give her a kiss for the cameras!" Darryl turned to me. I expected a kiss on the cheek, or a fast, chaste peck on the lips. I should have known my man better than that. He put both arms around me, pulled me close, and gave me a Bridges special . . . which I returned accordingly.

The distinguished ladies and gentlemen of the press reacted like a bunch of kids at a pep rally. Somebody hollered out, "Owwwwwww!" The rest were cheering, whistling, and clapping like lunatics. Dare took my hand then and led me off stage.

It had been a gratifying, but bone-breaking day. Much later that evening, Dare and I were in bed watching television. There had been a number of ten second news teasers about us all through the evening, and the late news carried a three or four minute feature segment on us. One part of it was a man-in-the-street deal, where various people were asked what they thought about our engagement. I thought one guy summed it up best: "I'm tired of hearing about them already."

Hear-hear, I thought, *so am I.*

After the news, the Tyrone Hyland Show came on, and as always, Tyrone started the show with a monologue. "Now, you *know* what I'm going to talk about tonight," he began. "The same thing everybody's been talking about all evening—Darryl Bridges's engagement!" There was a loud roar from the studio audience; mostly applause, cheers and whistles, but there were some boos, too. I didn't know if the boos were directed at Tyrone, for talking about us, or at us, for being engaged—probably some of each, I suspected.

In either case, I tensed—Tyrone was known for throwing heavy verbal punches. Darryl took my hand. "Now don't get uptight about this, honey. It's nothing personal. The man's just doing what he gets paid for." I *really* tensed then—the *last* time I'd been told something wasn't "personal" was by Dare's mother. And what she'd then said felt awfully personal to me.

But Tyrone continued, "The *first* thing I want to say to Darryl is: "Man . . . what *took* you so long?" The crowd burst out laughing. "I mean," Tyrone went on, "what were you waiting on, my brother—the Rapture?" The laughter got louder. "I mean," Tyrone persisted, "most of the *rest* of us are married—why should *you* be happy?" The laughter got still louder, with several "that's rights" thrown in. "Now let's talk about the future *Mrs*. Bridges."

The crowd quieted a bit. *Darryl* tensed this time. "Down boy—it's not personal, remember?" I said, trying to kid him out of being provoked by whatever Tyrone said about me. It didn't work. Darryl could take any amount of razzing about himself. But, like any man worth his salt, he didn't cotton to anybody making sport of his woman. I prayed Tyrone wouldn't go too far, not for my sake, for the sake of Tyrone's future health.

"Now let me say this right off. I know you've all seen clips of the press conference . . ." the audience clapped and yelled their assent. "Well, *I've* seen a tape of the whole thing, here in our news room." The crowd *really* got quiet then. "The lady's not in show business, so I've heard, but she stood up next to her man, and spoke her peace like a champ. If you think *that* doesn't take guts, *you* try it sometime. I take my hat off to her, the lady's got *balls!"*

"No, Tyrone. You're wrong there, my man," Darryl said, groping for me under the covers, as if to prove the point.

"Darryl! Stop that!" I laughed, slapping his hand away.

"My next point," Tyrone went on, "involves some of the comments I've heard about Mrs . . ." he consulted an index card, "Delaney. Comments like 'She's too old for him,' and, 'She's too fat.' Comments *mostly* from you ladies." I squinted my eyes then, in anticipation of the bomb that was coming. "All *I've* got to say is . . ." he took a "feminine" posture, "girls: your fangs are showing!" Most of the crowd howled then.

"Have you *seen* the tape? Have you *seen* that woman? *She's* not too old for *any* man! I wish I could get *my* hands on some 'too old' like that!" The men in the audience were whistling and yelling like crazy.

"And 'fat?' " Tyrone wasn't through yet. "The problem with you ladies is you listen to these freaky designers and whatnot, most of whom don't even *like* women!" Quite a few more women joined the booers on that one, but the rest were eating it up. "Well, they must not like you, seeing as how they want you to go around dressed like damn fools." He got a big hand then. "Instead of listening to them, listen to your men—your husbands and boyfriends—we'll tell you the truth. A man wants something he can hang *on* to, something he can get a good *grip* on!"

A bunch of guys in the audience called out, "Yeah!"

Tyrone went on, "Some of these models and things are so skinny, you could tie a whisk broom onto their feet, and use 'em to sweep down your front steps!" Some people in the crowd were actually crying now. "A man doesn't want to have to *search* for his woman in bed . . . 'Honey, where are you? Is that you? Oh, damn, that's the hem in the sheet! Oh, honey . . . Is *that* what you all think we want? *Hell,* no!"

Some of the audience were on their feet now, and a few men were waving their fists going "Woof! Woof!" Tyrone just blinked at them for a moment like he was wondering what they were all laughing about.

Then he said, "Look, folks, we've had a lot of fun with this, but I want get serious for just a minute." The audience quieted down a little. "I've met Darryl Bridges a couple of times, and he's one of the nicest people in show business. I just want to wish him and his fabulous lady all the happiness in the world." There was a lengthy and spirited round of applause.

"And one last thing. Take good care of her, brother Darryl, she's a hell of a woman. But if you ever get tired of her . . . *please* . . . give her my phone number!"

"You're right on that first point, brother man," Darryl answered him. "But as to the second . . ." He used one hand to click the TV off with the remote, and reached for me with the other, "Don't hold your breath!"

Thirteen

Through the Fire

I thought I knew what I was in for. I didn't. And despite Dare's vast experience in the public eye, he didn't either. Neither of us was prepared for the cascade of attention our engagement generated.

The calls started that first day. Every person I had ever known tried to call me. This included my first grade teacher, who, bless her heart, was now seventy-two, retired, and "having a ball" in Florida. My telephone in Lansing was still operative, but now the number fowarded calls to an answering service, which took messages, and passed them on to me. So many calls came in, we had to have the line disconnected. The great number of calls from people I didn't know, kept calls from people I *did* know from getting through. I tried to call all the people I wanted to be able to reach me, and hoped anyone I'd missed could reach me by contacting my family.

And that was another problem. Reporters were descending on my family like a pestilence. My Mom had no peace. She had to move in with her sister, who lived in the suburbs, until things settled down.

Darryl was right about posting a guard in my apartment. Somehow, word got out where I had lived. I don't know how—my telephone number was listed, but not my address. People began driving by the place and the security team there said the doorbell rang night and day. I couldn't understand this either, since we'd made it clear Darryl and I were in California.

Reporters constantly bugged my former neighbors, too, asking questions about me and Tiffani. I saw a clip of a group of reporters ganging up on one in the parking lot, asking him how I was as a neighbor.

"Well," he said, "she and her daughter were friendly, quiet people who minded their own business . . ." He glared at a reporter holding a mike right under his nose, and added, "A practice I highly recommend to *you*."

I called the apartment complex manager to apologize when I heard all this. "It certainly isn't your fault, Mrs. Delaney," she said. "I wouldn't have believed people could be such asses, if I wasn't seeing it with my own eyes." She asked for an autographed picture of Darryl before we hung up.

I had, of course, given my family, and my closest friends, the number at Darryl's house . . . I mean, *our* house. Calls to that number were routed to a switchboard attended twenty-four hours a day. And, of course, Darryl's family and closest friends had it. Well, apparently some of these people weren't as close as we thought, or somebody laid a bribe on the telephone company. We started getting all sorts of calls on that line, and that number had to be changed, too.

And the mail! Darryl's mail totaled several bags a week as a normal circumstance beforehand. After the press conference, it jumped to several bags a *day*. And *I* got "fan" mail! Personal mail—for me—not Darryl or both of us, but just me! I wouldn't have been surprised if I had gotten a few pieces of mail from Darryl's fans or other well-wishers, but the volume of my mail, at least at first, was almost as great as his! It came addressed as formally as "Mrs. Angela Delores Seymour Delaney (Bridges)" to as breezy as "Darryl's Fiancée, California, USA." Yes, the Postal Service delivered this one!

Most of my mail was heartwarming, like the letter I received from a lady in Little Rock, Arkansas, who was twelve years older than her husband. "We've been married thirty-one years last month," she wrote, "and every hour has been wonderful. Before our wedding, both our families, and all our friends, tried to talk us out of it. So, honey, don't you listen to blockheads who say you're too old for Darryl. What the hell do *they* know?"

Another one was: "Darryl is and always will be my favorite entertainer. He's brought me so much happiness over the years, and I'm tickled to death he's finally found someone to make *him* happy."

The vast majority of my mail, and Darryl's, was like that; people who were delighted by our engagement, and wanted to tell us so. The majority—but not all. I received another letter that read: "You bitch! Who in hell do you think *you* are, marrying Darryl? He deserves someone young, not an old biddy like you! If you really loved him, you'd step aside, and let him marry a *real* woman."

But that wasn't the worst. The worst one was: "I'll never let you marry Darryl! I'll never let you ruin his life! I know how to get to you, you gold-digging slut! I'll fix you so Darryl won't even recognize what's left of your body!"

I couldn't sleep that night. After that, Darryl refused to let me read any fan mail until it had been screened. He's always received death threats—his staff turned them over to the Postal Service for investigation, but it seldom amounted to anything. Apparently, people who were crazy enough to send hate mail *weren't* crazy enough to leave a trail. Anyway, we turned over to the authorities mail threatening me—and Tiffani. Yes, Tiffani—a threat was received directed at *her.* I didn't sleep for *two* nights after that one.

Three days after the press conference, Monroe told me I had a call from a Mrs. Delaney—a Mrs. *Iris* Delaney. I groaned; my former mother-in-law was about the *last* person in the world I wanted to talk to. I hadn't spoken to her in at least five years. It dawned on me then I should have called Iris to tell her about my engagement. After all, no matter what, she *was* Tiffani's grandmother, and should have been told how to reach her grandchild—that is, if she ever decided she *wanted* to.

I sighed and picked up the extension. "Hello, Iris? This is Angela. How are you?" I asked, determined to be civil.

"What do you mean, how am I? As if *you* cared one bit, Angela Seymour! I'm calling to see how you had the nerve to take my Bobby's only child to live on the other side of the country without even letting me know!"

This wasn't going to be easy. I took a deep breath. "Iris, you're right, I owe you an apology. I should have . . ."

"I had to call your sister to even find out how to reach you!"

"Iris, I *said* I apologize!" She was starting to get to me. I forced myself to stay composed. "And I am truly sorry, but . . ."

"Sorry? Seems to me you're always sorry about something, Angela Seymour! But not as sorry as I was the day my poor boy married you!" Now, as far as Tiffani is concerned, how dare you have that child with you while you have an affair . . ."

That's when I lost it. This woman was presuming to tell me how Tiffani and I should conduct our lives, when for the past twenty years she hadn't given a damn? *And* then to compound it by disparaging Darryl? That was the last straw.

"Iris, three things. One, my name is *not* Seymour, and it hasn't been for twenty years. My name is Delaney, the same as yours. And it will *remain* Delaney for the next three weeks. If you have to use a last name with me, use the right one.

"Two, Tiffani is not a child anymore, as you would know had you bothered to keep track of whether she was alive or dead. Where she lives is *her* choice now, not mine. She's here with my fiancé and me because she loves us—*both.*

"Three, Mr. Bridges and I will be married shortly. Maybe *then* you won't have such a hard time remembering my name!"

She hung up on me. It was no loss.

Outside of Pivot Pointe, we had no privacy whatever. We had to be accompanied by guards everywhere, and even guards couldn't protect us from the omnipresent staring and dissecting eyes. There was another kind of pressure, too. I rapidly discovered I had to look my absolute best whenever I ventured from home base. I was Darryl Bridges's fiancée. I had "hooked" the man many felt was the most eligible bachelor in the world. God forbid I should be seen with my nail polish even slightly chipped, or bags under my eyes from a sleepless night.

Later that first week, I was caught out looking less than "perfect," and the press hung me out to dry—literally. I had been on my way to meet Cassie for lunch, and gotten caught in a sudden downpour; no one had an umbrella. I wound up with half my hair plastered to my scalp, and the other half sticking straight up in a "do" any punk rocker would have been proud of. Of course, all my makeup ran, too. *This* face stared back at me from the front page of a national newspaper the next day, with the caption "Darryl's Angel Without Her Wings!" The devils. Even *I* had to admire the catchiness of the phrase! Darryl was royally pissed, and wanted to call the paper's editor, to ream him out.

"What right do they have to hound you and Tiffani?" he fumed. "*I'm* the one who makes a living on stage. I guess I'm fair game for their cheap shots. But you two shouldn't be subjected to this!"

"Darryl, this isn't about what's 'right' or 'fair.' It's about ratings, and subscriptions, and selling papers. You know that. And you also know calling that editor would only make the situation worse."

"I guess you're right," he reluctantly admitted, and then grinned. "Once again, the wisdom of age has prevailed. I knew it was a smart move to find myself a shrewd old broad to marry."

"I'll get you for that, rookie."

Darryl, of course, was the greatest target. One magazine said he didn't want to discuss our pre-nuptial agreement because it's terms would leave me penniless when—*when!*—we got divorced. Such a blatant falsehood burned me up. I thought Darryl should set the record straight, and I told him so.

He just laughed. "Honey, if you're going to get 'burned up' every time somebody puts out a lie on me, in six months you'll look like a charcoal briquette. Just forget it, Angel."

And on the subject of the name "Angel"—Darryl was the only one who had ever called me that. Up until *he* did, my nickname had been "Angie." It got out "Angel" was Dare's pet name for me, and suddenly strangers were calling me "Angel." I don't like a lot of formality, so that didn't really bother me . . . much. But what *did* was people assuming because they knew me—or more accurately, knew *of* me—that I knew them. At the other end of the spectrum were people who treated me like the Queen of Siam, and practically bowed at my feet.

"Both extremes are pretty much par for the course," Darryl told me during my ongoing lessons in "Handling Fame in the 90's." "That's one of the first things that impressed me about you; you didn't act either of those ways. Right from the first, you treated me like just another person, one you were glad to know; but still, just another person."

"Darryl, how can you say that when the first time you called I was so tongue-tied you had to ask if I was still on the line?"

"Well, naturally you were surprised. But, once you got over the initial shock of having this man with 'some small degree of prominence in the music industry' call you . . ." he gave me a wicked grin.

He'd run my own words back on me. "Ouch," I acknowledged.

"You were just friendly, not fawning. Friendly. And one of the first things you said to me was 'How are you?' "

"Well . . . so? Isn't it customary to hear something along those lines from someone you've just met?"

"Not for me it isn't. Although I do get asked all kinds of questions when I first meet people. Questions like, 'Can I have your autograph?' or 'Can you get me tickets for the concert?'; but very seldom just, 'How are you?' "

He studied my face. "You didn't know it was going to be this bad, did you, honey?"

I couldn't lie to him. "No, Darryl . . . I didn't."

"No more resale store shopping. No more going to the club on Saturday night. And no more career, at least, not the one you had. Are you sorry?" he asked very softly, as if afraid to hear my answer.

I touched his cheek. "No . . . don't you know I'd walk through fire to be with you?"

I was in my parlor one afternoon, pouring over some bridal magazines, when Tiffani came in with tears streaming down her cheeks. "Honey? Honey! What's the matter?" I cried.

"Oh, Mama . . . Darryl . . . Darryl . . ." she stammered, sitting down on the sofa next to me.

A bolt of fear flashed down my spine. "What about Darryl, baby? Is he hurt?"

"No, Mama. He . . . he just told me he wants to . . . to *adopt* me!"

"I know, dear. We discussed it right after he proposed, and decided he'd talk to you about it privately later, when he felt the time was right. But I didn't realize you'd be *upset* by it. I'd kinda hoped you'd *like* the idea. But it's your decision, hon—if you don't want . . ."

"Don't want? Oh, Mama I *do* want . . . I want it extremely much!" Not the most grammatical statement she'd ever made, but I got the point.

There was a knock at the door and Darryl peeked in. "What's going on in here? What is this, no men allowed?" He came into the room, and said, "Now, as head of this here household, I demand you womenfolk let me in on it when there's a Bridges family meeting." He looked at Tiffani. "This is a Bridges *family* meeting, isn't it?" His look became an appeal, "Or am I in the wrong place?"

Tiffani went to him. "No, you're not in the wrong place . . ." she said with her head on his shoulder.

For a house Darryl said he "rattled" around in before, the place was a virtual turnpike over the following weeks. Tiffani's new cousins came over, bringing their friends to meet her. People were coming in to prepare the house and garden for the wedding and reception. Darryl's few friends (my poor baby—it was a pitiful few) came over to meet me. And Darryl was conducting more of his business affairs—meetings, even some rehearsals—at home. "Now that I have something to stay home *for*," he told me.

During that first week, I read some fan mail and did a bit of shopping, but most of my time was spent setting things in motion for the wedding. This planning was wildly different from my first wedding; both easier and more difficult. More difficult because I had more decisions to make, and more complex ones. Easier because all I had to do was to *make* the decisions. Once I did, someone else was there to see they were carried out.

On Marcel's advice, I hired Jean Paul St. Claire, who Marcel said was the best wedding consultant in California. Darryl couldn't stand him, saying he was an "arrogant pompous ass." He *was* an arrogant pompous ass, but an arrogant pompous ass who knew his business, and was worth every penny of his astronomical fee.

No detail was too small for Jean Paul's notice or attention. A friend once told me, "You can have it fast, you can have it cheap, or you can have it right. But you can't have all three at once." Well, Jean Paul sure wasn't cheap; but fast and right? He set about arranging this major function with only mere weeks to work with, and as I quickly learned; he got things right the first time. I had but to tell him what I wanted, and he set about accomplishing it.

The following week, I was meeting with Jean Paul, discussing some aspects of the reception, when Tiffani burst into the room. Again there were tears in her eyes. *This* time, I knew right away they weren't tears of joy. She moaned, "Mama, this is the most horrible thing that's ever happened in my life! How am I going to face anybody again?"

"*What* horrible thing? What's happened? Tiff, what are you talking about?"

"Mademoiselle Delaney!" Jean Paul interjected, only he pronounced it "Dee-lawn-*nay.*" "I cannot perform with interruptions! Might it be possible for your daughter to postpone her discussion with you until we have concluded *our* conversation?" he demanded, rolling his eyes at Tiffani.

"No," I brushed him off. I turned to Tiff, "Honey, calm down and tell me what's the matter."

"This! *This* is the matter! Read this. Just read this!" Tiffani wailed, waving a newspaper around frantically.

"Tiff, I can't even *see* it, let alone *read* it, with you flapping it around like that! Calm down!"

I took a step toward her, but Jean Paul stepped in front of me. "Really! Mademoiselle, I *must* insist! We cannot be intruded upon by such adolescent histrionics! Do you not realize the wedding is less than three weeks away?"

Usually I could put up with, was even amused by, Jean Paul's self-important manner, but his timing was off *this* time. "Yes, Jean Paul, I know *exactly* when the wedding is! I'm the *bride,* remember? And stop calling me 'Mademoiselle'—I'm a 'Mrs.,' so it should be 'Madame.' Even I know that. Now sit down and shut up. My daughter has an emergency!"

Jean Paul sat down and shut up. I managed to wrest the paper away from Tiffani. The headline was, "I'll Slap His Face If He Hurts My Mother!" with the caption "Trouble in Paradise—Darryl Bridges's Step-Daughter's True Story."

Somebody had stolen Tiffani's diary, and that sleazy rag had gotten hold of it. The headline came from a section of the diary that read: "I don't care *who* he is! If he hurts my mother, I'll go to one of his concerts, find a way to jump up on stage, and slap his face!" The "newspaper" neglected to mention this entry was written the day I left to go to California that first time, weeks before Tiffani had actually *met* him. But they did manage to pick up from a later entry that Darryl was going to legally adopt Tiffani right after the wedding, a fact we weren't planning to make public until it happened.

It was all I could do to restrain Tiffani until Darryl, who had been at the studio, got home. And then it was *more* than I could do to restrain *him!* I'd seen Darryl angry before. Like most laid-back and even tempered people, it took a lot to get him mad. But once he was—look out! Even *I* was not prepared for his reaction to this latest journalistic outrage. The man was livid. I understood why he was so furious; this affront had involved Tiffani. He wouldn't have reacted half so powerfully if the attack had been directed only at himself.

"Those damn sons-of-bitches! Why won't they leave us alone! And who in hell gave them the diary in the first place?" I'd never heard Darryl talk like that before. Alex, Sam, and Jeff had come home with him. He turned to Alex. "Alex, you get the whole legal team on this right away. I'm gonna sue those bastards for every cent they do or ever will have!"

"Now, Darryl . . ." I began, but he ignored me.

"And Sam, what the hell kind of security operation are *you* running, when somebody can just come in this house, and steal something like a diary! I want to know who did it, and I want to know *yesterday.* Do I make myself understood?!"

I tried again. "Darryl . . ."

"Angela—what the hell *is* it?" he yelled at me.

That was the first time Darryl had ever raised his voice to me. I just stood there a second, then said quietly, "I'm sorry. I'll leave," and turned to walk away.

"No!" He came to me and took me in his arms. "Oh, baby. I'm sorry. I'm mad at those damn fools, and here I am acting a *bigger* damn fool, taking it out on you! Forgive me, sweetheart." I hadn't really been planning to leave, but I hoped if Darryl *thought* I was, it would bring him to his senses. It worked.

He looked at Sam. "I owe you an apology, too, man. I'm sorry."

"De nada, man" Sam said. "You wouldn't be human if you didn't lose it over something like this."

"Look, you guys, excuse us a few minutes, okay?" Darryl asked.

After they left, the three of us discussed the problem. "Darryl, are you mad at me?" Tiffani asked. "You know I'd never say anything like that now. I didn't know you when I wrote that."

"I know, honey. I know," Darryl said hugging her. "I'm just sorry this had to happen to you." The column had printed a lot of other information from the diary; entries about Tiffani's girlfriends and boys she'd dated. It was harmless stuff, but they were Tiffani's most private thoughts, and she was embarrassed—who wouldn't be? I'd forced myself to keep cool when I saw how enraged Darryl was—*both* of us on a rampage wouldn't do—but it wasn't easy. I was seething, too, and could have gladly strangled the person responsible.

Once everyone calmed down, we convinced Darryl not to file the lawsuit. He called the other men back into the room, "Alex, forget about calling the legal eagles," Dare told him. "But Jeff, I want a press release prepared right away saying how this whole unscrupulous episode has upset Tiffani, and how angry Angela and I are about it."

"Do . . . do you really think that's a good idea, man?" Jeff said nervously.

"A good idea? What do you mean?"

"Well . . . ah . . . you might be leaving yourself open to a lawsuit if you start claiming they . . ."

"Them sue *me?* Are you joking? They broke the law just being in possession of that diary, let alone printing it! They don't have one legal leg to stand on. What's gotten into *you?* Usually I'm the one holding *you* back from a confrontation with the press, not vice versa. No, I want that item released—*today,* my man."

There's an old saying: "What goes around, comes around." The weekly that printed Tiff's diary found out the truth of it in short order. There are a lot of teenage girls in this country, and a lot of parents, grandparents, sisters, brothers, aunts, uncles, cousins, and boyfriends who care about them. A large portion of this vast group pictured themselves or the girl they loved in the situation the weekly subjected Tiffani to—and they didn't like it. They flooded the paper with letters and telegrams and phone calls telling them so. A lot of subscriptions were canceled. And the authorities wanted to talk to the weekly's management, since the story was based on stolen property.

But Tiffani was still upset. I found her crying in her room one night, "I can't stand this, Mama! People watching me everywhere I go, having guards around all the time, people prying into every little thing I do! I can't live this way! I love you, and I love Dare, too—but after the wedding I'm going back to Michigan! I'll go to State, and live in the dormitory."

There was no going back. She was, all but officially, a world famous multi-millionaire's daughter now. But I knew it wouldn't do any good to reason with her then. To explain the life she was talking about was forever out of her grasp. So I just asked her to wait until Dare and I returned from our honeymoon, for the three of us to discuss it, and she agreed.

But that *still* wasn't the end of it. A few days later, Jeff called to tell us about an article in a Detroit paper. "Iris Delaney is suing Darryl Bridges, and his fiancée; her former daughter-in-law, Angela Delaney. The suit was generated by a rumor Bridges is planning to legally adopt Angela Delaney's daughter, Tiffani, who was born during Angela's marriage to Iris's son, the late Robert Bristol Delaney. Mr. Delaney died in a tragic automobile accident when Tiffani was less than two years old, and the suit is to block her adoption by Bridges. 'That child is all I have left of my son; all that's left to show he even existed,' said a tearful Mrs. Delaney senior. 'Darryl Bridges's money has bought Angela, but I'll never let him buy my son's child.' "

The fireworks I launched made Darryl's look like the minor leagues. Darryl just barely kept me from flying to Detroit to confront that spiteful biddy! He and Tiffani finally got me to listen to reason, making me see that of course her suit was ridiculous, and had no hope of succeeding. She was just trying to get my goat, and probably also get any of Mr. Bridges's aforementioned money she could lay her hands on. Darryl said he'd send one of his attorneys—and Alex—out to talk to her.

The following day, Darryl and I were on our way to his attorneys' for another reason. Our marriage created a host of legal details that had to be addressed: wills, bank accounts, deeds, stock options, credit cards. The list went on and on.

"Babe, I want you to have a good handle on our financial status. I'm no fool. I've got myself an astute businesswoman here. I'm not going to let all that expertise go to waste. It's real convenient when you sleep with your most trusted advisor every night."

The attorneys also needed signatures from me to settle my affairs: breaking the lease on my apartment; transferring title of the cars to my mother and Marlowe; closing my bank accounts.

"Darryl," I said while we were en route, "I've never asked you—and you know it doesn't matter one whit to me—but so I don't appear *totally* ignorant when we start the meeting . . . how much money *do* you have, anyway?"

He laughed and said, "Well, counselor, it fluctuates due to changes in property values, stock prices, and whatnot, but as a ballpark figure *we* have . . ." and he told me.

Several seconds passed before I gulped, "You're kidding."

He shook his head, "Nope." After several more seconds, he added, "Uh . . . close your mouth, dear."

We were at the attorneys' for about three hours, and were finally preparing to leave when Sam came in and pulled Darryl aside. Darryl looked exasperated as he listened. Then he turned to me, "Honey . . . we've got a problem."

"What Darryl? Is it Tiffani?"

"No, darling, no. Not that serious a problem. Somehow word got out we're here, and there's a crowd downstairs."

We'd been so careful in planning this trip. No one knew but Darryl's top people, and we'd tried to mask our identities by both wearing hats and dark glasses. "Word got out? How?" I asked.

"Don't know, baby," he shrugged. "The phantom strikes again." He turned to Sam. "This crap is starting to get out of hand. I think we're going to have to run another security check on everybody. We'll talk about it later." Dare turned back to me. "Anyway, it'll be all right, the building security people will help our guys get us to the car, and we'll be outta here."

I wasn't prepared for how big the crowd was. There must have been three hundred people outside. Cortez (I'm sure illegally) had pulled the limo up over the curb, onto the sidewalk. It was sitting some ten or twelve feet from the building exit. We'd brought Sam, Alex, Cortez, and another guy with us, and building security provided us with another four men—Darryl owned the building.

"Piece of cake, honey," Darryl said. "Just stay right beside me, and follow that guy in the hat," he pointed to one of the "borrowed" guards.

The minute we set foot out the door, the crowd started screaming and yelling. "Angel! Angel, Hi!" some of them cried. I waved, and they cheered. Women were blowing kisses to Darryl, and everybody seemed to be hollering, "Congratulations!"

As we walked along, I caught a flash of something bright in the crowd, at waist height. I looked up into a face that defined madness incarnate. She lunged forward abruptly, roughly pushing aside the few people in front of her. Her eyes were blazing with a hatred that could only have been born of insanity. "You whore!" she screamed. "I'll *kill* you before I let you take him away from me!"

She raised her arm. I had forgotten about the flash—her gaze had distracted me from all else. But now I saw she was holding a long, thin knife. She rushed forward, closing the few feet between us to inches. As she raised her arm, I tried to step to the side, but bumped into someone standing next to me. Then, in one split second, I went from staring into her deranged eyes, to looking at Darryl's back. My upraised hands brushed his shoulder blades as he stepped in front of me.

And then slowly, so slowly, he was falling. As he fell, the eyes of the people he had blocked from my sight came in view, wide with horror and disbelief. She dropped the knife, the tip now covered with Darryl's blood, and started to scream, "No! Oh, no! Her! Not you! Never you, darling!" Darryl fell on his back, his eyes closed, his right arm flung backward, toward me. A bright red stain bloomed on his shirt, and began to spread.

I felt air rush into my lungs as I gathered in one long, tremendous breath. It was as if I couldn't take in enough oxygen, as if I never wanted to take the next breath and let time move on. But finally, the gasp surged out as I screamed Darryl's name. The force of the scream hurt my throat.

I tried to fall forward, to drop to my knees at Darryl's side, but something held me erect. I felt confined. I looked over my shoulder. Alex was behind me, his arms around my waist. I began to struggle, "Alex! What are you doing?! Let me go! I have to get to Darryl! Let me go!"

"No, Angela," he said, pulling me backward with him. "I have to get you out of here!"

"Are you crazy? Can't you see? Darryl's hurt! He may even be dying!" When that thought registered, the world grew suddenly darker. Words I'd spoken to Tiffani in New York flashed though my mind: "Darryl would die before he'd let anything happen to me." My fight to be released increased ten-fold. "Let me go, Alex! I have to get to him! I have to *help* him! Let me go, damn you!"

Alex continued to pull me backward, away from where Darryl lay. The crowd closed around Dare and obscured him from my view. "Angela," Alex panted, "Sam and Cortez and the others are out there. They'll never leave without Dare. They can help him now a lot more than you can! And the best thing I can do for Dare right now is protect *you!*"

We finally arrived at the limo. One of the building security men guarding it opened the back door and Alex pulled me inside with him. He practically sat me in his lap to restrain me as I continued to struggle. After what seemed an eternity, the door opened again, and Sam and another man thrust Darryl inside. The front and one sleeve of his shirt were soaked in blood, and his eyes were still closed.

They gently laid him on the seat across from us. I dropped to my knees in the seat well in front of him, softly calling his name over and over. Sam and the other man got in, sitting on the seat behind me with Alex. Cortez got behind the wheel, and the other guard jumped in the front on the passenger side. The car shot off into traffic as Cortez gunned the engine, blowing the horn to alert other motorists this was an emergency.

"This guy's a doctor," Sam said of the stranger.

"Melvin Neal," the doctor said. He was wearing a tee shirt and jeans, and looked about twenty, but I was hardly going to question his credentials.

"Dr. Neal," I whispered, wanting to ask the question, but unbearably terrified of the answer. I made myself choke out, "Doctor, is he . . . is he . . ."

"No . . . no, Angela. He's alive, and I don't think he's gravely wounded. But he's losing a lot of blood. We need to get him to a hospital as soon as possible."

"Mt. Olive is only about ten blocks from here. We'll be there in no time flat!" Cortez called out. The other guard was on the phone with the hospital.

Darryl stirred and his eyes fluttered open. He examined me. "Angel?" he said faintly. "Are you all right? Were you hurt, honey?"

"No, darling, I'm okay, but don't talk now. We're taking you to a hospital. We have a doctor here with us and he says you'll be fine. Just lie still, sweetheart."

He raised his hand weakly and touched my cheek, "Don't worry, baby; I'll be all right."

At the hospital, a doctor and two orderlies with a gurney met us at the emergency room bay. There were crowds all around. The emergency room staff was trying in vain to clear the area. They wheeled Darryl into an examination room.

When I tried to follow, a nurse blocked my path. "We can take care of you in room two," she directed.

"I'm not injured," I told her, trying to go past.

"Are you sure?" she insisted, stepping in front of me, staring at my chest. I looked down. The front of my dress was heavily spotted with blood. I felt moisture on my face. I touched my cheek, and there was blood there, too, probably from when Darryl touched me.

"Yes . . . yes . . . I'm sure. I wasn't hurt. Please let me by!"

"You can't go in there now—the doctors are with him!"

"I don't give a damn *who's* with him!" I again tried to maneuver by, but she pushed me back.

"I *said* you can't go in there now! It's against hospital policy . . . and that policy was devised to keep hysterical women—like you—from fluttering around in the doctors' way!"

I stopped and looked her dead in the eye. "I'm not hysterical. I'm angry and frightened out of my mind, but I'm *not* hysterical. Now look—that's my man in there. I know him—you don't. And I know he needs to know *I'm* there." I pointed my finger an inch from her nose. "So you and your hospital policy better get out of my way or I'll *move* you out of my way!" I shoved her with my shoulder and went past. This time she didn't try to stop me.

The doctors looked up when I entered the room, but they were too busy to worry about me. They'd cut off Darryl's shirt, and were washing the wound to examine the injury.

"There's an artery nicked!" one of them yelled. "Get an operating room ready, stat!" I stood silently by while they clamped the artery and prepped Dare for surgery. One of them approached me, "Mrs. Delaney, we don't think Mr. Bridges's injuries are critical," she said, "but we need to go in and repair the artery. And he needs a transfusion. He's lost a lot of blood."

"I'll be the donor."

"It's not that simple. The blood types have to be . . ."

"I'm type O, RH negative," I cut her off.

The doctor didn't object further. My blood type made me what's known as a "universal donor." "I know if he has to have blood, he'd want me as the source." I told her Darryl and I had just taken blood tests for our marriage license the week before and gave her the name of our doctor.

She looked at me for a moment, then said to her nurse, "Get Myron Phillips's office on the line—now!"

I felt dizzy and my mouth was dry. An affectionate voice was calling, "Angela? Angela, honey, can you hear me?"

"Mama?" I croaked.

"Yes, dear, I'm here. Open your eyes, honey."

I did, and saw not *my* mother—but Darryl's. But if Sylvia was here! Darryl! . . . I struggled to sit up, but was too groggy.

"Just lie still, dear. You gave a lot of blood and they gave you a sedative, to help calm you."

"But, Darryl . . ."

"He's right here, Angela, look," she gestured to the side. Darryl was asleep in a bed right next to mine. Except for a large bandage on his shoulder, he looked like he always did—wonderful.

"Is he all right?" I asked anxiously.

"He's fine. They just brought him in from the recovery room. He's still sleeping off the anesthesia, that's all. The artery repair went smoothly. The doctors say there was no other significant damage. He should be back up and about in a few days." She smiled, "You won't even have to postpone the wedding." I stared when I realized the relevance of those words coming from her.

"They told me how you acted after the attack and here at the hospital. My son needs a wife who'll stand by him, who'll fight for him if she has to—a wife who loves him." She stroked my hair. "I'm glad he's found one," she added softly.

I smiled back . . . then remembered, "But Tiffani! My family . . ."

"Tiffani's right outside. She was out with Tameka, Barbara's oldest, when this happened. The two of them came directly to my house. I called your mother myself, to let her know you and Darryl were all right. It's a good thing I did, too. The poor woman was beside herself. The initial news reports said you had *both* been stabbed."

Suddenly, Darryl shifted, and said sluggishly, "Angela . . . Mama?"

Sylvia went over to him and had to tell *him* to look over where *I* was, before she could tell him anything else. He was determined to get up to find me. Then she left, saying, with a smile, "I'll send Tiffani in . . . in a few minutes."

Darryl looked at me and started to get up, "Oh, no!" I asserted. "Don't think you're getting out of marrying me in eleven days by falling out of bed on your keister!" I was still shaky, but better than when I'd first woke up, so I crept the few steps over to his bed and lay down next to him. Then I lay my head on his uninjured shoulder, and cried.

"What's wrong with you, crazy woman?" Dare asked in astonishment. "I came to while they were wheeling me up to surgery, and asked about you. The doctors said you were a tower of strength, and half the nurses in the ER were scared of you. And now you're wimping out on me?"

"Darryl, you could have been killed!" I sobbed.

"You could have, too, my love." He kissed my forehead, "I'd have rather died . . . than live without you."

"Oh, honey, if you had . . . if anything had . . ."

"Well, nothing did—but I sure wouldn't mind something happening to me now," he said, reprising this infamous statement from his Chicago solo mission. He tried to put his other arm around me, but groaned in the attempt. "Well, I guess we'll have to wait a couple of days for the more strenuous calisthenics, but you *could* kiss *me,* lady."

"The least I can do for the man who saved my life."

Just as we were really starting to perfect that kiss, the door opened. Then I heard Sam say, "Hell, there's nothing wrong with them! They're at it again already!" In came Tiffani, Alex, and Sam, followed by Sylvia. Tiffani hugged and kissed us both, then followed her mother's sterling example by bursting into tears.

Alex put his arm around her, but seemed awfully stiff. And his face was scratched up. Darryl noticed it, too, and asked, "Hey, man, what happened to *you?* Did a riot break out?"

"No. A *riot* I can handle. Your blushing bride is what happened to me, man." Alex rolled his eyes. "Darryl, are you sure you want to marry this Tasmanian she-devil? If you ever get her ticked, my advice to *you,* my brother, is—duck!"

Later, Dare was asleep, his pain medication made him drowsy. We'd had Sam and Alex push our beds together. I was in my bed reading, when Sam came back. "Dare asleep?" he whispered.

"Yes, Sam." Then I saw his face, "What is it?"

"Something he really needs to know about, Angela."

"From the look on your face, I gather the 'something' is not good news."

"No, Angie, it sure ain't."

"Well, I'll not have him disturbed right now for any reason, especially not bad news. He needs his rest a lot more than he needs more problems heaped on his already wounded shoulders. Whatever it is, you and I will just have to deal with it the best we can, for now."

Sam looked at me thoughtfully for a moment, then said, "Okay, Angie. Can you step down the hall?"

I put on my robe and slippers, and went with him, pressing him to tell me what was wrong. He would only say, "You've got to hear this for yourself." He took me down the hall to a small, enclosed waiting room with a glass door. Inside were Alex, Jeff, Cortez, and Dare's parents. They were looking somberly at a woman seated at a table. Her head was down on her arms, and even though I couldn't hear through the glass, it was obvious from the heaving of her shoulders she was crying. As

I entered the room she looked up, and I could then see it was . . . Jasmine!

Even through her tears, her face hardened when she saw me. When nobody spoke, I said, "Well, is anybody going to tell me what this is all about?"

"I think Jasmine has something to tell you, Angela," Sam replied, with a look to Jasmine that said, "Jasmine *better* have something to tell you!"

"No, I don't!" Jasmine spit out. "I don't have *anything* to say to *her!* This whole thing is *her* fault, not mine!" She looked at Sam accusingly. "You said you were going to talk to *Dare!"*

"Dare's a little under the weather just now, as you may have heard," Sam said sarcastically. He put both his hands down on the table and leaned toward Jasmine menacingly. "I think you'd better talk to Angela, while you've got the chance. My patience is running real thin right now, Jazz. Don't push me."

Jasmine looked sullenly at me. "Everything was fine until *you* came along, and then . . ."

I was tired. It had been a long, harrowing day. I was exhausted and weak, and I wanted to go back and see to Dare. "Look, Jasmine, I've already seen your dog and pony show, okay? And I already know you think Darryl is making the mistake of his life marrying me instead of you. And I also know Darryl's told you in no uncertain terms how *he* feels on that score. I don't give a flying fig what *you* think. So let's cut to the chase, shall we?"

Before Jasmine could give me more lip, Sam leaned farther across the table and glared at her. I didn't think Sam would hit a woman, but evil as he looked at that moment, *I* wouldn't have taken the chance. Jasmine apparently agreed with that assessment. She looked down at her hands and murmured in a defeated tone, "I'm the one who's been putting the information out about you and Darryl."

"I beg your pardon?" I asked incredulously.

Her head snapped up, defiant again, "You heard me, bitch!"

The men surged forward. I guess thinking my reaction might

have been a slap. But I wasn't going to lower myself—although the thought *did* cross my mind. I held up a hand to tell the guys it was all right and looked sharply at her. *"You're* the one who sent my address to Chet Mitchell a month or so ago?" I cross-examined her bluntly.

"You got it," she replied flippantly.

"And *you* stole Tiffani's diary?"

"Yep—little brat left it in the music room one day Dare had rehearsal at the house."

I let that one pass—for now. "And you put the word out Darryl and I were at his attorney's today?"

Her cockiness disappeared, "Yes . . . yes . . . I did . . ." she started to cry again. "But I didn't want anything to *happen* to Darryl! I thought I'd die when I heard . . ."

" 'Die' is exactly what *he* could have done. And me too, for that matter, though I imagine *that* wouldn't cause *you* much grief. But let me ask an analytical question here, Why? Why did you do it?"

"You're not good enough for Dare," she spat out bitterly. "*You* could never make him happy. When I found out he went to . . . *Michigan,*" she said "Michigan" as though it was the Black Hole of Calcutta, "to see *you,* I realized he was serious about you, and I knew I had to bring him to his senses. I had to force it out in the open so he'd see that nobody could accept *you* as his woman; make him see how wrong you were for him, so he'd forget about you!"

This time *I* leaned forward on the table and looked her dead in the eye. "Didn't work, though . . . did it?" Her face turned dark, but I went on. "All you did was almost get the man you profess to love killed. You don't really *love* Darryl, anyway. You don't even *know* him—and you're not capable of *understanding* him." I straightened, then said, "All right, let's have the rest of it—who helped you?"

"What?"

"I said who helped you? Have you gone deaf now? You know what I'm talking about. Dare told me there was no way you had access to that information. Somebody had to have given it to you, and I want to know who!"

Jasmine sat looking insolently at me and didn't say a word. Then Sam said softly, "You can talk to us . . . or you can talk to the police—your choice, darlin'."

Jasmine turned then, looking to the side where Alex, Jeff and Cortez were standing. "Well, lover, I tried . . ." she said brazenly, "but surely you don't think I'm going to sit here and take the rap all by myself?"

I looked at Cortez in amazement, but it was Jeff who turned pale and shouted," Shut up! Shut up!" He looked at me, "She's lying! Don't believe her! I didn't have anything to do with this!"

"I didn't hear her say you did," Q.T. said quietly. "She didn't give a name, son."

Sam got the truth out of Jeff in short order. Seems Jeff had the hots for Jasmine. She knew it—and used it. She gave him just enough of what he was hot for to get him to give her Darryl's phone records and personal address book. The photo Chet received *had* originally come from a fan—one who mailed it to Darryl, asking that he autograph it. After that first time, Jasmine blackmailed Jeff, telling him she'd blow the whistle on them *both,* if he didn't do what she said.

Sam and Alex had things under control, and I was truly done in then, so Q.T. saw me back to the room. Darryl was awake. "Hey, where you been?" he said, blinking at me woozily. "I thought you'd run off with the mailman."

"Not a chance. He's not my type—he's got big feet."

Q.T. told us both goodnight, and that he'd see us the next day. After he left, Darryl asked me, "What's going on, honey? Who were you talking to? Is something wrong?"

"It was nothing, sweetheart. Nothing worth a second thought. I'll tell you about it tomorrow, baby. But for now, go back to sleep."

Fourteen

Going to the Chapel

Mrs. Lillian Seymour
requests the pleasure of your company
at the wedding of her daughter
Angela Delores Seymour Delaney
and
Mr. Darryl Douglass Bridges
at four o'clock in the afternoon
Saturday, September 7
at
Pivot Pointe Estate
Eventide, California

R.S.V.P.

The bride and groom respectfully request you wear white, black, or red.

The invitations were engraved in black ink on heavy, pure white stock with a raised double border of black. The border enclosed an inner border of embossed red roses. The printer had been obliged to work around the clock to get them to us within a week after we announced the engagement. We wanted them in the mail three weeks before the wedding, since so many people were coming from a distance. I had people coming from Detroit, Lansing, Chicago, New Orleans, Atlanta, and Toronto. And my nephew, who was in the Air Force, was flying in from Germany. Needless to say, Darryl had people coming from all over the globe.

Darryl and I decided we wouldn't invite anyone with strictly a business connection. This applied much more to Darryl than to me, especially now, since for the first time in twenty years, I was unemployed.

An invitation to our wedding rapidly became the most sought after one of the season. But we stuck to our guns and only invited people we felt sincerely cared about us and rejoiced with us in our happiness. There was, however, one "wild-card" we hadn't considered. A number of the people we invited were single, and, as is customary, those invitations were addressed to Mr. Single and companion, or Ms. Single and escort. These single folk quickly became some of the most popular people around.

The doctors said I could go home, but they wanted Darryl to stay at least overnight, for observation. I flat-out refused to leave without him, so they *had* to let me stay the night, too. Tiffani spent the night with Sylvia and Q.T., along with several of the cousins, who rallied around her.

Dare was indeed able to go home the next day. We had just finished dressing and were waiting for the doctor to formally discharge him, when Alex peeped in the door, motioning for me. "What's up, honey?" Dare asked as I left the room.

"Oh, I asked him to bring something for me," I said over my shoulder. "Be right back."

When I returned a minute later, Dare took one look at the bouquet I was carrying and called out, "Hey! Who are those from? Nobody gets to give you red roses but *me,* baby."

"They're not *for* me, they're *from* me . . ." I kissed him as I handed him the flowers, "to you."

When we went out—Dare with his arm in a sling—there

was a crowd lining both sides of the street. The minute they saw him, they burst out in applause and a tremendous cheer. Dare was being pushed in a wheelchair. He had the bouquet of roses on his lap. I was walking along side, holding his hand. A picture of this scene later made the cover of several magazines. Dare, always gracious, let go of my hand long enough to take the roses and wave them to the crowd, which went wild. The limo was parked right by the exit. Sam helped Dare into the car, while Alex held the door on the other side for me.

We got Dare home, took him straight upstairs, and put him to bed. The doctors had only agreed to discharge him so quickly on the promise he'd spend at least the next two days in bed. I knew Mr. Bridges; left to his own devices, he'd do anything but rest, so I stood guard. After we gave him his pain medication, he started to get sleepy, so I kicked all the relatives and friends, who'd come to welcome him home, out of the room. I sat on the bed next to him, singing softly and stroking his hair, as he fell asleep. I thanked God for not taking either of us away from the other.

About twenty minutes later, Monroe came knocking softly on the door—the police were on the line. I went down to Dare's office to talk to them. It was a Detective Hurd of the LAPD. He wanted to come out to discuss the stabbing. I told him Darryl was sleeping, and asked if it was possible to delay any interrogation with him until the next day.

"*I'm* available today, detective, but I'd like Darryl to spend the entire day resting, if at all possible."

"There's no rush, Mrs. Delaney. It looks as though we're not going to press charges against the person who did it, anyway."

"What? What do you mean, not press charges? Why on earth not? She couldn't have gotten away. I heard several people in the crowd grabbed her and held her until a patrol car arrived."

"That's right, but since then . . . well, the lady, quite obviously, had a major head problem before the attack, and now . . ." He went on to tell me what the police had discovered so far.

Her name was Sarah Davis. She was a working mother of two. Her husband was, understandably, in a state of shock. When the police called him, he had refused to believe it was his wife they were holding until he went down to the station and saw her for himself.

He said Sarah had always been a huge Darryl Bridges fan, since before he met her. The husband's name was Darrin, and he said Sarah insisted on calling him "Dare." They'd treated it as kind of a joke. He'd teased her from time to time, telling her "you should have married that other guy, since you're so nuts about him."

Darrin Davis gave the police permission to search their house. The cops found nothing unusual, until they got to the basement. There was a small closed room Darrin said had been a coal bin, before a gas furnace was installed. He said the door to the room had been stuck since they bought the house. The cops found the door was not stuck, but locked. They forced it open. The room was very small, about seven feet square, but every surface, including the floor and ceiling, was covered with pictures of Darryl. Except for one small corner, where the pictures were not of Darryl, but of me—every one of them slashed or otherwise defaced.

A shiver ran down my spine. "I understand the question here, of her sanity, detective, but won't some sort of court action be necessary for that to be legally determined, to commit her to an institution?"

"She's already in one, and from the looks of things, she may well be there the rest of her life. After the attack, she struggled with the people holding her, trying to get to Mr. Bridges. From what her captors told us, she kept saying things like, 'You know I'd never hurt you,' and 'Forgive me, sweetheart.'

"Then someone in the crowd called out, 'Oh, my God! He's dead!' She stopped fighting then, and went into a state of complete catatonia—she hasn't moved a muscle or said a word since. Our staff psychologist suspects the guilt of thinking she's killed the man she 'loves' is more than her mind can take. She's completely withdrawn from reality, and there's no telling when—or if—she'll ever come back."

The last thing he told me really filled me with horror. A tourist in the crowd had a video camera, and had taped the whole thing, which was shown on TV. From the angle of the knife, and the position of my body, there was virtually no doubt: I would have been killed had Darryl not intervened. The knife had been aimed right at my heart. Darryl had truly, in point of fact, saved my life. The tape showed that just before the knife reached him, Darryl grabbed Sarah's wrist, so that only the tip, rather than the entire shaft of the knife, penetrated his skin.

Detective Hurd said he'd be out to talk to us personally in the next day or two. "The regs require it, and anyhow, I wouldn't miss this chance to meet you two for the world!"

Sylvia and Q.T. were still there, having come to bring Tiff home and make sure Darryl and I were all right. I told them what the Detective said. "Yes, we know, Angela," Q.T. told me quietly. "Most of that has been all over the news last night and today."

I hadn't watched TV or read a paper since the attack. I had no idea the magnitude of response from people everywhere. The interest in our engagement and marriage had been phenomenal before—now it was mind-boggling. One of the major networks had scheduled a ninety minute prime time special about Darryl and me; our engagement, the attack, and our effect on the public. I could understand how the "Cinderella" aspects of our meeting and falling in love could touch a person's romantic side. Now, since "Prince Charming" had risked his own life to save that of his fair lady, it seemed we'd become an international obsession.

I went upstairs to check on Darryl. He was awake and hungry. Monroe brought up lunch and after we finished eating, I told him about Jasmine and Jeff.

"I don't believe it! Jazz; yes, I can believe that of *her*. But eff? He's been with me over five years! What could have possessed him to *do* such a thing?"

" 'Possessed' is an accurate term for what happened to Jeff. t refers to having one's body seized by a demon, does it not? eff had his body seized by Jasmine, and if that doesn't fit the lefinition, I don't know what does!"

Darryl started laughing. "Now, Angie, that's not nice, baby!"

"Maybe not, but it's nonetheless factual."

"Well, I'm glad they've been uncovered. I was losing sleep rying to figure who it could be and wondering when they'd trike next. But now I've got a dancer *and* a public relations chief to replace.

"I'd already started scouting for a dancer. You missed it, but asmine really cut up the day we told the crew we were engaged. I knew she wouldn't straighten up. And I also knew my new wife wouldn't appreciate one of my employees draping herself around my neck at every opportunity. Jazz's days were numbered, anyway.

"But Jeff! That's the shocker! And what a time to be without a PR man! He's going to be much harder to replace. I need someone who knows the ropes, has contacts, is a fabulous writer, and most of all, is someone I can trust. And with the media breathing down our necks 24-7, I need him quick, fast, and in a hurry! Where am I going to find somebody like that?"

He stopped cold and looked at me. I looked at him.

"Are you thinking what *I'm* thinking?" he asked.

"I think so."

"Think he'll do it?"

I handed him the phone. "Only one way to find out."

Chet jumped at the chance, quitting his job at the paper that very day. By evening, the paperwork was all completed and he was officially on Dare's payroll.

And not a moment too soon. The get well telegrams, letters, and flowers, in addition to the mail we were already getting before the attack, were more than even Dare's large staff could handle. Chet prepared a press release from Darryl and me explaining this. It thanked the public for their kindness, but requesting well-wishers make contributions to Homes, USA, instead. Then Chet went down to talk to the network airing the special. He tried to get them to cancel it altogether, no dice there, but he *did* get them to cut it back to an hour and to minimize coverage of the attack.

Another network offered us ten million dollars to broadcast the wedding. We, of course, told them no. They came back and offered twenty million to tape the wedding, to be shown at some later date. We politely told them no—again.

Sam told us he expected all hell to break loose after the stabbing, but he was wrong. He never saw a crowd act more responsibly at the scene of a crisis. A Marine sergeant stepped out of the crowd and ordered everybody back, so Dare could get air. The Marine then enlisted ten or twelve of the burliest bystanders, and had them join hands and form a circle around Dare, to hold back the crowd. Dr. Neal stepped forward then, and after he swiftly examined Darryl, asked if anyone had something he could use as a compress to slow the bleeding. Several people started peeling off shirts, but a woman stepped forth with a department store bag full of towels. She said she'd just bought them, and handed the entire bag to Sam.

If we could, we'd have personally thanked everyone who was in the crowd that day, but that was impossible. We were, however, able to trace down the Marine sergeant (Sam remembered his name-tag), and the towel lady (from her credit card receipt, in the bag). Both Sergeant Wjotowitz and Mrs. Wright refused the monetary reward we discreetly offered; but eagerly accepted an invitation to the wedding. We invited young Dr. Neal as well, and, unknown to him, paid off his sizable student loan from med school. "After all," Dare said, "it's merely payment for professional services rendered."

By the time Mama, Celeste, and Marlowe arrived, a week before the wedding, Dare was up and about. He was still wearing the sling, but only because he was taking no chance of retarding his recovery. He was determined to not wear it at the wedding, "and I don't want anything in my way on the wedding *night* either!" he told me.

The days flew by then, and suddenly, it was the day before the wedding. As large as Pivot Pointe is, with its twelve bedrooms, it wasn't nearly big enough for the out-of-towners. We were able to put up my mother, Dare's parents, Celeste and Tony, Ida and Roy, Cassie and her husband, Barbara and her husband, Bev, and Reverend and Mrs. Matthews.

Except for the parents, all of these folks were members of the wedding party. Celeste, Cassie, Bev, and, of course Tiffani, were bridesmaids. Roy was giving me away. Mate was the flower girl. Dougie was the ring-bearer (and we needed his Mama there, to keep him happy). Sam was Dare's best man, and Alex, Tony, Larry, and Dare's good friend, Jason Papadapolous, an L.A. screen writer, were ushers.

Getting everyone *to* the wedding was a major exercise in logistics. We had one of the best on our side. I finally got to meet Anita Giles, and she became our general for the massive influx of guests. In several cities with a large number of guests, like Detroit, we just chartered a flight. Anita was also able to cut a deal with the Beverly Hills Regal, and several other hotels, due to the large number of rooms we were reserving.

Since so many participants weren't coming out until the day before the wedding, we held the wedding rehearsal that day. It's considered bad luck for a bride to rehearse her own wedding, so "Charlene" stood in for me, giggling and making eyes at Alex the whole time.

After the rehearsal, we all went into the dining room for the rehearsal supper. Alex had everyone in stitches, telling us about Dare's bachelor party the night before, and how Dare fell out of his chair when the inevitable scantily clad young woman jumped out of a cake.

Dare and I decided to turn in early, we didn't want to look worn out at our own wedding. We said goodnight to our family and friends, who were still whooping it up, and went upstairs entwined in each others arms. We agreed not to spend the night together. Another tradition is the couple not seeing each other on their special day before the wedding. That's kind of hard to do if they wake up next to each other. So we decided to spend the night in our own rooms with the door between closed. That was the first time that door would be closed since the night Darryl proposed and I resolved right then it would also be the last.

We were sitting on my balcony, on the swing sofa there, watching the last of the sunset fade from the sky. Below us was the white, circular gazebo, containing the altar that had been constructed on the lawn for the wedding. Dare put an arm around my shoulders. "Last chance, honey," he whispered. "Last chance to change your mind."

"I'm not going to change *my* mind. How about you?"

"There's only one earthly person who could stop me from making you my wife tomorrow . . . *you.*"

"If *that's* the way it goes, looks like there's going to be a wedding!"

Darryl pulled me close. "You know," he said softly, "I'm not so sure you're an *earthly* person, after all. Maybe that's why God moved your parents to name you 'Angel.' "

"The name's An-ge-*la,* my love," I put in.

"Well, names can change. My plan is to change your *last* name about nineteen hours from now."

We decided to turn in. I walked with Dare to the connecting doorway. He took me in his arms and gave me a deep, lingering kiss. "Well, I guess this is goodbye . . . Mrs. *Delaney.*"

"Yes, I guess so. Been nice knowing you . . . world's most eligible bachelor." I kissed him and he walked into his room, closing the door behind him.

As I started to walk away, I heard a soft knock. "Angel!" he whispered from the other side of the closed door.

"Yes, darling?"

"I love you."

"I love you, too. See you in church."

About a half hour later, Tiff knocked at my door. "Mom? You awake?"

I had just taken a shower, and was toweling off, "Yes, honey, come on in."

She stuck her head in the door. "You alone?" I smiled. A few months ago she never had to ask that question. Adjusting to having a man around had come easily for both of us. But then, look who the man was. Dare wasn't hard to take as either a husband or a father, as we had both found out, albeit unofficially.

"Yes, hon. Dare's in his room tonight."

"Oh, Mama . . ." Tiffani said hesitantly. "I . . . I just wanted you to know how happy I am for you, and for Dare . . . and for me. I didn't mean it when I said I was going to leave. I miss Lansing, and Detroit, and everybody there, but I couldn't make it without my Mama . . ." she looked at me shyly, "*or* my . . . Dad. Mom, when Dare got hurt, I realized how much *he* means to me, too."

I hugged her then, my heart too full for me to speak for a moment, then I said, "Why don't you tell *him* that? It would make him very happy."

"You think so?"

"I know so." I walked with her over to the adjoining door.

"Hey," she said suddenly, "what's he doing over there, anyway?" She looked at me in panic, "You two didn't have an argument, did you?"

I laughed. "No, dear. It's a tradition that the groom not see the bride before the wedding on their wedding day."

"Oh . . ." she said with a puzzled look, not comprehending the ways of us hopeless romantics.

When she knocked at the door, Dare called out, "Hey! No fair! I can't be strong if you put temptation in my path, you lascivious creature!"

"Uh . . . Dare, *Tiff's* here with me. She wants to talk to you."

"Oh . . ." he said quickly. "Sure, come on in, honey."

Tiff kissed me goodnight, hugging me tightly, and went through the door into Dare's room.

I opened my eyes to the sun streaming brilliantly through my balcony doors—my wedding day! I stretched my arms above my head and smiled. Before this day was done, I would be Darryl's wife! Just then, the telephone rang. It was my groom. "Morning. Were you awake?"

"Yes, darling. Good morning, did you sleep well?"

"Like a rock, although this sleeping alone is for the birds."

"Amen. Well, look at it this way; last night's the last time." Someone was knocking. "There's someone at the door. Call you back in a bit, sweetheart."

"Okay . . . oh, I almost forgot . . . there's something for you by our door. 'Bye."

I went to the connecting door and picked up the red rose my darling had left there for me. "Come in!" I called out, putting on my robe.

I was expecting Tiff, or my mother, or my sister. It was all three, with every other woman in the house, *and* several of my other friends and relatives, who were at nearby hotels. "Surprise!" they cried out, rushing in en masse, carrying trays of food and gift wrapped packages.

"Wha?" I stammered.

Bev came up and hugged me. "You don't think we'd let you get married without a proper shower, do you? We waited until today for everybody to get here!"

I'd forgotten about a bridal shower! My friends hadn't—they'd just waited until they all got to California to have it. A wedding day bridal shower breakfast! Well, why not? We had a fabulous time, playing silly games and opening my gifts.

Bev gave me a nightgown so flimsy, brief, and seductive that, even in a room full of other women, I blushed. "This is your shower gift," she said, "but you be sure to tell Darryl it's also my *wedding* gift . . . to *him!*"

Everybody had to hear all about how Darryl and I met, and our courtship, even those who'd heard it before. They all had questions about Dare, and listened in awe as I told them about him. But I didn't tell them the "glamour" stuff. I told them about the man I loved; his goodness, his sweet nature, his playfulness . . . his love.

"Angela, will you introduce me to him after the wedding?" timidly asked my friend Helen from Toronto.

"Are you kidding? You get one of the first dances with him at the reception—*after* he's danced with his wife!"

At about noon, the party started to break up. It was time to start dressing for the wedding. After everybody left, I called over to Dare's room.

"Hey, what was all that ruckus over there?" he said. "I thought I was going to have to call the cops!"

"Dare, they threw me a shower! That was my bridal shower! Wasn't that sweet of them?"

"Yes, it was, honey. I was just kidding. I knew about it. They told me last night. In fact, they put me up to calling, to make sure you were awake."

"You *knew?*"

"Sure . . . but you didn't expect me to *tell* you and spoil the surprise, did you?"

We chatted a few more minutes until my hairdresser came to the door. "See you at four," Darryl said. "Don't be late! Don't make me have to come and find you!"

"It's a date. You'll know me—I'll be the one in the veil . . . I love you, Darryl."

"I love you, too, my Angel."

In the next few hours I was washed, blown dry, curled, massaged, powdered, perfumed, and polished. Shortly after three, I could hear the murmur of voices as the first guests started to arrive. Next, I heard the sound of strings as the strolling violinists started to entertain the early birds. By three-thirty I was ready. My two moms and my bridesmaids came in to sit with me during my last few minutes of "freedom." No one had seen my wedding dress, except Tiffani, and they all proclaimed it's loveliness.

"I hope Darryl likes it," I said wishfully.

My bridesmaids looked enchanting in their elegant floor-length gowns of red chiffon. The dresses were off the shoulder, with a soft pleated edge surrounding the plunging neckline, the center of which had a large red chiffon rose. When I'd first picked the dresses, Jean Paul was aghast. "Ma-*dame! Red?!* For ze bridesmaids?" Jean Paul's accent got thicker when he got frazzled. "It is just not done!" he went on. But I insisted, and even *he* had to admit, once he saw them in the dresses, they were "magnifique."

The sounds outside became louder: people talking and laughing, the orchestra beginning to play. At a quarter to four, my brother came for us. "Time to go, ladies," he said, splendidly handsome in his white shirt, black swallow-tail tuxedo, and red vest. The usher's were dressed identically. All of the men were also wearing a single red rose as a boutonniere. There probably wasn't a single red rose left in the entire state of California, because that was the only flower at our wedding. My bridal bouquet, the men's boutonniere's, the mother's corsages, the flowers decorating the gazebo—all red roses. And each woman guest was to be presented with a single long stemmed red rose when she arrived.

Roy looked at me. "Baby sister, you are absolutely gorgeous! I hope that man of yours knows how lucky he is!"

"Roy, where *is* Dare? I don't want him to see me yet."

"He's already outside, honey. He went down about ten minutes ago. Man . . . is he nervous! The poor guy was shaking so bad, Alex almost had to help him down the stairs. This man stands on stage in front of millions of people cool as a cucumber, but gets a near terminal case of the shakes at his own wedding. Go figure!"

Alex was waiting at the bottom of the staircase. He looked up and watched as I descended the stairs, reaching up to take my hand, and help me down the last few. "Ahh . . . Angela!"

he sighed. He took my other hand and stepped back, holding my hand apart as he studied me. "You're a vision! If I didn't know Dare would hunt me down and beat the crap out of me, I'd steal you away and marry you myself!"

He turned to Tiffani, who was standing next to me. "And no Queen ever had lovelier ladies-in-waiting," he said, kissing Tiffani's hand.

We went down the hallway to the small room off the kitchen that contains the center door to the terrace. This was where I'd make my entrance. The others were to enter from the side terrace exit in the kitchen, slightly to the left of where I was. Jean Paul was there, and in his element—bossing everybody around.

The strolling musicians and the orchestra had been playing for the past hour. The last item in the pre-wedding musicale was a solo by Sylvia. Many a bride would have paid a king's ransom to have Sylvia Bridges sing at her wedding. Even though my wedding was also her *son's,* I wasn't sure Sylvia would do it, even for *us.* But when I had timidly asked, her face beamed in that wonderful smile she'd passed on to Dare. "I'd love to Angela, thank you for asking me."

I had asked Roy to come for me a few minutes before Sylvia's solo. Even though I couldn't be outside, I could still hear her. She sang "Bless This House." Her voice had not changed over the years—it was still rich and full, and no one could phrase a song like Sylvia. Shortly after she finished, Barbara came in, tears running down her cheeks. "Barbara! What's wrong, honey?" I asked.

"Nothing, Angie. Oh! You look so beautiful! It's just Mama singing again. There's hardly a dry eye in the house. I just came in for some tissue before I disgrace myself!"

Right after Barbara went back, Sam escorted Sylvia, wearing her lovely black and white print silk, to where we all were, for her and my mother to be formally escorted to their seats.

"How's Dare, Sam?" I asked.

"Well, I finally got him to stop trembling, honey—I think he's going to survive." He looked me over. "Hmmm-*Hmmm,* girl, you're a sight to behold! I'd better be ready to catch him if he faints when you make your entrance!"

"Oh, God, Sam. Is he *that* nervous? Do you really think he might *faint?"*

"No . . . no, Angie. I'm just kidding, darlin.' The old boy's gonna make it. Don't you worry. But I bet his blood pressure goes up a notch when he sees *you!"*

Sam went immediately back out, because it was time for the seating of the mothers, the traditional signal the ceremony was about to begin. As head usher, Alex had the honor of escorting these important ladies to their seats; Sylvia first, and then my mom.

He turned to Sylvia. "Ready?"

"Yes, Alex." When she looked to me I said, "Oh, Sylvia, your solo was glorious! Thank you!"

She just smiled the Bridges smile again and hugged me, pressing her cheek against mine instead of a kiss, so as to not smear my face with lipstick. "Welcome to the family," she whispered. We looked at each other joyfully. We both knew—*this* time—she meant these words with all her heart. Then she took Alex's arm and walked with him to the side exit. Q.T kissed me and followed. We watched as the three of them walked down the center aisle, and Alex seated them, on the front row right.

Now it was Mama's turn. She hugged me, too. "Darling, I'm so happy for you. Darryl's a wonderful, wonderful man; the kind of man who deserves a woman like you." In the week Mama had been there, she'd gone absolutely bonkers over her future son-in-law. She'd even taken to wearing an official Darryl Bridges fan club button a fan had given her. But she wasn't wearing it today. Today she looked radiant in white and red satin. Alex had returned for her, and she blew me a kiss as they walked away.

As soon as Mama was seated, front row left, Dare, Sam, and Reverend Matthews came out of the guest house to the right rear of the gazebo. I caught my breath. Darryl was princely in his all white tuxedo. He, too, was wearing a red vest, and had a single red rose in his lapel. He looked jittery, but happy, giving the assembled guests a shy, but very definite smile. I couldn't stop staring at him. This incredible man was waiting at the altar to marry *me!*

As Dare, Sam, and Reverend Matthews made their way to the right front of the gazebo, the ushers started down the aisle, single file. They lined up behind the other men.

The orchestra gave a flourish. This was the signal the processional was about to begin. Mate was first. "Is it time for me to go, Aunt Angie? Is Uncle Dare already out there?" Like all the rest of my family, Mate had fallen completely in love with Darryl. Mercifully, the grandeur of the day had apparently gotten through to her and she was more subdued than I'd ever seen her—except when she was asleep. She looked like a confection escaped from atop the wedding cake, in her floor length dress of white lace.

"Yes, honey, he's there. You remember what you have to do, right?" I quizzed her.

She nodded, and Jean Paul escorted her to the side door. As soon as Mate reached the top of the terrace steps, the orchestra began to play the Second Movement of Beethoven's "Pathetique Sonata." Mate went down the terrace steps and started down the aisle. Mate didn't toss flowers petals, as flower girls usually do. She had a more important function—she was carrying my bridal bouquet; a huge bouquet of red roses, in a backdrop of white lace, with red, black, and white satin ribbons streaming from it.

As soon as Mate arrived at the altar, Jean Paul started Dougie, unspeakably elegant in a white tuxedo "just like Uncle Dare's," he had proudly proclaimed. We held our breath on this one. After all, Dougie was only three. He didn't have my real ring though; that was safely on Sam's pinkie. Tiffani had Darryl's ring on her left thumb.

Dougie made it down the aisle—after stopping once or twice to wave at people. Bev was next. She hugged me and went out the side door. When she started down the aisle, John, who had lined up with the other ushers, started up the aisle toward her. They met in the center, John bowed, and handed Bev the single long-stemmed red rose he was carrying. Then Bev took his arm, and they proceeded down the aisle, separating at the gazebo, Bev to the left and John going to end of the line of men to the right.

This procedure was repeated with Cassie and Tony, and Celeste and Larry. Tiffani, the maid of honor, was last. "I love you, Mama" she said with tears in her eyes. She hugged me and started down the aisle, to be met by Alex.

"Now, Madamios . . . er, Madame Delaney. Now is the time of the bride," Jean Paul needlessly prompted.

"Ready, baby girl?" Roy asked, offering his arm. I smiled, nodded, and put my arm through his.

I heard Reverend Matthews's organ of a voice say, "Please stand."

Roy and I walked to the center terrace doors, which Jean Paul ceremoniously opened. When we stepped out on the terrace, the trumpet section gave a long fanfare, as we made our way to the top of the steps. I heard the guests gasping and murmuring as they caught their first glimpse. But there was only one pair of eyes I saw. Darryl looked across the sea of guests directly at me. Even from that distance, I could see him sharply inhale when he first saw me. His eyes never left mine, but after a few moments a tender smile touched his lips.

There had been a great deal of speculation about my wedding dress. When I refused to disclose any information about it, the press went to all the major couture houses to discover who was commissioned to make it. They never found out because none of these fashion houses had been contracted. In fact, nobody knew except my very closest family and the man I *had* asked to make my dress, the man who'd made the dress I'd worn on my first date with Darryl—Marcel. And Marcel had consented to do something he said he hadn't done in years . . . make the entire dress himself, with none of his many assistants even knowing about it.

Some of the press said I was just trying to further hype the already monumental interest in "the wedding of the century." But I didn't care why other people thought I was so secretive. There was only one reason I did it that way. I wanted the dress to be a surprise to—and a gift for—my groom.

The gown's design was based on the dress I'd worn that first night with Dare. It had a strapless white silk bodice with a white chiffon overblouse that tucked into the wide white silk waistband. The waistband was ringed with embroidered red roses—Marcel had done every one by hand. The flared floor-length skirt was of white silk, with three layers of white chiffon overskirt. I was wearing a white petticoat, its lace edge was also ringed with embroidered red roses—they peeked out under the skirt when I moved. On my head, I wore a circle of real red roses, to which had been attached my veil; a cloud of white chiffon that reached my waist. My white satin one inch pumps had red roses at the vamp.

The string section started to play Bach's Air from Suite No. 3 ("Air for the G String"). As Roy and I started down the steps, Mate went to Darryl and handed him my bridal bouquet with a curtsey. He took the bouquet and bent to kiss Mate on the cheek. Then Darryl and Reverend Matthews started down the aisle toward Roy and me. The four of us met with Reverend Matthews facing Roy, and Darryl facing me.

"Who giveth this woman to be married to this man?" Reverend Matthews intoned.

Roy took a deep breath and responded. "On behalf of our mother, I do." Then he kissed me on the cheek and slipped down the aisle to join Mama.

Darryl's eyes were shining as he went down on one knee before me and offered my bridal bouquet. When I reached out to accept it, he kissed my hand. Then he stood, offered me his arm, and we walked together back down the aisle, following

Reverend Matthews, and up the three steps leading into the gazebo and the altar.

When Reverend Matthews had asked us what kind of wedding vows we wanted, we'd both replied, "short and sweet!" So the Reverend quickly got down to business: "Dearly beloved, we are gathered here, in the presence of God, to join this man and this woman in holy matrimony. If there be anyone here who knows of any reason these two should not be joined, let him speak now, or forever hold his peace."

Everyone at a wedding holds his breath at this point, although I've never been to a wedding, nor even know of anyone who has, where someone spoke up. So I was astonished when someone spoke up at mine!

"Ouch!" a voice said loudly. Everybody jumped.

It was Dougie. He'd been fiddling with the stickpin in his tie and pricked his finger! Everybody started to laugh, including Darryl and me. The outburst frightened Dougie and he started to cry. Barbara hastily left her seat in the row behind Sylvia and Q.T., and took her much alarmed child to sit in her lap, where he immediately stopped crying, now that he could put his head down on his mother's breast.

"Ahem!" said Reverend Matthews with a smile. "Uh . . . shall we continue?" There was a titter of laughter. He paused to let it pass, then said, "Darryl Douglass . . . do you take this woman to be your lawfully wedded wife?"

Darryl looked at me with his heart in his eyes. "I do."

"Then repeat after me: I, Darryl Douglass . . ." As Darryl repeated the time honored promise, his eyes never left mine.

"And Angela Delores . . . do you take this man to be your lawfully wedded husband?"

I looked at Darryl, and said softly, "I do."

"Then repeat after me: I, Angela Delores . . ." I looked into Darryl's eyes and he seemed to nod slightly at each vow, as if to say, "Yes, honey, I know . . ."

"Darryl and Angela wish to say a few words to each other as they exchange rings."

We'd told the Reverend this. He didn't know what we were going to say. *Nobody* knew what we were going to say, each of us had told no one—not even each other.

Darryl turned to Sam, who handed him my ring. Darryl's hands were trembling as he took my hand in his. "Angela," he said, looking deep into my eyes, "God has given me blessings beyond measure, in so many ways. But the greatest blessing He ever gave me came the day He brought you into my life." He placed the ring on my finger. "With this ring, I thee wed."

I took his ring from Tiffani, and turning back said, "Darryl, your genius is legendary. The man on stage has won my awe and admiration—but it's the man you are off stage who won my heart." I put the ring on his finger. "With this ring, I thee wed."

"Then," Reverend Matthews proclaimed, "by the power vested in me by God, and the states of Michigan and California, I pronounce Darryl and Angela . . . husband and wife." He leaned toward Darryl. "You can kiss her now, son."

Darryl and I turned to face each other. As he reached out, I saw his hands had stopped trembling. He gently lifted my veil, and pushed it back over my crown of roses. Then he tenderly cupped my face with both hands, leaning forward to kiss me. Just before he did, he looked into my eyes, and whispered, "Hello . . . Mrs. Bridges." His lips found mine softly, lovingly, and his hands left my face to circle my waist. I put my arms around his neck and stood on my toes to be even closer to him. Our guests were applauding, laughing, and yes . . . some were crying.

After Darryl kissed me, and after I blinked back the tears that suddenly filled by eyes, we turned to face our guests. The instantly recognizable intro to Darryl's biggest hit single "Step Lively," his standard concert opening number, came over the sound system. "Step Lively" was a scorching dance floor number. One of Darryl's aunts who was sitting behind Sylvia, leaned forward, and I heard her appalled whisper: "They're *not!*"

Sylvia grinned and replied, "Oh, yes . . . they are."

Darryl and I wanted our wedding reception, in the ballroom, to be a high-stepping celebration, where everybody could have a good time and enjoy themselves to the hilt. We set the tone right from our recessional from the altar.

We debated this at length. My husband (*husband!*) is one of the most admired songwriters and entertainers of the twentieth century. I felt it only fitting his music be some way incorporated in our wedding ceremony. We'd thought about using several of his ballads—many were beautiful love songs—but the bombshell hit me—us *dancing* back down the aisle! "The moment I know we're married, I'm going to feel like dancing for joy!" I'd told Darryl.

Darryl loved the idea, but we were both concerned people might perceive us as taking our vows frivolously. We didn't—to both of us, our vows would be the most serious words we'd ever spoken. So we decided, the hell with what people thought—this was *our* wedding. And we knew people who really cared would understand. As to those who didn't, who gave a damn?

I put my arm though Darryl's, he quietly counted off the four beats we'd agreed on, and we were off, doing the simple step he'd choreographed, all the way down the aisle! (That's one reason my shoes were low-heeled.) The guests clapped in time to the music and some even cut a few steps right at their seats!

The reception was just the way we'd planned it. Everybody had a ball. There was good food and drink, lively company, and great music. And *what* music! We had not one, not two, but three bands: the wedding orchestra, which had a full string section; of course, Darryl's band; and a big band Darryl hired because he thought some of the older folks might like it. And anyway, *he* likes a lot of the big band sound. The man is a musician, and he likes *good* music—of all types.

Darryl's crew made good on their promise, and put on a presentation of song and dance. Darryl had told them they were our guests and he didn't want them to *work*, but they insisted.

One of the background singers had written some lyrics to a song he called, "Darryl and Angel," sung to the tune of "Frankie and Johnny." It had people practically falling out of their chairs with laughter.

When it came time to throw the bouquet, I noted where Tiffani was standing before I turned my back. But my aim was off. I threw the bouquet not to my daughter, but my mother! I teased her about it a short while later. From her blushingly girlish reaction, I surmised she was closer than I thought to the widower she'd been seeing. Maybe that bouquet knew where it was going!

When Darryl removed my garter (to all kinds of cat-calls) and threw it to the cluster of reluctantly gathered single men, his aim was equally bad. It landed over at a nearby table, dead in Alex's lap!

But for me, the high point of the reception began when my husband stepped on stage and took the microphone. When it got quiet enough for him to be heard, he said, "Good evening. Angela and I thank you from the bottom of our hearts for sharing this day with us." Everybody started clapping and cheering.

"If I may, I'd like to do a song . . ." They really went wild then. I looked up in surprise. Darryl hadn't said anything about singing. He had to wait for them to quiet down before he could continue, "A song I've never performed before an audience before . . . and never will again, after today." *That* got everyone's attention, especially mine. The room grew silent.

"I wrote this song for my lady. In fact, *it* was my real proposal to her, before I got up the nerve to ask her in words. From this day forward, she's the only person who'll ever hear it again. But so far she's only heard it on a tape. So, if you'll bear with me, I'd like to sing it today . . ." he looked directly at me, ". . . for my wife."

The song was, of course, "Whenever We're Apart." I'd managed to make it through the ceremony, and so far through the reception without crying, but the tears flowed as Darryl sang that song to me.

All three bands combined to play accompaniment for him, the lushness of the sound was breathtaking. During a musical bridge, Darryl left the stage and came to the head table, and took my hand.

He led me to the dance floor and held me close as we danced to the applause of our guests. As the musical interlude ended, he led me to the stage, lifted me to sit on the edge, and finished the song holding my hand and looking deeply into my eyes.

We slipped away soon after, eager to be alone. Unknown to everybody but those nearest and dearest, we were spending the night in the guest house, before leaving for the Caribbean the next morning. Darryl insisted on carrying me over the threshold, even though his shoulder was not yet completely healed. He put me down, and we stood just looking at each other for a moment. Then, without a word, we slowly embraced, and didn't "come up for air" until morning.

Much later, we lay together, feeling the beat of each other's hearts. "Honey, can I tell you something?" Dare whispered.

"Yes, my husband."

"I prayed for you. I prayed to find someone who'd love me for myself. Someone I could love, and trust, and admire in return . . . and one week after this prayer . . ." he kissed me, "I met you."

"Oh . . ."

"*That's* why I call you . . . 'Angel.' "

The next morning we were dressing to go to the airport. Dare was sitting on the bed, while I was at a vanity, brushing my hair. He was telling me about the small island we were going to. "Oh, and honey, do you have any money with you? There are some great boutiques there."

"Well, I've got my checkbook and credit cards, sweetheart."

Dare walked over to the dresser and got his wallet. "A lot of those places don't take anything but the folding stuff, baby . . . here." He handed me a thousand dollars.

"Thanks, hon," I said, putting the money into my purse..

"Hey! You're slipping!" Darryl exclaimed, walking back

over to the bed. "Aren't you going to lecture me on how you don't want to spend my money?" he said with a grin, sitting on the bed again.

"Nope," I retorted, walking to the closet. "We're married now, pal. Spending *our* money is one of my marital duties."

"Is that right? Well, since you're so committed to fulfilling one's obligations, why don't you just sashay your body on over here . . ." He reached out as I walked by and pulled me down on the bed with him. "We can both fulfill one of our marital duties together!"

Epilogue

We've Only Just Begun

Darryl and I have been married almost two years now. I don't suppose anybody would believe this story if it hadn't really happened. I still wake up at night sometimes and it all seems like a beautiful dream, but then I turn and see Darryl lying asleep beside me.

After returning from our honeymoon, I worried how I would occupy my time. I was used to working, used to having a career. And it wasn't as though I had small children to tend to, or household chores to do.

I do some chores though, just because I want to. I've always loved gardening, and I'd missed it during the two years I lived in an apartment in Lansing. And sometimes I take it into my head to dust the music room, or mop the kitchen floor, just because Pivot Pointe is my home, and my husband and child's home, and I love it.

And I insist on ironing Dare's shirts. He laughed at me, at first, saying, "Honey, *why* are you ironing my shirts?" with a perplexed smile.

And I always replied, "Because you're my husband." After a while he stopped laughing and stopped asking—I think he likes it.

Darryl really tries to keep his room neat, now that he shares the "master compartment" with me, but it's hopeless. Frankly, it doesn't bother me a bit—but it bothers him. He told me, "Angel, if the mess in here gets to be too much for you, just close the connecting door, and I'll get the hint."

I agreeably replied, "Okay, hon," knowing full well even if he has stacks of junk up to the ceiling, I'll never close that door. But we *do* sleep most nights in *my* room.

And Darryl wasn't kidding when he said my business expertise would not be wasted. I started doing small things at first; auditioning back-up musicians, okaying Darryl's travel arrangements. But as time went on, Darryl asked me to take on more and more responsibility. At first I thought he was just concerned about me being bored, and wanted me to feel useful. But I soon found out, I *was* useful. I filled a void that had long existed in Darryl's organization. Mary was terrific, and she remained as his assistant (and mine), but as Dare told me, Mary's forte was the business end, not the creative one.

"Angel, Mary keeps my scheduling together, stays on top of my correspondence and messages, and a hundred other important things flawlessly. But she has no creative side whatever. So when a decision or opinion was needed about new costumes, or orchestration for a number, or picking new talent, I've had to do the stuff myself. Now I've got you, a musician with top flight business credentials, a brilliant imagination, *and* who knows my needs and my tastes almost better than I do. That frees me to perform, and . . ." he patted my butt "spend more time with my wife."

My PC skills come in handy, too. I use the PC to keep track of a lot of Dare's operation. I taught him as well, and he's become so adept he's seldom seen without his new lap top somewhere nearby.

About two months after the wedding, Alex left the company. The video he'd done for Darryl had been so critically acclaimed Alex received an offer to direct a feature film. A low-budget one, but a feature film all the same. He'd been nominated for an Oscar. He didn't win, but he then received an offer to direct a major big budget production, and last month he asked Dare to write and perform a theme—a love song—for the movie.

Alex isn't Dare's employee anymore, but he's an even closer friend, and a colleague. And it looks like one day soon, Alex will be our son-in-law. He came to Darryl one day, like a man, to tell Dare about his feelings for Tiffani. He was afraid Darryl and I would think he was too old for Tiff.

Dare laughed at that. "Man, *I'm* sure not the person to say an age difference should stand in the way! You're seven years older than Tiff. I don't think that takes you out of the running, and neither will Angela."

He's right—I don't. And neither does Tiffani—whose opinion, after all, is the only one that really matters. *Miss* Bridges is in her second year of college now, at UCLA. I just hope her graduation beats her wedding.

Tiffani's adoption went through quickly after our attorneys laid a big check on Iris. We didn't have to do this—Iris had no real case to stop the adoption. But she was, as always, a noisy nuisance, and her frivolous lawsuit could have delayed proceedings. And the press would have had a field day. So we paid her off, which after all, was what she was *really* after. I never asked Darryl how much she got. I didn't care. I figured whatever amount—to get shut of *her*—was cheap at the price!

Dare got stuck in a rare dry spell writing the song for Alex's movie. I made several suggestions, in an effort to rekindle his spark, and we wound up writing the song together! Darryl warned me to be prepared for some to say I hadn't really helped write the song. But I *did;* some of the melody, and most of the lyric. Then came the real bombshell—Dare wanted me to *record* the song with him!

"It's perfect for us, honey! This is the song I've been shooting for! I should have known the answer was for us to *write* it together!"

Ever since our marriage, Darryl had been looking for the right song for us to record as a duet. I kept ducking the issue. I didn't want to be like certain other women who'd married famous singers and tried to sing with them, when they never should have even been on the same stage.

Darryl said we sounded fabulous together on the song. "Some critics are going to dispute your part in *writing* the song, but *nobody's* going to quibble about that voice of yours, baby!" he proclaimed.

Usually, his assessment on musical matters was close to infallible, but I didn't trust his judgment on *this* one. Darryl was in love with me. It's a well known fact love can be blind—couldn't it be *deaf* as well? Unknown to Darryl, I asked Stew to listen to a tape of us and tell me what he honestly thought.

"Well, Angie," he said contemplatively, "I think this time next year there's going to be a Grammy *and* an Oscar in Dare's trophy room—with *both* your names on them!"

And that's not the half of it. Darryl's talked Tiffani into doing a violin solo as a part of the bridge! Talk about nepotism!

Which brings me to this evening. Me giving Dare a gift before each live performance is a custom that's evolved between us. I gave him a small pin shaped like a treble cleft the first time I attended a performance after we were married, and he reminded me of the rose I gave him that first concert. He got such a kick out of it, the gifts became a ritual. He called them his "break-a-leg" good luck charms. The gifts were never anything large or elaborate, but they were another small tie between us.

Dare and I came to Chicago, for a rare concert that was to be filmed and later televised. Sam came to the dressing room door. "Ten minutes, Dare."

"Be right out, man," Dare called. He looked at me. "How do I look, baby?" he asked, buttoning the sequined vest he'd just put on.

I grinned and gave him a thumbs up.

"Well?" he asked, looking at me pointedly.

"You look fantastic, honey," I evaded.

"No, I'm not talking about that. Aren't you forgetting something?"

"No . . . I don't think so . . ." I said innocently.

"Uh . . . my gift?"

"Oh, that's right . . . your gift," I said absentmindedly.

Darryl waited for me to continue. When I didn't, he said disappointedly, "You *did* forget, didn't you?"

"No, honey, I didn't forget."

He was getting frustrated now. "Well . . . where is it? Is it here?"

It was a struggle to keep a straight face. "Yes, it's here."

"Well, excuse me, Mrs. Bridges," he said with a frazzled look, "but would it be too much trouble for you to *hand* it to me?"

"I can't hand it to you *yet,* my husband—I'm still working on it . . ." I went to him, put my arms around his neck, and whispered, "and you're going to have to wait about another eight months before you can hold it."

I watched the flood of emotions crossing his face: first bafflement, then the dawn of comprehension, followed quickly by joy, exhilaration, pride, a touch of fear, quite a bit of worry, and finally, love. The look of love Darryl gave me then washed over me like a wave.

"Angela . . . sweetheart . . . when did . . . how long . . . oh, honey . . . are you . . . are you *sure?"* he stammered in an awed whisper.

"Yes. Dr. Phillips and I are both *quite* sure . . . Dad," I whispered back.

Darryl wrapped his arms around me and just held me close, not moving, not saying a word. After several moments I said, "Darryl Honey?" He pulled away just far enough for me to look up into his eyes. He blinked and a tear slid down his cheek. He touched my face and tried to speak, but the words wouldn't come.

By this time, I was crying, too. "That's okay, sweetheart, I know," I sighed, putting my head on his shoulder.

Sam came back to the door. "Hey, Dare, what's the hold-up? Are you . . ." Then he saw the two of us standing there holding each other, with tears running down our cheeks. "My *God!* What's happened? Did somebody *die?*"

"No, man. Just the opposite!" Dare cried out, hugging Sam, and dancing him all around the room. "Somebody's going to be *born!*"

About the Author

Raynetta Mañees has been an administrator with the federal government for over 20 years, and is a graduate of Wayne State University. She has performed as a solo vocalist in numerous venues in the Northwest and has had several non-musical acting roles. She currently is an on-air radio personality on AM 1180 WXLA. She lives in Michigan with her family.

Raynetta welcomes your comments at: P.O. Box 27493, Lansing, MI 48909.

8 7 6 5 TRI-MET :30 :00

4 3 2 1 PM

VALID FOR
BOARDING UNTIL
TIME SHOWN AT TOP

:30 :00

12 NOON 11 10 9 TRI-MET :30 :00

M849612

8 7 6 5 AM

VALID FOR
BOARDING UNTIL
TIME SHOWN AT TOP

:30 :00

KEEP THIS
TRANSFER AS
YOUR RECEIPT

DAY CODE			
M	J	I	E
X	D	B	C

All Zone	DAY	A	H	Y

2 Zone	3-2	2-1

Short Hopper	1	2	3

Globe Ticket and Label Co.® (S)260P

Unlimited Mileage with a Tri-Met Monthly Pass

When paying a 2-zone fare, please tell your driver whether you want to travel in zones 1 & 2 or zones 2 & 3. Your driver will punch that section of the transfer to show which zones are valid.

Retain this transfer as your fare receipt and for reboarding until expiration time torn at top. Transfer issued only at time fare is paid. Valid only on day of issue and for sole use of purchaser. Sorry, may not be upgraded. Failure to have receipt of fare paid may result in your being cited to appear in District Court and/or pay a fine.

If the driver questions the validity of this transfer, please pay the fare, retain this transfer and submit it with details, including bus route name and number and time of the dispute in writing to: Tri-Met Customer Service, 4012 SE 17th Avenue, Portland, OR 97202.

For information, suggestions, commendations and complaints call 238-RIDE.

TRI-MET

THANKS FOR RIDING!

Printed on recycled paper

Look for these upcoming Arabesque titles:

October 1996
THE GRASS AIN'T GREENER by Monique Gilmore
IF ONLY YOU KNEW by Carla Fredd
SUNDANCE by Leslie Esdaile

November 1996
AFTER ALL by Lynn Emery
ABANDON by Neffetiti Austin
NOW OR NEVER by Carmen Green

December 1996
EMERALD'S FIRE by Eboni Snoe
NIGHTFALL by Loure Jackson
SILVER BELLS, an Arabesque Holiday Collection